Praise for Jenny White

'In writing a thoroughly enjoyable and gripping crime novel Jenny White also makes a serious point about today's politics and invites us to think' *Scotsman*

'A compelling thriller. Bold characters seize an adventure occasionally tinged with melancholy, while White's anthropological heritage floods her brisk investigation with colourful detail' *Financial Times*

'In her highly accomplished first novel Jenny White, whose subject is Turkish society and politics, steers a clever course between action and background . . . A neat mystery and persuasive portrait of credible people is joined seamlessly onto a fascinating portrait of Turkey at a time of fateful transition' *Literary Review*

'A remarkable piece of fiction ... This is a fast-paced read with a breathless, page-turning pace, and a sense of mounting tension ... written in gorgeously sensuous language ... As well as being a gripping thriller, *The Sultan's Seal* is a knowledgeable portrayal of life in 19th-century Turkey, as it struggles to find a middle road between traditional Eastern values and the modern attitudes of the West' *Waterstone's Books Quarterly*

'A wonderful read, written by someone who can write about the exotic and fascinating world of the late Ottoman Empire with knowledge and understanding. An historical novel of the highest quality'

Iain Pears, author of *An Instance of the Fingerpost*

'*The Sultan's Seal* is a fascinating and remarkably knowledgeable look at a society in flux, its very appealing characters caught between East and West, Islam and Christianity, and bound in a web of murder and treachery that only the lucky few may escape'

Diana Gabaldon, author of *A Breath of Snow and Ashes*

'Ms White's prose glints like the shores of the Bosphorus she brings to life with breathtaking detail. An astonishing debut novel that is impossible to put down'

Dora Levy Mossanen, author of *Harem* and *Courtesan*

'Set in 19th-century Istanbul, *The Sultan's Seal* is a joyous celebration of love and desire that recognises no cultural boundaries. Even long after you have read it, the novel lingers in the mind like the strong, delightful smell of an incense you will remember the next time you catch it in the air'

Elif Shafak, author of *The Bastard of Istanbul*

'An impressive debut. Jenny White has woven a compelling story, rich with emotion and sparkling with historical detail. She immerses the reader deep in the opulence, beauty and danger of the fading Ottoman empire'

Tom Harper, author of *The Mosaic of Shadows*

Jenny White is an anthropologist and the author of numerous non-fiction works about Turkish society and politics. Her first novel, *The Sultan's Seal*, was shortlisted for the Ellis Peters Historical Crime Award. She lives in Massachusetts.

The Abyssinian Proof

Jenny White

PHOENIX

A PHOENIX PAPERBACK

First published in Great Britain in 2008
by Weidenfeld & Nicoslon
This paperback edition published in 2008
by Phoenix,
an imprint of Orion Books Ltd,
Orion House, 5 Upper St Martin's Lane,
London WC2H 9EA

An Hachette Livre UK company

1 3 5 7 9 10 8 6 4 2

A CIP catalogue record for this book
is available from the British Library.

ISBN 978-0-7538-2439-9

Printed and bound in Great Britain by
Clays Ltd, St Ives plc

For Suzanne Campagna,
whose memories make it
all come alive

The bird of vision is flying towards You
with the wings of desire.

– Rumi, *Mystic Odes* 833

1

Constantinople, 28 May 1453

Isaak Metochites and his family set off through the unlit streets. His son, Michael, pulled the cart with their belongings, its wheels greased and padded to make no sound. His wife and seven-year-old daughter, cloaked in dark veils, followed behind. Constantinople lay about them in a black stupor, as close to sleep as death is to the afterlife.

The silence worried Isaak. For weeks, the Turks had kept up a fierce bombardment, along with a constant barrage of noise from trumpets and castanets, presumably to weaken the nerves of the city's defenders. Only seven thousand armed men remained to defend the city, he thought, but they were not so easily rattled. It was rumoured that the Turks planned a great attack the following day and the sudden silence seemed like a great ingathering of breath by the barbarian god of war.

The night smelled of wet charcoal and decay. Isaak thought he heard the Turkish army stirring on the other side of the city walls. He shook his head sadly at the thought that all that remained of the thousand-year-old civilisation of Byzantium was this despairing city, the flat of the Muslim hand against its back, ready to tip it into oblivion. Over generations, the Turks had swallowed the outlying cities and provinces of the Eastern Roman

Empire, the high plains, pastures, ports, and olive groves of Byzantium, until only the capital city remained, the city Constantine had named after himself in the year 330 and anointed the capital of Christendom. A triangle of precious civilisation girded by its great walls and flanked on two sides by water.

In the spring of 1453, Sultan Mehmet II, the ambitious leader of the Turks, barely out of his teens, had built a fortress on the Bosphorus strait at its narrowest point, cutting off provisions to the city from the north. It was said that the young sultan, whose favourite stories were the biographies of Alexander and Caesar, had piled stone upon stone alongside his men.

Now the Turks were camped outside the city, preparing their final attack. From the land wall he had seen them pitch their elaborate tents amid a sea of soldiers in red turbans and glinting helmets. An enormous iron chain sealed the entrance to the harbour, the Golden Horn, but a month ago the Turks had shocked the population by transporting seventy-two ships by land, rolling them on greased logs over the hill of Pera into the harbour, trapping the Byzantine fleet. Then they flung a bridge of barrels across the Golden Horn and began to mine the city walls. The Venetians had promised to send their fleet to protect the city, but it had not appeared and soon it would be too late. Another Turkish fleet was approaching that would block the Sea of Marmara to the south.

Sprawled along the harbour, Constantinople had become a dark and lawless place. All who could had fled south before the blockade. The day before, Isaak had passed a man roasting a rodent on a small fire beneath the lower walls. Of rats there seemed to be an unlimited number these days. They stopped even in daylight in the middle of a lane, as if to remind the remaining humans that they would soon be evicted. The night before, Isaak had dreamed of his wife lying naked on a sandy shore, the tide coming in. Jolted awake, he had reached for Achmet's *Dream Key* and read that, if a man dreamed of his wife naked, he would see her grave.

Isaak and his family pulled their cart past a grove of olive trees beyond which rose the high wall enclosing the property of the Studion Monastery. Isaak halted by an iron gate surmounted by a double eagle, then felt his way along the wall until he came to a low door.

He took out a key, recently oiled, and inserted it into the lock. To his relief, it turned easily. He edged the door open, careful not to make a sound. His son unloaded the cart and, ducking under the lintel, passed everything inside to his father. Isaak noticed the palms of his hands were stained black by rust, as if the door were already covered in blood.

The family crouched low and hurried through the monastery garden to a small chapel. Isaak whispered instructions to his son, a young man of twenty, who crept back through the garden to get the rest of their belongings. They slipped out of the chapel towards the crypt, a square hole in the ground covered by an iron grate. As they left, Isaak passed his finger through the chapel's holy spring and anointed his daughter's forehead. Beside the crypt, he kept an anxious eye on the caretaker's quarters, a cottage built against the wall at the other end of the garden. The monastery was quiet. All the monks were in the main church. He could hear the rhythmic drone of their voices praying for deliverance. His son lifted the grate and Isaak made his way gingerly down the steps, his eyes useless in the dark, hands groping for the passage he knew to be there.

The air was cool and the walls wept with damp. Isaak's fingers felt along the slick stone, stumbling into burial niches until they found the cleft, hidden at the far end of the crypt behind a massive sarcophagus. He pulled himself through, and his son followed with their belongings. Deep under the earth, they lit torches.

Isaak returned to the garden to help his wife down the stairs, then lowered his daughter into the crypt, pressing his hand over her mouth to stifle her protests. There was a commotion below, then silence. Isaak took a last breath of the cool night air and spent a moment to consider the cold blanket of stars that would as soon crown a Muslim city as a Christian one, then moved back underground.

Behind the cleft, a tunnel led to an iron door. Isaak pushed it open. 'This cistern has a passageway that goes under the city wall right to the sea,' he explained to his family, their frightened faces looming in the weak light of the flares. 'The boat is docked by the Golden Gate, not far.' He hoped they would not be too late. He had remained in the city until the last minute, waiting for his partner's ship, for a reprieve, for the promised Venetian fleet to arrive and rout the Turks.

A scrap of air tore at the flame of Isaak's torch as he stepped inside the cistern. Stone columns rose about him, textured by marks of ancient chisels. High above, invisible beyond the arc of torchlight, was a ceiling of vaulted domes. He could just make out the glimmer of white marble, hints of their ornate capitals, and wondered who had constructed these elaborate underground cathedrals that held the city's water supply. Had they given refuge to the earliest Byzantines when they too were under siege?

How else to explain the warren of tunnels that connected the cisterns to churches and to the palace, and burrowed secretly under the city walls to the shore.

Isaak breathed in the musty odour of decay. Below the tiled platform on which he stood, a lake of water receded into the darkness, rocking shards of light from his torch; water born in the mountains and brought overland by the aqueduct to serve the monastery. He checked to make sure the rowboats were there, tied up to the platform.

As father and son laboured to carry the bundles into the cavernous room, one of the sacks fell open, revealing a gold plate, a ruby-studded chalice, and a gold incense burner. Isaak squatted down and, propping his torch against a pillar, opened the sack he was carrying. He spread a clean cloth on the tiles, then took out a purple velvet bundle heavily embroidered in gold. He undid the gold braid that tied it, revealing a simple silver gilt box, one hand's breadth wide and two long.

He regarded the reliquary with awe. It was the reason he was here and not manning the ramparts alongside Constantine XI, his emperor. God forbid – he crossed himself – perhaps the last emperor of Byzantium. The box would remain with Isaak and, upon his death, pass to his son, to be given to his eldest son. Now he had no choice; they must take the reliquary out of the city. It must not fall into the hands of the Muslims. Travellers who had been to Cairo and Baghdad had told him that entire libraries were devoted to writings about the object lying on the velvet cloth at his feet. The Muslims knew it was here; perhaps this was the very reason the Turks were storming the city? The reliquary would make them more powerful than any weapon they currently possessed. Isaak planned to take it to Venice, where his family had connections and could safeguard it in secrecy. A future generation of Metochites sons must return it to Byzantium when the city was once again safe in Christian hands.

On the lid was an image worked in black niello of Jesus standing on a cloud, face shrouded, a tablet falling from his slack fingers. Below him sat a man with a striped turban on his head, holding a miniature model of a church in one hand, the other reaching confidently for the falling tablet. Behind the man stood an angel with powerful wings, her right hand resting protectively on his shoulder. The angel was weeping. The Greek inscription read, 'Behold the Proof of Chora, Container of the Uncontainable'.

'Why is the angel crying?' His daughter had squatted down beside him, her voice magnified and oddly distorted.

Isaak thought for a moment. 'I don't know, Melisane.' He drew his fingertips across the niello figures. 'It's so old that no one knows what these pictures mean anymore.'

'Who's that?' She pointed at the man in the turban.

'That I can tell you. This is Theodore Metochites, the great-grandfather of your grandfather,' Isaak told her.

She looked confused. 'How many grandfathers is that?'

Isaak smiled and ran his hand through his daughter's black curls. She was his child by an Abyssinian slave, who had died in childbirth. Despite the objections of his family, he had acknowledged the child and taken her in.

He was aware that his son was listening too. 'Theodore lived more than a hundred years ago. You're descended from a great man. He was Grand Logothete – a minister of state and a diplomat. He was also a great scholar. Do you recognise the church he's holding? It's our church, Saint Saviour in Chora.' Isaak put his finger on the turbaned man. 'And he built it.'

His daughter traced the angel's wings with her finger. 'What's inside?'

'It contains the Proof of God,' he answered softly. 'It's something our family has promised to guard.'

'Is God in here? He must be very small.'

Isaak smiled fondly at his daughter. 'He's very small and very big, all at the same time. God is in everything,' Isaak took his daughter's pudgy hand and pressed it against the lid of the reliquary, 'but this is the closest we will ever get to him on earth.'

They remained like that for a moment, father and daughter connected through a mystery.

'I'll take very good care of him. I promise, Papa.'

'I know you will.'

He had never looked inside the reliquary and he had no idea what kind of proof resided within. All he knew was that he held in his hands the most powerful relic in Byzantium. It was said that one of his ancestors had brought the Proof from Abyssinia in the time of Theodore, almost a hundred and fifty years ago. Theodore had made the reliquary for it, and it had been kept in the vault of the Hagia Sophia cathedral. The emperor had charged the Metochites family with looking after it. Three weeks ago, Isaak had brought it back to the Church of Saint Saviour in Chora, the church designed by Theodore, who had lived the last years of his life in the attached monastery. Michael, Isaak's son, was now caretaker of the church.

Isaak looked up at the serious face of his son, who would henceforth bear the burden of this responsibility.

'You remember what to do?' They had been over their plan many times.

Isaak and his wife would go to fetch Isaak's mother. Later tonight, they would row the two boats through the underground channel, board the ship sent by his Venetian business partner, and leave this doomed city. They had spotted it that morning from the sea wall: a fast, low-slung galley flying the prearranged blue banner. By some miracle, it had slipped past the approaching Turkish ships.

Along with the Proof of God, Isaak had brought their most valuable belongings – a small, ancient icon and objects made of gold and precious stones that could be traded for their lives, their passage on the boat, and freedom.

Should the family be separated and unable to board, Michael was to take his sister and the reliquary and seek refuge with Melisane's Abyssinian relatives in the city. If the Turks took the city, Isaak believed the Abyssinians were less likely to be put to the sword than the noble families of Byzantium. The Abyssinians would protect the reliquary containing a treasure from their own land. When he was able, his son was to restore the reliquary to its rightful position or find a permanent hiding place for it.

Isaak could sense the Turks massing outside the cistern, beyond the heavy masonry of Constantinople's walls, their armour creaking, their lances stretching to the horizon like blades of grass. The city walls groaned against their weight. He imagined he could hear the mellifluous vowels of their language fall incongruously from their harsh throats. These Muslims did not drink wine, he had heard, nor did they eat pork. He imagined they stank of horse, sweat, and leather.

The chill of the cistern crept into his marrow and he began to shiver. Behind him, his wife was weeping. He went over and put his arm around her. She looked up into his face, and in her eyes he saw the sad devotion that had flattered him early in their marriage, and of which he had foolishly tired. He kissed her forehead and whispered something in her ear. She smiled, nodded, and pressed her face against his chest. For the first time in his adult life, Isaak was afraid.

Mary, Mother of God, Container of the Uncontainable, Isaak prayed intently, protect us now.

He cocked his head and listened, as if the sound of an invasion could penetrate the stone walls and soil that separated him from the besieged city. Michael stood beside him, listening also, a stricken look on his face.

Isaak went back to the reliquary. He reached down and brushed his fingertips over his ancestor's face in farewell, silently begging his forgiveness. In the wavering torchlight, Theodore Metochites' serious eyes seemed to look directly at Isaak, in admonishment for leaving him in such a forsaken place. Isaak wrapped the reliquary carefully and handed it to his son. Their eyes met and Michael nodded briefly.

Isaak pulled his wool cloak tighter around his shoulders. It was time to fetch his mother. His wife would have to accompany him to the gynaeceum, the women's quarters, as men were not permitted to enter. He knew his father would be on the ramparts with their emperor. At that moment, he realised with anguished certainty that he would never see his father again.

Isaak embraced his son and leaned down to kiss his daughter. She turned her cheek away in pique, so Isaak let his fingers linger in her curls.

Michael kissed his mother's hand and pressed it to his forehead.

'Come now,' Isaak said gruffly. 'Enough time for that later.' He reached for his wife's hand and drew her into the darkness. They felt their way through the tunnel, then crept noiselessly out of the crypt and through the garden into the lane.

They ran through the dark streets towards his mother's house near the land walls. These massive fortifications, constructed in the fifth century, had withstood Turkish onslaughts in the past, as they had those of Huns, Avars, Russians, Saracens and other invaders. But Isaak had heard of a new weapon fashioned for the Turks by a Frenchman, a cannon as long as five men laid head to foot, that they said could cut through walls like a scimitar through flesh. As they approached, they encountered more and more people running in the opposite direction.

A man stopped them and said urgently, 'It's started. You have to turn around.' As he ran off, he called over his shoulder, 'We're all going to the cathedral.'

A terrible cry rose from beyond the city walls, from the throats of eighty thousand men set loose. Isaak grabbed his wife's hand and they began to run. An unearthly thunder smashed the air and, a few moments later, a great blast of exploding masonry. The screams of men tore the night. Behind them, the bells of the ancient cathedral of Hagia Sophia, the church of the Divine Wisdom, began to toll.

2

Istanbul, 2 Teshrinievvel 1303, Rumi (14 October 1887)

Kamil Pasha woke with a start. As he got up from the armchair, papers cascaded from his lap on to the floor.

His manservant, Yakup, stood in the doorway balancing a glass of tea on a tray. 'No word yet.'

'What's taking them so long?' Kamil complained as he picked up the files from the floor and stacked them on his desk. He stopped for a moment to examine a rose-coloured bloom that had appeared on the potted *Cephalanthera rubra* sitting beside the files. It was one of dozens of orchids scattered about the rooms of his villa. A passionate collector, Kamil had had a winter garden built on to the back of the house for his more delicate varieties.

Kamil went next door to his bedroom. He poured water from a pitcher into a china bowl and stood for a moment, hands splayed on the cool marble of the washstand, frowning into the mirror. The lamplight accentuated the lean angles of his face and the tired smudges beneath his eyes. He looked like a ruffian with his unruly hair and moustache, black stubble, and dour expression. They say a man's fate is written on his forehead, he reflected, examining the lines that scored his brow, but it was just a map of where that man has been. He smacked the flat of his hand against the marble and turned away. A map would imply the existence of a Mapmaker, he thought grimly, and no God worth his salt would work with such flimsy materials.

Kamil dipped a tinned copper mug into a jar of spring water and drank it down, then went back to his study. He pushed open the window and leaned out. A slick of moonlight spread outward from the Beshiktash shore at the base of the hill. Beyond the strait hulked the black hills of Asia. The moon was high and the night too bright for subterfuge. Had their target spotted the gendarmes following him?

Kamil was a magistrate in the new secular courts, responsible for investigating and prosecuting crimes, especially those that could potentially undermine the state. He oversaw an area stretching from the Old City all the way north to the fishing villages and summer konaks of the wealthy that nestled into the European side of the Bosphorus. These days, the mood in the city was as brittle as tinder. Muslim refugees from the embattled Balkan provinces had been teeming into the city, thousands of them, with harrowed faces and tattered clothing, clogging the lanes with bullock carts, and bearing tales of massacres. The municipalities and charitable foundations were overwhelmed.

To make matters worse, valuable objects were disappearing at an alarming rate from mosques, churches, and synagogues throughout the empire. Two days ago, an icon of the Virgin Mary that the Christians believed had miraculous powers had disappeared from the Greek Orthodox Patriarchate. Christians and Jews had begun to accuse the Sultan's government of orchestrating the thefts in order to undermine their communities, as if the disappearing antiquities were phantom limbs and they feared in this way that they might vanish entirely.

Then, this afternoon, the spark had been struck that could set all of Istanbul aflame. A man had ridden up to a carriage that was carrying an aide to the Ottoman governor of Macedonia and, before the guards could react, had leaned inside and shot him in the head. The man had galloped off, but one of the guards followed and alerted the gendarmes, the military police attached to the governor's office. That had set in motion an elaborate trap, the jaws of which were about to close around the assassin and his co-conspirators.

When news of the assassination spread, a crowd of Muslims, their numbers swelled by desperate refugees, had gathered outside the Aya Sofya Mosque, still revered by Christians as the Byzantine cathedral of Hagia Sophia, and threatened to burn it to the ground. They were met by an equal crowd of Christian men. In the resulting melee ten people had been killed.

Kamil glanced at the message from the minister of justice lying on his desk. It appointed him special prosecutor charged with seeing that the entire situation be brought under control as quickly and as quietly as possible, and giving him full charge of the military operation.

The last thing the government wanted was to arrest Christians in broad daylight. Disguised military agents had followed the assassin to identify his co-conspirators and all those involved would be arrested at the same time, silently and efficiently, so none could warn the others. When the assassin had settled in for the night, Kamil would lead the gendarmes in extracting him from his lair. The man would be brought to the ministry and then disappear. For all the Christian community knew, he might have escaped abroad. Kamil preferred not to think about what would happen to him; the man had shot a government official, and there would be justice.

As soon as the assassin was captured, Kamil would focus on the thefts, the tinder feeding the fear and resentment. It wouldn't take much for the city to burn. Literally. If an angry mob torched a neighbourhood and the fire spread, as it had many times before, it would engulf large parts of a city still mostly built of wood. He had confidence in the military police and didn't wish to get in their way, so he was now forced to wait for their signal.

He got up and fetched the stack of files from his desk. The reports described missing gold and silver vessels, icons, illuminated manuscripts and books, massive silver candleholders, and even ancient tiles prised from the walls of mosques. He pulled out a drawing of the icon of the Virgin Mary, no larger than his hand, that was missing from the Patriarchate. The sketch showed Mary looking out calmly at the world, while the baby Jesus, his right hand slung around his mother's neck, stared intently into her face as if willing her to do something. The theft of this icon had raised the level of tension more than any other as, he supposed, the Christians believed their divine protection had thereby been revoked.

The thefts appeared to be the work of an organised ring. Many of the objects appeared on the market in Europe, out of range of the Ottoman police, just weeks after being stolen, despite strict new antiquities laws and closer customs inspections. Kamil had spent the evening reading the reports, looking for a pattern. He despaired of the shoddy investigations carried out by the police. No systematic questioning of possible witnesses, no collection of more than the most rudimentary evidence. If the culprit hadn't dropped a knife or a calling card at the scene, the police generally found nothing of interest.

The churches in Beyoglu, the foreigners' section of Istanbul, belonged to embassies and were well guarded, so the thefts were mostly from Istanbul's Old City, a jumble of districts inhabited by Greeks, Jews and Muslims. Especially hard hit were the areas of Fatih and Balat, a tangle of crumbling houses, gardens, ruins, and small villas that extended along the banks of the Golden Horn up to the old Byzantine city walls, the southernmost boundary of Kamil's jurisdiction.

Kamil knew who the recipients of the antiquities were – the same people in whose drawing rooms he had seen displayed Greek busts and sections of Roman friezes when he studied law and criminal procedure at Cambridge University in England four years ago. Europeans had fallen in love with some romantic image of the Orient, short of actually embracing its people. Really, it was more of a lust, Kamil thought, that required an unlimited parade of objects to satisfy it. But who was stealing these objects and how were they getting to Europe? There was something deeply disturbing about these particular thefts, as if his own home had been violated.

Yakup returned and held out a starched white shirt. The son of Kamil's cook Karanfil, Yakup was tall and wiry, with high cheekbones and alert, almond-shaped eyes under brows that arched like bows across his forehead. He reminded Kamil of a Seljuk, one of the thirteenth-century Turkish tribesmen whose faces still bore traces of their Asian ancestry. Kamil had seen drawings of them in a collection of miniatures in the library of his friend Ismail Hodja, a learned Sufi sheikh and leader of the Nakshibendi order. Yakup's father had been a Tatar.

Kamil slipped on the fresh shirt, then picked up a string of amber beads from his desk. 'These belonged to my grandfather and probably to his father.' He held them up to the lamp where the beads glowed like miniature hearths. 'If I sold them, I'd probably get only a few kurush for them. But they're worth more to me than almost anything else I own.'

'I know what you mean, bey,' Yakup responded. 'It's as if when you touch it, your fathers are speaking to you. Like a bell ringing and you can feel the vibration, even if you can't hear the sound.'

'That's it exactly. You're a poet, Yakup.' Kamil laid the beads aside, pulled open the top drawer of his desk, and took out a Colt revolver, a box of bullets, and a holster. He pushed the files aside and placed the revolver on the desk. 'Is there anything passed down in your family that speaks to you like that?' He strapped the holster around his waist.

'People like us don't have a history, pasha,' Yakup responded, using Kamil's hereditary title.

Kamil stopped and frowned at Yakup. 'But your father was a water carrier, wasn't he? He had a profession like anyone else.' Like Kamil, most Ottomans used only their given names, adding titles and descriptions to separate Ali the Water Carrier from Ali the Pasha, Grocer Ali from Bosnian Ali. Names passed away with their owners; they didn't accumulate history.

'Great families have histories and their possessions become steeped in them, like baklava in sugar. My father's water skin, on the other hand, rotted and we threw it away. Almost everything in our house was passed along to other families when our need for it was done. It's not the same thing, my pasha. That's how it always was and that's how it always will be.'

Astonished, Kamil said, 'I never knew you were such a fatalist. Come on, Yakup. You don't really believe that, do you?'

Yakup shrugged, his face betraying only a stolid attentiveness, although Kamil thought his eyes sparkled with repressed humour, perhaps even a trace of mockery.

'Your history, my history, it's all the same, Yakup,' Kamil said, reaching for the jacket Yakup held out. He picked up the beads and regarded them thoughtfully. 'You're right about possessions soaking up history, though. Every object contains a story about who made it, who owned it, and what happened to it. The older it is, the richer the story.'

'My father always said, "For the lean ox, there is no knife". If you're poor, no one can take anything away from you.'

Kamil slipped the beads into his jacket pocket and turned to face Yakup. 'Your father came from the Crimea, didn't he?'

'Twenty-five years ago, after the war with Russia. The Cossacks killed his parents, but they missed me and my mother. After the war, he tried to start over, but they told him his land was owned by Russians now. They suspected him because he was a Muslim and he was afraid they were going to arrest him, so my parents joined some other Tatar families and migrated here. My father wasn't even religious,' he added. 'He just wanted to work.'

'Your parents were very brave.' Kamil pulled on his boots, instinctively checking for the long, slim blade secreted in the shaft of one of them.

Yakup shrugged. 'They didn't have much to leave behind. All their wealth was walking beside them on the road.'

Kamil picked up his revolver and dropped a bullet into the chamber. It made a satisfying click when he rotated it. There was a rap at the entry door and Yakup hurried downstairs to answer it. He reappeared with a gendarme captain, who bowed formally and introduced himself. The soldier was young and held himself with easy confidence.

'Welcome, Captain Arif. What news?' Kamil finished loading his gun and snapped it shut.

'Pasha, we have him,' the captain said, standing to attention.

Kamil slipped the revolver into his holster, and pocketed a leather bag of extra ammunition. 'Let's go then.'

The last stage of the operation slid into place.

THE PRIEST STOOD outside the door of a shabby cottage, in an isolated corner of Balat. The house was wedged between the ruins of a Byzantine foundation and a small brick warehouse that backed on to the water. Across the lane, in the dark recesses of an alley, Kamil watched as the priest embraced a man who was standing inside the darkened entrance, then handed him a basket. When the priest had gone, a light appeared behind the closed shutters. The moon now rode low in the sky and the night was dark enough to conceal the platoon of soldiers surrounding the house. Others would be waiting for the priest at his residence.

Kamil lit a cigarette to keep himself warm, careful to keep the glowing tip hidden within the palm of his hand. Captain Arif came to stand beside him, an immaculate Peabody-Martini repeating rifle slung over his shoulder. Kamil offered him a cigarette.

'I thank you, Magistrate,' Captain Arif said in a low voice. 'Perhaps later. My men are in position.'

'Good.' Kamil smoked and thought about the best way to proceed. They had learned that the suspect's name was Marko and he was a member of a group calling itself the Macedonian Revolutionary Organisation. He was fifteen years old.

Kamil glanced at the rifle on the captain's shoulder, threw down his cigarette, and began to walk across the lane towards the cottage.

The captain chased after him. 'What are you doing, pasha?'

'I'm going to talk with him.'

The captain stopped. 'What do you mean talk to him?'

'I'm going to reason with him.'

'With all respect, pasha, you don't know what weapons he has in there.'

'You're not responsible for me, Captain Arif,' Kamil assured him. 'I'm armed.'

The captain didn't look reassured. 'Please, pasha. At least let me go in with you.'

'Stay just outside the door. I'll call you if I need you.'

The captain nodded reluctantly and whispered instructions to an aide.

Kamil knocked. When there was no answer, he knocked again. He could hear someone moving behind the door.

'Who is it?' The voice was indistinct, but sounded young. A boy, Kamil thought. They've sent an army to capture a boy.

'Marko, my name is Kamil Pasha. I'd like to speak with you. I guarantee that no harm will come to you while I'm with you.'

There was no answer.

'There is no reason for you to die.'

'There's no reason for me to believe you either,' the voice said. 'I'm sure you're not alone.'

'No, but I'll come in alone.'

'Why would you do that? Are you trying to prove your bravery?'

'I don't need to prove my mettle against a boy,' Kamil retorted, annoyed. 'I want to talk to you. There's an army out here. Take your pick.'

Captain Arif was pressed against the side of the wall.

The door opened and Kamil could see the shadow of a face beyond it. 'I agree that talking is better than dying,' the voice said, closer now. 'Come in.'

Kamil pushed through the door and slammed it shut behind him. He flinched away from a light held directly before his eyes. A moment later, the light receded. A dark-haired boy with a tired smile beckoned him into the room.

'Sit, Kamil Pasha. Thank you for honouring me with your visit.' He indicated a chair across the sparsely furnished room. There was one other chair, a stained mattress on the floor, and a basket containing food and a book.

As Kamil sat down, he realised his revolver was gone. He scanned the room. Marko was wearing trousers and a shirt, but Kamil didn't discount the possibility that the revolver or some other weapon was secreted in the boy's waistband. Marko brought the other chair to sit facing Kamil and placed the lamp between them. His face was attractive, still rounded with childish plumpness. A dark fuzz across his upper lip and uneven patches on his cheeks indicated the beginnings of a moustache and beard. He had not even begun to shave yet, Kamil observed, then reminded himself of the brutality of the boy's crime.

'What can I do for you, Kamil Pasha?' Marko's voice was deeper than his looks implied.

'I would like you to come with me quietly. The house is surrounded by forty gendarmes. The people who helped you have all been arrested.' At that, Kamil saw Marko's face collapse. For a moment, he thought the boy would cry, but then he saw anger in his eyes.

'What advantage would it bring me to go with you?'

'You would live.'

'Ah.'

They sat silently for a moment. Then Marko asked, 'Answer me this, pasha. If a man kills another man but feels no remorse, does that mean he is by nature a bloodthirsty brute?'

'That depends entirely on the context. A soldier who kills the enemy of his country may be justly proud of his service, while a man who kills another out of greed is an enemy of society.'

'Exactly so.' Marko leaned forward, his eyes shining with passion. 'But one people's just cause is another people's lost territory. Therein lies the dilemma. We Macedonians won our liberty from your empire, but now it has pulled us back like an abused wife who has run away and must be punished. We have an Ottoman governor, but he is simply the greatest of the bandits pillaging our land.'

'The empire's laws are just,' Kamil retorted.

'That's a dream. We're living a nightmare!'

'Why did you kill the governor's aide?'

'He dishonoured my sister.'

Kamil was taken aback. 'Why didn't you accuse him in court?' The moment he uttered the words, he knew how futile such a gesture would have been. The Balkan provinces were in such chaos that the rule of law had ceased to be applied, and judging by the tales of refugees, rape was probably a daily occurrence, one of many unspeakable crimes committed by each side against the other.

Marko nodded, acknowledging Kamil's confusion. 'You're a wise man, Kamil Pasha. I understand that you're devoted to your empire, as I am to my people. By killing the governor's man, I cleaned his filth from a small spot of our land, the size of my palm perhaps.' He held out his hand. 'You must imagine thousands upon thousands of hands, each cleansing the space before them. We will win because each man's ambition is the same. You will lose, pasha, because your empire is driven by the greed of a few men.'

'That's not so, Marko,' Kamil responded heatedly. 'The empire's system of laws . . .'

Suddenly Marko pulled Kamil's revolver from his shirt, held it to his own temple, and fired.

Kamil jumped up from the chair and staggered backward. The door slammed open and Captain Arif rushed in, followed by a dozen heavily armed soldiers. Marko lay on his side, the basket of food on the floor next to him spattered with blood.

'Search the room,' Kamil told the captain.

He picked the book out of the basket, where it had miraculously remained untouched. English poems by John Donne. Kamil opened it at the marker and read, 'Death be not proud, though some have called thee mighty and dreadful.'

'No other weapons,' Captain Arif announced, holding out Kamil's revolver.

Kamil took the gun and slid it into its holster. He steadied himself for a moment against the chair, then dropped the book into his pocket and walked out.

KAMIL MOUNTED HIS horse and let it wander at will through the sleeping lanes of the Old City. After a while, the sky began to bleed light. In the distance, Kamil could make out the dome and minarets of the Mosque of Sultan Ahmet, and those of its Byzantine sister, the Aya Sofya. The dawn call to prayer hovered in the air, snaking like mist from every corner of the city. Long shadows prostrated themselves before the orange light of the rising sun. This early in the morning, Karaköy Square was nearly empty. He passed two fishermen squatting by basins in which fish feebly circled. Trapped and tired, Kamil thought, feeling compassion for a fellow creature in similar straits.

Restless and unable to shake the image of the boy's face – his look of surprise at the moment of death – Kamil dismounted. He wanted to walk the rest of the way to his office, so he left his horse at a stable behind the square.

He bought a simit from a man balancing a tray of the circular breads on his head, then began the steep climb up High Kaldirim Road, a broad stairway lined with shops, most of which were still shuttered. Finding he had no appetite, Kamil offered the rest of his simit to a bony street dog. The dog sniffed it suspiciously, then took it with a delicate snap of its teeth before rushing off.

Kamil's yellow kid boots navigated the uneven steps. His mother had commissioned them from a master bootmaker in Aleppo. Despite the delicate leather and intricate tooling, the boots were almost indestructible, tanned by a secret method passed from father to son that made the leather impervious to knife and water. Their wearer was further protected by talismanic symbols carved inside the shaft. Ill with a wasting disease, his mother had whispered to him, 'So that Allah might lighten your step and guard your path', while the bootmaker's assistant took elaborate measurements of his feet. She didn't live to see the boots finished, but Kamil felt her love in them. It was this, rather than the talismanic charms, he believed, that gave the boots their singular effect.

The baker Ibo leaned out of his shop, hands and forearms white with flour. He motioned a glass of tea at Kamil. 'Do good and receive kindness. Come and rest a moment, Magistrate Bey.'

'Another time, Ibo.' Kamil was in no mood for idle chatter.

He reached into his pocket for his string of beads. As he walked, he drew them over his right hand, his thumb and forefinger smoothing each bead along its way, reading the inflections worn into the amber by his father and grandfather, and finding peace in that continual text. Marko's face receded and Kamil settled into the calm apprehensiveness that allowed him to wander among the facts, gather them up, sort them.

The Christian icon was different, he thought, from the other stolen objects. It was too well known to be sold or even displayed openly. That required a special kind of buyer.

By now he was almost at the top of the road of stairs, where it entered the Grande Rue de Pera.

'Bey, bey.'

Kamil was startled from his reverie by a tug on his jacket. He swung around, irritated to see that it was a street urchin. The boy stepped back but held his ground. Enormous eyes in a pale, fine-boned face focused expectantly on Kamil. A threadbare sweater and wide, much-patched trousers hung on the boy's slim body, held in place by a ragged sash. His bare feet were brown, although whether from the sun or the dirt of the streets was unclear.

The boy stuttered, 'Bey, I . . .' He lowered his eyes and began to back away.

If the boy were a pickpocket, he would have been long gone by now. Kamil reached into his pocket for a coin.

When the boy saw the kurush in Kamil's outstretched hand, his cheeks flushed red and he shook his head vehemently.

'Well, what do you want, my son?' Kamil asked.

The boy seemed to regain some of his courage. He reached into his sash, drew out an object, and handed it wordlessly to Kamil. It was a quill pen. Kamil took it, puzzled.

'Thank you,' he said, turning it over in his hand. It was a simple, common pen like those used in his office. He examined the boy's face. He looked familiar, but Kamil couldn't place him. Perhaps one of the apprentices at the hammam baths he went to every week, or the boy at the coffeehouse who refilled his tea and refreshed the tobacco in his narghile? They were all about the same age, eight or nine, and lean as street cats.

The boy was still looking at Kamil expectantly.

'What's your name?'

'Avi, bey. I am Avi. I brought you a message from Amalia Teyze,' he blurted out. 'You told me that if I learned to use this,' he indicated the pen, 'I should come back and see you.'

'Of course,' Kamil exclaimed. This was the young boy sent last year by the Jewish midwife of Middle Village to give him a message about a murder case. He had been so impressed by the boy's refusal to accept payment – because, the boy had insisted, he was only doing his duty – that Kamil had given him the first object within reach, a pen from his desk. He remembered Avi as the child with hungry eyes, taking in everything in the room. Someone eager to know things.

'Well, Avi. Of course, I remember you.' Kamil wondered what the boy expected of him. Despite the early hour, a small crowd had begun to form around them.

'Why don't we walk a bit together.' Kamil resumed his climb, the boy keeping pace beside him. Out of the corner of his eye, Kamil could see Avi trying to keep a serious demeanour, but his joy kept breaking through. It both amused Kamil and touched him.

'And did you learn to use the pen?' Kamil asked.

Avi stopped and turned to him with a wide grin.

'Yes, bey. Amalia Teyze taught me letters.'

Kamil was surprised. He had thought the midwife illiterate, like so many of the empire's subjects. 'And what can you write?'

They began to walk again.

'My name,' Avi said excitedly. 'I can write my name.'

'Is that so?' Kamil noted noncommittally. He found himself inexplicably disappointed that Avi hadn't learned more than just his name, but reminded himself that this was more than most people could do.

They stopped at a patisserie and he bought Avi a yeast bun stuffed with goat's cheese. The well-heeled patrons stared disapprovingly as the boy placed the bun on his palm and swiftly devoured it, using his other hand to shield it. Kamil wondered why the boy ate so quickly and furtively, as if someone might steal the bun from his hands, and realised he must be very hungry. But surely the midwife cooked for the boy? She had seemed a kind and efficient woman. He took a closer look at the boy's ragged clothing, his grimy face and bare feet. When Avi had come to his office the previous year, his clothing had shown signs of attention from a loving hand. Kamil remembered a colourful sweater and patched but clean trousers. Something must have happened. Had the boy run away? He would give Avi some tea and something more to eat at the courthouse, then sit him down and find out what this was all about. He bought some meat-filled pastries and cheese börek and then they resumed their walk down the Grande Rue de Pera.

When they reached the entrance to the courthouse, Avi stepped back into the street and, crossing his arms, began to shiver, his eyes shifting between the enormous, imposing door at the top of the stairs, Kamil's face, and the ground.

'What is it?'

'I really can write,' Avi said softly. 'But I'm not anybody.'

Kamil stooped down and told him, 'Well, come in and show me what you've learned.' He walked up the stairs. Out of the corner of his eye, he saw Avi trailing behind, awestruck.

Kamil greeted the burly doorkeeper. 'Good morning, Ibrahim.'

'*Günaydin*, pasha.' Ibrahim held open the door and bowed low as Kamil passed through.

Kamil suddenly heard a commotion and turned. The doorkeeper had taken Avi by his sweater like a mother cat lifting her kitten and was hoisting him out of the door.

'Ibrahim, let him go,' Kamil called out. 'He's here to see me.'

Ibrahim shrugged and dropped the boy, who scuttled to Kamil's side. Kamil saw that he was crying but trying to hide it. They walked a short way over the tiled floor, past the small room behind the doorkeeper's station, in which a teakettle was steaming over a brazier. Ibrahim followed with a lamp. At the end of the corridor, the door to the courtroom, still locked at this hour, loomed in the half-light. It was a massive double door, carved with swags of gilded roses, as if justice were a pleasure garden. Beyond was a horseshoe-shaped room that always reminded Kamil of a theatre, with magistrates and solicitors striding across the stage beneath the box that held the presiding judge. The audience would sit behind a waist-high partition, fidgeting and rumbling as if bored by the play.

They entered the suite of rooms that made up the magistrate's offices and waited while Ibrahim lit the lamps. The outer office was still empty of scribes at this hour. During the day, all manner of the empire's subjects sat, patiently waiting to pour their story into the ear of a scribe, who would then translate it into the stilted, self-aggrandising language of bureaucracy in the form of a petition. At the back were two doors to smaller rooms in which Kamil's legal assistants met with solicitors and their clients. A heavy gilded door, mercifully without a garden motif, opened on to Kamil's private office.

The light picked out Abdullah, Kamil's head clerk, snoring on a divan in the outer office. The soles of his feet showed brownish yellow through holes in his socks.

'Abdullah,' Kamil called testily. 'Get up.'

The clerk woke, startled, and rolled to his feet. 'You're here early, Magistrate.' Seeing Avi, he said, 'How did this street dog get in?'

'He's here to see me.'

Abdullah shrugged. 'I'll get the tea, in that case,' he said and, shoving his feet into leather slippers, shuffled towards the corridor.

'Bring two glasses and two plates,' Kamil called after him. He invited Avi into his office and pulled over a chair. When Avi didn't move, Kamil realised he was unfamiliar with chairs and the high tables that accompanied them, alien European contraptions. Kamil fetched a small portable writing desk and placed it on the carpet. Avi folded himself into a sitting position before it.

While they waited Kamil handed Avi his pen, showed him where the ink was, then placed a piece of paper before him. He moved the lamp nearer as the light from the window was still only a pale wash.

Avi touched the white paper reverently. 'I can write on something less good, bey.'

'If you want to be a scribe, this is what scribes write on.' Nonetheless, he was impressed by the boy's frugality and modesty. He noticed that the boy's hands were blistered.

'What happened to your hands?' he asked.

'An accident, bey.' Avi tucked his hands under the desk.

'Someone should take a look at them.'

The boy stubbornly shook his head.

'Can you write?'

'Yes, bey,' Avi responded eagerly.

Kamil stopped, unsure what to tell the boy to write and unwilling to give him a task that he couldn't do and thus shame him.

'Write the alphabet.' Thinking this would buy him some time, Kamil sat at his desk and began to go over his notes on the thefts.

'I'm finished, bey.'

Startled, Kamil walked over to see what the boy had done, prepared for a page of ink blots and scratches. Instead, he found a neat line of letters.

'Why don't you write your name at the top?'

He watched as Avi confidently took the pen, dipped it in ink, and wrote, 'Avi of Middle Village,' the coiled Arabic letters sweeping right to left across the page.

'Write my name.'

Avi wrote, 'Kamil Pasha.'

'Beyoglu Municipality.'

The boy wrote.

'Remarkable.' Kamil took a closer look at him. 'How old are you?'

'I'm nine.'

Kamil made a decision. 'If you'd like to apprentice with the court, Avi, I'll arrange it.'

Avi nodded shyly, eyes gleaming.

An orphan raised by the village midwife, Kamil pitied the boy. His own mother had died after a long illness, and his father had passed away the previous year.

Abdullah came through the door carrying a tray. He put it down on the table and bowed his way out of the room. Kamil opened the package of pastries and placed a meat pastry and a piece of börek on each plate, holding some aside for Abdullah and Ibrahim. He sat at the table before his own plate and watched as Avi climbed on to a chair to eat. The boy added so much sugar to his tea that the spoon almost stood up by itself.

'What would Amalia Teyze say about your working here?' Kamil asked him.

Avi became very still, clasped his hands in his lap, and refused to meet Kamil's eye. Finally, he said in a small voice, 'I know she'd want me to do this.'

It was obvious that Avi was hiding something, but Kamil decided not to press the matter. From what he remembered of Amalia, it seemed unlikely that Avi would have had reason to run away. Perhaps she was ill and couldn't take care of the boy anymore and he was embarrassed to say so. Either way, an apprenticeship would be the best solution. He'd send someone to check on the midwife.

Kamil got up and pulled the cord on the wall beside his

desk to summon Abdullah. The head clerk came into the room and waited just inside the door, pointedly ignoring the boy, who had slid from his chair and stood behind the magistrate.

'Abdullah, this is Avi of Middle Village.' Kamil pulled the boy forward. 'I'm putting him in your care. I'd like him trained as a scribe.' He showed him the paper in his hand. 'You can see that he already knows his letters. Let him learn the trade with the other apprentices and send someone to confirm this arrangement with his guardian, the midwife Amalia. And get him cleaned up.'

'But, Magistrate,' Abdullah sputtered. 'Look at him. He's a street urchin. He can't apprentice here.' He peered at the boy. 'Avi. That's a Jewish name. They can't even speak Turkish properly, much less write it.'

Kamil raised his eyes to look directly at his head clerk and said in an icy voice, 'The Jews are physicians and scholars and the padishah himself employs them. Who are you to claim otherwise?' He glared at Abdullah. 'You can conquer from the back of a horse, but you can't rule from the back of a horse. For that you need learned men.' He pointed his chin at Avi. 'And they start out like this, as young boys with promise.'

'Yes, Magistrate,' Abdullah answered with what Kamil was certain was feigned meekness. The clerk grabbed Avi's arm and led him out.

A few minutes later, the door opened and Abdullah stepped in again. He waited just inside the door, hands clasped before his belly, shoulders slumped.

'What is it now?' Kamil snapped. He despised the obsequiousness subordinates were expected to show their superiors. For all he knew, knife-nosed Abdullah spent his evenings making fun of Kamil in the coffeehouses.

Abdullah straightened. 'Magistrate, a letter from the Ministry of Justice has arrived.'

'Fine. Let me have it.'

Abdullah bustled importantly to Kamil's desk and placed a letter before him, then retreated to wait by the door.

Kamil broke the seal. Minister of Justice Nizam Pasha desired that he come to the ministry immediately. The minister would want to hear his report on this morning's raid, Kamil knew. Word of the arrests would have spread by now.

Kamil had never understood the origin of the minister's seeming dislike of him. He assumed it was because Nizam Pasha had been educated in the religious schools of the old empire, while Kamil represented the new generation of bureaucrats – young, educated abroad, fluent in every language but religion. The minister was in his sixties and still dressed in the old-fashioned robes of the kadi courts instead of trousers, frockcoat, and the jaunty pressed-felt fez that was the mark of the modern man. Kamil had never seen any evidence of corruption, though, and for that he respected the minister.

He set the letter aside and pulled out his pocket watch, another gift from his mother. It was only eight o'clock. The minister kept early hours. Kamil respected that as well, although he wondered why the minister had assumed he would be at the court at this hour when the offices didn't officially open until ten. Kamil had a sudden unpleasant thought. Did Nizam Pasha assume Kamil wouldn't be here, and thus when he failed to appear, could accuse him of not answering the minister's summons? Kamil decided he had no evidence for such a supposition, but the idea soured his mood.

'Get my horse ready,' he told Abdullah gruffly. 'I'll ride over to the ministry now.'

A CLERK USHERED Kamil into the reception hall of the Ministry of Justice. Nizam Pasha was sitting cross-legged on a raised divan, flanked by his advisors. At his feet sat three scribes, bowed over their writing desks. An army of clerks and other officials stood to attention along both sides of the enormous, gilded room. Kamil stepped forward and waited for permission to speak.

'Begin,' the minister commanded, his eyes implacable beneath a large white turban. He wore a black robe with frogged buttons, its wide sleeves lined with magenta silk.

Nizam Pasha listened expressionlessly to Kamil's report. When Kamil described Marko's suicide, the minister's face registered surprise. 'That's unfortunate. We could have obtained a great deal of useful information from him if you hadn't decided to play the hero.'

'I apologise, Minister.' Kamil imagined Marko in the hands of the ministry's torturers and understood the boy's decision. 'From now on, I'll devote myself to the thefts.'

'Now is not soon enough,' the minister said, drawing out his words. 'The entire situation is out of hand. Yesterday the Greek Orthodox Patriarch suggested that the government is involved in the thefts. Unbelievable.' His voice rose. 'He actually accuses us of ransacking their churches to pay for the wars. And now the Jews are starting to complain that their places of worship are being looted as well. They've lost sight of the fact that mosques are being stripped too. The minorities have tasted blood in the provinces and now they're rioting in the capital. These thefts pour oil on the fire!'

Kamil had seen the Muslim refugees from the Balkans.

There were too many for the mosque hospitals and soup kitchens to take care of, and they sat begging in doorways and on street corners across the capital, their eyes angry or simply blank. They bore the scars of massacres, neighbour killing neighbour without mercy. European countries were quietly supporting Christian populations that wished for independence from the empire, fanning the flames of nationalist movements that devoured everything in their way, friend and foe alike. Istanbul was a tinderbox of enraged Muslim refugees who had lost everything and angry minorities who were afraid of losing as much.

'It's not enough that the Europeans are taking our provinces and emptying our treasury.' The minister leaned forward angrily. 'They're stealing our culture too. There's a long pipe sucking the treasures of the empire into Europe and I want you to find it and shut it down. Is that clear?'

'Yes, Minister. I'm . . .'

'I'll give you one week, Magistrate,' Nizam Pasha interrupted. 'Seven days. If you haven't broken this antiquities ring by then, you're dismissed from the court. But if you do manage it,' he paused for several long moments, as if trying to decide whether he should go on or not, 'I can't promise anything, but, who knows, there might be an opening on the Appellate Court.'

Kamil was offended that the minister assumed he had to be bullied or bribed into doing his job. He had made no appeal to Kamil's professionalism or to any shared vision of public service. Kamil wondered if the spirit of public service that had animated his ancestors was now dead; these days, what you did was more important than who you were. There were advantages to this, of course. It allowed talented men to rise, but it also discouraged the enthusiasm that for generations had driven men to follow their families' tradition. Who cared anymore who one's grandfather was, when all that counted were results?

'I'll do my best, Minister,' he responded politely. The Appellate Court was the next level of appeal above the district court Kamil now represented. All were technically subordinate to the chief public prosecutor at the Court of Cassation, but Nizam Pasha insisted that the prosecutors report directly to him. Kamil wondered whether a promotion would give him a freer hand or just subject him to even more scrutiny.

'You'll do more than your best, Magistrate,' Nizam Pasha said in a low voice, then turned abruptly to speak to one of his advisors.

Kamil took that as his cue to leave.

He stepped through the portals of justice into the bustling avenue. The buttresses of Aya Sofya Mosque cast half the street in shadow. He marvelled, as he always did, that the stolid former cathedral was still standing after more than a thousand years, having survived wars and earthquakes. At the other end of the avenue, the slender minarets of Sultan Ahmet Mosque soared white and delicate like orchid stems against the china-blue sky. He had a vision of himself on an expedition in the eastern mountains, bending over a rare orchid. Yet he knew he couldn't escape the responsibilities of his birth. These days, the title of pasha meant little more than a lord, but once it had given a man a clear position and duties in society. His father had been a governor and head of the gendarmes. One grandfather had also been a governor, the other a judge. Kamil had always thought of himself as one of the empire's modern men, but maybe he was really a throwback, an idealist among the technocrats, a sheep jostling amid the goats.

Manoeuvring his horse around the carts and carriages that were beginning to fill the streets, he rode back across the Galata Bridge and up the hill to the Grande Rue de Pera. Boys scuttled by carrying trays of tea and stacks of warming tins, rushing breakfast to craftsmen already toiling in their workshops. Shopkeepers cranked open their awnings and washed down the pavements before their shops. The street was filling with servants purchasing fresh bread for the families in embassies and mansions who were at this moment still rubbing the sleep from their eyes and deciding what to wear.

He loosened the reins, closed his eyes for a moment, and listened.

3

Back in his office, Kamil took up a sketch of a chalice stolen from a mosque two days earlier. Someone had coloured in the precious stones, pink for rubies, yellow for diamonds. Like many in the Old City, the mosque had been converted from a church, and some of its Christian valuables were still kept in a storeroom. Probably not locked or guarded, Kamil thought, shaking his head at the foolhardiness of his countrymen. Constantinople had fallen to the Turkish armies more than four centuries ago, but Istanbul was still strewn with its bones. Byzantine walls, arches, cisterns, and artefacts came to light every time someone stuck a spade in the ground. The old city was encrusted with the new, but no matter how many palaces and mosques the sultans and their families built, the Christian city always found a way to remind the newcomers that it had been there first.

Abdullah brought in a new file. A note attached to the front asked that it be delivered to Kamil directly. Thinking the file might be important, Kamil opened it. A silver reliquary, he read, had been taken the previous day from a storeroom in the Kariye Mosque in Balat. Also a small prayer rug. An accompanying sketch of the rug showed elaborate borders of saz leaves and lotus palmettes, and an open field in the centre of which was a six-lobed medallion. There was a description but no sketch of the reliquary.

He read through the file again, running his hand through his wiry black hair. The streak of white over his left temple had become more pronounced since his father's death and Kamil's lean face appeared older than his thirty-one years.

A small rug and a tarnished silver box hardly seemed worth his while. Why had this file been addressed to him personally? He detached the envelope from the front and broke the seal. Before reading even the first line, his eyes were drawn to the sketch in the bottom right corner, a charcoal rendering of a fox. Above the drawing was the signature 'Malik'.

Kamil remembered Malik with a rush of pleasure. The swarthy, white-bearded man with a pronounced limp had appeared one day at his office soon after he became a magistrate to ask about the medicinal uses of orchid powder. Having spent years finding, sketching, and cataloguing specimens native to the empire, Kamil had been delighted to find someone else interested in orchid lore and invited Malik to his house to see his collection. On that first day, he remembered, they had discussed Kamil's favourite winter drink – hot, creamy saleb, made from the tubers of *Orchis mascula*. People believed it healed the spleen, helped in childbirth, and prevented cholera, something they had both agreed was unlikely. Saleb in Arabic meant fox, Malik had explained, because the orchid's tubers looked like the testicles of a fox.

Their conversation had quickly moved from plants to philosophy. Malik, Kamil discovered, was a remarkably learned man. They began to meet once a month at a café near Karaköy Square, halfway between Kamil's office and the Kariye Mosque, of which Malik was the caretaker. One day in late spring of this year, the café owner had handed Kamil a note in which Malik explained apologetically that a relative had come to town, so he wouldn't be able to visit Kamil for a while. He had signed it with a sketch of a fox. Kamil berated himself for letting six months go by without calling on his friend. What if he had fallen ill? It would have been a simple enough matter to find his house, but Kamil, absorbed in his work, had let it go.

Happy to see that Malik was well, Kamil read his brief note. In it, Malik asked Kamil to come to see him that day on an urgent matter. The note was polite and apologetic, but gave no further information about what was so important. Surely not a simple reliquary and a rug?

Kamil debated whether he should go. He had only a week to solve the thefts. How could he justify wasting time on an errand for a friend?

He reread the report and noted, at the bottom of the page, the name of the police chief responsible for Balat and Fatih, Omar Loutfi. He had met Chief Omar several times and was impressed by his intelligence and tenacity, but remembered him also as a man with a temper, an intemperate tongue, and little patience. Still, discussing the thefts with the police chief of Fatih would give him a legitimate reason to follow up on Malik's request and might even open up new leads. He had to start somewhere.

He left his office cheered at the prospect of meeting up with his old friend. In the antechamber, Abdullah was laughing with another scribe in the corner. When they saw Kamil, they fell silent and lowered their heads respectfully.

Kamil stepped out into the avenue and rounded the corner to the stables at the back of the court building. He waited in the dimness, breathing in the salty scent of hay and equine sweat while the stable boy brought out a strong bay. He swung himself into the saddle, glad of the activity. His horse wound its way through the narrow streets behind the Grande Rue de Pera, past the British Embassy, and down a steep hill to the Old Bridge across the Golden Horn, which shone like beaten copper in the morning light.

CHIEF OMAR WAS a big, rangy man with a greasy moustache and the brusque talk and manner of a soldier. He had soft brown eyes, the kind that would be irresistible to a woman, but which lent the rough policeman a rather doleful air.

'I read your report on the theft at Kariye Mosque,' Kamil told him.

'You came all this way because of a silver box? Not that you're not welcome,' he added graciously.

They were facing each other on low stools in a corner of the Fatih police station. Between them was a round copper tray on a stand that held a battered bowl and two glasses of tea. Despite the early hour, the Fatih station was busy. Several men squatted on their haunches against the wall. A heavily veiled woman sat on a low bench, telling her story to a policeman who stood by a desk. Her son had been missing for three days, she began. Whenever she finished a sentence, the policeman would repeat it to another man, sitting at the desk, who wrote it down in a ledger. Kamil could hear raised voices down the corridor, where they kept the prisoners.

Omar offered him a cigarette. The tea was too sweet for Kamil's liking, but he sipped it out of politeness.

'So, tell me about the reliquary and the rug. If they're so unimportant, why send us a report at all?' Kamil waved a hand at the room. 'You deal with such things all the time.'

Omar shrugged. 'I told the caretaker it would be wasting your time, but he insisted. I hear you've got your hands full with thieves and assassins.' He looked at Kamil with approval.

Kamil brushed off the reference to the previous night's raid. The less said about it, the better. He leaned forward, alert. 'How much do you know about the thefts?'

'What there is to know. A lot of it's happening right here. Fatih has always been a paradise for smugglers. They do quite well with all of Byzantium lying beneath their grubby hands. You should see some of their houses. Not much to look at, but inside they'd rival a pasha's konak.'

Surprised, Kamil asked, 'You've been in their homes?'

'I've been a policeman in this neighbourhood longer than you've been wearing a fez. I know everybody.'

'Why don't you just arrest them?'

'The jail isn't big enough. We watch them and we make sure they know that we're watching them. We've been busy chasing down a string of murders over the past few months. Had another one this morning. They've just brought the body in. Want to see it?'

Kamil didn't, but knew he had to. He followed Omar down the corridor to a small, tiled room. The body of a skinny young man lay on the table, a deep cut in his chest just above the heart.

Kamil walked around the corpse. 'Is there a pattern to the killings?'

'There've been a lot of them.'

Kamil wasn't amused by his flippant tone and regarded the police chief with irritation. 'Who is this?'

'Don't know yet, but bound to be a local, the usual

rabble, stabbed, like the others.' Omar bent over and looked at the hands. 'Chafed knuckles, went down with a fight. One unusual thing is the number of deaths, every other week another body, sometimes two, since midsummer. This was a pretty quiet district before. Nobody knows anything, so people start believing it's all a conspiracy.'

He signalled to an assistant to turn the body over.

'This is the other unusual thing.'

Kamil saw four intersecting cuts on the dead man's back. 'Torture?'

'I don't think so. There was no bleeding. Looks like this was done after he was killed. It's always the same pattern, although not all the bodies have it on them.'

'What do you think it means?'

'Beats me. Looks a bit like mountains,' he tilted his head, 'or wings. Clearly the murderer's mark.'

'A message of some kind?'

'It's not writing, but then most of these thugs can't read anyway, much less write.' Omar turned and led the way back down the corridor. He stopped and spoke to the policeman behind the desk. 'See if that woman recognises ... you know.' He nodded in the direction of the back room. The policeman got up and went over to the woman who had reported her son missing.

Kamil and Omar sat back down on their stools. Kamil lit a cigarette to take away the chill of death.

'A fight over territory between rival gangs of smugglers?' Kamil suggested as he held out his cigarette case.

An agonised wail rose from the corridor.

Omar pursed his lips and exhaled loudly. 'Now we know who the body is. That's the butcher's widow. Must have been her son.' He took a cigarette and rolled it thoughtfully between his fingers. 'If it is a fight over territory, that'd be something new. These smugglers have been doing it for generations. They're organised in families, not gangs. It would explain how that boy,' – he nodded towards the corridor – 'got involved. He's not a member of the smuggling families and they don't take kindly to outsiders. They have their own traditions and they don't get in each other's way. As long as they keep on our good side, we don't bother them either. It keeps the peace.'

'Your policemen take bribes to look the other way?' Kamil asked, watching as the policeman and a woman helped the bereft mother out of the station. 'Don't you think that encourages people to commit crimes?'

Omar looked at Kamil incredulously. 'Ah,' he said finally, as if he had solved a puzzle. 'Of course. They say you have to be ignorant to be a saint. Do you have any idea what a policeman's salary is?'

Kamil ignored Omar's implied insult and admitted that he didn't.

'Four hundred kurush a month.'

Kamil was taken aback. Even the lowest official's salary was fifteen hundred. Ministers earned more than fifty thousand, but they had to support an enormous staff.

'Do you know how much it costs to support a family?' Omar continued relentlessly. 'At least a thousand. Do you think the Ministry of Justice takes bribes into account when calculating a policeman's pay?'

Kamil didn't answer. Was it really corruption if policemen were paid so little that they were forced to take bribes to feed their families? The answer wasn't clear to Kamil, and this disturbed him. Taking bribes was stealing both from the citizens and from the state and it ought to be wrong, always. He thought he might ask Ismail Hodja about it next time they met. The wise old sheikh would surely have some insight.

Meanwhile, Omar continued, 'Just think of bribes as a kind of service tax that goes straight into the pockets of the civil servant, instead of through the government first. If you feed meat to the government, it comes out as shit the other end. Makes sense to give it to a man up front so he can feed his kids. You know the saying, "If one eats while the other can only look on, that's when doomsday starts".'

'It would make more sense for the government to pay the police a decent wage,' Kamil responded drily. 'There's no justice if it can be bought.'

'Like I said, you're a saint, Kamil Pasha.' The police chief flicked his ashes into the bowl. 'I agree, but we're not living in the Garden of Eden.'

'The Garden of Eden is overrated. Think of the snakes and the temptation!'

Omar laughed. 'Yeah, not too different from Fatih.'

'Tell me about the smuggling.'

'Until now, it's been mostly petty stuff that doesn't harm anyone. We don't let anyone get too big because that's dangerous. And we don't like it when someone starts trampling on our district. We're the only ones allowed to wear iron shirts around here.'

Kamil understood this to mean that whoever was responsible for the recent spate of thefts hadn't paid the traditional bribe to the police and was therefore unknown and unpredictable. A co-opted criminal was a predictable criminal.

'The problem is,' Omar continued, 'there are just too many places to hide. This whole area is full of cisterns and tunnels from so long ago, nobody knows where they all are. Sometimes I wonder why the whole district doesn't just slide in. The other day, Ali over there,' – he indicated with his chin the policeman who was again sitting behind his desk – 'was replacing a floorboard in his house and what do you think he found when he took it up?'

'What?'

'A whole goddamned cistern. His house, which, by the way, is as old as ten grandmothers, was propped on top of an enormous lake. One strong fart and the whole thing would have tipped in and sunk.' Omar laughed uncontrollably, knocking against the tray and spilling his tea. Kamil laughed too, picturing the serious Ali hunched over his ledger and breaking wind. He found Omar both disturbing and refreshing.

Omar called over to Ali, 'What happened to your hole?'

Ali looked up, confused. He was tall and gangly, with a jutting nose and hair cropped so close that his ears appeared overly large. His Adam's apple slid up and down like a small animal trapped just beneath the surface of his neck.

'The hole in your floor.'

'Oh,' Ali responded, smiling broadly now. 'I've been fishing. There are fish down there. Big ones.'

'Well, they've been down there for a hundred years, fattening themselves up just for you.' Omar turned back to Kamil. 'Now I've heard everything. Can you imagine fishing through a hole in your floor?' He shook his head in wonder. 'But enough of this. I'm sure you didn't come down here to have a laugh.'

Kamil smiled. 'It has done me good.' He refused an offer of more tea. 'Please tell me about the theft at Kariye Mosque.'

'The caretaker insisted I deliver the report directly to

you. He's an old friend of mine and doesn't usually make unreasonable demands, so I figured he had a reason. Maybe the box is worth more than he's telling me. You read his note? What did it say?'

'Just that he wanted to see me today.'

'Do you know him?'

'I consider him a friend, although I haven't seen him in half a year or so.'

'His nephew came to town around that time. I've seen less of Malik lately too. He's been spending a lot of time at home, probably in his library. I swear that man doesn't need to eat. He survives on books.'

'Tell me about him.' Kamil was curious about Malik's life beyond his own narrow experience of it.

'He's one of the Habesh, you know, the Abyssinians who live over in Sunken Village, next to Sultan Selim Mosque.'

Kamil remembered that Malik had dark-olive skin. 'That's the village inside the cistern, isn't it?' He had heard of this eccentric settlement. 'In the Charshamba district. I thought Malik lived in Balat, near the Kariye Mosque.'

'He does, but his family's in Sunken Village. Ever been there?'

Kamil shook his head no.

'It's a huge open cistern,' Omar explained, 'a hundred and fifty metres on each side and almost eight metres deep. A strange place to put a village. You're walking along the street by the Charshamba market, and then suddenly there's a roof at your feet. Stairs so steep, they make your nose bleed.'

'Is the village all Habesh?'

'As far as I know. Some of them have been there for generations, but new ones join all the time – retired and escaped slaves. Allah knows where they all come from.

The village reminds them of home, I guess. Although you'd think the eunuchs wouldn't be so eager to remember their homeland.'

Kamil remembered the Habesh slave in his father's household when he was growing up. Her skin had the burnished glow of early chestnuts. He had been in love with her, his young heart racing whenever she entered the room to serve coffee to his mother and her guests. It was for good reason, he thought, that Abyssinians were the most sought-after and expensive slaves; they were a beautiful people.

'On Fridays, the village fills up. Habesh come from all over for the ceremony.'

'What ceremony?'

'There's a hall where they sacrifice an animal and pray. Some kind of old Habesh custom. Then the men walk over to the Kariye Mosque and pray some more. You'd think that with praying twice on Fridays, they'd be more devout, but when they get back, there's a feast. They play drums and the men sit around drinking raki.'

'You seem to know a lot about it.'

Omar grinned. 'I like to drink raki and the Habesh are very hospitable. It gives me pleasure to lie inebriated eight metres below the ground in the shadow of a great mosque, letting the prayers of the faithful roll over me. It's like practising being drunk and holy for your coffin. Plus, they pray enough for all of us, so I don't have to bother.'

Kamil imagined Omar pretending to be drunk, all the while keeping a close watch on the community.

'Why do they go all the way to the Kariye when the Sultan Selim Mosque is right there?' he asked, puzzled. The Kariye Mosque was near the city walls and, he guessed, at least a twenty-minute walk from Sunken Village.

'They have some kind of special relationship with the Kariye. Malik is the caretaker there, but it goes back before him. The caretaker position is inherited, always a Habesh.'

'Does Malik have a son?'

Omar clicked his tongue. 'As far as I know, he never married. A sign of great intelligence. The position'll go to his nephew, Amida. Malik's sister, Balkis, is the priestess.'

'A priestess? I thought they were Muslims.'

'So they say,' Omar replied cryptically.

'Tell me more about the robbery at the Kariye.'

'Well, since you're here, I can tell you there are some interesting angles to this robbery. For instance, what the thief didn't take.'

'What do you mean?'

'Well, he took that old, tarnished reliquary, but he didn't take a gold chalice studded with rubies that was in the same room. There was even a box of coins and he didn't touch it. And the mosque has some valuable silver candle-holders, although those are heavy. He must have taken the rug to wrap the reliquary in.'

'Some thieves specialise,' Kamil reflected, 'while others take anything they see. Either this was a particularly picky thief, or he was disturbed and had to leave before he could take anything else.'

'I don't think he was chased off. About four in the morning, an apprentice was walking by on his way to stoke the fire at a bakery and he saw a man coming out of the mosque carrying something.'

'A witness!' Kamil exclaimed, excited at the prospect of a real lead. 'Why didn't you write that in your report?'

Omar looked sheepish. 'To tell you the truth, Magistrate, I thought you people never read them.'

Kamil sighed with frustration. That explained the skimpy police reports. 'Well, we do. At least, I do.' Now he would have to follow up each case individually, something that could take weeks when he had just seven days. He wished he had trained investigators on his staff, but he had to rely on the police, the gendarmes, and a roomful of lazy clerks. When this was over, he would approach the minister about training investigators for the new courts.

'I'm glad to hear it, Magistrate, although in this case you're probably wasting your time.'

'Without decent reports, the whole enterprise is a waste of time,' he couldn't help remarking. 'But the fact that you have a witness is excellent news. Did you get a description of the thief?'

'Short and stout, with curly hair that fell below his ears, wearing a wide jacket and a turban. Oh, and the boy said the man was bent over as if he was locking the door. Then he ran off with something bulky under his arm.'

'The reliquary wrapped in the carpet.'

'Right. But it's not much to go on. Short, fat, and curly haired. Could be anyone. Could be me.' He showed a row of tobacco-stained teeth beneath his moustache.

'You're not short.'

'True.' Omar rubbed his balding head.

'So the thief wasn't disturbed. But why take just a worthless box?'

'Exactly. You'd think he'd be tempted by the chalice. It was sitting there in full view in the storeroom.'

Kamil clicked his tongue in disapproval.

'There was also a spilled medicine bottle.'

'What do you make of that?'

'That the room wasn't only used for storage.'

'Let's go there,' Kamil suggested.

On their way out of the station, Omar stopped by the policeman Ali's desk, leaned over, and told him in a low voice, 'Go find our ear in Charshamba. I want to know if there's any new activity. The magistrate here wants to get his hands dirty.' He turned to Kamil. 'I should wear one of those necklaces the old warriors had where they strung up their enemies' ears. I swear, having informants in the right place at the right time makes the difference between being a policeman and a donkey.'

They stepped into Small Market Street, where a young officer was waiting with their horses. The sky had become overcast and thunder rumbled over the sunflower fields in distant Thrace. They turned down one, then another narrow lane. Kamil tried to remember their route but soon lost track. Wooden houses in various stages of decay listed into the lane on both sides, their protruding second storey almost touching overhead. Some of the houses were missing wooden slats, revealing naked laths beneath or gaping holes. The houses were set within a gap-toothed landscape of ruined brick walls, many with the characteristic striped pattern, alternating brick and stone, laid by Byzantine masons. The district looked wounded, Kamil thought, still festering after four hundred years. Late-summer carnations brightened crumbling windowsills and sagging balconies.

Except where the streets narrowed, they walked their horses side by side. Pedestrians, peddlers and their carts, and the ubiquitous cats scattered before them. As they rode, Kamil filled Omar in on the rash of thefts and the way antiquities were appearing in Europe within weeks of being stolen. 'This has to be an organised ring. For such a fast delivery system, they must have very good connections.'

Omar nodded thoughtfully. 'Not the usual family business then, although you'd be surprised how clever and connected some of these people are. I've heard rumours, though, about a new dealer who pays so much that he's driving the old-timers out of business. Unless they sell to him, of course. They call him Kubalou. That's all I know.'

Kamil's mind began to sort new possibilities. 'He's Cuban?'

'That's what they say. I've never seen him. For that matter, I couldn't tell a Cuban from a cantaloupe. He speaks English, does everything through middlemen so nothing leads back to him. Maybe that's what the killings are about. As you said, a turf war, but between the dealers, not the thieves. Kubalou's gang against the old families.'

'It's the extent of the operation that puzzles me. It's on an entirely different scale from anything we've seen before, things disappearing all over the empire and ending up in London. We tracked some items stolen in Bursa and Edirne to Istanbul, so it looks like the smuggling routes converge here. If we could find the Kariye thief, he might lead us to the next level up in the hierarchy. It seems unlikely that one man could be behind something as elaborate as this.' Kamil guided his horse around a cart piled with apples that was blocking the lane. 'All of these antiquities should be put in the Imperial Museum for safekeeping,' he grumbled.

'I agree. But that would have been like throwing chickens to the foxes when all the museum directors were European.'

'Well, Hamdi Bey is head of the museum now,' Kamil responded. 'And we have an antiquities law.'

'So we have teeth but nothing to bite.'

The road climbed upward. After a while, they passed a shade-dappled fountain and emerged into a small square that was dominated by a perfectly proportioned Byzantine church, its domes rising softly above the portico. It was now a mosque, of course, but after seeing the decay of the streets leading up to it, Kamil was touched by its survival. A teardrop shaped ornament capped its minaret and a patchwork of tile-roofed houses unfurled behind it like a cloak.

The classic imperial mosques built by master Ottoman architects like Sinan were more majestic by far, but to Kamil's eye, the former churches had a sturdy charm. Some people might find his admiration for Christian architecture suspect, but he didn't care. He had tried to believe in something beyond this world, especially after his father committed suicide the previous year. Blaming himself, Kamil had been plagued by nightmares and headaches. Ismail Hodja had encouraged him to meditate on Allah's presence in the world and he had done so, sitting in the Nakshibendi order's lodge high on a hill in Beshiktash, allowing the soothing poetry and prayer to penetrate him. At least the nightmares had faded. But the pretence of faith was too hard to keep up and he had sought his natural direction, as always, in science and rational thought, in the straight line of understanding rather than the straight path of Allah. Reason and routine didn't bring solace, but they brought some measure of peace, the kind of peace that came when one ceased to struggle. That was almost the solace of faith, he thought, though it did nothing to ease his headaches.

'That's Kariye Mosque,' Omar explained. 'The imam lives over there. We'd better let him know we're here.'

They dismounted before a small, whitewashed cottage. Omar raised the knocker and let it fall. After a few moments, the imam, a skinny man with a stained yellow beard and hastily wound turban, opened the door, squinting against the light.

'This is the magistrate,' Omar announced without preamble. 'He's here about the theft.'

The imam blinked nervously at Kamil. 'It wasn't my fault,' he stammered. 'That's the caretaker's responsibility. Ask Malik.' He started to close the door, but Omar leaned his shoulder against it.

Kamil noted that the imam's teeth had rotted to brown stubs and wondered whether the old man was in pain. That would explain the medicine bottle found in the storeroom. 'Hodjam,' he said, addressing him as teacher, 'I'd like to take a look at the room where the theft occurred.'

'Oh, of course.' The imam appeared relieved, and smiled ingratiatingly. 'Omar, you know where Malik is. Get him to unlock the door for you. I haven't finished my prayers.'

Nothing sweetened a man like respect, Kamil thought.

As Kamil and Omar approached the mosque, a tall, dark-complexioned man with a white beard rounded the corner. He was wearing a white turban and a brown wool robe fastened by a silver pin of intricate design. As he approached, his broad shoulders dipped with each step and his right foot dragged slightly. Beside him walked a slight figure in an apple-green charshaf.

Malik smiled broadly. 'Kamil, my friend, it's good to see you again. How are you?' He took hold of Kamil's shoulders.

'I'm well, Malik. I'm well.' Kamil was enormously pleased to see his friend.

The woman beside Malik held her veil pinched shut

beneath her nose so that it framed her eyes, which were green and held the light like liquid. They were trained curiously on Kamil.

'This is my niece, Saba,' Malik explained. 'She's one of my best pupils. Saba, this is Kamil Pasha, magistrate of Lower Beyoglu,' Malik told her in a meaningful tone, then leaned over and said something to her that Kamil didn't catch. There were undertones in their exchange that he found vaguely disquieting, and he had the feeling that this meeting had been prearranged.

Saba looked up at him and stepped closer. 'My uncle has told me about you, Kamil Pasha.' Her voice had the melodious resonance of a clarinet, sweet and tenacious.

Kamil placed his hand over his heart and bowed his head in greeting. '*Selam aleikum*, peace be upon you.'

'*Aleikum selam*, upon you be peace, Pasha. I'm glad finally to have the honour of meeting you.' Her eyes tilted slightly upward. Kamil fancied that they flashed with interest before she lowered them modestly.

'We'd be honoured if you would visit our humble home, Kamil Pasha,' she told him, then took her leave.

They watched the tiny green figure move off down the street and disappear around the fountain.

'A remarkable young woman,' Malik said to no one in particular.

Kamil was tempted to take this as an invitation to ask about her, but decided it would be indiscreet.

'My family lives over in Sunken Village,' Malik said.

'Omar was telling me the village is mostly Habesh.'

'There are about forty families. We make a living selling produce from our gardens.'

'And smuggling,' Omar interjected.

Malik looked at him reprovingly. 'That's just gossip.'

'Come on, Malik. Everyone knows that. I hear your sister, Balkis, is quite well off. There's no way she got rich selling vegetables.'

Malik frowned. 'Her husband passed away and left her well cared for. Why do you always kick over rocks looking for scorpions? Sometimes a rock is just a rock and covers nothing but plain soil.'

'The soil in this part of town is rich with manure,' Omar retorted.

Kamil wondered at the relationship between the mild old man and the gruff police chief. They quarrelled like an old married couple.

'I'm impressed by how much you know about what goes on in this area,' he told Omar.

'The coffeehouse,' Omar said with a grin. 'Everybody knows everybody. All you need is an ear and a strong stomach. But enough socialising. If we don't get this case solved by lunchtime, I'll starve.'

Kamil turned to Malik. 'You asked to see me. Is it about the theft?'

'I'm sorry to trouble you with it,' Malik answered, pressing Kamil's hand between his own. It was an unremarkable statement, but Kamil saw the urgency in his friend's eyes.

'On the contrary,' Kamil responded, 'an opportunity to meet up with an old friend is precious. And I hear there was a witness. There've been thefts from the Patriarchate, the Fatih Mosque, and other places in the area. One thief could lead us to others, especially the dealers they sell to.'

Malik looked relieved. 'I'll do whatever I can to assist. What else can I tell you?'

'You've heard the description of the thief?'

'Omar told me,' Malik replied. 'Long hair. Could it have been a woman?'

Kamil nodded thoughtfully. 'I hadn't considered that possibility. Do you have the key to the storeroom?'

'It's not locked. The keys to those old doors are long gone. The mosque was restored about ten years ago and we asked the Ministry of Pious Foundations to replace the doors, but they didn't see fit to do so. Only the outer door can be locked.'

'How many keys are there?' Kamil remembered that the baker's apprentice had seen the thief bend over the door as if locking it.

'Just one. Both the imam and I use it, so we keep it in a room behind the mosque to which we both have a key.'

Two men were arguing in the square. A group of men surrounded them and began to take sides. There was shouting and a scuffle.

Malik frowned in their direction. 'It's probably about the icon, the one that was stolen from the Patriarchate. You heard about it?'

'Of course,' Omar replied, his eyes on the quarrelling men.

'The Christians are blaming the Muslims for stealing it. It's ridiculous, of course. Everyone knows a theft is just a theft.'

As the tension in the square rose, Kamil waited for Omar's cue to act. It was his district. Just then, the imam appeared and spoke to a few of the men. They turned their backs angrily and left, and the argument seemed to subside.

'Let's see the key,' Omar suggested.

Malik led Kamil and Omar around to the back of the mosque, where a small, whitewashed structure had been built into the corner of a collapsed but still massive brick wall.

'This used to be a church in Byzantine times,' Malik explained. 'The name, Saint Saviour in Chora, referred to the fact that in those days it was in the country, outside the original city walls.' He laid his hand on the crumbling bricks. 'This is all that's left of the monastery. The monks spent their time copying old texts. They copied Greek manuscripts that have been lost in the original, and they translated Arab writings from earlier centuries. If it weren't for the monks, we wouldn't have Ibn al-Thahabi's medical treatise *The Book of Water* or al-Ma'mun's *Face of the Earth*, based on Ptolemy's geography. When you come again, I will show you some pages. I have a modest collection in my home.' He pointed beyond the rubble to a nearby two-storey house that stood alone in a small yard. 'You're welcome any time.' He looked directly at Kamil. 'Why don't you join me for breakfast one day soon? Perhaps tomorrow? As long as the weather allows, I put a table under the plane tree behind my house. It's very pleasant and the housekeeper supplies me with excellent cheese from her village.'

Beneath the pleasantries, Kamil heard the entreaty in Malik's voice. For some reason, he thought, Malik wished to speak with him alone. 'Thank you, Malik. I look forward to it.'

After a moment, Malik added, 'You're welcome to come too, Omar, but you know that.'

'Thanks, but I see enough of you already.' Omar was prowling the perimeter of the building, testing the windows. 'A child could open these windows,' he pointed out, teasing one open with a small knife.

Malik unlocked the door and led the way into a bright, pleasant room with blue-washed walls. 'Quran classes are held here now, so it's still a place of learning.'

The room was furnished with a threadbare carpet. A cushioned divan stretched along two sides, and more cushions, their colourful geometric designs stitched in wool, were stacked on the floor. Kamil saw several low writing desks, a shelf of books and papers, and a cabinet that presumably held writing supplies.

Malik opened the cabinet and took a heavy iron key from the top shelf. 'It's possible that someone saw where we keep the key,' he told Kamil. 'As you can see, it's quite large.' He slipped it into the pocket of his robe.

He let them into the mosque and lit a lamp. Kamil was surprised by the brilliant mosaics lining the domes and arches above him. He saw peacocks, trees, fruited branches. Jesus taking a woman's wrist. A woman kissing his hem. A diminutive Mary, her head caressed by an angel, approaching a woman on a throne, her hands outstretched. The dazzling images and colours were overwhelming. Kamil had never seen anything better, even in the Aya Sofya Mosque where fragments of gilded mosaics were still visible in the upper galleries.

Malik followed his startled gaze.

'Thirty years ago, this was all painted over. The plaster was cracked and filthy. Then there was a fire and Sultan Abdulaziz, may he be rewarded in heaven, allowed the architect Kuppas to restore the interior. During the restorations, these mosaics were revealed. Aren't they magnificent? These are scenes from the life of Mary. The Byzantines believed her to be the mother of God, the Container of the Uncontainable, the vehicle by which Jesus came to the earth. Chora also means the dwelling place of the Uncontainable.'

Kamil was puzzled. 'I admit they're beautiful, but surely depictions of the human form are prohibited, especially in a mosque. Why didn't they plaster over them again?'

'You're right, but this wouldn't be the first time that rule was broken. Persian and Ottoman artists have always painted scenes from the lives of important persons, pictures of hunts, battles, processions, picnics, circumcision parties, all kinds of everyday activities. Like most civilisations, the Byzantines used art to honour their leaders, especially those who had a lot of money.' He pointed to a faint figure painted on plaster against the outer wall. 'That's Theodore Metochites, the patron who paid for these mosaics.'

Kamil could barely make out the image of a man wearing a striped turban who was presenting a miniature of the church to Christ.

'Still, it's forbidden by the Quran,' Omar pointed out.

Malik looked at Omar with an expression Kamil put somewhere between respect and disbelief.

'There are two kinds of religion in the world, my friend,' Malik explained patiently. 'One is blind faith that requires only obedience and discourages thought. It's to the leader's advantage that you see only his heels, so he demonises all other views. That kind of faith is comforting, but it can lead you down treacherous paths. Another kind of faith encourages the faithful to think about what they're doing and why. These are people who praise Allah in the highest way they can imagine, through scholarship or art, or simply by consciously living as good Muslims. The rules don't matter as much as the principle.' Malik put his arm around Omar's shoulders. 'I'm worried about you suddenly becoming devout, my friend.'

'Well, it's true I don't know much about it,' Omar admitted reluctantly, 'but it seems to me that Islam is Islam and there are certain rules. I'm a policeman because I like to know what's what.'

'In the Quran it says that all the prophets back to Abraham were given the same message. Jews and Christians share the same prophecy as Muslims.'

'Of course, but Islam is different. Our Prophet is the last one.' Omar shrugged, then admitted to Kamil, 'I don't believe any of it, really, without proof.'

'Faith means believing anyway,' Malik explained.

'That's the problem,' Omar replied. 'But I still like to get the story straight.'

Kamil thought it was as perceptive a description of his own feelings as any he had heard, but said nothing.

Malik craned his neck at the mosaics. 'Regardless of the theology, these mosaics deserve to be displayed for their beauty alone. Look how the colours are striking, even after all this time. The craftsmen used gold and ground lapis. But they used simple materials too. Look over here. They used tiny pieces of pottery to make these amphorae. The theme of Mary as Container is everywhere, even in the structure of the building. Let me show you.'

He led Kamil and Omar to the end of the hall and a small door that stood open. Inside, Kamil could make out the base of a steeply winding stair that led to the top of the minaret, where the imam called the faithful to prayer five times a day.

'The walls are very thick here in order to hold the weight of the bell tower.' Malik pointed upward. 'There are also ceramic jars built into the corners with their openings exposed so that moisture doesn't build up inside the walls. They're called weepholes. The workers keep plastering them over, so they're hard to spot.'

'Clever engineering,' Kamil responded, thinking that

faith required a great deal of creativity to find signs in even the most mundane objects.

As if reading his mind, Malik said, 'You're a sceptic, Kamil, I know. And maybe the architects of this church had nothing more in their heads than keeping the walls dry. But the actors don't write the play.'

'I like to think we write our own scripts.'

'It's in our nature to try,' Malik responded good-naturedly.

'It's my observation,' Omar interjected, 'that someone else is always trying to write it for you. Your wife, your mother-in-law, the government . . .'

Malik laughed. 'A man whose nature is untamed by his heart. You should be grateful you have a wife who puts up with you.'

'Never marry a woman who was spoiled by her father,' Omar said to Kamil. 'A peddler's daughter loves beads.'

'Do you have children?' Kamil asked.

'By the will of Allah, it hasn't happened.' Omar looked uncomfortable.

Kamil felt sorry for the burly police chief. Having no children, especially sons, was considered a tragedy by many. It was said that a man without a son was a man whose hearth had gone out and it occasioned pity and sometimes scorn, especially for the man's wife, who was usually held responsible. Omar didn't seem the sort to appreciate people's pity.

'Where do you teach your pupils?' Kamil asked Malik.

'In the room behind the mosque. When I have female pupils, my housekeeper comes and knits. I'm hoping she's learning something just by being in the same room. I took Saba on as a pupil because she has a passion for the old languages and learns them as readily as birds take to the air. Allah has placed in her a yeast that I'm privileged to help rise.'

'Old languages?' Kamil asked. He had assumed Malik taught only the Quran.

'Greek, Aramaic, the sacred languages.'

Omar scoffed. 'Half the neighbourhood speaks Greek.'

'Modern Greek is infected with the street. It sheds history like a dog flinging rain off its pelt.'

'Those Greek dogs,' Omar joked. Malik laughed.

Kamil watched them, envying their easy camaraderie. He had few close friends. His American friend Bernie had returned home the previous year, leaving a gap that Kamil found he was no longer able to fill as easily with work and books and orchids. He wandered into the central prayer room, its walls decorated with marble panels instead of mosaics. He let his eyes try to puzzle out the patterns in the marble. They looked like the desert, a sea, snowy mountains. Art with no human intercession, remote and beautiful.

Malik followed him, seeming to sense his mood. Kamil was glad of his company. 'Those revetments were once Greek columns. To get these continuous patterns, the Byzantines cut the columns into thin slices that unfolded like fans.' Malik illustrated with the palms of his hands.

Kamil noticed Malik wore a gold signet ring on his right forefinger. It had a curious design engraved on it, a disc and crescent. The silver pin that clasped his cloak was also unusual, a geometric weave of lines. He wondered about the history of Malik's family. Had there been Abyssinians in Istanbul during Byzantine times? Perhaps they had been desired as slaves even then.

Malik stopped in the middle of the room and swept his hand towards the walls. 'The Greeks built their empire on top of what came before them, Constantinople was built on Greek ruins, and Istanbul is built on top of Byzantium. Nothing is wasted. There's a lesson there,' he smiled mildly at Kamil, 'but I'm not wise enough to know what it is.'

As they walked back to the corridor, Malik leaned closer and said in a low, urgent voice, 'Tomorrow morning. Please do come to my house. I must speak with you.'

Puzzled, Kamil assured him that he would.

'Thank you, my friend.' Malik squeezed Kamil's arm, then turned and walked away quickly.

Omar was in conversation with a tall, thin man by the mosque entrance. As Kamil drew closer, he recognised the policeman Ali. The two spoke in low voices and then Ali left.

'Our snitch in Charshamba has reported that there's going to be a big smuggling operation late tonight,' Omar told Kamil. 'Do you want to join us in the raid?'

'Of course.' So far, he had learned nothing about the thefts here, only about Byzantine architecture. He wondered what it was that Malik had to tell him.

'Good,' Omar said amiably. 'Let's go fishing and see what lands in our net.'

They went looking for Malik and found him sitting on a sarcophagus in a long, narrow room with a domed ceiling. More sarcophagi rested in niches along the wall. One side of the room was piled with sacks and chests. In the corner, someone had arranged a circle of cushions around a low tray.

'The reliquary that was stolen was silver and somewhat damaged. It's very old,' Malik explained, getting to his feet. 'The rug once belonged to Sultan Ahmet I, so I think it must have been valuable.' His face looked drawn and Kamil had the impression that his friend had aged in the few moments since their whispered conversation.

'What was in the reliquary?'

Kamil noted a slight hesitation before Malik answered.

'It was empty.'

'Where was it?'

'In here.' Malik went to the back corner and opened a dusty chest.

'How often was this chest opened?'

'Never, that I know of.'

Kamil pointed to numerous finger marks in the dust around the latch and lid. 'So these must be the thief's. Was the lid open or closed when you arrived?'

'Open. That's how I knew the reliquary was missing.'

'How did you know what was in here if the chest was never opened?'

Malik looked startled. After a moment, he said, 'I saw it open once and I remember seeing the reliquary.'

This seemed unlikely to Kamil. The chest was filled with a jumble of objects. Why would Malik notice an unremarkable reliquary with enough accuracy to be able to tell it was missing? It was also clear to Kamil that Malik was not accustomed to lying and it made him enormously uncomfortable. Malik wanted the reliquary found, yet he also wished it to appear unimportant. Perhaps, thought Kamil, that was why he had asked Omar to send for him, knowing he would investigate the matter out of friendship, despite the trivial value of the stolen object. Perhaps the reliquary had personal meaning for Malik and he could think of no other way to convince the authorities to look for it. Kamil planned to have his officers make the rounds to the other police stations that had reported thefts, but for the moment the reliquary was his only lead. He systematically checked the other chests and bundles in the room. The dust on all of them had recently been disturbed.

Omar pointed to one of the open chests. 'If I wanted to steal something, I would have taken some of these.'

Kamil looked over and saw dented gold plates, a chalice, and other objects he didn't recognise, some elaborately decorated with niello work and a few with jewels.

Omar lifted up a heavy gold chalice studded with rubies.

Kamil was flabbergasted. A chalice like this could buy a small villa. 'Why are these objects not under lock and key?' He thought of Hamdi Bey's museum with frustration.

Malik looked embarrassed. 'The Imam occasionally likes to do an inventory of objects.'

It could have been the Imam, then, who had drawn his fingers through the dust. Omar flipped open a small carved box, revealing a cache of coins, not a few of them gold liras.

'Tithes. The thief didn't take them either.'

'Was the box open?' Kamil asked.

'For inventory,' Malik repeated, then paused before pointing to a small, upended medicine bottle on the tray. 'The Imam has terrible toothaches. Sometimes he's a bit forgetful after taking his medicine.'

'Forgetful enough to leave the door unlocked?'

'I always check the door before I retire,' Malik insisted. 'Whoever came in here had the key.' Malik sounded so despondent that Kamil found himself wondering whether Malik had an idea who had taken the reliquary.

Kamil sniffed the mouth of the bottle. 'Laudanum.' The Imam had turned his pain into his own version of paradise.

'In the future, I'll add such details to my reports,' Omar promised, then turned to Malik. 'My brother, I've learned that up on their unholy hill of Pera, the magistrates actually read the crappy reports we send them. That alone will help me sleep well tonight.'

Omar was right, Kamil thought. The mystery lay in what the thief hadn't taken. He began to see that this reliquary might be more valuable than he thought. He placed his hand on Malik's arm. 'Each loss is a counsel,' he reassured him. 'There's much here to help us.'

4

Three young boys lay flat on the ground, heads hung over the edge of the cistern wall, frightened by the unprotected distance to the rocky earth below, but daring each other to creep closer. The wall was built in layers, five courses of brick and five of stone, scored at intervals by lines of large marble slabs, with moss and grasses growing from its crevices. Despite its great age and state of disrepair, the wall appeared massive and more enduring than any of the flimsy wooden cottages in Sunken Village below. At intervals, the cistern bent inward in shallow arches, revealing masonry the width of a man's reach.

The boys watched people emerge from their cottages and converge like trails of ants on the domed stone structure in the village square.

'Why are they going to the mosque? I didn't hear the ezan.'

'And look, the women are going too.' The boy raised his arm to point.

His friend pushed him and laughed.

The boy quickly pulled in his arm and grabbed a protruding stone to keep from sliding over the edge. 'Stop it,' he whined.

'They're slaves,' his friend pointed out proudly. 'You know what they do in Africa? They cut off their *yaraks*.'

'They do not. How do you know, anyway?'

'My uncle told me. He was there. He said that's where they make eunuchs.'

'Where?'

'Addis Ababa.'

'That's not really a place.'

'Is too.'

'Isn't.'

They tussled on the lip of the cistern until the third boy, who had been watching the line of people in the square below, turned and slapped them both on the ear.

ONE DAY A red line had appeared on Balkis's mother's wrist where she had cut herself on the tine of a monstrance, a top-heavy gold receptacle with a flattened face shaped like the sun. How and when the monstrance had come into the family's possession was unknown, but it must once have served Roman Catholics to display the wafer they adored as the body of their God. The red line had slowly but inexorably lengthened, reaching up along the inside of her mother's arm until Balkis imagined it had tied her heart up like butcher's string and stilled it. After her mother's death, Balkis kept the gold monstrance, tarnished by her mother's blood, on a shelf in the receiving hall. It reminded her of many things: to live, never to forgive.

This Friday, she had risen early and passed through the door at the back of her house that led to a small marble hammam bath. A servant fed the wood-fired boiler. Hot water flowed through ceramic channels beneath the floor and spilled from a spigot set over a marble basin. Balkis took her time bathing, allowing the heat to penetrate her muscles and release her from her body. The midwife Gudit, an old, square-shouldered woman with a face and neck like a bull, scrubbed her skin with a textured silk mitt and denuded Balkis's body hair with aghda, a mixture of sugar boiled with lemon juice, until the space between her legs was as smooth as an egg. After Gudit left, Balkis reached down and drew her fingers along the two lines of small round scars from the thorns that the midwife had used to pin her wound shut after circumcising her. A small pinhole at the centre, where the midwife had left a straw reed inserted until the wound healed, was the only opening that remained.

'Container of the Uncontainable,' Balkis thought sourly. They hadn't told her beforehand that the priestess became the container, never to be opened again, for ever empty. After performing the circumcision, the midwife had told her that she would look beautiful, but Balkis had felt only despair. Now, seventeen years later, her wounds had healed, but the rage she felt was still raw.

After her bath, Balkis lay wrapped in a towel on a bench in the cooling-off room, thinking through her plan. She was short and plump, with a round face, a patrician nose, and lips tightly pressed, a door slammed shut on an elegant ruin. Her golden complexion highlighted her alert brown eyes, framed in starbursts of wrinkles; the face of a once beautiful woman violated by time.

Gudit brought a glass of tea and withdrew.

Balkis ran her fingers over the designs cut into the crystal and thought about the community she led, the Habesh and their Melisite sect. She focused her mind on her two children, Saba and Amida, who would lead the sect when she and her brother, Malik, passed away. It was all well and good that Saba believed in their sacred mission, but the girl would have to stop reading long enough to learn the affairs of the community. Bees only rush to the hive with a queen bee in it.

She wished Malik took more interest in Amida, her beautiful boy who had become such an attractive, talented, but wayward young man. They had to find a way to channel his angry energy into the community. The Habesh needed his leadership so they would become prosperous again and so that the young people would stay in the village. Without a thriving community, the Melisite traditions wouldn't survive. Four hundred years of Melisite ancestors sat in judgement, should she fail.

The Habesh had long supported themselves by serving as intermediaries, buying stolen and forged items from certain families in Charshamba and passing them on to dealers in the bazaar. It was a risk-free business based on trust, and lucrative enough to have supported her village for generations. She remembered her own mother in the receiving hall of this very house, setting terms with men from the Covered Bazaar. But in the past year, the supply had dried up and the villagers were suffering. Young people were moving away to look for work. Their children would grow up Muslim, never knowing the joy of witnessing God, the blessing of their ancient community. She had to find a way to keep them here and the community alive. They must love her and, through her, their God. This sacred hunger, to which she fed her rage, was what kept her alive.

Balkis returned to the house. In the dressing room, Gudit rubbed her down with warm towels, then laid out the traditional garments worn by the priestess. Shivering with cold, Balkis put on a finely worked, backless linen robe held up by straps of pearls. She lowered her head so Gudit could place a gold chain, from which hung a key, around her neck. Gudit then settled a turban on Balkis's head and draped a welcome cloak around her shoulders.

Gudit said little these days and her expression, which had never been pleasant, was perpetually sour. When Balkis became priestess, she had initially avoided the midwife, the agent of her circumcision, but quickly realised that Gudit was very knowledgeable. Feuds among villagers, bad harvests, epidemics – these were recurring problems. Gudit remembered how they had been handled in the past. On her advice, Balkis had revived old institutions, such as her grandmother's informal court of mediation over which the priestess presided as neutral arbiter. She added her own innovations, for instance rotating crops so the harm of one season wouldn't pass easily to the next, and adding winter crops. A stand in the market now sold village-produced craft, providing income even when the gardens failed. When disease gripped the surrounding areas, Balkis took advantage of the natural boundary of the cistern wall to quarantine the village. For all of these schemes, Gudit had been a sounding board, until the young surgeon Constantine Courtidis came to the village and she had fallen sullenly silent.

Courtidis had begun to visit Sunken Village a year ago, offering to care for the sick at little charge. Although he brought modern European medicines, people continued to ask Gudit for her traditional remedies on the principle that two cures were better than one. But Balkis was certain Gudit felt pushed aside. The problem, she thought irritably, was of the midwife's own making. She was becoming old and had trained no one to take her place.

Balkis stepped from her dressing room into the opulently furnished receiving hall, which stretched the entire length of the house with rooms radiating out from it. The ceiling rose to the height of two men, lending grandeur.

Servants stood at the back near the doors to the kitchen and hammam, waiting for instructions.

She saw Saba perched on the divan at the front of the hall, oblivious to the requirements of running a household, head bowed over a book. Behind her daughter, the sharp tines of the monstrance radiated outward like a cruel sun. When Saba raised her head, the monstrance made a halo around it. Her skin was the colour of burnt sugar, her nose long and straight, with high, fluted nostrils like those of an Arabian horse.

Saba put her book aside. 'Are you ready, Mama?' she asked. 'Uncle Malik isn't here yet.'

Balkis nodded. Retrieving a long, narrow box from a corner of the room, Saba took from it a sceptre. It was a diamond-shaped cross of iron and brass, decorated with small stylised birds, attached to the top of a long iron stave.

Just then, Malik arrived. He stood inside the door to catch his breath before limping into the receiving hall and greeting them warmly. Saba hurried over to kiss her uncle.

'Ah, Priestess, you're ready. Give an old man a few minutes.' He leaned over so Balkis could brush her cheek against his.

He looked ill, Balkis noted. They were both getting old. She was almost forty and Malik three years older. She was plagued by a pain incubating deep within her belly and a fatigue that stole upon her like a blanketing mist.

An old servant with a wrinkled face the deep purple-black of aubergines took Malik's arm and led him towards the dressing room. 'Someday one of us will become worn out and have to be replaced,' Malik joked. 'Judging from the strength of your grip, it'll probably be me.'

The old man didn't respond, though Balkis saw a shy smile cross his face.

After a few minutes, Malik emerged in a linen robe and matching ceremonial cape similar to Balkis's. The caretaker's traditional garment covered him from waist to ankle, leaving his chest and back bare. A key, larger than the one around Balkis's neck, hung from a wide leather belt around his waist. His chest was bony and the olive skin above his belt sagged, but she thought he still looked magnificent.

'Use your fur-lined robe, brother,' Balkis admonished him. 'See. I have mine.'

'Next week, sister. I promise.'

Saba ran outside and returned with a freshly plucked peacock feather. She dipped its nib in molten wax from a candle and handed it to Malik.

'Thank you, my dear girl.'

Gudit reappeared, dressed in a red smock.

Their motions were routine, but Balkis saw the unrehearsed portends in the actors' ready lines, the advanced age of those carrying out the ritual, her brother's decline and foolish refusal to take care of himself, and Saba's naïveté. She was a child still, and attached to her uncle, who was filling her head with pious thoughts and ignoring her wits, which also needed to be developed.

They waited for Amida, but when he didn't arrive, they stepped out into the courtyard. The house of the priestess was an imposing structure set within the embrace of the cistern wall. Flanking the house were two cottages. The larger one backed against the cistern wall and was hidden behind a row of oleanders. Amida had recently had the doorway enlarged to accommodate a grand piano he had purchased. Six brawny men had manoeuvred the instrument like a giant scaled insect down the stairs from Charshamba, providing entertainment and gossip for half the district. In the evenings, Balkis could hear the halting canto of him practising.

A shabbier cottage, inhabited by Gudit, stood just before two columns with elaborate Corinthian capitals that guarded the entrance to the courtyard. Both cottages were made from wood, then plastered and whitewashed like the other village homes. They had been rebuilt many times. The ruins of similar cottages jutted from the weeds.

No one knew the age of the house of the priestess, the only substantial stone building in Sunken Village besides the prayer hall. Its walls, like those of the cistern, were courses of bricks alternating with bands of marble. A marble frieze – a mosaic of warriors engaged in violent encounters with lances and swords, archers on horses, women in elaborately draped robes and muscular men – wrapped around the house above the windows. Snakes, horses, and other animals, interspersed with acanthus leaves, paraded around a narrower band just below the eaves. Inset directly above the lintel was the carving of a winged lion. The outlines of the figures were blurred after centuries of scouring by the elements but Balkis never tired of studying them. The house and the ritual reminded her that she was one of a long chain of priestesses, each given a sacred trust.

Malik and Balkis crossed the courtyard, Saba behind them, followed by Gudit and the other servants. Balkis slowed her steps so Malik could keep up. It was mid-morning and the sky had darkened. The poplars slashed at the sky in a hard gust of wind, then were still again.

Amida strode across the courtyard and fell in place beside his sister. Balkis felt a surge of pleasure at the sight of her son. As they walked slowly down the lane to the village square, groups of men and women fell in behind them. People bowed as they passed. By the time they had crossed the square to the prayer house, a crowd had formed.

The Melisite prayer house was old, perhaps even older than the home of the priestess. Its walls were built of precisely cut limestone fitted seamlessly together in alternating bands of stone and brick. Its iron-studded wooden portal was shut and flanking the entry were two shoulder-height granite pillars scored by a series of thick horizontal lines and protruding circles.

The procession stopped before a large, flat stone in a clearing next to the prayer house. Lying on the stone was a young ewe, its fore- and hind legs bound, held in place by a middle-aged man in a red smock.

Balkis stood before the sacrifice and, together with Malik, began to pray. The villagers followed, their voices rising and falling.

Hail Mary, Mother of God,
Take us under your wing.
O Virgin of the Closed Door,
Who doth songs of David sing.
Hail Mary, Mother of the Word,
Hear those who bear your message,
Container of the Uncontainable,
Grant us your intercession.

When the prayer was done, Balkis nodded. The man in red pulled back the ewe's head and stroked its soft throat as tenderly as a lover. When the animal relaxed, he cut its throat, directing the blood into a large bowl on the ground.

Balkis used a cup to pour some of the blood into the hollows on top of the pillars by the entrance. Then Malik dipped the peacock feather in the blood and anointed the prayer-house door with one long stroke, followed by three short cross-strokes. He took the key from his belt and unlocked the door.

They waited while Gudit lifted the bowl and spilled its contents beneath a towering fig tree, its fruit plump and red veined. Then Balkis led the village into the prayer house. As the villagers entered, they each touched one of the pillars and then their forehead.

The interior of the prayer house was lined with marble, except for a mosaic inside the vault that depicted a gold crescent and disc against an indigo background. Oil lamps hanging from the ceiling cast a spiderweb of light over the congregation. At the front of the nave a wrought-iron divider separated the congregation from the Holy of Holies. Behind it, an iron gate guarded a room that only the priestess was allowed to enter. Inscribed on the gate was an angel with powerful wings, which were painted gold. Those permitted to approach could see that the angel was crying.

The floor was spread with carpets, like a mosque. The women's side of the room bloomed with bright colours, while the men's side reflected the stolid tones of earth and grain and vernal green. As the procession passed down the middle of the hall, the villagers bowed their heads respectfully. Balkis and Malik passed through the divider and stood before the gate, where they led the congregation in prayer.

Balkis unlocked the gate using the key on her chain and pushed it open. It made no sound on its oiled hinges. The congregation craned to see. Malik took a lit candle from a niche and handed it to Balkis. She walked through the opening and was immediately swallowed up by darkness. The gate swung shut behind her.

There was a faint scent of incense. Balkis could hear the muffled hum of conversation resume in the hall. She blew out the candle and closed her eyes. The dark power in this room, the Holy of Holies, penetrated her like heat in the hammam, taking control of her body and cleansing it.

She imagined her brother's majestic, cloaked figure on the other side of the gate, standing guard before the miracle. Malik, caretaker of the Melisites.

'Behold Balkis,' she heard him intone in a loud voice. 'Behold the Proof of God, Container of the Uncontainable. Behold the Key to all religions.'

The angel gate opened and Balkis stepped out into the light. She felt tall and commanding. She knew the villagers no longer saw her, but their priestess. Two fillets hung from her embroidered turban, framing the face of a woman comfortable with power. In her hand was the iron sceptre. The gate closed behind her.

Balkis stood for a moment, surveying the crowd, noting who had come and who had stayed away. She took her time, bestowing approving glances on those whose goodwill she needed to carry out the project she had in mind, and letting the few young people heedlessly flirting at the back of the room feel the weight of her gaze until they fell silent. Saba and Amida sat side by side at the front of the room before the elders, a place of honour. Saba, as always, was absorbed in the ceremony, perhaps imagining herself in the role of priestess. Amida looked bored and distracted. This saddened Balkis. She wanted her son to believe in the Melisites as she did, to love the sect. To love her.

Balkis put her sceptre aside and turned to face the gate, her eyes on the angel's powerful wings. She wondered, as she always did, why the angel was crying. She thought she knew.

The cloak slipped from her bare shoulders and pooled around her feet. Beside her, Malik, too, let his cape fall. They raised their arms to the angel gate.

'Behold the Proof of God,' Balkis announced.

'Adonai, help us,' the congregation responded. 'Virgin of Chora, Container of the Uncontainable, keep us.'

Balkis felt the fervour of their gaze on her bare tattooed back. Priestess and caretaker, angels before the angel gate.

5

Back in his office at the courthouse, Kamil combed through the files again, this time looking for links to the Charshamba district or the Habesh, but the files contained little more than lists and sketches of objects taken, and the names of places they had been taken from. None of the thefts had occurred in Charshamba itself. Kamil wondered if criminals had a code of honour that forbade them from stealing in the area where they lived, or whether the pickings were simply better elsewhere. A silver nielloed Byzantine ewer and matching plate, a solid gold plate, a chalice decorated with diamonds, and another with rubies and pearls had disappeared from the Fatih Mosque, just a stone's throw from the Charshamba market. The sketches were clear enough, but the report was illegible. The police required their officers to be literate, but in practice that could mean anything. He peered at the paper, unable to make out where in the large mosque complex the objects had been stored.

The other stolen items came from smaller mosques, churches, and synagogues all over the Old City. He assumed that these would be less carefully guarded than a venerable institution like the Fatih Mosque. But, he chided himself, on what basis was he making that assumption? What he had seen so far had convinced him that people at all levels of responsibility were careless with old things, probably believing them to be intrinsically less valuable than something new, even if they were made of precious materials.

The descriptions of stolen items corresponded closely to a list sent by the London Metropolitan Police Force of oriental objects recently sold in that city, including the ruby and pearl chalice. That sale and several others had been handled by Rettingate and Sons, dealers in oriental antiques, located at 58 Smythe Street in South Kensington. A good address near Kensington Gardens and the museum, Kamil noted. He remembered elegant rows of brick and stucco houses with black-lacquered doors and polished brass knockers. Perhaps the tent of facts could be anchored at that end. He penned a telegram to Detective Inspector Joseph Ormond, his contact at the Metropolitan Police, or as it was commonly known, Scotland Yard.

In the letter accompanying the list, Ormond had suggested Kamil contact Magnus Owen, the cultural attaché at the British Embassy in Istanbul. Kamil wrote a note requesting an appointment with Owen and gave it to Abdullah to deliver to the embassy, only minutes away.

HALF AN HOUR later, the door to the office flew open and an enormous man with a heavy beard fell into the room. With one hand, he extricated himself from Abdullah's grip, with the other he dragged Avi, who squirmed in pain.

Kamil jumped to his feet and bellowed, 'Drop that child right now. What is the meaning of this?'

The man stopped but didn't loosen his grip. Abdullah renewed his attempt to pull the stranger from the room.

'Let the boy go or I'll have you arrested.'

Reluctantly, the man complied. Trouble seemed to stick to this boy like metal filings to a magnet, Kamil thought irritably. He noticed that the man's sash protruded at the side, indicating a weapon, most likely a long-handled knife. With a stealthy flick of his fingers, he slid open a drawer, putting his Colt revolver within easy reach.

'Abdullah, take the boy out.'

Abdullah looked doubtfully at the intruder, but did as he was told. He left the door open.

'Your name?'

'The boy belongs to me,' the man said in the thick accent of Istanbul's back streets. His hands were scarred and his fingernails blackened. He took a wrestler's pose, feet apart, arms loose at his side.

'Your name?' Kamil repeated angrily. He smelled anise; the man had been drinking raki.

'Mustafa,' he muttered grudgingly.

'What do you mean, the boy belongs to you?'

'He works for me. His father gave him to me.' Mustafa became animated, gesturing with his hands. He took a step towards Kamil. 'I have the agreement.' He reached into his vest, pulled out a tattered piece of paper, and held it out to Kamil. 'He signed it and I signed it.'

Kamil took it and read it. 'This is a bill of sale for a young sheep,' he said finally. 'It says you paid five hundred kurush for it. That's quite a sum for a sheep.' There were two names at the bottom, Mustafa the Tanner and another name that was illegible, with an X penned under each.

Mustafa looked stunned. 'That can't be. Let me see.' He reached over the desk and snatched the paper from Kamil's hand. He looked at it intently, but it was clear to Kamil that the man couldn't read. He looked at Kamil helplessly. 'I paid him for an apprentice.'

'Didn't you go through your guild?' The tanners' guild regulated the hiring and training of apprentices.

Mustafa shifted nervously. 'I needed the boy to do some

extra work. It wasn't really an apprenticeship.'

Most likely something dangerous, Kamil thought, something the guild wouldn't agree to. Tanners worked with caustic chemicals that ate the flesh from hides and from the workers' hands. The stench of drying hides stung the eyes and throats of residents within a wide radius of the tanning sheds just outside the city wall.

'You can't purchase a free subject of the empire. The boy isn't a slave. And as far as I know, both his parents are deceased.'

Mustafa looked surprised, then said, with a sly smile revealing broken and blackened teeth, 'So he needs a home. I can give the poor orphan a home.'

'He has a home. And I'm going to report this to your guild to make sure you don't use up any of your other boys like kindling. You can go.'

The man glowered at Kamil, then turned and stomped angrily out the door.

Kamil heard a mutter, followed by a sharp scream of pain. He ran to the door and saw Avi collapsed in a heap on the floor, blood streaming from his head. Abdullah and Ibrahim were holding on to the bearded giant as more men ran towards them to help. But with a shrug of his massive shoulders, Mustafa broke free and ran away.

'Let him go,' Kamil called to Abdullah. 'I know who he is. Help me with the boy.'

They laid Avi on the divan. Kamil watched while Abdullah washed and bandaged the deep gash on the boy's forehead where Mustafa had hit him with the hilt of his knife. When Avi opened his eyes, he found Kamil sitting next to him, reading.

'Welcome back, my son,' Kamil said. His relief ran deep, but currents of anxiety still pulsed through him. He crossed his arms. Is this what people feel, he wondered, when they have children? That life can never again be taken for granted, and you can never know peace? It seemed a precarious way to live.

Avi smiled weakly. His eyes were bloodshot. When he tried to move his head, he whimpered in pain.

'When you're well enough to move, we'll send you back to Amalia Teyze in a carriage.'

Avi frowned and tried to shake his head.

'Don't worry. When you're well, you can come back.'

Tears spilled down Avi's cheeks. 'She's dead.'

Kamil paused. 'Who's dead?'

'Amalia Teyze,' Avi whispered. 'I didn't know she was sick,' he cried. 'I could have done something.'

This news didn't surprise Kamil, who already suspected something of the kind. But surely another family in the village would have taken the boy in. '*Bashin sagholsun*, my condolences, son. There's nothing you could have done. These things just happen. Tell me, where did you stay after that?'

'One of the men from the village took me to Tanner Mustafa and told me I had to work for him. But he beat me and I ran away. I'm sorry, bey. I'm sorry I lied to you. I was afraid you'd send me back there.' His thin body shook. 'Please don't send me back.'

Kamil fought down his anger. He would see to it that both sides of this devil's bargain would regret it. He took out a linen handkerchief and wiped the boy's face. 'Don't worry. You're not going back. We'll find you a place in the apprentices' quarters. But first you need to get better.' He placed his hand on Avi's hot cheek and held it there, thinking. Then he rose and told Abdullah to get a carriage ready.

*

It was a short ride to his sister Feride's mansion in the suburb of Nishantashou. The carriage swayed to a halt inside the stone gate, and three men dressed in scarlet and blue livery ran to greet him. The ambition of his brother-in-law, Huseyin, was emblazoned even on the backs of his servants, Kamil thought sourly as he gave them instructions to carry Avi inside. Kamil disliked his self-centred brother-in-law, a distant cousin and minor member of the royal family whose exact function in the palace bureaucracy was unclear.

Feride greeted him in the reception hall, a massive room decorated in the European style. Kamil thought the ropes of gilded plaster and oil paintings of fruit and dead pheasants an abomination of taste. He was certain it was Huseyin who had insisted on this décor. In contrast to the room, Feride had the calm demeanour and classical lines of a Roman marble. Her face was a long, pale oval, with a straight nose and thin lips that gave her an air of repose. She was fashionably but simply dressed, as always. A light silk scarf edged in tiny pearls fluttered from her head. He never understood why she had agreed to marry Huseyin against his advice when she had had her choice of men of good family seeking her hand.

Feride smiled happily and held out her hands to Kamil. 'My dear brother, what a wonderful surprise.'

He kissed Feride's cheeks. 'You're looking well, Ferosh,' he lied, using the affectionate form of her name. The strain of her marriage and their father's suicide had begun to show. Two deep lines had settled permanently above her nose, the beginnings of sorrow on her otherwise flawless face. He reached up and gently brushed away a strand of hair, then kissed her forehead. He was rewarded with a brilliant smile that made her look young again.

'You'll stay for lunch, won't you?' she pleaded.

The events of that morning were still fresh in his mind and he did not want to spend precious time in idle conversation, but not wishing to disappoint Feride, he acquiesced. He also wanted to ask Huseyin about Hamdi Bey.

He heard a distant patter of feet and squatted, waiting for his seven-year-old twin nieces to appear. They flew into the room, matching flurries of white and blue, and threw themselves into his arms. He kissed their red hair and breathed in the scent of soap and innocence. Feride prised them away and sent them to tell the cook to add a place at the table.

'Ferosh,' Kamil said, 'I've brought you a gift, another child. A boy, this time.'

Feride looked shocked, then laughed. 'You're always teasing me. I can't wait for the day when you really will be married and bring your children to see me. When will that be, my wild-blooded brother?'

'I'm serious. But he's not mine.'

'Whose then?'

'An orphan.' He told her about Avi. He had considered bringing the boy to his house, but thought Avi might benefit from staying with a family that had other children.

'The poor child,' she exclaimed. 'Of course he can stay here.' She swung her arms around wildly. 'There's enough room here for an entire city of boys.'

Feride gestured to a servant waiting at a discreet distance and consulted with her. The woman led them to the servants' quarters. There, they found Avi on a mattress under a quilt with a matronly servant squatting beside him, spooning broth into his mouth from a bowl. When Avi saw Kamil, he relaxed.

'This is Feride Hanoum, my sister.' His nieces peered

around his legs. 'And these are her daughters Alev and Yasemin.'

The girls giggled.

'You're welcome in my house,' Feride said, touching Avi's bandage and lifting the quilt. She turned to the woman. 'Bathe him and get him some clothes. And fetch the surgeon. This bandage needs to be changed.'

'You'll be well treated here, Avi,' Kamil said softly. 'When you're feeling better, I'll expect you back at your post.'

Feride looked at her brother in surprise.

Avi struggled to keep his eyes open, smiled, then fell asleep.

'YOU'RE FULL OF surprises today, dear brother,' Feride said when they were in the corridor. 'I heard the way you spoke to that boy. You care about him, don't you?'

'I suppose so.'

She beamed at him. 'It's a start. We'll domesticate you eventually. Come along. I have a surprise for you too.

'Elif is a distant cousin of Huseyin's from Macedonia,' Feride explained, as they made their way back to the main part of the house. 'She landed on our doorstep five days ago, as thin and dirty as a street urchin. And as tough. I can't believe what she has been through. I wouldn't have been able to survive it.'

'I think you'd be surprised at how tough you are.'

'I don't know.' She shook her head. 'They shot her husband right in front of her and then, when she was fleeing, bandits killed her five-year-old son and stole her carriage. Somehow she got hold of a horse and rode until she arrived here. What amazes me is that she seems so kind and considerate. I could never be so pleasant if I had gone through all that.'

Kamil thought that being pleasant was a survival strategy. The woman probably had nowhere else to go.

He let Feride draw him into the dining room.

'Where have you been?' Huseyin growled when he saw Feride, waving her in with one large, pale hand.

Face flushed, Huseyin sat at the head of a long table that was set with silver and fine china. He wore a frock coat with a wide blue sash and a large diamond starburst order on his chest. His thick neck was encased in a starched collar. Kamil found the medal to be an affectation when worn at lunch with one's own family. The woman sitting by Huseyin was partly obscured by a silver candelabra.

Spying Kamil, Huseyin jumped to his feet and hurried over. 'Brother-in-law, what a surprise.' He grasped Kamil by the shoulders and kissed him on both cheeks. He smelled of expensive French cologne. 'What are you doing away from the court in the middle of the day?' He gasped before each sentence, as if he couldn't get enough air. 'Did we commit a murder or did Nizam Pasha fire you?'

For Feride's sake, Kamil forced himself to smile.

'Not yet, Huseyin, but you'll be the first to know.'

Huseyin laughed too heartily and pounded Kamil on the shoulder. 'Come and sit.' He pulled out a chair next to his.

The woman turned her head towards Feride and a smile appeared on his sister's face. Kamil liked Elif already. He saw opposite him a delicate blonde woman with chin-length hair and clear blue eyes. She looked tired and thin. The planes of her face were angular, her cheeks hollow, and there were deep circles under her eyes. She appeared to be in her late twenties, although her ordeal might have aged her. A small silk kerchief was pinned to the top of her head, almost as an afterthought, concealing little. Her face and hands were tanned like a peasant's, but her neck was pale.

There was something intriguing and elusive about her. She wore no jewellery and her vest was unornamented. Even the kerchief on her head didn't have the usual fringe. She was trembling. Kamil remembered what Feride had told him about the young woman's experiences. He had heard stories about the fighting in the Balkans, some brutal beyond his imagining. He thought again of Marko's childish face as he'd pulled the trigger. How much horror the boy must have seen to have met death so serenely.

Feride watched him, and he thought he saw an element of calculation enter her eyes.

'Kamil, this is Elif.' She turned to Elif, who sat with her eyes down, hands clasped tightly in her lap. 'I've been telling Kamil about you.'

'I'm pleased to meet you, Elif Hanoum.'

Elif nodded her head in acknowledgement, but said nothing.

Servants bustled around the table, filling everyone's bowls with fragrant leek soup. Kamil realised he was hungry.

'Watch out, Elif. Feride's mission in life is to get her brother married off.' Huseyin pointed his spoon at Kamil. 'You're better off a bachelor. Wives are trouble.' He was already halfway through his soup.

Feride placed her hand briefly on Elif's arm, then pretended to busy herself with her food.

Elif, Kamil noticed, was not eating. He caught her looking at him before her eyes slid away. 'Elif Hanoum, Feride told me something about your tragedies and difficult journey. May the worst be over.'

Elif inclined her head, but still said nothing.

'It will be,' Huseyin grumbled, waving his spoon, 'now that Macedonia has an Ottoman governor again. I don't know how the Russians managed to grab it from us ten years ago, but I tell you, it won't happen again. They're like magpies, snatching territory here and there. Greater Bulgaria. What the hell is that? I ask you. It's a good thing we got Macedonia back. Now at least there's a chance it'll become civilised. A slim chance.'

'I'm not so sure,' Kamil responded, thinking of Marko. 'The Christians of Macedonia have tasted independence. It's not surprising that they feel betrayed – by their own leaders, by the Russians who gave them back to us, and by the British who brokered the deal. One people's just cause is another's lost territory.'

'We gave them a Christian governor, for Allah's sake. What more do they want?'

'They want control over their own land. They feel betrayed and now they're attacking their Muslim neighbours. Have you seen the refugees in the streets?'

Huseyin nodded. 'I've seen them, but I tell you the Christians are busy killing each other too. Take the Bulgarians. They had Macedonia for only the briefest moment, but to them, that still makes it part of Bulgaria. Now they cut out the tongue of anyone who even says the word Macedonia.'

Feride was puzzled. 'But surely the Bulgarians are Christians.'

'Bravo, my dear. The Bulgarian Christian guerrillas are fighting the Macedonian Christian militias. I say let them kill each other and save the governor the trouble.'

'How can you say that?' Elif cried out in an anguished voice. 'You have no idea what it's like there. Ordinary people are caught in the middle and slaughtered like sheep.'

'Couldn't our army protect you?' Feride asked with concern.

Elif's eyes flew up and met Kamil's. In their blue depths he saw an ocean of grief. 'The Ottoman army isn't blameless,' she said softly.

'We should just give the province up.' Huseyin gestured to a servant to refill his raki glass. 'We don't have control over it anymore. It's just a hole in our pocket.'

'You can't let the province go now.' Elif's voice was shrill. 'Thousands of people would be killed.'

'What do I care about Christians who want to kill each other? Let them, I say.' He shrugged. 'Whoever's left can try to run things without our help. They're so primitive, they wouldn't know how to govern themselves. They'll be barking in the trees like monkeys.' He chuckled, spearing a piece of meat. 'Monkeys,' he repeated, shaking his head.

'You don't understand, Huseyin. Most of the people don't want to fight,' Elif insisted. 'They're ordinary people with families. All they want is peace.' She appealed to Kamil. 'Our neighbours were Christians. Our children played together. When there's someone to keep order, people do get along. You can't just say, "We've had enough trouble", and walk away.'

'We wouldn't abandon Macedonia without making sure there's a government in place, Elif Hanoum,' Kamil said soothingly.

'Don't be an ass, Kamil,' Huseyin interjected. 'We've already gone. Look what happened to her.' He indicated Elif with his fork. 'They shot her husband. There's no law and order there. It's a sham. So it's better that we call it a sham and save ourselves the effort.'

Elif grimaced and pressed the palms of her hands against the table.

'What about the Muslim population?' Kamil countered. 'We just abandon them to be slaughtered?'

'Well, let them join the Ottoman army or get out. They're all coming here anyway.'

Elif sprang to her feet, swaying as if she might fall. Feride put her arm around her, but Elif pushed her away. She glared at them.

'You know the roads aren't passable.' Tears ran down her cheeks. 'There are bandits everywhere.'

Kamil remembered that her son had been killed on the road.

'Elif Hanoum,' Kamil began.

Feride reached out, but Elif shook her off again. 'The empire has a duty to protect its citizens,' she said in a harsh voice.

Huseyin looked amused and waved his fork at her. 'Sit down, Elif. Allah protect us. We have to be realistic.'

Before Kamil could object, Elif fled the room. Kamil noted with surprise that she was wearing men's trousers and a loose white shirt under her brocaded vest. Feride followed her out.

Kamil stood, unsure what to do. Huseyin seemed not to notice.

'So, are you working on any interesting cases?' he asked, peering at Kamil over the rim of his raki glass.

'Why did you taunt that poor woman, Huseyin? Hasn't she been through enough?'

Huseyin shrugged. 'She's got to get over it. It doesn't do her any good treating her like a victim. She arrived here half dead. I'm just helping to pull her back into life. Of course, it's not going to be easy. You know, sometimes I think people prefer to sink in their well of misery. Everyone else runs around and does things for them. Nobody challenges them. They live in a fantasy world in which the only thing that counts is what happened to them. You see how she's dressed. That's how she arrived, dressed as a man. I suppose it helped her to get here, but it's time she put on a skirt. I won't let her out of the house in that get-up. She'll be arrested. Hell, we'd all be arrested. I don't think her attitude is healthy and I won't stand for it in my house. If she wants to be coddled, she can go elsewhere.'

Kamil sat back down and lit a cigarette, offering one to Huseyin. Much as he hated to admit it, what Huseyin said made a certain sense. 'Give her time, Huseyin. Go too fast and your cure might kill her.'

Huseyin clicked his tongue. 'She's as tough as camel hide, Kamil.' He drew on his cigarette. 'She's a member of my family, and as you well know, we're all tough bastards.' He grinned mischievously.

Feride came into the room and heard the last sentence. 'That's certainly true,' she agreed, prompting a guffaw from Huseyin.

Elif returned to the table. 'I apologise,' she said softly to no one in particular.

The servants replaced the untouched food with plates of warm rice, lamb, and aubergine puree.

'Eat,' Huseyin ordered Elif.

For a while, the only sound was the clink of cutlery.

When he had eaten all he could, Kamil pushed his chair back. 'You asked about my cases, Huseyin. I have a challenging one.' He told them about the antiquities thefts in the Old City and, to amuse Elif, he added the story of the policeman Ali's discovery of a cistern beneath his house. She smiled when he described Ali fishing through his floorboards.

'So all these Byzantine structures are still there. What happened to the people?' she asked.

'They survived,' Huseyin explained drily. 'Mehmet the Conqueror allowed his soldiers three days of looting, and then there was peace. The Byzantines became Ottomans. End of story.'

'That's horrible,' Feride exclaimed. 'Why punish a population that has already surrendered?'

Huseyin shrugged. 'That's war. The Byzantines lost and that's how armies paid their soldiers in those days. Anyway, it was only three days. After that, he built the empire we still have four hundred years later.' He swept his hand expansively around the room. 'Civilisation. You don't know a thing about gardening, Feride, but let me tell you, the best roses bloom in shit.'

Feride ignored him and asked Kamil about Balat and Fatih, where she had never been. Kamil tried to describe the districts, leaving out the filthy streets and gangs of thieves.

'I would love to see those places,' Elif said, surprising everyone.

'Not in that outfit,' Huseyin growled.

'You could draw them,' Feride said with excitement. 'I could come with you.' She turned to Kamil. 'She's a wonderful artist. You should see her drawings.'

'I'm not having my wife and cousin drag themselves like whores around the worst areas in the city,' Huseyin interrupted. 'But Elif,' he pointed at her with his elbow, 'no one can tell her anything.' He grinned. 'Isn't that right, Elif? The apple doesn't fall far from the tree. The rest of you might have come from monkeys, but our family is descended from a goat.' He laughed so hard, he nearly choked.

Feride hurried over and patted him on the back. 'Definitely a goat, my dear,' she agreed, trying to smile.

'Where did you learn to draw?' Kamil asked Elif, sensing that this was a safe topic and one that might engage her.

'Paris. My family sent me there as a child when the troubles started. I lived with my aunt and uncle. Have you been to Paris, Kamil Pasha?'

'No, regrettably. I've been to London and Cambridge, but no further. I'd like to see more of Europe someday. Perhaps when you have the time you would consent to tell me more about Paris.'

'I'd be delighted. In exchange, you will tell me about the Old City?'

'Agreed.' Kamil could see Huseyin's point about a stubborn streak. It had probably helped her survive.

Feride followed the exchange with a satisfied smile on her lips. Huseyin also observed them closely over his spoon of pudding, but said nothing.

'Show him your drawings, Elif,' Feride urged.

'They're nothing special,' she demurred.

'Don't be so modest. That's not a family trait.' Huseyin turned to Kamil and said jovially, 'If I say her drawings are good, I know you'll believe me because I never say anything good about anyone.' He looked at Feride. 'Isn't that right, dear? Why don't you go get them, Elif, and let Kamil have a look?'

'I'm sure he's not interested,' Elif responded shyly.

'On the contrary, I'd be honoured if you would share them with me.'

Elif rose from the table, but then just stood there. She had begun to tremble again almost imperceptibly.

Feride put a hand on her arm and said, 'Sit, Elif, dear. I'll go and get them.'

Elif nodded and sat back down, her face the colour of chalk. Huseyin caught Kamil's eye and raised an eyebrow.

After Feride left, Huseyin pushed himself to his feet and led the way into a sitting area just off the dining room. A fire crackled in the fireplace.

'Join us, cousin,' he called to Elif. 'It's warmer in here.'

As Elif came around the table, Kamil saw she was barefoot. Her clothing was a striking combination of East and West, with no ornamentation at all beyond the carnelian-coloured vest. Still, dressing as a man was unacceptable and dangerous for a woman. He understood his brother-in-law's concern.

Huseyin cut the end from a cigar. 'Whatever the evidence to the contrary, Elif, you're still young and accommodating. Just wait till you bloom and then see how many thorns you have. Right, Kamil?' He took a couple of shallow puffs. 'My brother-in-law is an expert on flowers.'

'Only orchids,' Kamil replied, smiling at Elif. 'I like to read about them. I used to go on botanical expeditions. There are so many varieties of orchids in the empire, but you rarely hear about them. I have some rare specimens in my winter garden. Occasionally,' he added shyly, 'I try to capture one on paper.'

'What medium?' She took a seat by Kamil's side, crossing her legs, her bare foot arched like a Roman bridge. Kamil could see her leg pulsing with each heartbeat. Huseyin was in the chair opposite him, cigar clamped between his lips, engrossed in a newspaper.

'Pardon?' Kamil asked Elif.

'Watercolour? Paint? Charcoal?'

'Watercolour mostly. I like watercolour because the delicacy of tone and transparency of the colour allow me to capture those qualities in the flower.'

They talked in this way for a few minutes before Feride returned and laid a battered binder on the side table.

They gathered around the table, watching as Elif paged through the drawings and watercolours one by one. 'This is all I managed to save,' she explained.

Rather than the usual facsimiles of life through detail, the landscapes pulsed with shape and motion brought alive by colour. They reminded Kamil of the Paris Impressionists. He had seen several of Monsieur Monet's feverish and intensely coloured paintings in the London drawing room of a wealthy Ottoman collector. These were easily as good. There were also studies of a young boy's head, some quick sketches, others more detailed, showing his delicate lashes and the seashell of his ear.

'Who's this?' Kamil asked.

'My son,' she responded in a barely audible voice.

As she turned a page, Kamil saw on the back a charcoal sketch of the boy with his eyes closed, mouth slightly ajar, a brown smudge at the corner of his lips that looked more like dried blood than paint. Elif quickly hid it under another drawing. Huseyin caught Kamil's eye and nodded slightly. Kamil understood. It was the boy's death mask.

'These are brilliant,' he said honestly. 'Are they in the Impressionist style?'

'Yes.' Elif seemed pleased that Kamil recognised it.

'They should be in a museum,' he insisted, sweeping his hand towards the drawings.

'They're good, but not good enough,' she said, her mood darkening again. 'I wasn't able to finish my training.'

'Why not?'

She said nothing for so long that Kamil thought she

wouldn't answer. 'I married a fellow artist,' she said finally. 'A painter. When I had a child, he insisted I stop working and return with him to Macedonia. But it's not work,' she said, her anguish breaking through. 'He of all people should have understood that.'

Elif gathered up her drawings and put them back in the binder, carefully tying it shut with string. 'I knew an American painter in Paris, Mary Cassatt. I studied at the Académie Julian, but it was Mary who helped me develop my own style.'

'I saw one of her paintings in London,' Kamil said. Painting was a subject Elif felt comfortable talking about and he wanted to draw her out. 'It was of a woman holding a baby. Remarkable. The brushstrokes were loose, as if it were a sketch, but somehow it looked more real than if she had painted in every detail.'

'During my last summer there, Mary took me and my son to her summer house at Marly. It had a beautiful garden. Mary's mother was there, and her nieces. We did nothing but paint all summer, despite my husband's wishes.'

'We don't have much of a tradition of painting or drawing of this kind,' Kamil said. 'Except for Hamdi Bey. He paints in the European style.'

A servant brought coffee and a platter of fruit which no one touched. Elif picked up her coffee and took a sip. Her eyes seemed focused on something beyond the room.

'Hamdi is a remarkable fellow,' Huseyin agreed. 'He's painting a portrait of himself with turtles.'

'Oh really,' Feride scoffed.

'It's true. I saw the painting in his studio. It's of a man with a pointy beard feeding his turtles. Looks just like him. He denies it, of course. Claims it isn't finished.

Maybe if I irritate him enough, he'll put my face on it.'

'On the turtle, you mean,' Feride sniped.

Kamil was glad to see his sister showing some spirit. She hadn't always been this assertive. Their father's death had changed her, made her less willing to bend. There was a brittleness about her now, but also a new strength.

'I don't know where he finds the time. He's head of the Imperial Museum now and he's also heading up our first archaeological expedition.'

'Soon we'll be able to kick those thieves masquerading as archaeologists right back to Europe, eh, Kamil? Dig the stuff up ourselves,' Huseyin said, showing his fist. 'I wish we could throw the Franks out of our treasury too. People think the Franks shit gold. What they don't realise is, it's our gold.'

'Huseyin,' Feride scolded. 'You're a beast.'

'Don't I know it.' He winked at her.

Kamil saw Feride suppress a smile and wondered at the complex and, to him, utterly mysterious bond between husband and wife.

Elif had gathered up her binder and was hesitating by the door.

Kamil got to his feet. 'It was a great pleasure to meet you, Elif Hanoum,' he said with feeling.

'Also my pleasure, Kamil Pasha.'

Feride kissed him on both cheeks. 'I'll leave you to Huseyin now, brother dear, but do come again soon. Elif and I would love to see you. And,' she whispered, 'don't worry about the boy.'

Elif overheard. 'What boy?'

Huseyin echoed her.

'A young apprentice named Avi.' Kamil explained what

had happened. 'I had hoped he might stay here for a few days until he's better.'

'Of course,' Huseyin boomed amiably. 'What have we got all this space for if it isn't to take in strays.'

'Can we see him?' Elif asked Feride.

'Yes, let's see how he's getting on with Alev and Yasemin.'

Huseyin rolled his eyes. 'More of those family roses, Kamil.' He raised an index finger and braced it with the fingers of his other hand. 'They've already got thorns as long as your finger.'

When the women had gone, Kamil remarked, 'So you know Hamdi Bey quite well.'

'Yes. Why?'

'I thought as director of the museum, he might know some of the antiquities dealers in Europe. I want to see what I can find out about the buyers.'

'I suppose you want me to set up a meeting.'

Kamil swallowed his distaste at asking his brother-in-law for a favour. 'If you could.' He suspected Huseyin took pleasure in his discomfiture.

Huseyin reached for an enormous red peach, peeled it, cut it up, and divided the quarters between their plates. 'I'll let you know tomorrow.'

As Kamil rode through Nishantashou on his way back to his office, he thought about Elif. What happened to people who had lost everything and had no family to take them in? The scent of roses and jasmine defied the rusts and reds of autumn creeping over the gardens beside the road, but Kamil's eyes were on an inner scene of savagery, of neighbour slitting the throat of neighbour or turning away when a friend was threatened. He wondered what Elif had lived through and found himself wanting to cradle her small golden head. He worried that she would break in Huseyin's well-meaning but compassionless hands.

He passed the city's water-pumping station and the artillery barracks looming over Taksim Square. Prayer services in the mosques were over and groups of men were walking back to work or meandering to coffeehouses or home. Behind the French Hospital, the streets of Tarla Bashou were crowded with shabby two- and three-storey houses, now deep in shadow. The Grande Rue de Pera, in contrast, was a broad boulevard lined with shops, cafés, and brasseries. A woman sat huddled at the corner of an alley next to a French café, an infant in her arms.

Kamil dismounted and put a gold lira in her lap, enough to rent a room.

'May it bring you blessings,' he muttered, embarrassed.

Surprised, the woman looked up for a moment, and Kamil saw that she was no more than twenty, her face ravaged by sorrow. She attempted a smile. Then, as tears flooded her eyes, she hid her face and, clutching the child, began to rock back and forth.

Kamil crossed the street and asked the gatekeeper at the French Hospital what he knew about the refugees on the street.

He shook his head in dismay. 'There are more every day. They sit there and beg. Some of them just sit. They look like they've left this world already.'

'What happens to them?'

'The hospitals pick up the sick ones. Mostly the mosque hospitals, but this one too.' He motioned towards the entrance behind him. 'The merchants of Pera don't like people in rags lying in front of their shops. Bad for business. So the shop owners' organisations and the foreign churches pay to have them picked up. I hear they take them to centres where they can get food and maybe learn some skills to support themselves. Especially the women. You know, sewing, needlework, women's stuff. Maybe even find them husbands.' He smiled shyly. 'If I had the guts, I'd take a look there myself. These were decent people.' He shook his head sadly.

'Would you make sure she's taken care of?' Kamil pointed to the woman by the café, still huddled over her infant. He handed the man another gold lira.

The gatekeeper craned his neck and looked across the street. His face registered surprise, then softened. After a moment, he nodded. 'Of course, but I can't take money for doing a kindness.' He gave Kamil the lira back.

Kamil thanked him and rode down the Rue de Pera to his office.

As soon as he entered the antechamber, Abdullah handed him a letter embossed with the seal of the British Embassy.

6

The threatened rain didn't materialise, and Sunken Village basked in the unexpected warmth of a late autumn afternoon. The shadows of the cistern wall crept into the orchards and gardens, but hadn't yet reached the village square. After the ritual in the prayer house, the Habesh men had gone to the Kariye Mosque for afternoon prayer. Two prayers are better than one, Balkis always said when explaining this tradition. Abundance reaped abundance. It was a law of nature. In the morning, the men had set to roast over a charcoal pit the sheep Balkis always provided. She knew that many of the villagers filled their bellies with cabbage the rest of the week and looked forward to the Friday feast.

Having returned from the mosque, the men joined their families lounging on carpets spread before their homes and in the square, spooning rice and mutton from their bowls. Children ran through the chatting groups. Gudit brought a tray of more generously apportioned plates to the big house, where Balkis rested on the divan. She had removed her ritual clothing and put on a gold-embroidered robe. Malik had remained at the Kariye Mosque.

Saba sat on a cushion on the floor. She leaned back against the wall, eyes closed as if asleep, fingers curled quietly in her lap. Such a lovely child, Balkis thought wistfully, but they praise a horse's swiftness, not its looks. Saba needed to wake up.

Amida sat opposite Balkis on the divan, still in his jacket, his back straight, as if rebuking the cushions that invited him to recline. He had her build, short and portly, but his father's dark complexion and eyes – small, deepset, and unreadable. Wavy brown hair fell to his shoulders and Balkis found herself wondering what it felt like. She sensed he wouldn't like her reaching out to touch it. Was it soft or coarse? When he was a boy, before he went away to the monastery in Abyssinia, it had been light as angel feathers. Balkis remembered suddenly that she had never touched her husband's hair, not once. Why was it that those closest to us often seemed like perfect strangers?

Saba offered Amida some grapes. When he refused, she joked, 'When you were little, you were angry at me once when I wouldn't give you my fruit ice. Do you remember?' She laughed. 'Mama made me give it to you, though. She really spoiled you.'

'He was older than you, Saba,' Balkis interjected. 'And he was going away for a long time.' Children remembered the oddest things. An ice, from so long ago, yet it stuck in her daughter's memory like a fishbone.

'That's right. She got to stay while I was shipped off for eight years to that rat-infested pit in the mountains. You thought a fruit ice would make up for that?'

'Was it really so bad?' Balkis asked, taken aback by the bitterness in his voice.

Amida looked at his hands. 'It was a school run by old men who've spent their entire lives on that mountain,' he muttered. 'What do you expect?'

If Amida had had a bad experience at the monastery, Balkis thought, it might explain some of his anger. Malik had never spoken about his years at the monastery either. She had mourned her son's childhood passing without her, but had never given much thought to what monastery life was actually like. Young men of the priestly Melisite line were always sent there to be educated. There had been reports that Amida had run away, sometimes disappearing for months before the monks tracked him down and brought him back, but she had put it down to the rebelliousness of youth. After leaving the monastery for good, Amida had taken his time returning to Istanbul, lingering for almost a year in Cairo. What had he been doing there?

'Well, you're with your family now,' she consoled him. 'And when you become caretaker, I'm sure the things you learned at the monastery will make sense.'

'You can't draw milk from a dead sheep.' Amida adjusted a cushion on the divan, then pushed it away. 'Anyway, I told you I don't want to be caretaker of a mosque where nothing ever happens. It's a waste of time.'

Balkis looked squarely at her son. 'Being caretaker isn't about the mosque. It's about four hundred years of tradition and our family's duty, your duty, to guard the Proof of God. You're going to be caretaker and Saba will be priestess. You'll be leaders of the Melisites, just as it's always been.'

'Leaders of what?' Amida scoffed. 'Nobody believes that Melisite crap anymore. The young men in the village are Muslims. They don't plan on raising their kids in the old way.' He raised his hand to his chest and pleaded, 'But if you let me, I could modernise things. We could make decent money and build proper houses, instead of these shacks. Make Habesh a term people respect, instead of assuming we're all slaves.'

Balkis was dismayed. She knew he was unenthusiastic about becoming caretaker, but this was the first time she sensed the depth of his scepticism about the sect itself. His rejection was seamed with anger. That meant he couldn't be lured back by argument or appeals to his faith. He had to be cajoled, brought into the stable like a skittish horse. She would tread carefully so as not to drive him away. She couldn't bear to lose him again.

'You're right, my son. Our business is failing and I'm glad you have some ideas about how to set that right. What do you propose to do?'

Amida flashed her a smile, leaned back against the cushions, and crossed his legs. 'The way we do things now is a waste of time. We're just middlemen between Charshamba and the bazaar. The bazaaris sell the stuff to someone else and pocket most of the money. I say we bypass the bazaar and go straight to the buyer.' He clapped his hands. 'We take orders, meet customer demand.'

'But we've been working with the bazaaris for generations,' Balkis cautioned. 'We have obligations.'

'This is the modern era. You make contracts for services, not vague promises that last for generations. A business has to be able to change with the times. You say the merchants are our friends. Well, you know what friends pay friends: nothing. When you're in bed together, the services are free.'

'Amida,' Balkis chastised him. 'We deserve your respect.' He was smart and he had courage and determination, she thought, qualities the Habesh needed in their leader. But the bird doesn't fly with one wing. She had yet to see much evidence of character and maturity. The pain in her stomach increased. Her eyes rested longingly on the glass-fronted cabinet across the room where, in a crystal bowl, lay the envelopes of powders Courtidis supplied her with.

Amida looked uncomfortable but didn't apologise. 'The

Charshamba families are working for one man now. That's why they don't need us. He has his own shop, so he can buy with one hand and sell from the other. We could start working with him.'

Balkis had suspected the families had found new channels that bypassed the Habesh, but she had thought they were selling to the shops in Beyoglu. She hadn't realised her competition was a single person. 'You know this man?'

Amida shrugged lightly.

'What's his name?'

'He keeps that to himself.'

'How can you trust him if you don't know who he is?' Balkis asked, incredulous.

'He's legitimate, not small trash like the Charshamba people,' Amida answered defensively. 'This is business. We don't always have to do things the old way. The modern world lets us reinvent ourselves. In fact, we don't have a choice.'

'There's always a choice. Even the blind man can smell. Business has to be honourable.'

'A choice between starving and going hungry. Where's the honour in that?'

Balkis decided she had nothing to lose with a meeting. At the very least, she'd learn something about her competitor.

'All right. If he wishes to speak with us, bring him.' She saw the light in Amida's eyes and was glad.

'Mama,' Saba asked in a soft voice. 'Have you heard about the killings in Charshamba? Maybe we should get out of the business altogether and do something else? I don't see that there's anything honourable about associating with men like that.'

'Like what? Let our young men become porters carrying

burdens on their backs like snails? We've invested many years in our trading connections. Why throw that away? Our men have to work.' Balkis thought Saba was sounding more and more like Malik with his useless idealism. 'If you were priestess, we'd all starve,' she added irritably. 'You don't know a kurush from a stone.'

Undeterred, Saba told Amida, 'You overlook our true wealth, brother. After all, we're custodians of the Proof of God.' She spoke the name reverently.

Amida rolled his eyes.

'But it's our greatest strength,' Saba insisted. 'The community needs an income, that's true, but its spiritual centre is what holds it together.'

'Just look at this place. You think we're special? We live in a hole in the ground! At least half the people have no teeth because there's no hygiene. People get sick and die because no doctor will come down here.'

'Constantine Courtidis comes here,' Saba corrected him.

'That quack! We all know what he wants.'

Saba's face flushed. 'You're wrong about that.'

Balkis knew why the young Greek surgeon bothered with a small village like theirs, but she didn't know whether Saba reciprocated his interest. Saba had always kept her feelings to herself, even as a child.

'I'm worried about the young people too,' Balkis said, hoping to draw Amida back in. 'Are they really as disengaged as you say? I know there isn't much for them to do. There used to be all kinds of jobs related to the rituals, but now only Gudit knows how to do them.'

'She's so unpleasant, Mama,' Saba complained. 'Why have you put up with her for so long? When I was little, she used to pinch me when you weren't looking, but now it's worse. A few weeks ago, I saw her in the laundry room, sniffing my dirty clothes. That's disgusting. And she spies on me, even in the hammam.'

This worried Balkis. Was Gudit preparing to initiate Saba? Surely she wouldn't do so without her permission. Saba hadn't yet borne an heir. 'There are a lot of important things only Gudit knows how to do, my dear. But you must come and tell me your concerns, not keep them to yourself.'

'I'd feel better if you retired her. Let some of the girls apprentice to her so they can learn her skills.'

'The girls only last a few weeks, then leave. It's a hard job. There's a lot more to being a Melisite midwife than delivering babies. The tattoos, for instance.'

'Why does it have to be the midwife who does the tattoos? I'm sure you could get apprentices from Charshamba,' Amida suggested. 'They'd jump at the chance to learn a trade.'

'The tattoos aren't just for decoration. They're part of our ritual. Some things have to remain within the sect. You forget who we are.'

'Please, mother. I'm whoever I make myself.'

'You're the caretaker, Amida. You will always be the caretaker, and your son will be the caretaker.'

'You talk about becoming caretaker as if it's like becoming the grand vizier.' Amida got up and began to wander around the room. 'Malik doesn't seem to have a say about anything.'

'Malik has never cared about leading the community,' Balkis said. 'He thinks being caretaker means sitting in his library reading or daydreaming under his linden tree. That's why we're in such a sorry state.'

'That's not fair, Mama,' Saba broke in. 'He's very well

known. People all across the city read his *dawa*, his calls for ecumenical discussion.'

'While he's holding theological debates, no one's leading our young people,' Balkis said, her eyes intent on Amida. 'That's why we need you, my son. You've got the energy and the ideas to revive the community. But you have to respect the traditions.'

'How much power does the caretaker have, then, in the tradition?' Amida asked, pointedly emphasising the last word. 'And none of this happens until Uncle Malik dies, right?'

Balkis was taken aback by his unsentimental enquiry. 'Once people in the community learn to trust you, they'll follow your lead.'

'I understand that, but what I want to know is how much power the caretaker has. If the caretaker is someone who can really do his job, unlike Uncle Malik, then he's in charge, right? The priestess is just a figurehead.'

Saba's head jerked up in surprise.

'The priestess is the equal leader of this community,' Balkis told him, aghast. 'She's joined to it for ever, so you should never underestimate her.' The last thing the community needed was a power struggle between her children. 'Think of the priestess as a cornered animal,' she added in a low voice. 'Reach out your hand and she'll reward you. But never, ever cross her.'

Amida looked at her open-mouthed. 'So a woman is the leader and the caretaker's some kind of servant? I'm supposed to feed the animal?' He laughed. 'I'm in a zoo!'

Balkis got to her feet. 'Watch your tongue,' she barked.

Saba rose from the floor and faced her brother. 'There have been women leaders before,' she scolded him. 'It's nothing new. The Queen of Sheba. Mary, the Mother of

Jesus. There was our founder, Saint Melisane.'

'Melisane is just a legend, like her ridiculous reliquary. I've never seen this Proof of God, have you? Who knows if either of them ever existed. And even if they did, so what? We live in the modern world. Where do you see a woman in charge of anything?'

Balkis was speechless. If this was what Amida thought, then her plans for the community were as likely to succeed as a fish in a poplar tree. She wished there were more young men in her line who could be trained as caretaker. But Amida was the last. It was him or no one.

'There must be some truth to the stories if they've held the community together for so many years,' Saba insisted. 'If we could show people the Proof of God, it would revive their faith, but it's forbidden.'

'I bet if I went through that gate into the Holy of Holies, there'd be nothing there. What about that box Malik found? He says it's the Proof of God, but how can that be if it's in our prayer house like you claim,' he taunted his mother. 'It's all just a bunch of lies.'

'It's true that the Proof of God is a mystery,' Saba admitted, 'but there's a miracle behind it.'

Amida looked at his sister with exasperation. 'There is no Proof of God, Saba. It's all just a story. And the reliquary is just an empty box.'

Saba looked at him in surprise. 'What do you mean empty?' she asked.

That fool Malik, Balkis thought. What had he really found?

'What I mean is anything that old would be worth something, empty or not.' Amida laughed. 'Those Europeans would buy a rat's turd, if it was old enough. If you can convince them that a worthless box is the Proof of

God, well, money will rain from heaven. That would be a blessing, if ever I heard of one.'

'Don't even joke about selling it,' Saba snapped.

'Malik's reliquary is gone, so someone has already had that bright idea.'

Balkis listened incredulously to this exchange. She was furious at Amida's wholesale dismissal of all that was sacred in their lives. 'Even though you are my son,' she said, 'you are a fool.'

'Well, I won't be the donkey pulling your cart.' Amida headed for the door.

'We're a community, not a vehicle for your ambitions,' Saba called out behind him. She turned and left the room.

Balkis was surprised at the strength of spirit she had glimpsed in her normally quiescent daughter. Bent over in pain, she shuffled to the cabinet, opened the glass door and reached inside for the envelope of powder.

7

Kamil found the British cultural attaché slouched on a bench in the Municipal Gardens at the crest of the Pera hill, one lanky leg draped over the other, revealing an expanse of white silk sock. Between thumb and forefinger of his right hand, he pinched a thin cigar, the picture of the insouciant gentleman. Pink clouds had begun to gather to the west as the sun weakened.

'Mr Owen?' Kamil asked.

The man turned his head. He was in his forties, with a long, pleasant face, an aquiline nose, and thin lips curved in a friendly smile.

Owen's pale blue eyes regarded Kamil with amusement. 'You've found him,' he drawled, and then motioned with his cigar for Kamil to sit beside him. 'Like to come up here and sit?' He leaned back and took a deep breath. 'Get away from those ghastly fumes.' He looked to Kamil for sympathy. 'The price of progress, eh?'

Kamil sat down. 'I'm afraid so.' As the weather grew colder, a suffocating haze from the coal and wood with which people heated their homes had descended on the city. The public gardens were atop a bluff and a steady breeze kept the air relatively clear.

Owen wore a well-cut gabardine suit, a brocaded waistcoat, and a shirt that Kamil recognised as the work of a Beyoglu shirtmaker. Kamil owned several shirts made by Tailor Pepo, with their trademark rounded collar and distinctive stitching, and he was surprised to find Owen wearing one. Tailor Pepo was a well-kept secret. He could make only a limited number of shirts, so his devoted customers generally didn't share his address.

Owen pulled out another cigar and offered it to Kamil. 'Rare, but the best.'

'Thank you. I prefer cigarettes.'

'Your English is good,' Owen remarked. 'Been to the home country?'

'Cambridge.'

Owen looked at him with interest. 'Well done.' He puffed on his cigar. 'Been to London, of course.'

'Yes, it's a marvellous city.' Kamil reached into his jacket for sketches of the missing objects. 'Let me show you . . .'

'Are you much for classical music?' He leaned towards Kamil. 'Mozart? Bach?' He shook his head distastefully. 'Germans, I know, but what's to be done? No one better. Do you play?'

'If you mean the piano, no, I'm afraid not, although I do appreciate good music when I hear it.'

'Dash it. I miss my music. I play piano. Not bad at all. But, without an audience . . . you know what they say, if a musician plays to an empty room,' he smiled, showing a row of gleaming white teeth, 'is it really music?'

'There's some good music in the city. The concert and theatre season has just opened. I don't remember seeing Bach on the programme, but there's a performance of Bizet's *Carmen* this week at the Palais de Cristal.'

'Thank you for the tip, my friend. Will I see you there?'

'No time, I'm afraid. Would you mind taking a look at these?' Kamil held out the sketches. 'They were stolen recently. I'm particularly interested in these.' He pointed to the sketches of the icon and the diamond chalice missing from the Fatih Mosque.

Owen lifted one of the sketches up to his face. 'Are these jewels?'

'Diamonds.'

Owen whistled.

'The icon is unique and, if it appears on the market, could easily be traced.'

'Then it'll be sold privately.'

'That's what I'm worried about.'

'What makes you think I know anything about them?'

'My contact in the London police suggested you might be able to help. Many of the stolen objects are ending up in London, but we don't know how they're getting there so quickly.'

'Makes a certain amount of sense, but I'm not sure what we can do to help you, short of searching every shipment that leaves the country and the baggage of every British traveller.'

'I wish that were possible,' Kamil admitted. Ottoman customs agents had few rights to search British citizens, leaving huge loopholes in the antiquities laws.

'But, of course, it's entirely impractical,' Owen pointed out. 'The embassy barely has enough staff to handle its own shipments.'

'There's more at stake than the actual thefts,' Kamil explained urgently. 'You're a man with political experience. You know that when people lose their heritage, it ignites deeper fears, especially these days.'

'It's a tragedy what's happening in the provinces. Her Majesty's government is very concerned.'

Kamil knew the British wanted a strong Ottoman Empire to stand between themselves and the Russians.

The empire was the prey that kept the bear occupied.

'Then I'm sure you'll be willing to help us. We'd like permission to search the cargo of any vessel leaving for England. You're welcome to send a representative to oversee the operation.'

Owen raised his eyebrows. 'I'll ask the ambassador.' He puffed on his cigar. 'Don't expect too much.'

Kamil was disappointed but not surprised by Owen's lack of enthusiasm. He frowned into the distance, where smoke rose from what appeared to be a large fire. The smoke drifted upward, a dark smudge against the sunset.

'How long have you been here?' Kamil asked, momentarily distracted by the fire.

'Arrived six months ago,' Owen answered.

Kamil turned to him. Something had struck a discordant note. 'It's odd, but I feel sure we've met before.'

'You must be mistaken, old chap. Tall, balding, blue-eyed Englishmen are as plenty as blackberries, as Shakespeare would put it.'

Kamil thought of the former British ambassador, another tall, balding Englishman with faded blue eyes. Owen was probably right.

'How do embassy personnel send things home?' Kamil asked, remembering the frail former ambassador and his daughter Sybil standing forlornly on the deck of the ship that would take them back to England.

Ash from Owen's cigar fell on to his knee and he brushed it off with an angry flick of his hand. 'Diplomatic pouch. There's a special steamer that goes directly to London. Why?'

'Just curious. Does everyone at the embassy use the pouch?'

'It's for diplomatic correspondence,' Owen explained,

'not your auntie's quince jam.' He rose, threw his cigar on the dirt path, and ground it under his shoe. A sparrow fluttered down and pecked at the red and yellow label. 'My good man,' he extended his hand, 'it's been a pleasure, but I must get back.'

'Of course.' They shook hands. 'Thank you for your time. I'll call on you again, if I may.'

'Absolutely, old chap. Perhaps we'll meet at the Palais de Cristal. And I'll see what I can find out about your problem. I'll be in touch.' He flashed Kamil a smile and, with a wave, turned and strode down the path.

8

Dressed in a charshaf that exposed only her face, Saba stood inside the door, hand on the jamb, looking out at the candlelit windows of the village. Beyond the cottages and gardens, the cistern wall rose like a black page. A group of men clustered in the road outside the courtyard. She could hear their low voices and an occasional laugh. When they saw her, they bowed respectfully, but didn't disperse. They, like her family, were waiting for a man named Kubalou.

The men's voices rose suddenly like the sound of leaves in a great gust of wind, then fell silent. Saba saw a lamp approaching and hurried into the receiving hall.

'He's coming.'

Her mother sat regally on one side of the U-shaped divan, arrayed in her most imposing gold-stitched robe and brocade kaftan, with a silk scarf wound over her hair that was pinned in place by a diamond brooch. Her right hand held the Melisite sceptre, the other lay calmly in her lap. All the lamps had been lit, and the high-ceilinged room blazed with light. Servants were lined up at the far end of the hall, out of earshot, but ready to spring into service. She noticed Bilal, Amida's servant, among them. He was a comely boy, a few years younger than Amida. They had returned from Abyssinia together and were inseparable.

Saba surveyed the room with pleasure and thought

about all the other women of her blood that had sat here over the centuries, confident and powerful. She wondered whether she could absorb that confidence just by being in its presence.

A few moments later, Amida came in carrying a lamp. While he paused to place it on a chest, a tall, heavyset man in an ill-fitting suit strode past him into the hall, as self-confident as if he were in his own living room. Saba disliked him immediately. His watery brown eyes met hers and she felt the cunning in him like a blow. He wore a bowler hat, but swept it off as he entered, revealing a halo of orange hair. She wished Uncle Malik were here, but he rarely interested himself in the business of the community and she doubted her mother had even told him about the dealer's visit.

The man's eyes rested a moment longer than necessary on Saba, appraising her, then his face broke out into what she was sure was meant to be a charming smile. Black spaces showed at either end of his grin where teeth were missing.

'Ma'am?' he said to her in English. He had an odd, high-pitched voice, totally incongruous with his bulk. But what did she know about how the English spoke? Uncle Malik had taught her some English and French – 'The tongue is sharper than the sword,' he had told her, 'and the master must know how to wield every kind of blade.' – but she had never heard a native speak. And if this man were Cuban, as his name suggested, then she knew less than nothing, since she had no idea what that was.

Amida led the man to the side of the divan opposite the priestess. Kubalou's eyes roved among Amida, Saba, and the stately woman on the divan before him. He probably wasn't used to dealing with women, Saba realised, and didn't understand that he should address the priestess. Her mother looked wary.

Saba was shocked to see Amida sit down at the priestess's right hand, when he knew their place at a formal audience was on the third leg of the divan. He clearly wished to show himself to Kubalou as having more standing than he had. Saba debated whether she should sit in the appropriate place, but then decided she wouldn't let her brother alone claim equal status with the priestess. She sat at her mother's left hand, feeling awkward at breaking the rules. She stole a glance at her mother's face, but saw no reaction to the unusual seating. Her eyes were riveted on the visitor.

'*Selam aleikum*, peace be upon you. We welcome you to Sunken Village.'

Amida translated into broken English, and there ensued an exchange of customary pleasantries interrupted by awkward pauses while Amida wrestled with the words. The servants brought tea in crystal glasses and pastries on plates, morsels as small as the end of Saba's finger. Bilal served Amida, and Saba saw a fond look pass between them. She saw that Kubalou had noticed it too.

Saba listened to Amida mangle the translation. She considered offering to translate instead of her brother, but to do so would humiliate him. Hopefully, she thought, we'll have no future dealings with this man anyway. She also found herself struggling to understand Kubalou's English. She noticed that he left words out, didn't play by the rules, parried when he should have thrust straight to the heart of the subject. She adapted quickly, though, and his meaning was soon clear: work directly for me and I'll make you rich.

She could see the priestess had also understood, despite Amida's tortured translations.

'How long would this agreement last?'

'It's a bottomless cup.' Kubalou smiled agreeably. 'We can drink from it for ever and not let it run dry. I understand from Amida that you can get hold of some particularly, what I'd call, interesting items.'

Amida looked frightened at this, and Saba noticed that he mistranslated Kubalou's words as 'You have access to many places.' Had Amida told him about the Proof of God? Impossible. Surely even Amida wouldn't reveal the central secret of the Melisites. Saba suddenly felt chilled, remembering their conversation that afternoon. Did Kubalou have the stolen reliquary?

Kubalou regarded Amida with a bemused smile, as if aware of his translator's counterfeit. He took a piece of pastry in his big fingers and washed it down with tea.

'Who would make the decisions about which objects are taken, from where, and how?' Balkis asked him. 'What would be the role of the Habesh?'

'We're only interested in certain items. We tell you where they are, your men get them, and we pay for them.' He spread his hands, palms up. 'Very efficient.'

Saba noticed they were covered with yellow calluses. What kind of high-status dealer had hands like this? She also wondered about his too-tight clothes.

'The Habesh work as a team.' The priestess sat stiffly upright. She hadn't touched her tea. Saba felt proud of her mother and, as always, awed by how flawlessly she inhabited the institution of priestess.

Kubalou shrugged. 'I don't care how you work, as long as you deliver.'

'What is the chain of command?'

'Ma'am,' Kubalou explained pleasantly, 'you can be the Queen of Sheba as long as we get what we ask for.'

Saba was furious and saw that her mother recognised the insult just from his tone of voice. If she were priestess, Saba decided, she would have ended the interview right then. Unlike her mother, Saba understood what had been said. Uncle Malik was right. Knowledge was power.

Balkis looked pointedly at Amida but he avoided her eyes and didn't translate. She turned back to Kubalou and waited, her face betraying nothing.

'If you want your son here to head up some kind of group,' he added, 'that can be arranged. I mean, assuming he can get them to follow his orders.' He gave Amida a fatherly smile.

Amida looked uncomfortable and glanced at his mother but the priestess showed no emotion.

'What I mean is, do we deal directly with you or does someone stand on the ladder of authority above the Habesh?' Balkis asked again, rephrasing her question.

'We have some men in Charshamba. They'll be in touch and let you know what we need.'

Balkis thought for a moment, then said, 'The Habesh work alone. We make our own decisions. This will only work if we deal directly with you. We can then tell you whether or not your assignment can be carried out.'

Kubalou shook his head in frustration. 'Ma'am,' he said, 'we can't deal with a hundred separate gangs. Ask your son there.' He nodded at Amida. 'He's a smart kid. He'll tell you success lies in organisation.'

'You misunderstand us. The Habesh are not a gang.'

'Fine, you're a minority. It doesn't matter if you're Hottentots. There's got to be a chain of command. I told you we'd include your son. Or did you want in on this? I mean, that might be a little awkward seeing as how you're, well, a female person.'

Saba noted that Kubalou's frustration had begun to break through.

Her mother closed her eyes for a moment and suddenly looked weary. But when they opened again, Saba saw no weakness there, only a simmering anger. She wondered if her wrath was directed at Kubalou or Amida.

Saba felt suffocated by her own silence. She wanted to speak her mind, in English, to this arrogant foreigner. She felt sure that of all the people in the room, she could handle him best. Kubalou was a predator, she saw that clearly. She imagined him as a wild boar with sabre-sharp tusks. She looked directly at the man for the first time. He appeared startled by her direct gaze, but immediately caught it, locking his eyes with hers. His thick lips curved into a slight smile.

The way to deal with a predator, Saba thought, was to treat it as prey, never taking your eyes from it. She had learned that from her mother.

Kubalou's eyes hardened and he turned back to the priestess.

'Well, have you thought it over, ma'am?' he asked her impatiently. 'What do you say?'

'We decline your offer.'

The lines around Amida's mouth deepened. He looked angry.

'Christ. Women and business,' Kubalou muttered, shaking his head in disbelief.

'Mother,' Amida said urgently, 'this is our big chance. There aren't any other jobs that pay as well as this and it's not something we don't already do. You said yourself we have to do something to stop the young people from leaving. What else have we got to offer them?'

'Heart,' Balkis said simply.

Kubalou asked Amida what had been said. When Amida told him, he snapped, 'You'd be better off using your head.'

Amida hesitated, then translated for his mother.

Balkis turned her icy gaze on the man who now stood before her. 'Thank you for making us this generous offer, Kubalou Efendi. I regret the Habesh cannot join your organisation. I bid you good night.'

'Oh, I ain't Mr Kubalou, ma'am. Mr Kubalou couldn't come, so he sent me instead. But I speak for him, don't think that I don't.'

Saba could see that her brother was as surprised as they were.

'Who are you?' Balkis demanded.

'No need to get all worked up, ma'am. I never told this boy otherwise. I assumed he knew I wasn't Mr Kubalou. Never occurred to me he didn't know, or I would've set him straight. But it makes no difference, as I told you. My word is his word. I'm what you might call his right-hand man. Name's Ben.'

Amida staggered through the translation. Even Saba could make little sense of some of the words.

The man put his hat on. 'Well, ma'am. I'm sorry to waste your time, and you mine. Good night to you.'

'Go in peace,' Saba heard her mother say.

Outraged as much at Amida as at the man she had thought was Kubalou, Saba rose to her feet. As the man passed her, he said in English in a low voice, 'I hope we meet again some time, Miss Saba.'

He must have noticed that she had been following the conversation, Saba realised, and it chilled her that he knew her name. She wondered what the real Kubalou was like. What kind of predator were they dealing with?

'I doubt it,' she responded coolly in English, then turned and walked away.

Amida passed her and followed Mister Ben out. She saw from the surprise and alarm on Amida's face that he had heard her speak English. What did he want with this counterfeit Kubalou?

She looked over at her mother and saw that she was slumped forward.

'Mama, Mama. What is it?' She ran to her side.

Balkis's mouth was open, her breathing erratic. 'Nothing, dear,' she gasped. 'Get me my powder.'

Saba opened the glass-fronted case and took out a slim envelope. She unfolded it and poured the powder into a glass of water, then took it to her mother.

'Get Gudit,' Balkis said weakly.

But Gudit had already appeared, as she always did, seemingly out of nowhere. She helped Balkis to her bedroom and closed the door behind them.

Amida didn't return.

Saba hovered around her mother's door until Gudit emerged.

'She'll be fine,' the midwife told her gruffly. 'Stop hanging about like an unweaned calf.'

Saba slipped on her shoes and went outside into the cold air. She felt emotionally exhausted, but also exhilarated. She had felt a power in herself tonight that she hadn't known she possessed. A fulcrum that had found its centre.

Her ears became aware of a commotion in the village square. Pulling her charshaf close about her, she ran down the road. In the square, she saw Amida and the ginger-haired man, surrounded by some of the young men of the village, talking in excited voices. A dark stranger with long, gangly limbs stood beside the counterfeit Kubalou, looking bored. Saba saw him whisper something to Amida, then pull on Mr Ben's sleeve.

She stopped outside the glow of the lamp and watched, feeling her anger rise again. There would be only one source of power in this community, she decided. There was more at stake than a simple village and a way of life. Amida chose to ignore that at his peril. Perhaps he no longer believed in the Proof of God, in the mission of the priestess and caretaker, the charge left them by Melisane and Michael, their founders. People with no imagination believed survival depended on money. She would see to it that Amida didn't sell the kernel of their faith so cheaply.

She suddenly remembered her mother's face before she had drunk the powder. It was grey with pain. Her mother, she realised, was sicker than she let on. As she walked back through the darkness, Saba was suddenly afraid. If her mother died, there would be no one but Uncle Malik, who might not be much help against her brother and Kubalou. She stopped under the poplar tree just inside the courtyard. There would be no one by her side, no one to support her. She had never felt more alone.

Her mind wandered to Kamil Pasha. Why had Uncle Malik spoken so often about Kamil if he hadn't meant for them to be together? Leaning her cheek against the tree trunk, she began to cry.

Aware of someone standing behind her, she turned.

'Pardon me, Saba Hanoum. I apologise for intruding.' It was Constantine Courtidis. 'Someone rode over and told me your mother was ill, so I came right away. Are you all right?' The concern in his voice irritated her because it made her want to cry even more, and she had to force herself not to lean forward on to his chest and allow him to minister to her as well as to her mother.

She took a deep breath and said, 'Mama is in her bedroom, Constantine. Come in. Thank you for coming so late.'

'I'm the slave of your eyes, Saba Hanoum.'

She thought his eyes brimmed as if he too were about to cry. Her melancholy needed stronger medicine than this well-meaning but artless young man.

Saba led him into Balkis's bedroom. Gudit always disappeared as soon as Courtidis was sent for. Balkis was asleep, her chest rising and falling evenly, but her face retained traces of anguish.

'What's wrong with her?' Saba asked in a small voice.

Courtidis looked closely at his patient and felt her forehead. 'She won't let me examine her, so I don't know.'

'What do you mean?'

'In cases like this, I need to see, beg your pardon, all of my patient. There must be an infection somewhere.'

Saba looked puzzled. 'I'm surprised. I didn't think she was conservative about things like that. She's always been very practical. Have you explained it to her?' But as she said this, Saba realised she too had never seen her mother naked. Gudit always helped her with her clothes and in the bath. Perhaps Balkis was more prudish than Saba thought.

'I'll talk to her,' she promised. 'Can it wait until she's awake?'

Constantine regarded his patient and suggested, 'Shall I stay, Saba Hanoum? I'd be happy to keep watch over her.'

Saba saw the worried frown on his face. Suddenly distressed, she asked, 'Is it that serious?'

'Oh, no, I didn't mean to imply she's that ill.' He took another look at Balkis's face and felt her forehead. 'Nothing like that.'

'Then please get some sleep yourself, Constantine. Will you come by in the morning and check on her?'

'Of course.' He beamed. 'Anything. Anything at all.'

Saba laid her hand on his arm. 'Thank you.'

Courtidis was overcome with confusion. He bowed himself backward out of the room as if she were a sultana. When he was gone, Saba vowed not to think badly of him anymore. He was kind and generous. She wished Amida had some of his qualities.

Saba wondered uneasily why Amida was so disloyal to his family. Why such unnatural feelings in a son? Amida had been gone for a long time, nearly nine years, but that didn't absolve him of the responsibility to act decently towards his mother. She remembered Amida as a quiet, shy boy. Their mother had doted on him, even more than on her daughter. Saba remembered the fruit ice, but without rancour. Had something happened at the monastery to change him?

They would have to learn to work together. If there was a key to understanding her brother, she was determined she would find it.

9

At one in the morning, Kamil rode across the Old Bridge to Oun Kapanou Square. Against a backdrop of enormous stone warehouses and shuttered shops, the only light came from a few fires around which slumped shadowy figures. They were probably peasants from the countryside, Kamil thought, looking for work and huddled together for safety in the square near the police station. He was relieved and excited to be taking action again, although he hoped that this night would end better than the last. Marko's face remained vivid in his mind.

Kamil dismounted and gave the reins of his horse to a policeman on guard by the station door. Inside, six men sat around a table playing cards. The table was littered with half-full tea glasses, a bowl of cigarette butts, and the remains of a meal.

'You're killing me.' Omar threw his cards on the table and pushed back his chair. 'Tea, Magistrate? Are you hungry?'

The other men ignored him and concentrated on their game.

When Kamil tipped his chin to indicate no, Omar asked, 'Are you armed?'

'Of course.'

'Let's go, then.'

THEY RODE SLOWLY along Djoubalou Boulevard, the padded feet of their horses making almost no sound. The line of shops gave way to warehouses and depots. In the dark, Kamil couldn't read their signs, but knew they contained the empire's stocks of oil, flour, tobacco and other export goods. To his left stretched a long open lot where heaps of scrap iron made fantastical shapes in the dark.

'I told you our ear in Charshamba heard that a big shipment of antiquities is going out tonight,' Omar said in a low voice. 'But we don't know where they're loading. One possibility is the wharf behind the Ottoman Tobacco Works.' He spat on the ground. 'Ever since the French took over the tobacco monopoly, all we get is shit.'

Kamil agreed. 'I heard that the Greeks and Armenians have moved their factories to Egypt.'

'Can't blame them. The women work for less money there. Although I hear someone reads to them while they roll cigarettes.'

'Reads to them?'

'Beats me. Keeps their fingers limber?' Omar threw out with a snort. 'My cousin was stationed there. Saw it with his own eyes. Someone reading newspapers out loud to the workers. I think it's a bad idea. Limbers up their minds too, never a good thing in a woman.' He smiled broadly and smoothed his moustache with his forefinger. 'They should be limber elsewhere.'

'The Tobacco Works next to the Golden Horn, isn't that the office where they print the tax stamps? It must be well guarded.' Kamil remembered a hulking brick building with large windows overlooking the water.

'That's right. The actual depot is on Hissar Altou Street. But the smugglers aren't interested in the offices. There are archways leading from the basement of the tobacco works to the pier. No guards back there. We think the basement connects to a tunnel. Someday, I'd like to see where the other end comes out, but the French don't appreciate the police poking around in their basements unless we can prove there's a reason.'

'But if you know stolen goods are coming through there, why haven't you raided it?'

'We were waiting for a big shipment. Otherwise, we'd have wasted good knowledge on small results. By the will of Allah, tonight we'll have our proof.'

When they came to a marble depot, Omar pulled his horse up next to Kamil's and whispered, 'From here, we go on foot.' He pursed his lips and cooed like a dove. Five men in uniform emerged from behind the marble slabs, like Greek statues coming to life. All of them were armed and two carried large lamps. Kamil recognised Ali from the Fatih station and nodded to him. Ali grinned, clearly pleased that Kamil remembered him.

One of the policemen was so young that he had only black down above his lips instead of a moustache, although his white, bony wrists had outgrown the sleeves of his uniform. Ali seemed to have taken the young man under his instruction and Kamil heard him explain in a low voice, 'Rejep, never take your gun out unless you're willing to use it. If you hesitate, someone will get it away from you and then use it against you. Just keep your eyes open and your gun tucked away unless the chief tells you otherwise.'

One of the other three men was short and stout like a barrel, but unexpectedly agile. The other two were unremarkable, short and slim like many local men. If Kamil had been able to see their features more clearly, he would have expected gaunt, prematurely old faces, perhaps some missing teeth, incongruously youthful dark eyes, and luxuriant moustaches.

With Omar and Kamil in front, the group, keeping close

to the wall of the depot, made its way single-file down an alley leading to the port. There was no moon and the stars were obscured by clouds. Kamil's world consisted of the sound of his own heartbeat and the bulk, felt rather than seen, of Omar before him.

They reached the wooden pier and turned left, keeping close to the enormous warehouse gates. To their right, the thick, almost tangible blackness of night on water pressed against them.

Suddenly, Kamil felt the spring of wood give way to flagstones beneath his feet.

Omar stopped and put his lips to Kamil's ear, 'This is the wharf. There's another pier straight ahead.'

Kamil nudged him and pointed to a pinprick of light that had appeared on the water.

The light went out. They watched and waited until it blinked again. Suddenly, in front of them a door opened, emitting a dim light, but was shut again almost immediately. They heard scurrying sounds, footsteps on wood, scraping as if a heavy object were being dragged towards the water. Finally, the noises stopped and low voices drifted towards them from the pier.

His senses fully alert and his heart racing, Kamil whispered to Omar. 'Now.'

As Omar passed the signal to his men, Kamil calmed his breathing. Cloaked in darkness, he crept silently forward on to the pier, followed by Omar and the five men.

When the voices were close by, Omar gave another signal and the two policemen quickly lit their lamps and rushed forward, illuminating the scene: a rowboat in the water piled high with sacks and a large wooden chest. A man balanced in the boat, securing the load. The three men on the pier were momentarily blinded by the sudden brilliance. Kamil ran past them and sprang on to the man in the boat. As they struggled, the boat rocked wildly. The other smugglers turned and ran along the pier with Omar and the policemen right behind them, shouting at them to stop. Panicked, one of the smugglers jumped into the water. Kamil heard him struggle, then call for help. Kamil realised that the man couldn't swim.

Kamil subdued the man in the rowboat and used a piece of rope to tie his hands, then threw a length of rope in the drowning man's direction. 'Grab the rope!' he called out, but the man continued to flail and, with a surprised gasp, he suddenly disappeared.

Kamil hauled his prisoner out of the boat and on to the pier. There he found the policemen squatting over the other two smugglers, their heads pressed against the wooden planks, arms pinned behind them. Kamil handed his captive over.

'He's finished,' Kamil answered to Omar's questioning look at the water. 'Let's see what we've caught.'

While Omar held the lamp, Kamil stepped back into the boat, slipped his knife from his boot, and slit open one of the sacks. He pulled out a tin box with a red lid. On the lid was the image of a silver sickle moon and star and the words, RÉGIE DES TABACS DE L'EMPIRE OTTOMAN, CONSTANTINOPLE. He opened it, then turned and showed Omar. The box was filled with cigarettes, the musky odour lifting pleasantly to their noses. Kamil could see Omar was as disappointed as he was.

'May it profit Allah,' Omar exclaimed, throwing the box into the water in disgust. 'For it hasn't profited us.'

Kamil took out another box and looked at the cigarettes closely in the light. 'No tax stamps.' He slit open the other sacks and soon the boat was knee-deep in tin boxes and cigarettes.

'Run-of-the-mill smugglers' fare,' Omar said dejectedly. He handed Kamil a heavy-bladed knife.

Kamil used it to prise open the wooden chest, fully expecting it to hold more of the same. But when Omar held the lamp closer, both men smiled broadly. The light glinted from a hoard of gold and silver items, some set with jewels. Kamil recognised objects from across the ages, a highly decorated Roman silver platter, a gold Byzantine chalice, and what appeared to be a silver candleholder engraved with the sultan's seal that could have come from any imperial mosque. He pulled aside some of the pieces and spotted a nielloed ewer. He pulled it out and examined it.

'This was stolen from Fatih Mosque,' he concluded.

'So we're on their tail,' Omar said with undisguised pleasure. 'Let's go and sit on these thugs and see what information they spill.'

They closed the chest and hauled it on to the pier, then turned to the policemen standing proudly over their captives.

'Well done,' Omar told them. His good mood infected the men, who grinned and nodded at one another.

Omar pulled aside the stout policeman. 'You, Shishko, I want you to ride as fast as you can to Oun Kapanou station. Tell them to send five more armed men and two wagons. When you get back, take the prisoners to the Fatih jail in one wagon and that chest to the Fatih station in the other. And hurry.'

The man pressed his fist against his heart and bowed his head. 'On my honour.' Then he ran off into the night.

'And you,' Omar singled out one of the older policemen, 'make sure the chest is still here when he gets back.'

'Chief?' The man looked confused.

'Aren't we going to wait for them?' Kamil asked Omar.

Omar stared at the archways at the back of the building. 'I'd like to look for that tunnel,' he confided to Kamil in a low voice. 'They won't use it again, but we need to see where it goes.'

'Better in daylight,' Kamil cautioned. 'You've got your proof now,' he pointed to the boat, 'so the French will allow you to search the basement. At least wait until reinforcements get here.'

'If we wait, they might block off the tunnel.'

'That may be so, but it's too risky. We don't know how many men are in there.'

Omar walked up to the door the smugglers had used and yanked it open. Beyond was darkness. 'They're long gone.'

'You don't know that.'

Kamil took stock: three trussed prisoners and four policemen, now that Shishko had been sent for reinforcements. If he and Omar went into the basement, four armed men should be enough to guard the prisoners. Kamil could see the policemen's faces in the light and found them to be energetic, muscular young men, not the faded civil servants he had imagined. One was a particularly handsome youth, with a head of dark curls and an easy smile. They were joking around, but Kamil sensed this was to cover their apprehension.

'These donkeys stink,' the older man said. 'Shall we roll them off the pier and wash them before they stink up the station?' He nudged the captive at his feet with his boot and asked him, 'Can you swim?'

Two of the captives struggled crablike against their ropes, eliciting more laughter from the policemen. The third, the man Kamil had subdued in the boat, lay still. At first, Kamil thought he was unconscious, but then he noticed the man looking about him with hard, observant eyes.

Kamil called Omar over and pointed him out. 'That's their leader.'

Omar watched the prisoner for a moment, then nodded and went over to speak with his men. Kamil saw their hands moving to their revolvers.

When the prisoner realised he was being observed, he closed his eyes.

Omar returned, Ali and Rejep trailing behind. 'Coming?' he asked Kamil.

'If you take Ali and Rejep, there'll be only two men to guard the prisoners,' Kamil objected. 'What if the other smugglers come back?'

'My men are armed,' Omar pointed out. 'And if there are others, they'll be inside and have to get past us first. We won't be long. I just want to find the damn tunnel before they have a chance to block it off. They could be doing that right now while we're standing here jabbering.'

He took a baton from one of the policemen and walked over to the prisoners. He bent over and neatly and systematically bashed each of them on the head once, hard enough to make them go slack but not hard enough to draw blood. A master in full control of his tools, Kamil thought grimly.

'Was that necessary?' he asked.

'Just putting your mind at rest. They won't be giving anybody any trouble.'

'It's not them I'm worried about.'

The policemen remaining behind looked serious now. They shifted about, staring into the darkness. Kamil snapped open his cigarette case and held it out to the young men. They shoved their revolvers into their holsters, accepted the cigarettes, and cupped hands for each other to light them, grateful for something to do.

'Omar, don't do this,' Kamil appealed one last time.

'We'll be back before they finish those cigarettes. Friends, have your guns ready.'

The men snapped to attention and pulled out their revolvers. Kamil wondered if any of them had ever fired a gun before.

'Ali, Rejep, come on.' Omar grabbed the second lamp and headed through the door. Kamil swallowed an expletive and followed the men into the basement.

THEY PASSED ALONG a damp corridor that smelled of mould and urine and led steeply downward. Despite his wool jacket, Kamil was chilled. Omar's light wavered up ahead. They emerged into a large room with brick walls and Kamil could just make out a vaulted ceiling. The room felt limitless and cold as a grave. The lamplight picked out carcasses of rusted machinery, broken crates, piles of crumbling bricks.

'Ah, you decided to join us, Magistrate,' Omar said, his voice magnified in the cavernous space.

'If the basement is as large as the building, you'll be here for hours.'

'We're here now. Let's see what we can see.' Omar moved forward with the lamp. Greek and Roman capitals sprouted like enormous mushrooms from the dark rubble of the floor and marble pillars were stacked like firewood, some cut into roundels to be used as building material.

Despite his unease, Kamil found he was fascinated. He remembered what Malik had said about empires building upon the remains of earlier civilisations. Given its size and the pattern of brickwork, Kamil guessed the basement had once been the foundation of a Byzantine palace. Perhaps these columns had been harvested by the Byzantines, sliced and stacked and inventoried in their own version of technological progress. The Ottomans had built a modern factory on top of it all, full of printing devices, stamping and calculating machines, the clatter of modernity. But in its hidden recesses, the Ottoman Tobacco Works was infested with history, its subterranean heart riddled with ancient tunnels. They passed the rusting hulk of a large machine that looked like a press or printing device. A thick iron square hung suspended in the air like a giant hand blessing the unidentifiable remains beneath it.

Suddenly Omar stopped and pulled out his revolver. Kamil and Ali followed suit. The light picked out the whites of Rejep's eyes. He looked very young and frightened.

'What is it?'

'Over there. See them?' Omar whispered, pointing.

Just beyond the edge of the light, only metres away, Kamil could make out what appeared to be a group of men facing them. He heard Rejep's sharp intake of breath and Ali whispering to him to stay calm.

Kamil signalled to Omar, then stepped sideways into the darkness. He moved quickly and soundlessly towards the waiting men while Omar held the light in their eyes.

Suddenly, one of the figures toppled over.

'They're dummies.' Kamil walked into the circle of light, pulling one of the figures behind him, its cloth body black with mould, straw and wool swelling through its disintegrating skin. 'Dressmakers' forms. Look, this one still has scraps of some kind of uniform on it.'

Omar started laughing, the sound multiplying as he did.

'Quiet,' Kamil commanded. 'If there are men around, they can hear us.'

Suddenly one of the figures moved its head. An enormous rat glared at them before hurling itself from its perch. Its piercing cry rattled Rejep, who whispered to Ali in a frightened voice, 'Maybe it's like the magistrate says. Maybe it'd be better to come during the day. I heard some of these rats eat children.'

'Go on, you drag tail,' Ali teased him, pushing him ahead. 'That's a rat and you're a man.'

Rejep moved closer to Omar, who held the lamp. Rats scuffled close by, but Kamil thought the men all felt easier now, as if their laughter had sucked the poison from the night.

Rejep turned around to Ali, smiling. 'That was some rat,' he chuckled. But before he could finish, he stumbled to a halt and said Ali's name in a breathless, quizzical tone. 'Come on, don't joke with me like that.'

'What is it, Rejep?' Kamil asked.

Omar had forged ahead and the edge of the lamplight receded from them.

'Omar,' Kamil called in an urgent whisper. 'Omar.'

Omar turned and held up his lamp. 'What?'

'Ali's gone.' Rejep's voice trembled.

Omar walked back to them. 'What do you mean, gone?'

'Gone. He was here a second ago. Now he's gone.'

Omar and Kamil held their revolvers ready. Omar held the lamp high as they searched the room, calling Ali's name, but the only response was the squeak and scrabble of rats. The darkness seemed to swallow the light.

Rejep followed behind. 'They took him,' he said in a wavering voice. 'It's my fault. I should have kept him in my sight. I looked away and now he's gone. It's my fault.' Rejep raised his gun with a shaking hand. 'They're going to kill him,' he cried. Then he pulled the trigger.

The report shattered the air with a violent sound that filled the basement and rolled over them from all directions like a physical force.

'Allah protect us,' Omar exclaimed.

Kamil peered intently into the darkness, ears alert for any movement.

Rejep was on his knees, eyes wild, breathing raggedly, his revolver fallen to the floor.

'I'm sorry. I'm sorry,' he repeated.

Omar took his collar and yanked him to his feet. 'Get up,' he bellowed. 'What are you, a virgin? I'll fuck you if that's what you need. Get up like a man. Take your gun.'

Still trembling, Rejep reached down for his gun, failed to find his holster, so stuck it in his waistband.

Omar shook his head. 'Now we're all deaf,' he snarled.

They continued the search for Ali, calling his name. Finally, Kamil had had enough. 'We're getting out. We need more light and we need help,' he said in frustration. 'Give me the lamp.'

Omar hesitated, then handed it over.

'Let's go,' Kamil said curtly. 'Watch our backs.'

Kamil retraced their steps, orienting himself with difficulty by the pillars and piles of bricks and machines, until he saw the corridor. Relieved, he ran along it, then pushed through the door and on to the pier. It was dark. The other lamp was gone. So were the prisoners and the two guards.

Omar cursed. 'They must have come from the station and taken the prisoners. Where are the extra men?'

Kamil laid a warning hand on Omar's arm and pointed

to the pier at their feet. Pieces of cut rope snaked across the wood. They exchanged a sharp look.

Kamil drew his gun once more and gestured to Omar to follow him to the end of the pier. Kamil held the lamp out over the water. The boat was gone. He leaned over further. Bobbing against the pilings of the pier were the bodies of the two policemen.

Kamil wondered how long they had been in the basement. It seemed like for ever but he thought it had only been a few minutes.

Omar walked up to the shaking Rejep and took him by the collar. 'Take one of the horses from the marble works and ride as fast as you can to Oun Kapanou station and get help. That's the closest station. Don't let anyone there put you off, you scrawny-arsed bastard. Overturn their card table if you have to. Understand? Tell them there are two dead policemen and there may be more if they don't get their arses over here. Do you think you can do that?'

Kamil could see from Rejep's face that anger was beginning to displace his fear. Kamil was furious at Omar for insisting on this disastrous adventure, but at some level he had to admire the police chief's understanding of men.

When Rejep was gone, Kamil gave Omar his revolver, took off his jacket, and let himself fall into the water. It enfolded him, absolving him for a moment of the need for thought. His boots clung to his legs like a second skin and seemed to buoy him up. Then his head broke the surface and he found his nose just a hand's breadth away from the younger man's curly hair. He tucked the man under his arm and dragged him through the water to the wharf, where Omar waited to pull him on to the flagstones. Kamil went back for the second man. He saw the body of the drowned smuggler snagged under the pier, but decided to let the police fish him out.

They laid the policemen out in the lamplight. They were handsome men, Kamil thought. Both wore slim gold bands. Their wives might have admired them like this in sleep, their faces defenceless, easier to adore. He remembered the younger man's smile and imagined that they had been happy, rich in life if not in wealth. Perhaps they had children. He pictured a young black-eyed boy with curly hair and an easy smile and felt inexpressibly sad.

Omar shook his head, clicked his tongue, and pointed to the single slash in each man's uniform just above the heart. 'Perfect cut.'

A master of his art admiring the handiwork of another, Kamil thought angrily. If Omar hadn't stubbornly insisted on looking for that tunnel, his men would still be alive. But then he saw Omar's face and reconsidered his wrath. The police chief looked harrowed.

'Stupid,' Omar whispered harshly to himself. 'Stupid to risk the lives of my men. I would never have done that in the war. For what? So I could prove there was a tunnel. Of course, there's a tunnel. Allah. Allah is the enemy of pride.'

'That's probably where they took Ali,' Kamil pointed out in a neutral voice, not trusting himself to say more.

He heard a commotion and looked around to see Rejep jump from his horse and run towards them, Shishko at his heels with the original back-up force. They were too late, Kamil thought.

DOZENS OF POLICEMEN with lamps and torches swarmed through the basement of the Tobacco Works, islands of light floating through the darkness.

'It's got to be here,' Omar shouted, flinging debris aside. 'I know it's here. It has to be here.'

Kamil wiped his face and walked over to him. Omar sagged suddenly, as if the puppet master had dropped his strings.

'We've gone over every fingernail's worth of this wall. Nothing. So the entrance has to be through the floor, but look at the size of this place.' Omar swept his hand around. 'And it's full of junk. We'd need an army to look under everything.'

'Let's keep looking,' Kamil responded tiredly, walking over to a large, draped object. He pulled at the cloth but had to retreat, choking on the dust he had dislodged. Why couldn't they find the tunnel entrance? he berated himself. Ali hadn't just disappeared into the ground. Or had he? Kamil looked down at the patchwork of cracked marble and grimy stone slabs that extended beneath his feet.

'You know, the number two rule in the army is to watch out for your men.' Omar's eyes were red and feral, like a rat's. 'You never leave one behind.'

'What's number one?'

'Stay alive, no matter what.'

Those two rules contradicted each other, Kamil thought, but didn't say anything.

He surveyed the enormous space. 'We'll never find him this way. Let's get a few hours of rest. Then we can think what to do next.'

'Rest,' Omar spat. 'You go. I'm staying.'

'The men will continue the search, Omar,' Kamil said sternly. 'You've only got two hands and two eyes. Let the men do their job. They're just as anxious to find him as we are.'

Djoubalou Boulevard was unrecognisable in the daylight when he and Omar emerged. Kamil checked his watch and realised it was almost noon. They rode past the scrap-iron yard. Farther along, storefronts were festooned with painted signs, and displays of wares spilled from doorways. Kamil found the colour and motion of everyday life somehow obscene, as if the world should be in mourning for the men lost that night.

He left Omar at the police station in Oun Kapanou Square. Men stood in small groups in the yard, smoking and looking anxiously towards the street. Kamil pushed his horse through the crowd in the square and crossed the Old Bridge, his eyes on the water as if he expected to find Ali there.

KAMIL RODE SLOWLY along the crest of the hill, past the cypresses of the Turkish cemetery and the municipal gardens. His clothes had almost dried but felt clammy. Some distance behind him another rider followed. Kamil had first noticed him crossing the Old Bridge at Oun Kapanou and since then he had kept glancing back, keeping the rider in his sight, his hand near his gun.

Kamil traversed the shadow of the British Embassy's high wall and turned down Hamal Bashou Street, where he dismounted, leaving his horse in the care of a boy. He stepped into the mirror-lined dimness of the Brasserie Europe and sank into a chair in the corner, far from the other diners and facing the wall. Recognising Kamil, the waiter brought him a glass of water, then another when he drank the first down.

Just as Kamil expected, after a few moments the man who had been following him entered. Before the man's eyes could adjust to the gloom, Kamil had sized him up in the mirror. He was long-limbed, with black hair and a moustache, and was wearing a fez, Frankish trousers, and a short, tight jacket. His thick calves and shoulders and thin joints gave him the appearance of a large articulated insect. Kamil didn't recognise him, but felt sure the man had followed him from the Tobacco Works. By the time the man's eyes found him, Kamil was engrossed in the menu.

Kamil took his time eating a generous portion of lamb nested in smoked eggplant purée. When he emerged into the street, his head was clear again. He walked his horse the rest of the way to the court building, aware of the man still following a short distance behind.

At the courthouse, Kamil took out his watch and placed it on his desk. It wasn't fifteen minutes before Abdullah knocked and announced a visitor who wished to speak with him about a case. Kamil slid his desk drawer open and sat back as the man walked into his office.

'Good afternoon, Magistrate. My name is Remzi.' His voice rasped and he continually cleared his throat. Several of his front teeth were missing and the rest were stained a dark brown.

'Please sit.' Kamil motioned towards the chair in front of his desk, but the man remained standing. He looked around the office carefully, as if systematically noting potential weapons and exits. Kamil wondered what his real name was.

'A bird sang to me about what happened last night.'

'Pardon?'

'Last night. At the Tobacco Works.'

'What do you mean? What happened?'

'The police pushed one of my friends into the water and he died.' The man looked genuinely sad, Kamil thought. Even thieves mourn friends.

'I'm sorry to hear that.' Kamil noted that the dead friend couldn't have told Remzi what happened. Either Remzi had been there himself or the escaped smugglers had told him. 'Why are you here?'

The man laughed drily as if Kamil had told a joke. 'I always go right to the top.'

'Where do you live, Remzi?' Kamil was in no mood to play games.

'Here and there.'

'If you want me to help you,' he said angrily, 'I need to know who I'm dealing with. Your address?'

'I live in Fatih.'

He sat back in his chair and regarded Remzi levelly. 'What do you want?'

As if Kamil had given him a cue, Remzi sat down in the chair before Kamil's desk. He leaned back with a knowing smile on his face, his unfortunate friend forgotten.

'I'm here to pay my taxes.'

'What? Don't waste my time.' Kamil wondered where this elaborate ruse was leading.

'I'm a good citizen,' Remzi said slyly. 'I pay my taxes, then I get taken care of. That's the deal.'

'What are you talking about?'

'My friend, he always said, "Go right to the top".'

'What do you want?' Kamil kept his exasperation in check. This man knew the smugglers – he was probably one of them. The bit must be inserted slowly so he didn't buck.

Remzi seemed to struggle with himself, perhaps wondering if he should leave, but then a confident look appeared on his face. He took a small, heavy sack from his pocket and placed it on Kamil's desk. 'Go ahead and take a peek, Magistrate, and tell me if this isn't the best deal you've been offered in a while.'

'What is it?' Kamil asked.

'My taxes. Come on, Magistrate. Take it or leave it.' He showed his stained teeth. 'I've never yet seen anyone leave it.'

Kamil leaned forward threateningly, his hand near his desk drawer. 'Are you calling a magistrate of the court a thief?'

Abdullah opened the door and looked in enquiringly but Kamil waved him away.

'No, Your Honour. No.' Remzi looked flustered. 'Just taxes.'

Kamil pulled the sack over and looked inside. It was full of gold lira coins, a year's salary for an official. He pushed the sack back to the middle of the desk.

'I'm asking you for the last time. What do you want?'

'Leave your hands off our business.'

When Kamil opened his mouth, the man interrupted. 'Don't go asking what business, as if you're some innocent virgin. We do business like anybody else and you have no right busting us up.'

'Smuggling isn't business. It's a crime.'

'Oh, and what's this?' Remzi indicated the sack with a dirty hand.

'I haven't accepted it.'

'Allah save us from whores who play virgins,' Remzi grumbled and got to his feet.

Kamil repressed his desire to smash his fist into the man's face and then clap him in irons. He needed more information. 'Sit,' he commanded.

Remzi was reluctant but sat back down. The sack of gold coins lay unacknowledged and unclaimed on the desk between them.

'What do you "export"?'

'The usual stuff,' Remzi answered grudgingly.

'Tobacco? Gold? Jewels? What?'

'Not our customers. We've got what you call,' he drew the words out, 'a steady clientele.'

'And who is that?'

Remzi didn't answer.

Kamil smiled pleasantly. 'Of course. Your professional discretion is admirable. What is it, then, that you'd like me to avert my eyes from? I have to know what it is, don't I, so I know what I'm not seeing.'

He could see Remzi's mind frantically winnowing what could be told from what could not.

'My boss does business in antiques. Strictly legit.'

'Of course.' Kamil leaned back comfortably.

'There are regular shipments and he doesn't want them disrupted.'

'Of course not.'

'So you keep the police off our backs.'

'At the Tobacco Works?'

'Not just there,' Remzi responded petulantly.

'Well, you have to tell me where,' Kamil said reasonably. 'Otherwise, how am I supposed to keep the police away?'

'There's a mark on the stuff. You tell them whenever they see the mark, they let the shipment go through. You tell them it's a legit shipment.' He pulled out a piece of paper and showed it to Kamil. It was the same mark as the one on the body at the Fatih station.

Kamil suddenly remembered some lines burned into the top of the chest of antiquities they had found behind the Tobacco Works. He hadn't realised their significance.

'The mark refers to your master?'

'Yes, no. I mean, it's his mark.'

'So let me get this straight. You want me to tell the police all over Istanbul to let through any shipment carrying this mark?'

'Now you've got it.'

'What makes you think I have such a wide reach or that anyone would listen to me?'

Remzi looked incredulous. 'You're the magistrate,' he said. 'And you're a goddamned pasha. What do you think?'

It worried Kamil that the man knew he was titled. Did they also know where he lived?

'Can you narrow the area down? Istanbul is a big city. I could do a better job if I knew where to concentrate my efforts. My resources aren't unlimited.'

Remzi thought this over. 'From the Old City up through Beshiktash.'

'Well, that narrows it down,' Kamil said sarcastically.

'That's all I can do,' Remzi answered harshly.

'And what do you have to offer me besides this?' Kamil tilted his chin at the sack of liras.

'Well, the magistrate's got balls,' Remzi snickered. 'You want to come work for us, maybe?'

'Where's the policeman?'

'What policeman?'

Kamil rose and walked nonchalantly but swiftly behind Remzi's chair and before Remzi could rise, had slipped the knife from his boot and was pressing its blade against his throat. 'I could slit your throat and claim that you came here to bribe me,' he said quietly, 'and when I refused, you attacked me. Who do you think they'd believe? I'm asking you again. Where is the policeman?' Kamil put enough pressure on the blade that it cut the first layer of skin. Tiny drops of blood beaded along its edge.

Remzi took shallow breaths, trying not to move. 'Can't talk,' he choked.

Kamil released the pressure, but kept the knife poised over Remzi's throat.

'He's in Charshamba.'

The knife moved closer.

'I don't know where they're keeping him. I swear it.'

'Who are they? Give me names.'

'They don't give us their names. We're just hired help. I wasn't there. That's all I know.'

'Where does the tunnel lead?'

'What tunnel?' Remzi's question ended in a gasp as the knife drew blood.

'Sunken Village is what I heard,' he whispered. 'Please.'

When Kamil was satisfied he had obtained all he could from the man, he called out for Abdullah.

Abdullah's eyes widened when he saw the knife and the blood.

'Get Ibrahim and some rope.'

As Abdullah and Ibrahim tied Remzi's hands, Kamil wiped his knife on a handkerchief and slipped it back into his boot. 'Arrest this man,' he instructed them, 'and charge him with attempting to bribe an official.'

Kamil grabbed a pen and paper. 'Tell the guards to take him to Chief Omar at the Fatih station.' He sealed the letter and handed it to Abdullah. 'And give Chief Omar this note. Hurry.'

Putting his face close to Remzi's, Kamil said softly, 'If anything happens to that young man, I'll consider it your fault.'

From the look of fear in Remzi's eyes, Kamil suspected it was already too late.

10

Kamil put on a clean set of clothes he kept in his office, took a fresh horse from the stable, and threaded his way through crowds and traffic back across the bridge to Oun Kapanou Square. He stopped at the police station, where he learned that Ali had not been found and the search inside the basement of the Tobacco Works had been abandoned. No one knew where Omar had gone.

Kamil rode as fast as he could down Djoubalou Boulevard, focused on avoiding the heavy midday traffic of carts and porters. In the distance, he saw the great dome and minarets of the Mosque of Sultan Selim I, which stood on a high terrace overlooking the Golden Horn. He turned left and spurred his horse up a steep dirt road. They couldn't search all of Charshamba, but he hoped he might find someone in Sunken Village who knew where Ali was. He didn't know the exact location of the village, but it wasn't far from here and he thought it should be visible from the mosque.

He dismounted and walked into the courtyard, which was framed by columns of stone and marble. In the centre was a fountain shaded by a plane tree. The rhythmic chant of men's voices sounded from within, reminding Kamil of the Friday afternoons of his youth, when his father used to take him to the mosque near the governor's mansion. After they moved to Beshiktash, Kamil had spent his afternoons exploring the forested hills instead of praying. His father also gave up prayer when he lost his position as governor. Kamil wondered what measure of duty had made up his father's faith.

He suddenly felt weary and remembered that he had barely slept the past two nights. He bent over a spigot used for ablutions and let the cool water run across his wrists. He dried himself with a handkerchief and walked to the back of the courtyard, past the great tombs of sultans and their families. There, the terrace fell off sharply. He stood at the edge of the land and looked down into what he assumed was Sunken Village, its whitewashed cottages like toys in an enormous brick box set deep into the earth.

He rested for a moment on a patch of wild thyme in the shade of the great türbe of Selim I. He needed to think before going down into the village. If Remzi was right about the tunnel, then finding it might lead to Ali. But the only person he knew in the village was Saba and he hadn't even seen her whole face. It would be inappropriate for him to arrive there, a strange man, and ask to speak with a young woman. He would need to be accompanied by the imam or village headman. Perhaps he should have gone to fetch Malik first. He now remembered his promise to meet Malik for breakfast that morning. The search for Ali had driven it from his mind. He'd see what he could find out, now that he was here, then ride over to Malik's house to apologise and, if he hadn't been successful in the village, ask him about the tunnel. Saba's father, he remembered, was deceased, so perhaps a male relative was the headman. He would ask him for permission to speak with her.

Through the window of the türbe, he could see the sultan's catafalque draped with embroidered velvet, an enormous turban at its head. Regardless of how much velvet is piled on top, he mused, in the end we're all just scraps of bone. The thought made him profoundly sad. Yet here he was, chasing down a man so that death wouldn't take him. Why? Because he was young and fished through a hole in his floor? Because he had a mother and father, sisters, perhaps a wife or a girl he wished to marry? Why did he care? Our families cloak us with life. He thought of Avi, without a family. He thought of himself. Would someone go to so much trouble to save him? Who loved him besides Feride and his nieces? The scent of thyme mingled with the breeze among the tombs and the dull timpani of prayer.

Between the treetops at his feet, he could make out a large house in the village and, behind it, a yard where peacocks strolled. A woman in green looked up at him.

KAMIL ASKED A villager for the headman and was led to the large house where a servant brought him into a high-ceilinged reception room. The furniture was ornate and gilded, the rugs of expensive silk. Servants waited attentively at the other end of the long room. A woman in a green caftan received him, her long, hennaed hair and powdered face uncovered, although beneath the powder, he thought she looked ill.

When Kamil bent to take off his boots before stepping into the carpeted room, she said in a surprisingly commanding voice, 'That's not necessary.'

'I am Kamil, magistrate of Lower Beyoglu.'

She surprised him again by saying, 'I thought so. I am Balkis.' She led him to a long U-shaped divan and bade him take a seat opposite her. 'Will you drink some tea?'

'No, thank you.'

Kamil noticed a large gold starburst on a stand above the woman's head.

'It's a monstrance,' she explained. 'The Christians put a wafer in the centre that represents the body of their God.'

Kamil nodded. Endless superstitions.

She picked up a long chubuk pipe and pulled on it, releasing the smoke through her mouth and nose. On her right forefinger was a gold ring carved with a crescent and disc that appeared identical to Malik's.

'You are welcome here.'

'Thank you. I am pleased to be here. I'm honoured to consider myself a friend of your brother, Malik.'

She bowed her head in acknowledgement. 'Then consider this your home. Malik has spoken often of you, Kamil Pasha. What is it you seek?'

'Do you know Remzi of Fatih?' he asked her.

'No one by that name lives here. Who is he?' Her voice was seductive and threatening at the same time, like a cat growling low in its throat. He couldn't read her, but she did look sincerely puzzled.

'We're looking for a policeman who was lost inside a tunnel under the Tobacco Works. We're told the tunnel leads here. Do you know of it?'

Balkis stared at him, her expression inscrutable. 'Maybe my son knows something about this.' Kamil read a faint note of disapproval in her voice. She signalled to one of the servants. 'Get Amida.'

A door opened and Saba came into the room, lithe and elegant as a cypress tree. She looked directly at Kamil and greeted him.

Kamil was momentarily speechless. Her face was uncovered and she didn't wear the usual outer tunic that would have camouflaged her shape. Kamil felt as if he had come upon her undressed for sleep. She wore a red robe, stitched with tiny white carnations, over a soft cotton chemise. A silk girdle emphasised the tiny circumference of her waist and a vest gathered her breasts, swelling them beneath the flimsy material of the chemise. Her chiselled features were framed by black curls escaping from her gauze veil.

Kamil knew he should look away, but he couldn't. 'Saba Hanoum? I'm honoured.' She was spirited and aloof, he thought, someone who would never be tamed – or satisfied with the life of a humble village woman.

Balkis noticed his appraisal of her daughter and frowned.

Embarrassed, Kamil turned his eyes away. 'I had the honour of meeting your daughter with Malik at the Kariye Mosque,' he explained quickly.

Saba had pulled her veil across the bottom of her face.

'Saba,' Balkis began in a stern voice, but was interrupted by the arrival of a short, powerfully built man of about twenty. Kamil noticed that he didn't remove his boots either, as if he were an honoured guest, and had tracked dirt on to the carpet.

He looked Kamil over before extending his hand, European style. 'Amida,' he announced. He held his left arm stiffly, as if it were injured.

Kamil shook his hand.

'My son,' Balkis added.

The woman and her son looked too much alike to be anything else. Saba was different. She must have taken after their father.

'My mother tells me you're looking for someone,' Amida said in a voice inflected by the enthusiasm of youth.

'A man called Remzi of Fatih.' Kamil described him.

Amida shook his head. 'I don't know of anyone by that name.' His eyes gleamed with what Kamil thought might be amusement. He was sure Amida was lying.

Balkis looked away, her lips tightly pursed.

A son going his own way, perhaps a son beyond her control. Kamil remembered what Omar had told him about the generations of smugglers who had developed their own rules and traditions, like any other trade. Had Amida been apprenticed to the smuggling trade? He sensed an iron will in Balkis. He could see how a power struggle might develop between the two.

'That's too bad,' Kamil said to Amida. 'He told me some things about Sunken Village that I'd like to know more about.'

'Like what?'

'That there's a tunnel leading between the Tobacco Works and Sunken Village. I need to know where it is.' Kamil kept his eyes on Amida's face. He noticed Balkis watching her son carefully too, as if she didn't trust him.

'Who is this Remzi anyway?' Amida asked dismissively. 'Why would he know anything about the village?'

'He's under arrest.'

Amida blinked. His mouth opened, then closed, the words unsaid.

Kamil got to his feet. 'Would you see me out, Amida? I have a few more things to ask you.' Amida clearly knew Remzi, and whoever knew Remzi would probably know where to find Ali.

Balkis gave her son a hard, thoughtful look.

Saba came to Kamil and offered him her hand. He hesitated, wondering if it was proper, but then took it in his. Her hand was cool and firm, like polished marble, but her eyes seemed troubled. He noticed the green was flecked with gold. Something passed between them that Kamil tried, unsuccessfully he feared, to keep from communicating to her. The imprint of her hand in his was a moment too long, the pressure of his hand on hers a degree too hard. For a brief moment, he was unable to move his eyes from hers. She's concerned for her brother, that's all, he told himself.

'Kamil Pasha,' she said. 'I hope you'll keep my brother's youth and inexperience in mind.'

Her words surprised Kamil, since she appeared to be younger than her brother. He saw Amida's face twist with anger.

'I hope we can meet again.'

Before he had a chance to compose himself enough to reply, Saba disappeared through a door at the side of the room.

Balkis's frown, meanwhile, had deepened. A woman who has seen much unpleasantness, Kamil guessed, and has learned to brace herself for more. She seemed relieved when Saba left and turned her attention back to Kamil.

Kamil thanked her and started to leave, but Balkis detained him. She asked him questions about his family, who they were, where they lived. Kamil tried to answer politely, but without revealing too much detail. Amida looked embarrassed.

Finally, her son said with mock sternness, as if he were the parent and she the child, 'That's enough, mother. We mustn't be rude to our guest.'

Balkis flushed bright red and leapt to her feet. 'How dare you speak to me like that. Get out.' She turned her back, and didn't respond to Kamil's polite farewell as Amida led him out the door.

*

As they walked across the courtyard, Kamil turned Saba's unexpected words over in his mind – that he should keep her brother's youth and inexperience in mind. He thought it might have been a warning.

'Do you live in the house?' Kamil asked Amida.

'No. I live over there.' Amida pointed to a cottage built against the cistern wall. Kamil walked up the dirt path, Amida anxiously trailing behind him.

As soon as Kamil entered the cottage, he recognised the rug on the floor from the sketch in the police report. It was unmistakably the carpet in which the thief had wrapped the reliquary. Had Amida stolen the reliquary from his own uncle? If so, was he connected to the mysterious dealer, Kubalou?

'That's an interesting rug,' Kamil noted.

Amida looked momentarily disconcerted. 'That rug? It's been in my family for generations.' He pointed to an armchair. 'Please sit.'

A dark-skinned boy of about fifteen hurried into the room. He stopped short when he saw Kamil, and the smile slipped from his face, but not before Kamil had witnessed his unguarded adoration when he looked at Amida.

'Bilal, go fetch us some whisky,' Amida told him.

The boy cast a curious glance at Kamil, then disappeared down a corridor.

The room was furnished in the European style, with a sofa and armchairs crammed into the small space. Several Venetian lamps stood on occasional tables, their delicate glass bellies filled with oil. The sofa rustled when Kamil sat. Cheap local manufacture, he thought, stuffed with straw and covered in cotton, its wooden arms gilded. Amida had expensive tastes, but not enough money to complete the picture of fine living. The furniture in

Balkis's house, by contrast, was finely made. She clearly kept her son on a short financial leash.

'Do you play?' Kamil asked, indicating the Steinway piano in the corner. It must have cost a fortune.

'Amateur,' Amida said enthusiastically. He went over and slid his hand along the sleek black lid. 'Isn't it magnificent?'

Amida reminded Kamil of a puppy, one moment earnest, the next playful as he trotted up with a favourite scrap of bone. Not gang material, Kamil thought, and wondered whether the young man was in over his head.

The boy brought a tray with a decanter and two glasses. He poured each man a drink, then squatted against the far wall. Amida offered Kamil a cigarette, then took a small ormolu box from the table, clicked it open, and pushed a lever. A flame shot up. When they had lit their cigarettes, he tilted the box towards Kamil so he could see the elaborate mechanism inside.

'Clever, isn't it? Every day there are new inventions. To be really modern, you can never rest. Railways, for example, are changing everything. Soon we'll be able to get on in Istanbul and step off in Paris. Have you heard about something called centrifugal force?' He seemed to have forgotten all about the reason for Kamil's visit.

'The tendency of rotating bodies to fly outward,' Kamil answered. 'I've read about it.'

'In America, they have a train based on centrifugal force, a gravity switchback train. It was built on an island called Coney. They call it the Gravity Pleasure Ride.'

Amida seemed starved for conversation. 'You know,' he continued, 'I spent nine years away, in Abyssinia mostly, but on the way back, I spent a year in Cairo. I met the most fascinating people there. Have you heard of

Shepheard's Hotel? It really gave me an appreciation for the modern life. I met an American there, Charles Freer, one of the new men of industry. He runs factories and collects art and antiquities. The two marks of the modern man, he told me, are money and taste. Have you been abroad?'

'I was in England for a year,' Kamil said.

'London, Paris, New York. I'd love to see those places.'

'Are you planning to travel?'

Amida's mood changed. 'I have responsibilities here. I'm going to modernise the family business. Once that's done and it can stand on its own, I plan to travel.'

'What's your family's business?'

'Export,' Amida answered blandly.

'I see, and what do you export?' Kamil could see the jeweller's wheels spinning inside Amida's head.

'Carpets,' he said finally.

No carpet dealer would put the prayer rug of Ahmet I on his floor and walk on it with dirty boots, Kamil thought. Did Amida's 'family business' send Remzi to bribe Kamil? Whoever was behind the Tobacco Works kidnapping was well organised, and, unlike the old smuggling families, brutally careless of life and unafraid of the police. Omar thought they were a new and dangerous group. But they had sent Remzi, a common local thug, so perhaps it was only the leadership that was new.

Was that leader Amida? Kamil regarded the young man and thought it unlikely. He didn't appear to possess the steely bloody-mindedness that made a leader. No one would follow him. Perhaps it was someone else in the village, someone not so obvious. Balkis, perhaps. But she hadn't recognised Remzi's name.

'When there are so many interesting new things, it

seems a shame to be wasting our time on old pieces, like the reliquary your uncle Malik reported stolen from the Kariye Mosque,' Kamil ventured.

Amida hesitated for a moment, as if sensing a trap. 'I agree, modern is best.'

'Did you ever see the reliquary?'

'It's just an old box.'

'So who do you think would take it?'

Amida shrugged. 'Some people like that old stuff.' He refilled his glass, knocking the decanter against the rim.

'Do you know people who buy antiquities?'

'Me? No.' He stood. 'Look, I'm sorry I can't help you.'

'Let me try this again,' Kamil said calmly. 'I'd like you to take me to the tunnel that leads to the Tobacco Works.'

'I don't know what you're talking about. The Tobacco Works is over by the Golden Horn.'

Kamil waited.

'Look, I heard about the policemen killed over there last night. Word gets around. But I have nothing to do with that,' Amida insisted. 'And I don't know what tunnel you're talking about.'

Kamil wondered whether that could be true. Amida looked nervous, but it might simply be because he thought Kamil was trying to link him to the murders. He considered again the possibility that Remzi was lying, saying the tunnel connected to Sunken Village in order to cast suspicion on Amida and away from someone else. He decided to apply more pressure.

'There's a policeman missing. If you help us find him, we'll overlook your role in all this. But if we find out that you knew about it and didn't help us, then you'll be spending the rest of your life in a dungeon. He was taken into that tunnel and I'm going to find him. I know the tunnel ends in this village and I'll find out where. I might begin by tearing your house apart, starting with your piano.'

Amida's expression swung between confusion, outrage, and fear. 'Go ahead and look,' he said. 'You won't find a tunnel in the piano or anywhere else.'

It was clear to Kamil that Amida wouldn't tell him where the tunnel was, even if he knew. What was he afraid of?

'You've been warned,' he told Amida ominously. 'If you change your mind, you can find me at the Beyoglu Court. Believe me, you'll wish you had talked to me sooner.'

He walked out.

He could arrest Amida for stealing the carpet and the reliquary later. Right now, Amida was more useful to him as a potential link to the dealer, especially since his other link, Remzi, was in jail.

KAMIL STOOD AT the base of the cistern wall, a massive expanse of rough, broken stone, wondering where to start looking. He walked the perimeter of the cistern, working his way systematically into breaks and around fallen sections. Some homes, like Amida's, were built right against the wall with bricks taken from the cistern itself, as if they were parasites. He soon generated a trail of curious onlookers, mainly children. He passed out some small copper coins, and the children led him to a rotted wooden door. He prised it open and squeezed into the corridor behind, but it soon ended in a pile of rubble.

The entrance had to be inside one of the houses, Kamil concluded, when he returned, dusty and sweaty, to the village square. He studied the cottages and the enveloping cistern for a few moments, noting the mounds of debris that had collected against the walls. If you multiplied that debris over several hundred years, he realised, the ground was probably five metres higher now than when the cistern was built. He had been looking in the wrong place. Any tunnel built back then wouldn't be at this level, especially if it had been used for water. It would be far below ground.

He looked around, envisioning a trapdoor in every cottage that led to a rabbit's warren of steps and paths running underground in every direction. Omar was right. This was truly a smuggler's paradise. He wondered if Balkis or Malik knew or would tell him anything. He doubted it. There was a secret to this place, strange undercurrents that disoriented him. He wanted to go back and smash a chair into Amida's piano until he told him where the tunnel was. What held him back was the faint possibility that Amida was telling the truth and Remzi was lying.

And how much did Saba know? The thought of Saba set off a cascade of feelings. This was a new sensation, different from his deep affection for Sybil, the ambassador's daughter who had returned to England, and entirely removed from his physical attraction to the French actress who had been his mistress some years back. Consummation was impossible, of course. Saba was a protected young woman from a respectable family. And if he were to marry, it would be to someone of his own class, not a Habesh woman from Sunken Village, no matter how deep the attraction. Forget about Saba, he told himself crossly. It was a foolish fancy, no different from the actress. Listen to your head, not your loins. The image of Elif's delicate golden head and haunted eyes came suddenly to his mind, and he felt foolish and slightly guilty.

He stopped before a stone house in the village square. Two shoulder-high pillars flanked the entrance. He examined one, running his hand across the protruding circles carved into its side and exploring its concave top. His hand came away smeared with rust. He brought his fingers to his nose. Blood. Then he noticed the sacrificial stone. For animal sacrifice, just like at any other Muslim shrine. He was beginning to see blood everywhere, he chided himself.

It was late afternoon and the square was empty. The villagers were working in their gardens. Women were inside preparing the evening meal, their daughters helping. Little boys napped in the shade. Kamil climbed the steps out of Sunken Village up to the market district of Charshamba. The rhythmic recitation of ilahi drifted into the street from the Sufi tekke at the corner. He paid a boy to deliver a message to Malik, apologising and saying he would come to breakfast the following morning. Then he mounted his horse and rode off in the direction of the Fatih police station.

11

'May I come in, my dear?'
'Of course, Mama.'

Saba's room was furnished with a low cushioned divan below the window, a Persian carpet on the floor, a wardrobe, and a narrow wrought-iron bed. Shelves held books, stacks of papers, and manuscripts. A cluttered table was pushed against the wall. It didn't look like the room of a young girl, certainly not the room of a woman thinking about marriage. There was not a single piece of embroidery or tatting.

Saba sat on the divan by the open window.

'You'll catch a cold.' Balkis went over and closed the window. Then she stood, wondering what to say next. She was glad Saba hadn't witnessed that last scene with Kamil and Amida. It was her own fault. Balkis had let her emotions rule her, something she had promised herself years ago never to do again. Kamil's resemblance to his father had overwhelmed her. Every detail Kamil revealed about his family had brought her closer to them. It had been irresistible, foolish, and painful.

'Do sit, Mama. You look tired.'

Balkis slumped down beside her, her belly pushing against her breasts. She bit down the pain that seemed to come from everywhere and nowhere.

Saba arranged the cushions behind her mother's back. 'You're ill, Mama. Can I do anything?'

'I want to talk to you about Courtidis.'

'Mother, please. I don't want to talk about him. I know you rely on him and I know he's helped all of us a great deal. You don't have to worry that I'll say something to put him off, but I don't want to marry him.'

'Why not, my dear? He wants to marry you. He's a good, generous man and he'll treat you well.'

'Why the sudden rush to marry me off?'

Balkis heard the querulous tone and cautioned herself to tread carefully. 'You know that you and Amida are the last of the line.'

'But we're still young. There's no hurry.'

Balkis's stomach turned at the thought of Gudit's circumcision knife wavering over her daughter's tender flesh. What was the point of this tradition now when it was more important than ever for the priestess to bear children? Balkis knew she could never allow it. She would have to make this clear to Gudit, who would take Balkis's forbidding of the ritual as one more betrayal.

'My mother told me that in her mother's time, there were lots of candidates for priestess and caretaker. There was even rivalry between siblings and cousins. Whole groups of boys went to the monastery together. But by the time Mother was chosen to be priestess, there were only three eligible people.'

'What happened to everyone?'

'The plague hit the last generation very hard, dear. Who knows what else there was? All I know is that we're at a bad turning. If you and Amida don't have children, the line comes to an end.'

'Why didn't Uncle Malik have children?'

'You know him. He's never shown any interest in that sort of thing.'

'He doesn't have to be celibate?'

'No. That's his choice.'

'May I ask you something, Mama?'

'What, dear?'

'Why didn't you remarry? You could have had more children.'

Balkis sighed. How could she explain without revealing the savagery of the ritual? 'After my initiation as priestess, I, well, I wasn't interested in that sort of thing anymore.'

'What is the initiation like?' Saba asked cautiously.

She wanted to tell Saba, to lift her kaftan and show her what had been done to her. Balkis realised at that moment why a young girl must be brought to the ritual like a ewe to the sacrificial stone. She would never have agreed to go through with it if she had known. Why were women willing to spill the blood of their daughters, knowing what it felt like themselves? She had a sudden image of bullnecked Gudit as executioner. A hundred Gudits down the generations, knives in hand, ready to splice the priestess to her faith. And it had worked. She had been made priestess against her will, but after the circumcision she had had no choice but to clothe herself in all the power the Holy of Holies and the community bestowed. There was nothing else.

Balkis looked at her daughter. She didn't need to be sacrificed to the sect in order to rise as its priestess. Saba had faith, something she lacked. The blood rite was for the faithless. That was the secret of four hundred years of continuity.

'Does something happen during the initiation?' Saba asked worriedly.

'Yes, my dear. But it's not something you need to worry about. We'll talk about it later. We have time.' She gave her what she hoped was an encouraging smile.

Saba didn't look reassured. 'Is there some reason you want me to have a child now? There's something you're not telling me, Mama.'

Balkis patted her on the arm. 'I told you not to worry. I simply want you to be settled. It's time. And Courtidis is a very good candidate.'

'But he's a Christian.'

'That's immaterial as long as he agrees to live here and your children are raised as Melisites.'

'Why would he want to live here? He's not even Habesh.'

'I think the good surgeon will live wherever you ask him to. Why don't you like him?'

'It's not that I don't like him, Mama. I'm not attracted to him like . . .'

'Are you in love with someone else?'

Saba flushed. 'Kamil Pasha.' She said it so softly Balkis wasn't sure she'd heard correctly.

'Who?'

'I'd like to marry Kamil Pasha.'

Balkis froze. 'Pashas make mistresses of the likes of us,' she snapped. 'They don't marry girls from Charshamba.'

'I can make him love me.'

'You've only just met him. You have no idea who he is. Perhaps he already has a wife. Have you considered that?'

'He's not married. Uncle Malik told me all about him.'

'What did he tell you?' Balkis asked warily.

'He said Kamil Pasha would always be there for me and that I could rely on him. Why else would Uncle Malik have said that if he didn't mean for us to be together?'

The fool, Balkis thought, her mind in turmoil. How dare he introduce her daughter to Kamil without her knowledge or her permission. Now Saba had misunderstood and believed Kamil would marry her. It could never happen.

She grasped her daughter's hands. 'I won't force you to marry Courtidis. But if you don't choose him, then you must choose someone else. The village is full of good-looking, ambitious young men. Pick one. In six months, there will be a wedding. If you don't choose someone, I'll do it for you. But I forbid you to see Kamil Pasha again.'

Tomorrow, Balkis decided, tomorrow she would tell Saba the real reason she couldn't marry Kamil. Today she felt too ill and too upset. Meeting Kamil for the first time had struck open a fissure of pain and longing she had thought long healed. She wanted a last chance to dream her own story, before sharing it with others who might dismiss it as nothing more than a sordid affair. Tomorrow, she would start at the beginning and give Saba the gift of her life as she had composed it, before others had come to carve it to their own design. She wanted Saba to love the only part of her mother's life that she had loved.

Balkis steeled her heart against the broken look on Saba's face. She recognised it. It had been her own face eighteen years earlier.

BALKIS STOOD ON the terrace of the Sultan Selim Mosque, which towered over Sunken Village, watching men leave the mosque after prayer. She could see each man's face as he emerged from behind the leather curtain that spanned the main door, squinting at the light, then bending down to put on his shoes. The pasha had sought her out, those many years ago, in the Charshamba market. She was eighteen and already married, her baby at home swaddled and asleep in his cradle. He had come up to her in the sweet afternoon light and bought a handful of peaches, telling her, as he bent to count the coins into her hand, that her cheeks put the peaches to shame. They burned, even today, those cheeks, when she thought of the timbre of his voice, lush and low, casting everything in gold. She had said nothing at first, but she couldn't stop herself from hurtling wilfully into his life like a basket of peaches overturned. She had never wished it otherwise. All she wanted was for him to return.

She knew he was dead now, yet she continued to stand there every afternoon, hoping to see his face, guarding her emptiness.

AMIDA PUSHED BILAL away and sat down heavily on the piano bench. He took a big gulp of whisky. His hands were shaking. Kubalou must have sent Remzi to the magistrate to point the finger at him. There was no other explanation. Did Kubalou think he had squealed about the shipment last night? Someone had told the police, but it hadn't been him. The image of Remzi stabbing the two young policemen in the heart so efficiently and nonchalantly was etched into his mind. The younger policeman had been about the same age as Amida, no more than twenty, his eyes full of intelligence and yearning. He could have fallen in love with that policeman.

Now there was another policeman missing. Didn't those fools know that killing policemen would bring retribution raining in upon them from every direction? This couldn't have been Kubalou's plan. Remzi must be acting on his own, sheltering under Kubalou's money and power to play his own sick games. Did Kubalou even know? He should tell him that Remzi's bloodlust would destroy his operation. Maybe then, Amida allowed himself to think, Kubalou would trust him and give him more responsibility, even his own gang. Then he wouldn't need to run to his mother for permission for every fart.

They had arrived home near dawn and he had barely slept. Each time he closed his eyes, he saw the blood spurting from the young man's chest. Bilal had curled himself around Amida. In his fitful sleep, Amida dreamed a hand had reached into Bilal's chest and torn out his beating heart.

Amida emptied the rest of the decanter into his glass and drank it down. After Kubalou's man Ben had left yesterday evening, Amida had celebrated with his favourite whore, a boy with a harelip whose family had sold him to a brothel. Amida had bought him and kept him in a rented room on the outskirts of Charshamba. The boy kept his face veiled when they did the act. Amida found it more exciting that way, the satin expanse of his belly, his tight nipples, the gleaming pink snail between his thighs rendered forbidden, vulnerable, even more naked by the black cloth covering his face. He could be anyone.

And then Remzi had come to the door of that rented room with his rough men, smiled knowingly, and demanded that Amida come with them. An initiation, he called it. No Habesh were needed that night, just him. And he had gone, wondering how they had known where to find him. No one in Sunken Village knew about the rented room. He worried about the boy. He wasn't safe there anymore.

He opened the lid of the piano and let his fingers slide across the keyboard, then looked at the score and began to pick out Mozart's *Fantasia in D minor*. He played badly, despite a year of lessons in Cairo, but the cool ivory responding to his fingers soothed him. He played until his arm hurt so much that he could barely move it, then closed the lid and held out his hand to Bilal.

Later, Bilal's smooth copper-coloured flesh hot beneath him, Amida imagined a sleek, blond boy like the ones he had seen on the verandah of Shepheard's in Cairo, his skin white and taut as the belly of a fish and cool to the touch even in the heat. Afterward, Amida lay in the dark, eyes open, wondering how the future that had been so tantalisingly clear yesterday, had become so murky today. A man had to make himself. He decided to speak directly with Kubalou. He would find a way to bypass Remzi. The wound on his left arm, four slashes from Remzi's knife, throbbed under its bandage like a second awkward heart-beat grafted on to his body.

12

When he saw Kamil, Omar jumped up from his chair in the corner of the police station and greeted him. The room was subdued. The desk by the door was unoccupied, the ledger lying open, seemingly untouched since Ali had sat there yesterday noting down other people's misfortunes.

'Thanks for the gift,' Omar grumbled. 'Wrapped like a butcher's portion. Where did you find that scum?'

'He followed me from the Tobacco Works. Did you find out anything?'

'He squealed like a calf when we used the bastinado. The tougher a man's hide, the thinner the soles of his feet. Allah is just.'

For once, Kamil had no qualms about Omar's method.

'Ali?'

Omar frowned, flung his cigarette on to the floor and stamped on it. 'Nothing. He said he didn't know anything about it. I think that's a bad sign. If Ali were still alive, this motherfucker would have tried to bargain.'

Kamil slapped his riding gloves on the table in frustration. An officer brought tea, but the men let the glasses sit untouched between them. Kamil told Omar about his conversation with Amida, the carpet that proved Amida had stolen the reliquary, and his fruitless search for the tunnel.

'Amida looked pretty rough, like he hadn't slept. And he

was holding his arm stiffly, as if he'd been wounded. He denied knowing Remzi, but I'm sure he recognised the name. He's involved, but I don't see him as a killer.'

'No, his main vice is chasing arse, which I couldn't care less about. I kind of like the kid, pathetic as he is. Growing up in that strange family, all that weird sect crap, then being sent off to some mountaintop in Africa for eight years. That would screw up anyone.' From Omar's red eyes and chin thick with stubble, Kamil was sure he had neither gone home nor slept.

Kamil shook his head. 'It doesn't add up.'

'You're right. There's something wrong with Remzi's holier-than-thou story. He didn't look scared enough, even after I let some of the men take out their disgust on him. It's like he knows he's got Allah on his side.'

'What else did he say?'

'That Amida had hired him and some other men from Charshamba to run the shipment that night.'

'So he's deflecting attention away from his real boss by pinning everything on Amida.'

'Which is like trying to pin an elephant on a flea.'

'What about the tunnel?'

'He claims he wasn't there on the docks when the men were killed. He was the innocent lookout at the other end of the tunnel.'

'You found it?' Kamil's voice betrayed his excitement.

Omar looked disconsolate and shook his head. 'He said it was in a house in Sunken Village, but they went there at night, so he couldn't tell us where, just that it was dark and you had to go down a stairway into the ground. That's all we could get out of him. Believe me, we tried.'

'How did he get there if he doesn't know where it is?'

'Apparently Amida led them there.'

'Why would he do that? From what I've learned, the Habesh are very protective of their secrets. And it puts his whole family at risk. I can't believe Amida wouldn't know what kind of men these are.'

'The young look at a desert and see an oasis.'

'Any way we can loosen their tongues?'

'I think they're more afraid of their boss than the bastinado. He must be the devil himself!'

'Amida is giving away Habesh secrets and attracting busybodies like us snooping around. Someone must want to stop him enough to talk to us.' Kamil picked up his riding gloves. 'I think I know who that might be. I just need to find a way to speak with her privately.'

Omar raised an eyebrow and gave Kamil a knowing look.

Irritated, Kamil asked, 'Don't you ever think about anything else?'

Omar shrugged. 'I'm a married man,' he said. 'Imagination is my only refuge.'

13

Feride met him in the hall and whispered enthusiastically, 'Hamdi Bey is here, Kamil. What a nice, gentle man. Do you know he studied art at the same academy in Paris as Elif? They've been talking non-stop since lunch. Would you like some . . .' She stopped in mid-sentence and took a closer look at Kamil's face. 'My brother, are you ill?'

'Just tired,' Kamil answered gruffly, annoyed that the conversation would now be monopolised by art instead of the more serious business of the antiquities thefts. Huseyin had sent a message saying Hamdi Bey, the director of the archaeological museum, would be coming to their house at five that afternoon. It was now after six.

Feride took Kamil into the parlour, a room rarely used except when Huseyin entertained important visitors. It was furnished with Frankish sofas, tables, and chairs. Heavy blue drapes kept the room in semi-darkness.

Elif was dressed in loose black trousers and a long white tunic, less masculine but still unconventional attire. She sat on the yellow sofa, talking to a bearded man with a prominent nose and receding hairline who sat opposite her. His hair and beard were flecked with grey and a pair of spectacles lay on his knee. They were speaking French, Elif leaning forward and gesturing. She had dispensed with even the token scarf, and her bare feet seemed white and vulnerable against the blue and red carpet. A stack of drawings lay on the table beside them.

Huseyin rose from his armchair. 'Well, brother-in-law, glad you could make it.' He looked over at Hamdi Bey, who had also risen. 'My brother-in-law's a busy man, but he's been anxious to meet you.'

Elif smiled up at Kamil. He bowed graciously, then turned to Hamdi Bey. He saw a kind man in an old-fashioned suit, quick to smile. He was anxious to consult with him, but could see that Elif wanted to continue her discussion. In any case, it would be unthinkable to impose his own agenda on this gathering without first playing the role of guest. He reached for the glass of water a servant held out to him and tried to relax.

Elif told him excitedly, 'Kamil, did you know that Hamdi Bey also studied at the Académie Julian? Under Gustave Boulanger. Before me, of course, but we know many of the same people. It's so exciting to find someone here who knows what it was like.'

Hamdi Bey beamed at her and said to Kamil, 'I know the passion for art that animates those who are drawn to that life. I was sent to France to study law, but Paris was such a paradise for creativity, I could do nothing else but paint, paint, paint.' He turned to Elif. 'Although I've recently taken up photography. It's a remarkable thing, like painting with light. Have you tried it?'

'I haven't had the opportunity,' Elif responded, 'but I'd love to see how it works.' Her cheeks were flushed and her eyes blazed.

'You will have to come to our house at Eskihisar and meet my wife. She's French. I'd like her to see your sketches.' He thought for a moment, then asked, 'Would you be interested in teaching at the Istanbul Academy of

Fine Arts? I'd have to look into it, but I think it might be possible.'

Clearly stunned, Elif responded, 'I didn't know you had an academy here. I would be honoured.'

'Hamdi Bey founded it four years ago,' Huseyin interjected. 'Are you still the dean?'

'No longer, Huseyin. A man has just two arms and two eyes. Being director of the archaeological museum takes most of my time and this year I'm directing the excavations in Sidon.'

The look of sheer pleasure on Elif's face moved Kamil.

'Thank you, Hamdi Bey.' She reached out to kiss his hand, but he withdrew it gently and patted her on the arm.

'This is a remarkably talented young woman,' he said to the room. 'It is I who am grateful for the opportunity to take advantage of that talent for our school.'

Elif wiped her eyes, unable to stop smiling.

Huseyin broke in. 'Well, enough good news. Let's hear the bad, Kamil. Tell Hamdi Bey about the thefts.'

Kamil flashed him a grateful look and began to recount the problem of the stolen antiquities and the London dealer. When Kamil finished, Hamdi Bey shook his head. 'I'm not familiar with Rettingate and Sons, but I'll make some inquiries for you. I presume you want to know the names of the current owners and any connections they might have here.' When Kamil nodded, he continued. 'I'll see what else I can discover, Kamil. Thanks be to Allah for devoted servants of the state like you.'

Kamil expressed his gratitude and added, 'We need more guarded locations to store antiquities, like your museum.'

Hamdi Bey sighed. 'Think of the empire as a plump piece of baklava. Each layer is studded with artefacts, entire civilisations,' he gestured broadly with his hand, 'ancient cities, temples, enormous stone sarcophagi, friezes, mosaics, statues, an endless array of objects. The layers near the top have preserved clothing, carpets, inlaid wood, documents. Those near the bottom are littered with clay tablets and bones. The layers in between are endless, each as replete as the next. There aren't enough museums in the world to house all our treasures.' He smiled in a self-deprecating way. 'We are embarrassingly rich.'

'Isn't it better to leave the things in the ground then, instead of digging them up so people can steal them?' Feride asked.

'That's a good point,' Hamdi Bey conceded. 'I wonder that myself sometimes. But our curiosity is too great and we keep excavating. It's a wonderful thing to know about the people who lived on this earth before us. I think it helps us be more tolerant towards our neighbours. The fact that they speak to God rather than to Allah is a minor difference, a matter of semantics, really, compared to the lives of the Romans and Greeks who lived on this very same spot.'

'Didn't they feed their Christian neighbours to the lions?' Huseyin asked with a laugh.

Hamdi Bey stood. 'Unfortunately, I must depart. I leave for Sidon tomorrow. But I'll be in touch with you, madame,' he bowed low to Elif, 'and with you, Kamil, about the thefts. It's rare that in one afternoon I am allowed to contribute, even if in a minor way, to two such important projects.'

AFTER HAMDI BEY had gone, Huseyin commented, 'He has a tongue that could sweeten vinegar. He should be in parliament. If we had a parliament.'

Kamil responded, 'That's how he gets the government to support all of his projects.'

'After he's gone, we should gild his tongue and display it in the museum.'

Kamil couldn't help but laugh. 'You're jealous.'

Huseyin stuck out his tongue at Feride. 'Mine's already gold, isn't it, wife?'

Feride blushed and ran after Elif, who had gone to put her drawings away.

Kamil got up to leave.

Huseyin clapped him on the shoulder. 'Brother-in-law, you look like a camel on the far side of the desert. Just skin, bones, and determination. Sit with me for a moment before you rush off back to that desert of yours.'

Kamil allowed Huseyin to lead him into an adjoining sitting room. He settled in an armchair by the unlit fireplace and took the glass of Scotch Huseyin handed him. He set the glass down, then drifted off. He was awakened by Feride pulling at his sleeve. Next to her stood Avi, a bandage on his head, watching Kamil intently.

'Well, my boy,' Kamil said, sitting up straight. 'How are you feeling today?'

'I'm very well, bey,' Avi said in a firm voice. 'I'm ready to come back to work.'

'Good riddance.' Alev's little-girl voice floated across the room.

Huseyin laughed. 'No golden tongues in this family.'

Feride scolded Alev. 'Don't be impolite. Avi is our guest.'

Alev folded her arms and scowled. No doubt the girls weren't used to sharing the adults' attention. Yasemin was perched on a chair, admiring her embroidered skirt that was splayed across her legs like a fan. Kamil wondered which moments in childhood predict the adult.

Then he noticed Elif, or rather, he caught the scent of her as she approached the back of his chair. It was a fresh, green scent, not floral like that of other women. She sat in the chair next to him and crossed her legs. Her foot arched elegantly, animated by the beat of her heart. Her toes were long, but not bony, the clefts between them almost erotic, a tiny country of vulnerabilities. There was a slight plump rise on the inside of her foot near the heel. He wanted to press his mouth there, feel the resilience of the flesh at her instep, at the span of her arch.

Elif was watching him, her face flushed. Kamil was embarrassed. Had he been asleep and dreamed this? He looked down quickly. Her feet were tucked under her chair. She was asking Avi about his life in Middle Village.

14

That evening, Kamil was in the winter garden, repositioning his orchids to compensate for the shifting autumn light. He set the pot of *Orchis lactea* down carefully. Its long spikes were densely set with milky white conical flowers flushed with rose. He had discovered the plant growing in a patch of wildflowers just outside the city walls, despite the stench and effluvium of the nearby tanneries, and had managed to bring it to bloom in his winter garden for the second time this year. The *lacteal* orchid, however, was a simple fishwife compared to its delicate, high-born cousin in the next pot, the rare *Orchis pinetorum*, which grew only at high altitudes in the Taurus Mountains and whose pure white blossoms looked like tiny hummingbirds feeding on the stem.

He thought he heard a tap on the glass and peered out the window. In the half-light, he made out Malik's worried face.

'Malik, welcome,' Kamil said. 'Please come in. Have you eaten? The cook has made some wonderful kabak dolmasou.'

Malik stood in the winter garden, looking about as if he had never been there before. Kamil was concerned. 'Has something happened?'

'May I sit for a moment, my friend?'

'Of course.' Kamil gestured towards two comfortable cane chairs under a potted palm. 'Let me take your cloak.'

Malik ignored his request and sat down in the chair, eyes closed.

Kamil waited, trying not to show how tired he was. The light had faded, leaving a grey pall that infected the air and made the colourful blooms of his orchids look like the wings of dead moths. When Yakup appeared at the inner door with a lamp, Malik turned so his face remained in shadow. At a look from Kamil, Yakup retreated without a word.

'I need your help,' Malik said finally in a weary voice, 'but more than that, I need your silence.'

'You have my loyalty as a friend, Malik, but you should know that if you tell me anything about a crime, I can't keep that to myself.'

'Of course. I would expect no less from you. This is about a crime that I need your help in solving, but there are other things that must remain between us.' He leaned back and regarded the palm fronds above him. 'It's so restful here.'

'What is it you wish to tell me?'

'It's about the reliquary.'

Kamil nodded.

'It's more important than I told you.' He leaned forward, his face in his hands.

Kamil reached out and laid his hand on Malik's arm. 'Is there something valuable in it?'

Malik looked up at Kamil with red-rimmed eyes. 'I know I must tell you, but understand that this is difficult for me. If word gets out about its true nature, there will be more death.'

'No silver box could be that valuable, Malik.'

'You see, that's my dilemma. If I don't tell you about it, I know you'll do your best as a friend to locate it, but I'm not ignorant of your other priorities. If I do tell you, I'll be revealing a four-hundred-year-old secret and putting my community at great risk.'

Kamil waited, but Malik was silent, clearly struggling with his decision. Kamil got up and opened the door into the house. Yakup reappeared immediately, the handle of a revolver protruding from his belt.

Kamil nodded towards it. 'That won't be necessary, but you can bring us some coffee and water. Just leave it here,' he pointed to a small table outside the door, 'and knock. Make sure we're not disturbed.'

He closed the door, sat down again and, after a few moments, said gently, 'I'll do whatever I can, my dear friend. You know you can trust me.' He wondered what secret could agitate the old man so deeply.

'I'll tell you what I can. You are one of us, in a way.'

'What do you mean?'

There was another long silence. Dry leaves skittered across the glass ceiling.

'Let's discuss that tomorrow at breakfast in the light of the new day. Here in the darkness, let me tell you a story.'

Kamil settled back in his chair. He was having difficulty keeping his eyes open.

'Sunken Village is home to a sect,' Malik began, 'called the Melisites. It dates back to the time of the Conquest.'

This was not at all what Kamil was expecting. He was suddenly wide awake. 'I've never heard of them.'

'There's a reason for the secrecy.' Malik shook his head. 'No, not because of any criminal activity, although . . .' He took a deep breath and let it out slowly. 'Although Omar isn't wrong. They do deal in stolen goods. I've kept out of it myself. My sister runs the commercial affairs of the village.'

Kamil kept his excitement at bay. He knew a door had opened, and that he must enter slowly so it didn't swing shut again. He waited for Malik to continue.

'But these aren't the people you're looking for,' Malik added quickly. 'Everything's on a small scale. The Habesh don't steal, so much as provide a service to those who do. They buy stolen items from professional thieves in Charshamba and sell them to merchants in the bazaar. They've been doing this for generations.'

He held up his amber-skinned hand, then turned it and looked curiously at his palm. 'I am Habesh, so I suppose I'm culpable. You understand that I would rather discuss the reliquary.'

'As you like.' One door opened, another shut. They led to the same place.

'Since the Conquest, the Melisites', Malik continued, 'have been custodians of a reliquary said to contain a priceless religious artefact that gives it miraculous powers. It's called the Proof of God.'

'Said to . . .' Kamil echoed.

'No one actually knew what was in it.'

'In four hundred years, no one was curious enough to open it?'

'No one knew exactly where it was.'

'I'm confused.'

'The Melisite congregation believes the reliquary resides in the prayer house in the village.'

'But it doesn't.'

'No. It never has. Only the leaders of the sect know it is missing and they pass that knowledge on to the next generation of leaders when they are initiated. We have always carried out the ceremonies as if the Proof of God were there in the Holy of Holies.'

A sect built on lies, Kamil thought, but perhaps no different from most sects built around some shrine or object.

'So a sect grew up around a reliquary that no one knew the contents or the location of?'

'Faith, Kamil, is more powerful than knowledge. Sheikh Galip has shown us that reason can be duped by logic, but faith . . .'

'I'm sorry, my friend,' Kamil interrupted, a bit testily. 'I'm too tired to follow Sufi allegories right now.'

'Forgive an old man's desire to rest in the garden of philosophy for a while.'

There was a knock at the door. Malik stood quickly and put his face to the orchids.

Kamil went to the door and returned carrying a large tray containing two cups of coffee, glasses, and a pitcher of water. The cook had added plates of baklava and fruit. Kamil set them on a table within reach. Malik sat down again and Kamil handed him a small china cup of coffee and a glass of water. 'You can rely on Yakup's silence.'

Malik took a sip of water, then set the glass down. 'It's not my safety I'm concerned about. There's much more at stake. The Melisites believe they're a chosen people,' Malik explained, 'who were given the reliquary for safe-keeping during the Conquest of Byzantium. Shortly after the Conquest there was a battle between the caretaker of the reliquary and a false prophet, and the reliquary disappeared. The leaders of the community at the time believed the reliquary was still in the Church of Saint Saviour in Chora, as it was known then, and that the caretaker had hidden it before he was killed. They believed it would be just a matter of time before it was found again, so they told no one it was gone.' He pointed to himself.

'Each descendant of the original caretaker has searched for the Proof in his own way. Perhaps over the generations some lost hope. My father, for instance, no longer believed it was there. He said it would have been found by now.'

'You found it, didn't you? This is the reliquary that was stolen last week.'

'Yes.'

'How did you ever find it?'

'The building remained a church for a hundred years after the Conquest. As you know, when it was turned into a mosque, its mosaics and other features were plastered over. After the renovation revealed them again for the first time in three hundred years, I began to see possibilities.'

'The Habesh men pray at the mosque, don't they? Are they Muslims or Christians?'

'Does it matter?' Malik sighed. 'All the faiths of the Book received the same prophecy.'

'It doesn't matter,' Kamil shrugged, 'I just find it intriguing.'

'The Melisites converted so they could continue to worship at the church after it became a mosque.'

Kamil took that in. No wonder Malik was worried his community would be at risk if this information got out. 'Who is their leader?'

'Balkis is the priestess and I'm the caretaker, both hereditary positions, usually held by a sister and brother. The Melisites are named after the original caretaker's sister, Melisane. Amida and Saba are the last of their line.'

'I noticed your sister has the same ring.' Kamil pointed to Malik's right hand.

Malik rubbed it with his thumb. 'They're said to have come from Abyssinia along with the reliquary, and they're handed on whenever a new caretaker and priestess are initiated.' He regarded Kamil with surprise. 'I didn't know you knew my sister.'

'I went to the village today and spoke with your family about an incident that happened last night. Two policemen were killed and another kidnapped.'

'A terrible thing. But why were you asking my family about it?'

'The murders happened on the pier behind the Tobacco Works. We believe the missing policeman was taken into a tunnel that leads to Sunken Village. He might still be alive. Do you know anything about this tunnel?'

Kamil fully expected Malik to deny having any knowledge of such things, and was astonished when he asked, 'Was Amida involved?'

'Probably.'

'He's not a murderer.'

'I know that.'

'There are many tunnels, but I don't know of any leading to the Tobacco Works. I'm sorry. What makes you suspect Amida?'

'An accusation. Perhaps it's wrong. It's possible the man accused Amida in order to draw suspicion away from himself.'

'I see I was right that you have other things to worry about.'

'I'm honoured that you feel you can confide in me,' Kamil said earnestly. 'I'll do my very best to find the reliquary, but you must know that the stolen objects are being sent abroad. It's possible the reliquary is already in London. Did you tell anyone you had found it? That would have been important news.'

'No, not straight away.'

'Why not?'

'A selfish reason unworthy of me. I wished to study it. And I didn't know what would happen if I gave it to my sister. The sect isn't what it was. So many years without a touchstone has eroded the faith of its leaders.'

'So how did anyone know about it?'

'I recently told Saba. She can read some Aramaic.'

'Aramaic?'

'Yes. It's written in Aramaic.'

'I thought it contained a relic.'

'In a way, it does.' Seeing Kamil's confusion, he continued. 'It's a document. A very old and invaluable document. The parchment was preserved in a lead sleeve that fitted inside the reliquary. It's extremely fragile. That's why I wanted to make a copy of it before I told anyone else. I planned to copy it and then I wanted Saba to study it with me.'

'What exactly is it?' Kamil wondered why Malik hadn't told him this to begin with. Clearly it wasn't the reliquary he was concerned about, but its contents. Secrets within secrets.

Malik stood and paced nervously along the gravel path of the winter garden. Reflected in the night-blackened glass panes, a dozen faint Maliks split and recombined in a cascade of ghosts. The crunch of gravel suddenly ceased.

'Please forgive me. I can't tell you any more. The less the world knows about the document, the safer it'll be. It needs to be preserved and protected. Then it can be made public. I sometimes wonder whether it wouldn't be better just to hide it again, until humankind is worthy of such a gift. But I'm afraid it'll crumble away.'

'I can see why getting the reliquary back is so important to you, with such a fragile treasure inside.'

'You misunderstand. The reliquary that was stolen is empty. I took the document out.'

Kamil was stunned. 'Why concern yourself with the empty box, then, when you have the document? Surely that's the important thing.'

'I understand it's just one object among dozens that have gone missing, but there are two reasons for you to bend your mind to finding this particular empty box, Kamil. The reliquary confirms the Proof of God. It gives provenance to the document within.'

'What do you mean?'

'On the lid is an engraving of Theodore Metochites, a historical figure who we know was associated with the Proof. The inscription is "The Proof of Chora, Container of the Uncontainable". It names the Proof and links it to Theodore's church. That's how we know it's real.'

Kamil thought that wasn't a very compelling reason to be wasting his time on finding the reliquary right now. Malik must have known that. It was probably why he hadn't mentioned sooner that the box's valuable contents were actually safe.

'What's the second reason?' he asked.

Malik appraised Kamil silently, then said, 'Someone else has worked out what it was. Perhaps they read the engraving and understood its significance. When I took the text home to study, I left the reliquary hidden in the storeroom at the mosque. I thought it was less conspicuous to carry the document in its sleeve. No one but Saba knew what I had found. I didn't even tell my sister until it was stolen. Why would someone bother to steal a battered box and leave behind much more valuable items unless they knew what it was and thought it contained the Proof of God? It's a powerful relic, Kamil. Although I know you don't believe in such things, others do. I'm afraid if one person knows, then others will hear of it and be drawn to Istanbul like scavengers to blood. I'm afraid it'll fall into the hands of men who will either destroy it or use it to incite hatred among the religions.'

Kamil was sceptical, but seeing Malik's earnest face, he felt guilty at having doubted his friend's sincerity. Clearly people believed deeply in the power of this object, enough to sustain a four-hundred-year-old sect. The doubts of one magistrate did nothing to tip the scale.

'I'll inquire about the reliquary,' he assured Malik. 'And you make sure that document stays safe. I won't tell anyone about our conversation tonight. Where's the document now?'

'Hidden where no one will find it without my guidance. By now, whoever took the reliquary will have discovered it's empty and they'll be back. They'll want the Proof of God from me, but they won't get it.'

Was Malik saying he thought his life was in danger? Kamil wondered whether he should tell Malik that it was his nephew who had stolen the reliquary. He didn't think Malik had much to fear from Amida. The young man must have learned of the Proof of God from Saba or perhaps overheard them talking about it and seen an opportunity. A man who sells his patrimony. What else was he capable of? Perhaps he had underestimated Amida. But if he told Malik about Amida's involvement, he might decide to confront his nephew on his own and Kamil wanted to avoid that. Amida's possible involvement in the murders and with Kubalou made the situation too sensitive.

Kamil decided that since the Proof of God was safe for now, the best thing to do would be to find out what Amida had done with the reliquary. He wouldn't be surprised if he had sold it in the bazaar.

'I promise to look into it.'

'Thank you. You're a good and kind man.' Malik placed his arm around Kamil's shoulder. 'If you come for breakfast tomorrow, I can show you the document. I'll ask Saba to join us. I've wanted you to meet her for some time, but Amida's arrival and translating the Proof have kept me busy for the past few months.' He looked at Kamil thoughtfully. 'Things will become clearer to you then.'

Kamil was puzzled. What answers could Saba give that Malik could not? 'I look forward to it.'

Malik got up from the chair. He reached into his sash and pulled out a sealed letter, which he handed to Kamil. Kamil saw it was addressed to Saba.

'I'm imposing further on our friendship, Kamil, but I need this additional favour from you. If anything should happen to me, would you please give this letter to my niece?'

'Are you ill?' Kamil asked with alarm.

'Age diminishes me year by year, but, thanks be to Allah, I am well enough.' He gripped Kamil's forearm. 'Will you do this?'

Touched, Kamil said simply, 'I'd be honoured. By the will of Allah, may this letter never need to be delivered.'

'Inshallah,' Malik repeated, releasing Kamil's arm.

At the door, Malik paused and said, 'Watch over her. She'll need your help.' Malik left, his bearing lighter than when he had come.

Kamil watched him through the window and puzzled over his request. He was pleased at the prospect of seeing Saba again, but disturbed that he was somehow expected to take responsibility for her. He heard the gate close, and eventually the creak of a carriage from the lane above.

Kamil didn't believe the reliquary had any miraculous properties. Reason was more likely to be duped by faith than by logic. The world was peopled with believers whose faith caused them to act against all reason, to steal, to wage war, to kill and maim their neighbours. If they believed the reliquary or its contents was sacred, then they could cause great harm. The icon stolen from the Patriarchate had already demonstrated that.

Kamil found the file and reread the description of the box. He had wondered why there was no drawing of it. Malik must have thought making a likeness was too risky. A niello engraving showing a turbaned man, an angel, and the figure of Jesus. A partial inscription that fitted what Malik had told him. The surface pitted with age. Malik was right. Why would anyone think this was an antiquity worth stealing unless they knew what it was? And who would buy it from Amida unless they too knew of its importance? A bazaari might buy it as scrap. But it would be a big coup for a dealer who realised its importance. He wondered if, after all, Malik's reliquary would lead him to the mysterious dealer and the connection to Rettingate and Sons in London. No ordinary dealer would be able to handle the missing icon or the Proof of God.

15

The imam put down his lamp in the entryway, out of the rain, hefted the enormous key into the lock, and used both hands to turn it. Several times he had sent a petition to the Ministry of Pious Foundations requesting a modern door with a more manageable key, but he had never received a response. He supposed the ministry had more important things to worry about than the pockets of an elderly imam being ripped by the weight of a Byzantine key.

He took up his lamp and stepped across the stone threshold into the corridor that ran along the front of the Kariye Mosque. Directly before him was the archway leading to the prayer room. Starlight sifted through its windows, illuminating faint trails of dust in the air. He turned to the right and walked down the corridor towards the stairway that led up into the minaret, from which he would call the faithful to their first morning prayer. Mosaics gleamed in the arches above him, reflecting the lamplight.

He looked up and came face to face with an enormous mosaic of Jesus, whose eyes seemed to follow him as he walked. When the mosaics were revealed, the sultan's heathen architects had been so enthralled that they had insisted on restoring them, over his objections and entirely heedless of the Muslim prohibition against the representation of the human form. The corridor, they claimed, was so dark that the restored images would disturb no one if they kept their eyes piously to the ground.

The imam was relieved that the reconstruction was limited to the public areas and not the smaller room that he used to entertain his friends in private, and where he kept the chalices, plates, reliquaries, and other objects he had found over the years secreted in the former church or its grounds. At the back of the mosque, behind the caretaker's house, amid the ruins of a large building, the ground yielded interesting objects every spring, pushed upward by the frozen earth from where Byzantine hands had buried them on the night of the Conquest.

The caretaker should have swept the hall the night before, the imam noted, but the tiled floor still looked dirty. There was also a stench in the air, perhaps a dead pigeon that had not been cleared away. Carelessness, thought the imam. When a man inherited his right to a job, why should he care to do it well? All in all, though, he had few complaints about Malik, except for a disquieting feeling that his caretaker was more learned than he. Still, the imam could recite all of the Quran in Arabic. Since this was the language Allah spoke through an angel to the Prophet Muhammad, peace be upon him, it was much more important than any other languages the old caretaker might have acquired. The imam sometimes wondered where Malik could have gained so much learning since he came to the mosque as a young man to replace his father. It was true that Malik had always been curious. Right after his arrival, while exploring the Byzantine ruins behind the mosque, he had fallen into an abandoned cistern and broken his leg. His friend Omar had pulled him out, but the leg had healed badly.

A large bundle blocked the entrance to the minaret

stairway. The imam, fearing he was late for his ezan, pushed at it with his foot. When it didn't budge, he leaned over and pulled at the black cloth. He fell backward, landing hard on the floor, the cloth still in his hand. The stench was overpowering.

The lamplight fell on Malik's ghastly, bloodied face. His robe had been slashed open and his body sown with innumerable cuts.

The imam felt his heart pause with fear. He took a breath, then tried to calm himself by whispering a prayer, but his eyes roved the dark corners of the mosque and his ears strained to hear whether or not the person who did this was still in there. He tried to shake Malik's cloak from his hand, but the cloth was swollen with blood and stuck to the imam's arm, as if some vital essence of the caretaker was holding fast to him in a final desperate plea. With a shout of alarm, the imam struggled to his feet and ran outside into the driving rain. From the minaret of a neighbouring mosque, the call 'Allahu akbar, Allah is great' drifted over the imam as he woke the neighbourhood with his cries.

SQUALLS OF RAIN flung themselves against Kamil's bedroom window as if someone were throwing handfuls of pebbles. He massaged his forehead against the pain that had settled inside his skull. Ever since his father's death, he had been plagued by headaches. Sleep was impossible, so he rose and slipped on his dressing gown. The predawn call to prayer was muted by the weather, but the plaintive cry worked its way into the house and followed Kamil down the stairs. He could hear the chink of glasses and china in the dining room.

Yakup appeared with a glass of tea on a tray.

'Just tea. I'm having breakfast with a friend this morning,' Kamil told him. Not under the plane tree, he thought, peering out of the window at the rain. He looked forward to seeing Malik and to continuing their conversation, but he'd wait for dawn before setting off.

He took the previous day's newspaper, which he hadn't had a chance to read, and carried his tea into the winter garden. Yakup lit the lamps. Kamil relaxed into a chair and looked up at the wet, black panes. The newspaper dropped from his hand.

'Bey, bey.'

Kamil awoke with a start, wincing with pain as he moved his head. Yakup stood above him, his face imperturbable, as always.

'What is it?'

'The police chief of Fatih, Omar Loutfi, is here.'

'What time is it?' Kamil squinted. He could just make out the shapes of the rosebushes in the garden.

'Five thirty,' Yakup replied.

Kamil pushed through the door into the house.

Omar was streaming water on to the carpet of the receiving room. 'Malik is dead, Allah protect us. He's been murdered. The imam found him in the mosque when he went to call the first ezan.'

'What?' Kamil was stunned, remembering Malik's furtive visit the previous night. He pressed his palms against his forehead. Malik had as much as told him he was afraid for his life, and what had Kamil done? Nothing. He had sent him off to his death with a handshake.

Kamil pulled on the raincape Yakup held out to him and headed for the front door.

Omar grabbed his arm and said, 'There's one more thing. Remzi has escaped.'

Kamil halted and turned on Omar. 'How could that happen?'

'Someone must have bribed the guards. Believe me,' he added grimly, 'when I find out which one, I'll rip out his liver.'

THE ASHEN-FACED imam held Kamil's bridle as he and Omar dismounted. The rain had turned into a light mist that crept along the ground and clung to hollows. Residents peered out of their windows at the commotion and a crowd of men had begun to gather in the square. The imam began a steady stream of low-pitched commentary as they made their way to the mosque.

Kamil squeezed the string of amber beads in his pocket, aligning himself with the fingertips of his father and grandfather, who had ticked off each bead with a prayer, one of the ninety-nine names of God, or, like him, with a string of thoughts. This morning, he gripped the beads in his fist. He should have pressed Malik about who he thought might come after him. Men who would use the Proof of God to incite hatred among religions, Malik had said. That didn't sound like Amida.

A policeman stood guard by the door and saluted when he saw Omar. Following the imam's lamp, they stepped across the threshold of the mosque. There was a fetid smell, not of decay but of excrement. He took a linen handkerchief out of his pocket and held it across his nose. The imam extended a silver rose-water sprinkler, but Kamil waved it off.

'The windows don't open, you see,' the imam explained. 'I would have moved the body outside, but I didn't want the neighbours to see it.'

'It's better this way,' Kamil assured him. 'I can learn

more if the body isn't touched. Nothing should be moved.'

'No, Magistrate bey. Nothing's been touched.' He grimaced.

Omar had gone ahead. Kamil could see him standing like a statue in a pool of lamplight at the far end of the corridor.

'Wait here,' Kamil told the imam, and joined Omar by the ruined body of their friend.

Although he was wet through and the thick walls trapped the cold, Kamil's face was covered in a sheen of sweat. He knew his distress was not just a result of his headache.

Omar's face was grim. He glanced at Kamil, then looked again more closely. 'Are you well?'

'I'm fine,' Kamil answered through gritted teeth. He closed his eyes for a moment, then took a deep breath and forced himself to look at the scene slowly and methodically.

Malik's turban had fallen to the side and his wispy hair was matted with blood. His mouth was a rictus of pain. His robe was splayed open and revealed his chest, raw with cuts that were already thick with flies. Judging by his frame, Kamil thought, he must once have been a large man, but age had withered him. His feet were bound together with rope.

They each grasped the body and turned it. Malik's hands were bound behind his back.

'Do you have a surgeon assigned to the Fatih police?'

'That's Fehmi. I'll send one of my men to get him.' He thought for a moment. 'Fehmi might be gone. In that case, they'll bring in Courtidis. Damn.' He was unshaven and his face sagged with sorrow and fatigue.

'What's the problem with Courtidis?'

'Let's go outside.' They stepped into the square and Kamil waited while Omar instructed one of his men.

When Omar returned, he led Kamil into the small mosque garden. They stood in a dry area protected by the wall, smoking. 'Courtidis is another one of those people who have sudden unexplained wealth.' Omar narrowed his eyes. 'I hate people like that. It makes me want to know everything about them down to the direction they piss in.' He threw his cigarette to the ground. 'He's a Greek, lives near the Crooked Gate. I get tired of hearing what a great guy he is, how he treats the poor, even if they can't pay.'

'That sounds admirable.'

'Why would anyone do that? And if he's giving it away for free, where's he getting his money from?'

'You know and you're about to tell me.'

'He's a small-time drug dealer, that's where. Makes the stuff at home and sells it all over Fatih. Dishes it out like halvah. Not enough to bother about, but I like to keep people like him on a long rope, so I can reel him in if I need to.' He made a sweeping motion, ending with his fist before Kamil's nose.

'That's an unusual combination,' Kamil laughed weakly, 'a philanthropic, drug-dealing surgeon.'

'Let's not take the charity thing too far. He gets something out of it. Think of all the grateful mothers with nubile daughters.'

'Not everyone thinks like you,' Kamil teased, glad that Omar seemed to have regained some of his equanimity.

'The world would be better off if they did.'

'I take it that none of those mothers has managed to marry off a daughter to him yet.'

'He's besotted by Saba. You can understand why. But he

doesn't have a chance. She's much too proud to take up with a bastard like him. I mean that in the best sense of the word. He doesn't know who his father is. When he was five, his mother tried to walk out on his stepfather and he bludgeoned her to death. The stepfather married again and the new wife decided she didn't want someone else's spawn, so they shipped him off to the monastery out on Heybeli. And suddenly he reappears as a surgeon. How is that possible? I ask you. Something stinks. I don't think he really is a surgeon,' Omar grumbled. 'And besides, an apple doesn't fall far from the tree.'

'People take charge of their own fates. For all we know, the darkness this man saw as a child might have spurred him to climb towards the light. I'm sure the monks on Heybeli helped him.'

'You mean they enlightened him?' Omar joked.

'I mean they educated him.'

'As I said before, Kamil, you're a saint.'

'Well, whether he's a real surgeon or not, we have to take what we can get. Where can we bring Malik?' Kamil couldn't get himself to say the word body.

'There's a hammam just down the street.'

'Have your men take the body there. We'll need some hot water.'

'Already arranged,' Omar said in a rough voice and turned away. 'Ready?'

Kamil nodded and followed Omar back inside. His head still ached, but the cigarette had helped.

Two policemen lifted the body on to a stretcher. They covered it with a sheet, then carried it outside. One of the men was retching, a dry, barking sound.

Kamil looked around. The stench emanated from a sticky puddle where Malik's body had lain.

The imam bustled in breathlessly, then retreated to stand by the open door. 'I did another inventory of the mosque's valuables,' he reported. 'A silver candleholder is missing. That's all.'

Kamil scanned the corridor, then pointed to a candleholder glinting in a dark corner. 'There.'

Omar picked it up. Its blunt end was slick with blood. 'Looks like they used it to bludgeon him.'

'It might have been just one man,' Kamil countered. 'Maybe the same man the baker's apprentice saw during the first robbery. He didn't find what he was looking for the last time and came back.'

'True, but if it was one man, he'd have to be young and strong. Malik, may Allah accept him into paradise, was old, but he had steel in his arms.'

They went outside and followed the policemen carrying Malik's body.

'I suppose that lily-arse Amida will become caretaker now. That's the way it is with that family. Malik's father was caretaker before him. My own father knew him. They probably sat together in the coffeehouse just like me and Malik. It must have been almost time for old Malik to retire,' he shook his head in disbelief, 'but I wish he had left that way and not this.'

He leaned closer to Kamil. 'All last week Malik looked worn out, like he wasn't sleeping.' He thumped his chest. 'Something was wrong. I felt it here.'

'He might have been worried about the stolen reliquary,' Kamil ventured.

Omar thought for a moment. 'He claimed it wasn't valuable, but there must have been something important about it. Otherwise he wouldn't have badgered me to write to you. And why you?'

'Maybe because he knew me.'

'Maybe.' Omar didn't sound convinced.

'That's his house, isn't it?'

They stopped before the half-buried remains of a massive brick arch. Behind the ruin was a narrow two-storey building with an overhanging second floor. The men carrying Malik's body disappeared around a corner.

'Let's take a look,' Kamil suggested.

'Why not? There's no hurry now, is there?' Omar added bitterly. He pushed open one of the tall iron double doors.

They paused in the entryway to let their eyes adjust to the gloom. The house felt abandoned. Kamil wondered idly how houses knew when their owners were gone. He opened the door to the ground floor and felt his way through the hall into a large, central room. It was dark and something crunched underfoot.

Omar leaned out to open the shutters.

The light fell on a scene of destruction. The room in which they were standing appeared to be the sitting room. It was furnished only with a chair, lying on its side, a glass-fronted cabinet, now empty, its contents scattered across the threadbare carpet, and a low, old-fashioned settee, its horsehair innards protruding like weeds through slashes in the upholstery.

'Allah protect us,' Omar exclaimed.

A mattress had been dragged into the sitting room and disembowelled there. It had been slashed and turned inside out, brown clots of wool and straw stuffing strewn everywhere. Like its owner, Kamil thought.

In the adjoining room, a small chest of clothes had been emptied on to the floor. The kitchen was a graveyard of broken crockery.

Without a word, Kamil turned to the stairs, Omar

following. The upstairs rooms had also been systematically violated, the furniture smashed.

'Look at this,' Omar called from an adjoining room.

Kamil stood stunned just inside the door. The walls were lined with shelves, all empty. The floor was a blizzard of pages that lapped at his feet. Malik had used the room not as a bedroom, but as a library, and someone had ripped out every page of every book and thrown them on the floor. Splayed spines hovered in the drifts of paper like birds massacred in flight.

'Crazy. This is the work of a crazy person,' Omar exclaimed, taking up handfuls of paper and throwing them back down. 'Do you know how long it must have taken to rip out all these pages?' He shook his head. 'I don't get it.'

Kamil looked round and thought. 'Whatever they were looking for,' he said slowly, 'must be something that can be hidden inside a book.'

He was thinking about the pages of Aramaic text that Malik said had been inside the reliquary. He wanted to tell Omar, but remembered Malik's desperate desire that this remain secret, even from his own sect. Kamil shifted uncomfortably under the burden of other people's secrets. It was against his nature and his principles to sit on information in an investigation. And yet, he wasn't sure what was at stake here.

'I remember when I was a soldier,' Omar mused, examining one of the spines, 'people used to hide their jewellery in books, thinking soldiers don't read. Carved out the middle of a book so it looked gnawed by rats and then put their stuff inside.'

Kamil didn't ask Omar which war – there were enough to choose from – nor did he ask how the soldier Omar knew where people hid their jewellery.

'Nothing was taken from the mosque,' Kamil said, 'so robbery doesn't seem a likely motive. Unless the killer was looking for something specific and didn't find it. Or found it here. You'd better post a guard at the door. I wonder why they killed him in the mosque.'

Omar waded through the drift of paper. 'They wanted something from Malik, otherwise why the multiple cuts? It's a filthy way to kill someone. It takes a lot of time and a strong constitution. There are easier ways.'

'Maybe the reliquary wasn't what the thief thought it was and he was trying to persuade Malik to tell him where to find what he wanted.'

'The wrong box?' Omar scoffed. 'You don't do this sort of thing over a wrong box. You have to be powerfully motivated, if nothing else just to stand the smell. Death doesn't have to be dirty, Kamil, believe me. I was in the war. For this type of death, you need more than just a missing box. You need hate, revenge, greed, something that doubles the size of your liver.' He kicked at the papers, then stomped out of the room.

Omar was right, Kamil thought. Amida's liver wasn't strong enough for this. Who had he sold the reliquary to?

They emerged from the dark house. The sudden change from dark to light intensified Kamil's headache, and he stood blinking on the stoop, taking shallow breaths. When he focused his eyes, he found Omar looking at him curiously, but the soft-eyed man said nothing.

When they returned to the lane, they could hear raised voices coming from the direction of the mosque. Knots of men were gathered on either side of the small plaza and there was a rumble of angry muttering. Kamil could see the dark shapes of women listening at their windows behind curtains and wooden lattices.

'Looks like there might be trouble.'

'I'll take this side of the square,' Kamil offered. 'We can separate the groups.'

Omar squinted at the scene. 'I know all of these men. I think it'd be better if I just talked to them.'

Kamil hesitated.

'Crowds are like children,' Omar explained. 'You have to distract them. But having an outsider involved won't help. Let me handle this my way.'

'Agreed. I'll go see about the autopsy.'

'That's the hammam.' Omar pointed to a dun-coloured dome studded with circular glass windows that was just visible down a narrow lane.

Suddenly one of the men in the square shouted, 'You Christian son of an ass. How dare you push me.' Kamil couldn't see who it was, but the crowd began to swirl inward.

Omar strode into the square, took out his baton, and smacked it on the side of the fountain beside the mosque. The crack caught the crowd's attention and it paused for a moment, a hydra-headed creature intent on destruction but nonetheless curious.

Omar took this moment to raise his voice. 'If you want to know who killed Malik . . .'

He waited as the crowd disengaged and people turned towards him expectantly.

Omar drew out the tension until someone called out impatiently, 'Well, who the hell did it?'

Omar lowered his voice so the men had to move closer to hear him. The groups mingled as the men pressed forward. 'I'm pleased to think that Lame Malik was my friend, and I know he was a friend to many of you, Christian and Muslim alike. He was a learned man.' He paused.

'We all respect learned men, no matter what their religion.' There were mutters of agreement. 'We want to punish whoever did this.' Shouts of approval.

'So who did it?'

'Well,' Omar answered slowly, 'we need your help to find that out, don't we?'

A few of the men laughed, realising they had been cleverly strung along. Others groaned.

'Did any of you see anyone last night who didn't belong in the area? How about you, Gyorgio?'

'I was sound asleep in the coffeehouse.'

'Because his wife kicked him out of the house,' a man called out from the crowd. The men laughed.

Kamil could only admire Omar's defusing of the tension. Now he circulated among the men, asking questions. Kamil turned and walked down the lane leading to the hammam. The rain had stopped and the mist cleared, but the air was still dark, as if a stain had fallen on the world.

A MAN IN his late twenties sat on the low wall before the hammam, his horse tethered beside him. When he saw Kamil, he jumped up and strode towards him.

'Are you the magistrate?' he called out. His grey trousers were frayed at the cuffs and his jacket was missing several buttons. His black curls were cut tight under a fez that badly needed to be cleaned and pressed. A carefully trimmed moustache ended in a curl at either side of his lips.

'Yes.'

The man broke into a smile, showing a row of alarmingly large teeth. 'Constantine Courtidis, surgeon, at your service. Call me Constantine.'

So this was the shady drug dealer, Kamil thought. He

didn't know what he had expected, but it wasn't this friendly, enthusiastic young man. He found himself simultaneously drawn to Courtidis and repelled by him. Judge on the evidence, Kamil reminded himself.

'Thank you for coming. I take it the surgeon assigned to the Fatih police couldn't come?'

'That's Pericles Fehmi. He's taken his family to the coast. He's an old man now, and even healers need time to heal. I'm the next best thing. Never take a holiday. Tried it once and couldn't handle it. Too hard on my behind. All that sitting and staring at trees and squinting at the sun. Not for me.'

'There's been a murder,' Kamil interjected abruptly. 'We'd like you to tell us what you can about how the man died.' The surgeon's levity seemed sacrilegious, given the circumstances.

Courtidis rubbed his hands with what to Kamil looked strangely like glee.

'Let's get started then. I love a puzzle.' He picked up his leather bag and turned towards the hammam entrance. 'In here, right?'

As they made their way single file along the outside corridor that hid the entrance of the bathhouse from public view, Courtidis kept up a non-stop monologue.

'You saved me from the usual routine, you know. Pregnancies, haemorrhoids, fevers, diarrhoea. Last week this couple came to me because they'd been married a year and she hadn't conceived yet. The bride complained about pain during, beg your pardon, you know, intercourse. You're not going to believe this, but when I examined her – with her husband present, of course – she was a virgin.' He stopped, turned, and blocked Kamil's path. 'Can you even guess what was going on?' He smiled happily up at Kamil.

Kamil gritted his teeth. 'No, I can't.'

'They had been, beg your pardon, fucking in the urethra.' Courtidis whinnied a laugh.

'Urethra?'

'Where she, beg your pardon, pees.'

Kamil found himself laughing. 'No wonder she complained about pain.' Despite himself, he began to warm to the prattling surgeon. A man must be forgiven his childhood, he thought. Omar was sometimes too harsh in his assessment of his fellow man, seeing evil everywhere. It was a policeman's weakness.

They had come to the central room of the hammam, where the men had deposited Malik's body on the central platform, the bellystone, and covered it with a tattered sheet. A cauldron of hot water steamed nearby on the floor. The warm, buzzing smell of offal bloomed into the room from the direction of the body.

Kamil nodded at the ranking policeman. 'Take your men and wait outside, but stay within earshot.' The men made quickly for the door, unable to hide their relief.

Courtidis strode up to the body and slid the cloth off, throwing it into the corner.

'His name is . . . was Malik,' Kamil explained. 'Caretaker of Kariye Mosque.' Until a few hours ago, this had been a scholar with pupils and a library in his home. A man with secrets. A friend. The caretaker's hands were still tied behind his back and he lay awkwardly at an angle. Grief and fury made Kamil turn his head away. It felt as though iron bands were compressing his head.

The surgeon stared wordlessly at the body, hands dangling by his sides. He looked shocked.

'Did you know him?' Kamil asked.

'Yes,' he whispered. 'Who killed him?'

'We don't know. Can you tell us how he died?'

Courtidis walked over and squatted before one of the low marble basins. He turned on both spigots, releasing ropes of cold and hot water. When the basin was full, he plunged his head into the water and kept it there until Kamil thought he was trying to drown himself. Finally, he pulled his head out, drenching his jacket and the floor about him. He continued to squat there, holding his head in his hands.

Kamil handed him a towel.

'Thank you,' Courtidis said. 'For every death, a baptism.'

'You must have known him well. *Bashiniz sagholsun*.'

The surgeon towelled his hair dry and took off his jacket. He let it fall on to a marble bench, then sat down next to it, his eyes fixed on Malik's body.

'You know, Magistrate, I didn't really know him that well, but I know that he was a great and generous man.'

'What do you mean?'

'I didn't have a lot of opportunities when I was a child,' he said finally in a strained voice. 'My mother and father had passed away and I had no one to give me direction, to help a young whippersnapper with more balls than brains get off the street. I was like one of those mangy mutts that lie in the sun and then hang around the butcher's door. You know what they say, if you could get a skill by watching, then every dog would be a butcher. I'd do anything for a free scrap. And, beg your pardon, I mean anything.'

He got up and stood over Malik's body, a haunted look on his face.

'This man gave me a life. He just handed it to me. It's as if the butcher had opened his shop door and said,

"Come in, eat all you want." I thank God I was smart enough to reach out and grab the opportunity.' There was a strained smile. 'Or desperate enough.'

Courtidis reached out and gently caressed Malik's forehead. He slid his hand over Malik's eyes to shut them, and told him softly, 'Your eyes are in my heart.'

Kamil stood quietly nearby, careful not to interrupt the surgeon's requiem.

Courtidis shook himself and began to examine the body. He looked at it carefully from head to foot, at first touching nothing, at times bending so close that his nose almost touched Malik's robe. Finally he opened his bag, and took out a thin sharp blade. He reached behind the body and cut the rope tying Malik's wrists. The arms fell stiffly apart. Courtidis pulled the arms forward and settled the body on its back. He pulled the gold ring from Malik's finger, rinsed it in the basin, and observed it for a few moments before handing it to Kamil.

Kamil saw that the surgeon's face was wet with tears. He wrapped the ring in his handkerchief and slipped it into his pocket.

'First he fed me,' Courtidis continued. 'Then he paid me to sweep the mosque. Then he showed me the magnificent illuminated manuscripts he has. Have you ever seen them? He let a simple child with dirty hands hold his masterpieces. It was like training a wild bird to come closer and closer until it eats the grain right from the palm of your hand. Because then, you know what he did? He taught me to read and write.'

As he spoke, Courtidis pulled the blood-soaked wool away from the body, then cut and removed the undergarments. Malik's body on the bellystone was blue-white and shadowed, like a hard-boiled egg released from its shell.

The sight of the birdlike bones of the old man's chest, the wiry grey hairs around his sagging nipples, filled Kamil with pity and grief. By the time Kamil had seen his dying father, he had been wrapped in a quilt that padded his fragile, broken body. Now, in the thin-skinned, pathetic presence of death, Kamil was reminded that even fathers are frail and that this was something most sons never acknowledged. He averted his eyes from the white worm of Malik's shrivelled but clearly uncircumcised organ.

Every Muslim must be circumcised. The story of the Melisites and their reliquary became more real. Christians masquerading as Muslims for hundreds of years. They must have had a reason. The Proof of God?

'So you know,' Courtidis said, continuing to wash the body. 'Otherwise you would have been exclaiming from here to Baghdad, "What's this? He's not a Muslim!"'

Pink water pooled on the marble.

'How did you know?' Kamil asked him.

'I didn't, but it makes sense from what I know about his family. He was Habesh. They pray like Muslims, they say they're Muslims, but they have their own rites.' He stopped, momentarily overcome by grief. 'He was the finest human being I have ever met.' He looked up at Kamil suddenly. 'You won't tell anyone, will you? You know there are people who would call this blasphemy and make trouble. Let Malik keep his dignity.'

'If I need to share this information with the police in order to find his murderer, I will do that. But otherwise I don't see why any of it should become known.'

'Thank you.'

After he had cleaned away the blood, Courtidis bent

over and repeated his close inspection of the body.

'Look at these.' He swept his hand across a battlefield of cuts and punctures between Malik's groin and chest. He gently inserted a probe into the middle of one of the cuts, then moved it sideways. He did the same to another. 'The wounds all have the same strange pattern. They're flat, deep in the middle and shallow at the ends.' He pointed to Malik's stomach. 'One pierced the intestines. That's where the smell comes from and, of course, from the usual evacuation.' He probed around Malik's chest. 'Another one pierced his lungs. But here's the strangest thing of all. Do you see these pairs of puncture marks? It's as if something with two sharp teeth bit his chest all over.'

Admiring his professionalism, Kamil observed that focusing on the puzzle of piecing together the cause of death seemed to have calmed the young surgeon.

'Yes, I can see that,' Kamil said. 'What do you think it could be?' Kamil steeled himself to look closely at the wounds. The thought of Malik's prolonged agony nauseated him.

'The puncture marks occur at the same places as the other wounds. I'd say the weapon had an odd-shaped blade and two sharp protrusions. But I haven't got a clue what it could be.'

Kamil thought about this. 'Perhaps some kind of knife used in a particular profession. Skinning animals, maybe?' He thought of Mustafa the Tanner.

'Help me turn him on his side.'

The surgeon grasped Malik's hips and Kamil his right shoulder. Together they tilted the body forward so his back was visible.

Much of the blood had been soaked up by Malik's heavy

robe which now lay on the table. Kamil looked through the pile of wool. Malik's silver brooch was gone. He wondered whether robbery had been a motive after all. It seemed a lot of effort to kill someone in this brutal manner for a small piece of jewellery.

'Would you soak this in hot water?' Courtidis asked Kamil, handing him the sponge.

Kamil held Malik's shoulder while Courtidis swept the sponge back and forth across the back. When the blood was gone, they both leaned over, speechless.

'The lost angel,' Courtidis said softly. 'You have fallen to earth and been destroyed.'

On Malik's back was tattooed a pair of wings that stretched from his shoulder blades to below his waist. The powerful wings were folded shut. Every deep blue feather was detailed. Over time, the ink had begun to bleed and blur the outlines, giving the feathers the appearance of having been ruffled, disarranged.

'Do you know what they mean?' Kamil asked.

'A tolerance for pain. That would have taken hours with a sharp needle.'

Kamil ran his fingers down the span of wings. 'The detail is amazing. I've never seen anything like it.' He had seen tattoos on the arms of sailors and prisoners, and on the faces and hands of tribal women from Hakkari and the Sinai. But those were crude tracings compared to the wings on the dead man's back. They looked so real he expected them to unfurl and take flight at any moment.

'I had a Habesh patient once – with a bad cough that eventually killed him – the man had a tattoo of this quality on his chest. Not wings, though. The face of Jesus. So real, I expected Jesus to open his mouth and bite my hand. I didn't see his back.'

'Do you know where he had his tattoo done?'

'The Sunken Village midwives were famous for their tattooing. There's only one left now that knows how to do it, a water buffalo named Gudit. Secret ingredients in the ink, she told me.'

They laid Malik on his back again. Courtidis dipped a hammam bowl into the cauldron of hot water, soaped his hands, and rinsed them, leaving a red scum in the bowl. 'I think Malik was alive for a while after they did this. They're shallow cuts, most of them, painful, but not immediately life-threatening. He was killed by a blow to the head. Look here.' He showed him an area of matted hair speckled by fragments of bone.

'The murderer used a candlestick from the mosque.'

'Bastard. Who would do this to a harmless old man? Why?'

'We'll do our best to find out. He was my friend too.' As Kamil said it, the truth of it came to rest painfully in his chest.

Courtidis walked to the corner, retrieved the sheet, and flung it in the air so it came to rest slowly over Malik's broken body like a wing. 'When you find the devil,' he said viciously, 'saw off his tail with a blunt sword. And I don't mean the hind one.'

KAMIL EMERGED FROM the hammam and was surprised to find it was still day, that the sun was shining and that people were going about their business as normal. It seemed incomprehensible. His head throbbed. Propping himself against a ruined wall, he reached into his pocket for his beads, but instead his hand encountered the pocket watch. It was twelve o'clock.

Time. Things in their place. He sighed and fished out a

clean handkerchief to wipe his face and hands. He had washed them in the hammam, but in the daylight he saw there were still flecks of Malik's blood beneath his nails. Courtidis joined him, rummaged in his bag, and took out two cigarettes. He offered one to Kamil, then lit them both with the same match.

Kamil inhaled deeply. The acrid smoke scorched the back of his throat. Perhaps patients in this part of town didn't pay well.

'You look pale, Magistrate, if you want my professional opinion.'

'It's nothing.'

'Headache?'

'How did you know?'

Courtidis flashed his equine smile. 'Two things cannot be hidden – love and a headache. The area around your eyes is tense and you look like you're balancing a water jug on your head.'

Kamil managed a weak smile, then took refuge in his cigarette. The tobacco was much stronger than the Egyptian cigarettes he usually smoked.

Courtidis rummaged in his bag again. He clicked open a tin case and plucked out a small brown ball. He extended it to Kamil. 'Chew that.'

'What is it?' Kamil sniffed it. It was sticky and had a sharp, unpleasant smell.

'Trust me. It'll cure your headache.'

'No, thanks.'

'Works every time. Myrrh, cedar agaric, aloe, a pinch of charred tobacco, marjoram, and a few other things. Can't tell you everything. Proprietary information, like Gudit's ink. I call it Balat Balm. It's very popular, if you'll excuse me beating my own drum.'

Kamil thought about it, remembering Omar's suspicion that Courtidis was a drug dealer, then popped the ball in his mouth and chewed. What was the difference between medicine and drugs when one was ill?

'It tastes like vinegar.'

'The ingredients are dissolved in vinegar, then mixed with honey so they stick together. Go home and get some sleep. I guarantee you'll feel better tomorrow. If you still have problems, I live by the Crooked Gate. Ask anyone. You're welcome to visit. Even if you're not ill.'

As though embarrassed, he added, 'You know, Malik made it possible for me to study and become a surgeon. It pains me not to be able to help him.' He examined his cigarette. 'I promised myself a long time ago that I would always be there for his family. He has a niece, Saba.' He crushed the cigarette in his fingers and flung it to the ground. 'This will break her.'

He shook Kamil's hand awkwardly, showed his teeth in a half-hearted smile, and disappeared around the corner.

Kamil leaned against the wall, thinking about Courtidis and Malik. It fitted with what he knew of the old scholar that he would see the most potential in those who had fallen the farthest. Courtidis, Omar had said, was infatuated with Saba. Kamil could understand that: she was beautiful. But the young man's bond to Saba and her family was much deeper than that. Kamil found he was relieved that Saba had such a devoted protector.

He walked through the ruins towards the Kariye Mosque, where he found the square now oddly deserted. The mosque door was open and he went inside. Someone had cleaned up the blood and the hall smelled of vinegar. He followed the light into the main room, lit by three high windows and carpeted for prayer. Kamil squatted in a corner and looked up at the marble revetments. At the back of the room, the marble was the grey and white of mist and bones. The patterns looked like women, he thought, one bowing, the other lifting her dress. One woman emerging from another, white, the red of clotted blood, white. A woman giving birth, the pubic bone rising sharply to either side of the head of a child emerging from the womb. What was it Malik had said? Mother of God, Container of the Uncontainable. Muslims did not believe that Jesus was God, of course, simply a prophet like others before him. Disturbed by the images in the veins of marble, Kamil fled through the corridor and out into the square. His headache was gone, but he was seeing visions.

16

He looks like his father, Balkis thought. The same eyes that seemed to see into everything, the chiselled features. Her daughter sat huddled beside her. They were both dressed in white, the colour of mourning. Word of Malik's death had arrived within minutes of the imam finding his body.

'I see that you already know, but I wanted to tell you in person. Your brother Malik has passed away.' Kamil handed Balkis Malik's ring. 'I'm very sorry. *Bashiniz sagholsun.*'

Balkis took the ring and held it against her breast. My heart, she thought, my heart has ceased to beat. She had railed so long against her brother's irresponsibility that she had forgotten his gentle humour, his boyish enthusiasms. All this came rushing into her mind as she clutched his ring: the fat-cheeked boy who had brought her fistfuls of poppies from the ruins; the young man who had found her pregnant, distraught, and almost destitute in Beyoglu and brought her back to Sunken Village; the man who had stood up to Gudit after her circumcision. The only man who had always stood by her.

Balkis cried out and doubled over in pain. Saba threw her arms around her, weeping. Balkis reached out and stroked her daughter's head, then pushed her gently away. She turned Malik's ring in her hands, trying to focus her mind through the pain.

'Who killed him?' she asked Kamil, who stood by the

door, eyes on the floor as if ashamed to have brought such news.

'We don't know. He was found in the mosque, stabbed. It must have happened late last night. When did you last see him?'

'At the ceremony on Friday.' Kubalou's man had come that night, but that had had nothing to do with Malik.

'Why would anyone kill Uncle Malik?' Saba wailed. 'All he ever did was help people.' She rocked back and forth on the divan, keening softly, her veil pulled across her face.

Balkis put an arm around her.

'I'm very sorry,' Kamil said. 'We'll do our best to find whoever did this. If I may, I'd like to ask you some questions.'

Saba looked up and dried her eyes on her veil. 'I'm sorry, Kamil Pasha,' she said in a shaky voice. 'Look at us. We should be helping you instead of falling apart.'

Balkis looked at her daughter gratefully, surprised at how quickly the girl had pulled herself together. Her own tongue had grown numb. It was as if nothing she said could ever again be of any importance, so her mouth refused to form any words. She couldn't even find the energy to despise her brother's killer.

'What do you want to know?' Saba asked. 'I didn't see Uncle Malik after Friday either.'

'Do you know where the Proof of God is?' Kamil asked.

Balkis and Saba both stared at him.

'Malik told me about it,' Kamil explained. 'He asked for my help in locating a reliquary that had been stolen from the mosque. He said it was important to your sect.'

Balkis looked at him, shocked. 'He told you about the Melisites?'

'He told me in confidence and I have no intention of

telling anyone else unless it becomes necessary,' he assured them. 'But it's important that you talk to me now. I think whoever has the reliquary might be the same person who killed Malik. Who else knew that this reliquary contained the Proof of God?'

At that, Balkis saw Saba suddenly raise her head and become still and alert, like a deer scenting danger. She tried to focus. Malik had told her after the ceremony on Friday that he had found the Proof of God. She hadn't believed him, thinking he had unearthed an old box and that his fanciful imagination had got the better of him. He told her that the reliquary had been stolen, but that the Proof itself was safe. She had mocked his incompetence, joked that he had managed to lose even the Proof of God. The shame she felt now was only a fraction of the punishment she deserved. Why else would someone kill Malik? Perhaps he really had found the Proof of God.

'Amida knew.' Saba pressed her veil against her mouth.

'Why would he steal something from his own uncle? Much less kill him? That's impossible.'

But Balkis knew Malik would try to protect the Melisites no matter what. Had he told Amida he wouldn't allow him to become caretaker, threatened to send him back to the monastery? Balkis knew it had been on his mind. Malik didn't think Amida was ready and he was worried that the boy would reveal their secrets to outsiders. She had assured Malik that he would outgrow his infatuation with money and travel and that other distasteful interest he had brought back with him from the south. Once a man tastes leadership, it goads him like salt on the tongue.

'Where was Amida last night?' Kamil still stood near the door as if he did not want to track dirt as well as bad news into someone's home. Balkis bade him come in and sit.

When he had settled on the divan opposite her, she told him, 'He was at home.'

'You saw him?' Kamil asked her.

'I heard him playing the piano.'

'But he could have gone out. Surely he didn't play all night.'

'Well, let's ask him,' Balkis said, exasperated. She signalled to a servant and instructed him to bring Amida.

'I think we should consider the possibility that if the reliquary is so important, someone in the village might have heard about it and stolen it. It would probably sell for a lot of money, but only if it were complete. And, of course, the thief would have to know where to sell it.'

Balkis knew he meant Amida.

'Malik told me about the smuggling in the village,' Kamil added.

'Malik didn't know what went on here,' Balkis answered wearily. 'He came once a week for the ceremony and the rest of the time he lived in his head. If you've seen his library, you'll know he had a very active imagination. Don't believe everything he told you. He was probably angry that his reliquary was stolen and wanted to blame someone.'

If her brother hadn't been so headstrong, he'd still be alive, she thought.

Kamil asked a few more questions and seemed anxious to leave. A few minutes later, the breathless servant returned and announced that Amida hadn't been seen since the day before.

Kamil stood. '*Bashiniz sagholsun*,' he offered again and bowed deeply, his hand on his heart. 'If I can be of any service to you, you have only to send a message.'

*

KAMIL MADE HIS way through the gardens towards a stairway leading out of the cistern. A breathless Saba appeared at his elbow. 'Kamil Pasha, may I speak with you?'

'Of course. This has been a difficult day for you,' he said kindly. She held her charshaf closed under her chin. Her face was blotchy from crying, but she still looked beautiful, he thought. In his haste that morning, he had forgotten to bring Malik's letter. He would give it to her the following day.

She led him to a secluded part of the garden by the wall, where the arches of an old arcade had collapsed, leaving a row of tall brick scallops. They sat on a bench under one of the niches.

'I apologise. The shock was so great, we forgot our hospitality,' she said softly.

'There's no need. On a day like this, it's you who should be taken care of.'

Saba signalled to a servant standing some distance away, who then approached, set down a heavy tray, and withdrew.

This was no chance meeting, Kamil realised, and wondered where the conversation would go. He waited while she filled their glasses from a steaming pot and she placed a lady's navel on his plate. The plump mound of dough, soaked in honey, was indented in the centre by a tiny jewel-like pistachio. She added a small pickled cucumber. 'To cut the sweetness,' she explained.

'My mother used to do that.' Kamil smiled. He took a bite of the lady's navel, then was glad of the vinegary pickle to take away the scorching sweetness. As he wiped his fingers and took his tea, Saba added another pastry and pickle to his plate. The combination of sweet and sour was making him feel slightly ill, but it would have been rude to refuse. He ate the second pastry, then politely declined any more.

'Is there something I can do for you?' Kamil asked, hoping to draw out the reason for this unusual picnic.

There was an awkward silence.

'I'm worried about my brother,' she said finally. 'Are you sure you won't have more tea?'

He shook his head no.

She got up to refill her own glass and when she sat down again, she was nearer to Kamil on the bench.

'Now that my uncle is gone,' she said, her eyes welling with tears, 'there's no one to keep Amida on the right path. I'm afraid he's in over his head. He thinks his bravado will get him through, but he's dealing with people who are truly dangerous.'

'Who are these people? What do they want with your brother?'

'They're from Charshamba. He's hired them to do jobs for him, but in reality he has no control over them. The Habesh have never had anything to do with people like that. You must believe me. It puts us in a bad light. I wish it would stop.'

'I understand, but what is it you'd like me to do?'

'Arrest Amida.' She startled Kamil by letting the charshaf fall back from her hair on to her shoulders.

'I don't think being in jail will keep him safe, Saba Hanoum. Do you know these men from Charshamba? Someone named Remzi or Kubalou, perhaps?'

'No, of course not.' She dropped the spoon into her empty tea glass, a loud, dissonant clatter.

'I apologise,' he said. 'Of course not. Yet you seem so well informed.'

'This is a small village. People hear things.'

'There's a policeman missing.' He looked hard at her. 'Have you heard anything about that? We think this Charshamba gang was involved. If we can find him alive, he could testify against them. That way, they'd be in jail and your brother would be safe.'

She appeared genuinely shocked. 'I didn't know. If I hear anything about that, I'll tell you.'

'Do you know about a tunnel between here and the Tobacco Works?'

When Saba didn't answer right away, Kamil added, 'It's not a secret anymore, now that Amida has let the Charshamba gang in on it. You might as well tell me. We think the policeman might be there. His name is Ali. He's a decent young man with a family.'

'If I help you find this man, will you help me with the two things I want?'

'And what are they?' Kamil asked.

'The Proof of God.'

'Of course,' he said, surprised. 'We're already looking into that.'

'Not the reliquary. The document that Malik took out to study. Did he tell you where he put it?' she asked urgently.

'No. He just said he'd hidden it.'

'I want you to help me find it,' she said. 'It's what Malik would have wanted. Amida must never get his hands on it.'

'Why not?' Kamil wondered if this was sibling rivalry.

'He doesn't respect it.' She held out the palms of her long, delicate hands. He noted the elegance in the tilt of each finger.

'Where do you think he would have hidden it?'

'In his house or in the Kariye.' She withdrew her hands and shrugged off her charshaf. 'It's so warm today.' Her skin looked as golden as the honeyed pastries on the tray. A fat bee buzzed about the plate, then settled delicately on a lady's navel. Kamil could see its legs and antennae quivering as it sampled the sweetness.

'Uncle Malik spoke about you,' Saba said softly. 'He always told me you were a person I could trust. He said we would have a special relationship. I felt I knew you even before we met.'

She had let her slippers fall to the ground. The tips of her toes were red with henna. Kamil's heart contracted at the brutal contradiction between her tiny feet, so like the chubby feet of his nieces, and their flushed tips.

'He told me to go to you if I ever needed anything,' she continued. She put her face close to his. 'Why do you think he said that?' she asked curiously, like a small child confident he would have the answer.

'I don't know. He never spoke to me about his family but last night he came to see me and told me something similar. He seemed worried about you and thought I'd be able to help.' He spread his hands and said more formally than he meant to, 'I'm available, of course, should your family need assistance, Saba Hanoum. But I'm also investigating a crime. I can't promise to help someone who's guilty.'

Kamil saw the disappointment on Saba's face and felt ashamed.

'Of course not,' she answered, pulling the charshaf briskly back over her shoulders. There was an undertone of anger in her voice.

'He also gave me a letter for you. He said I should give it to you if anything happened to him. I think he knew he was in danger.'

Saba sat up. 'A letter?'

'I don't have it with me. I'll bring it next time.'

'But it might be important,' she insisted. 'May I come to get it now?'

Kamil was shocked that Saba had suggested she accompany him to his home. Perhaps she had some notion that she was honouring Malik's wishes by befriending Kamil.

'I'm sorry, Saba Hanoum. I won't be home until much later. I'll bring it tomorrow, if you like. We can talk more then. Perhaps you can give me some idea where to search for the Proof of God. Maybe there'll be something in Malik's letter.' He considered asking her permission to open the letter, but remembered his promise to deliver it, presumably unopened. 'And if you find any information at all about the missing policeman, send a messenger to my home no matter what time of day or night.' He told her his address.

Saba stood before him as if willing him to change his mind. Then she gave a sad smile and said, 'Tomorrow, then. I'll be waiting for you.'

He bowed. 'Thank you for the tea.' Smiling, he added, 'You haven't told me your second wish.'

Saba stepped close and inclined her head so it was almost resting on his chest. Finally, she said in a soft voice, 'Another time.' She looked up and searched his face. By her expression, Kamil decided, she couldn't find what she was looking for there.

'I'll see what I can find out about the tunnel.' She stepped back and then was gone.

As Kamil mounted the stairs to Charshamba, he noticed Saba, wrapped in her charshaf, standing by a fig tree in the gardens below, watching him.

17

As Kamil rode through Fatih towards the Galata Bridge, he wondered why, after two nights with little or no sleep, he felt so energetic. Colours assaulted him from the drab streets, from women's patterned trousers, their bright sweaters and headscarves, as they sat on doorsteps and pavements knitting and talking. Laundry stretched between the houses above his head snapped like spinnakers. He thought he heard whispers from behind the latticed windows, a susurration of speech like receding waves. It was disturbing and exhilarating. Ahead, red- and blue-painted ships, boats and ferries traced criss-crossing wakes across the broad triangle of water where the Golden Horn joined the Bosphorus and emptied into the Sea of Marmara.

He crossed the bridge at Karaköy, then turned on to the shore road. Here, the buildings were substantial, made of stone: the stock exchange, banks, the customs house, the armoury, Foundouklou Mosque with its enormous green leather curtains at the door and an ornate public fountain. To his right, the Bosphorus was a deep turquoise, the colour of the rarest Iznik bowls. Light chased across the surface like children at play. Kamil almost felt happy despite the tragic events of the day.

ISMAIL HODJA'S WHITE beard was neatly trimmed and his robe and white turban were spotless. Kamil looked down with distress at his own cuffs, discoloured with blood and grime from his unpleasant task in the hammam. But the distress lifted again and Kamil felt buoyed, his mood a cork bobbing easily to the surface. He was disturbed by this feeling, unmoored. He wished to be sad. Anything else was disrespectful to his friend.

The Sufi sheikh led Kamil into his study. While Kamil filled Ismail Hodja in on the events of the previous two days, the sheikh's driver, Jemal, brought them glasses of tea on a tray so dainty it was almost lost in his large hands. Kamil had always wondered about Ismail Hodja's aversion to servants. He lived in a house farther up the Bosphorus and during the day came to these rooms in a dervish lodge high on a hill over Beshiktash to work and meet with his disciples. In neither place had Kamil seen a large staff, although the rooms were always tidy. Most people of his class had several dozen servants. Instead, Jemal seemed to take care of everything. It wouldn't be a matter of money. Ismail Hodja came from a wealthy family. Kamil supposed he simply preferred to live alone.

Ismail Hodja sat beside Kamil on the low divan. He leaned forward and looked at him thoughtfully.

'You don't look well, Kamil.'

'What do you mean?'

'Your face is flushed and there's an unusual brilliance about your eyes. Do you have a fever?' he asked with concern.

Kamil wondered whether he should tell him about the hallucinations in the mosque, but he felt too weary to add yet another story to the day. In any case, he felt certain these effects were due to Courtidis's balm and planned to ask the surgeon about them. The experience was interesting and not entirely unpleasant, but it wasn't something he wished to discuss with Ismail Hodja. The feeling would pass. He was puzzled, though, by the duration of the balm's effects. He had thought earlier that they had worn off, and was surprised to find himself again affected. He wondered briefly about the lady's navels Saba had given him, but dismissed the idea.

'I'm just tired, but thank you for asking. I was wondering if you knew anything about a sect called the Melisites.'

'They've been around for four hundred years or so. The sect was founded right after the Conquest. How did you know about it? Not many people do,' Ismail Hodja asked curiously.

Four hundred years was a remarkably long period of time compared to a man's lifespan. Malik would have had something wise to say about that, Kamil thought, remembering their conversations. He felt a tide of sadness rising in him and welcomed it.

'Do wings have any special significance for the Melisites?' he asked.

Ismail Hodja rose and went to one of the shelves in his study. He pulled one manuscript or book out after another, flipping through, then replacing it. Finally, he took down a slim, leather-covered volume. He cleared the tea glasses away and placed the book on the table before Kamil, open at a page with an engraving of a seated woman holding a girl child suckling from her right breast. Powerful wings rose from her back. In her left hand, she held an elaborate cross on a stave. Next to her a bearded man dressed in a simple robe bowed down and presented her with a small jewelled book or box.

'This book is about a sect of Jewish Abyssinians. They revere a holy woman who is always depicted with wings.'

Kamil noticed a symbol of a crescent and disc above

the woman's head that was the same as the engraving on Malik and Balkis's rings. But they weren't Jews. He told Ismail Hodja about the rings and the blood-stained columns before the prayer hall.

'Some of those old rituals, such as animal sacrifice, were once shared by Jews, Christians, and Muslims alike,' Ismail Hodja explained. 'The Jews and Christians don't practise them anymore. I've never had the privilege of seeing one of the Melisite rituals as the community is very secretive, but they have good reason to keep to themselves. Some believe that the Melisites are really Christians living as Muslims, although who's to say what that means. But ordinary people aren't interested in philosophical debates, and they tend to be quite unforgiving about that sort of thing. They say that he who prays at two altars is without religion.' Ismail Hodja leaned forward to refill their tea glasses. 'It's a remarkable feat, if you think about it, to hide their identity for such a long time.'

Kamil felt certain that by sharing Malik's secret with Ismail Hodja, he wouldn't be revealing anything the old scholar didn't already know.

'Malik said he had found something called the Proof of God.'

'He found it?' The empty tea glass dropped from Ismail Hodja's hand. He stared at Kamil in amazement.

'Malik didn't tell me much, just that it's somehow central to the Melisites.' Kamil began to reevaluate his assessment of the reliquary. If it elicited this much of a reaction from the ordinarily unflappable Ismail Hodja, it might be as important as Malik had said.

'I think he was killed for it. I wish I had listened to him,' Kamil said bitterly, balling his fists. 'Last night he told me that he was in danger and I didn't do anything about it. If

I had asked him to spend the night, he'd still be alive.'

'You can't protect someone by locking them up, Kamil. You know that. The minute he walked out of your door in the morning, he would still have been a target.'

Kamil took a deep breath. 'I know.'

'The Proof of God disappeared after the Conquest. I didn't realise the Melisites were involved.' Ismail Hodja pulled at his beard and thought for a while. 'It makes sense. If this is indeed the authentic Proof of God, it would be important enough for a sect to have formed to protect it, especially after the fall of Byzantium.'

'What is it?'

'A relic stolen from Jerusalem by Christian Crusaders early in the twelfth century. They claimed to be protecting pilgrims in what they called their Holy Land, but in fact spent their time digging secretly under the Dome of the Rock. They claimed to have found the Ark of the Covenant. Reports at the time describe a casket, but we're fairly certain it wasn't the Ark – that had already disappeared from Jerusalem long before the birth of the Prophet Jesus. It's said that King Solomon's son Menelik took the Ark back with him to Abyssinia, where it remains to this day in a temple at Aksum.'

'Do you believe that?'

'I believe that armies have crept across the earth stealing objects that they think are powerful. Whatever it was that the Crusaders found allowed them to become wealthy and strong. They called themselves Templars. They raised an army and carved out their own little fortified kingdoms all over this region. It was shameful. These men acting in the name of Christianity sacked some of the greatest Christian cities of the time. When they were finished, there was almost nothing left of Byzantium. I suppose the Turks can thank the Templars for weakening Constantinople over the centuries. When Mehmet the Conqueror finally plucked the apple, the city was almost bankrupt. The Templars took their treasure to Acre and then to Antioch, staying one step ahead of our armies. In Antioch, they entrusted it to a young man, Philip of Stark, who was to take it to Aksum in Abyssinia. You can see how desperate they must have been to give the casket to a boy of sixteen. He arrived there in 1291, by their reckoning.'

'How did it get from Aksum to Istanbul?'

'The Abyssinian king thought that the Templars were trying to steal the Ark of the Covenant, their Ark, which I think is quite likely. In 1306, when the situation became too dangerous, Philip took the treasure to France, to their main temple in Paris. He was accompanied by Sophia, his daughter by a local woman. Sophia must have been around thirteen.'

Ismail Hodja drank some tea and continued. 'The poor young man escaped from the river only to drown in the sea. On the same boat with Philip and his daughter was an Abyssinian mission to the Christian Pope. It's believed that they warned the Pope that the Templars were planning to overthrow him.' Ismail Hodja shook his head and clicked his tongue in disapproval. 'These were all supposedly religious men, yet they were scheming against each other. It's remarkable that the Christians have thrived for so long.'

'Luck,' Kamil offered.

'Guns,' Ismail Hodja corrected him. 'And convenient ethics. Just a few months later, the Pope convinced the French king and other European heads of state to hunt down the Templars and confiscate their wealth, like a sow devouring its own brood.'

'What happened to Philip and his daughter?' Kamil

asked, now thoroughly drawn into the story.

'Philip was arrested and executed by burning in a public square. Sophia and her treasure turned up here in Constantinople. The Byzantine Church wasn't on friendly terms with the Roman Pope, so it was a natural destination. The Byzantine emperor put the Proof of God under the the protection of the statesman Theodore Metochites. He was probably grateful to acquire such a powerful, sacred object, since almost all of their relics had been stolen by the Crusaders and taken to Europe. In sacred terms, the city was naked.'

'There's an image of Theodore on the reliquary. Malik said the reliquary gives the Proof of God provenance.'

'Ah, even God must prove his authenticity,' Ismail Hodja remarked with a half-hearted smile.

'How have you learned all this?' Kamil asked in amazement.

'Muslim scholars kept track of the relic. It had been stolen from one of our holiest sites and they hoped to get it back. Every generation has its choniclers. The Templars used the object to advertise their own importance, so for a while it was easy to follow. The chronicles were collected in the library at al-Azhar University in Cairo. I had the honour of contributing a brief account of the Proof's sojourn in Byzantium.'

'How did the Proof arrive in the hands of the Habesh?'

'Sophia was half-Abyssinian, remember? She married Theodore's son.'

'So Sophia's descendants kept the Proof of God and built their sect around it.'

'We don't know for sure. The Metochites family was given custody in perpetuity, but the Proof was actually kept in the vault of the Hagia Sophia cathedral. The chronicles end there. No one knows what happened to it during the Conquest. Some believe it was taken out of Constantinople, perhaps to Venice. Over the years, many have tried to find it. It's extraordinary to hear news of it again.'

Kamil was stunned and humbled to realise that generations of scholars had tracked and written about the crushed reliquary he had so cavalierly dismissed as worthless.

'Malik told me it was lost after the Conquest during a fight between his ancestor, the caretaker of the Church of Chora, and someone he called a false prophet.'

It felt odd that he, Kamil, was contributing some small part to the tale of the Proof's odyssey. It occurred to him that he might be adding to history that would be written down and preserved in the library of al-Azhar. It was thrilling, but he felt guilty, as though he were feasting on Malik's death.

'What else did he say, may he rest in peace?' Ismail Hodja's excitement bled through his measured tone.

'The Melisites thought the reliquary was still somewhere in the Church of Chora, so they kept one of their members there as caretaker, even after it became a mosque. What's odd is that they never admitted to the members of their sect that it was missing. The congregation still thinks it's in a room in their prayer hall.'

'Secrets are the lifeblood of sects. The Melisites must have been very secretive indeed. I'm surprised word didn't circulate that they claimed to be guarding the Proof.'

'The prayer hall isn't very impressive. It would be hard to believe an object of worldwide importance was being kept there.'

'And you say Malik found it in the Kariye Mosque? Did he say where he found it?'

'No. I wouldn't be surprised if it was in one of those tunnels or cisterns that seem to honeycomb all those old churches.'

'Perhaps,' Ismail Hodja said thoughtfully. 'But that would be like hiding a grain of sand beneath a dune. Whoever hid it four hundred years ago wanted it to be found, but not by the wrong people.'

'And probably a little sooner.'

'Did he say what was in the reliquary?'

'A document written in Aramaic.'

Ismail Hodja closed his eyes and laid his hand across his beard. He was silent for a long while. 'It must be the real thing,' he said at last. 'There's no other explanation.' He looked at Kamil, eyes shining with delight. 'Until now, this has been nothing more than an interesting tale with no ending. Now a new chapter is being written. You cannot imagine how important this document is, Kamil. I would do anything to read it. I'm one of the few people in the empire who can read the old languages.'

'What does Aramaic look like?'

Ismail Hodja took a leather box from a cabinet and opened it. He handed Kamil a piece of parchment covered with angular writing. 'It's a copy, so don't worry about handling it.'

Kamil studied it. 'It looks a little like Arabic, but I can't make out anything.'

'It's a distant ancestor of the Arabic alphabet. Few people today can read it. '

'Malik was training his niece to read it. She's the next priestess.'

'That would make sense. He was preparing her to lead

under these new circumstances. Whoever possesses the Proof will be immensely powerful. She must understand it to wield it properly.'

'Because it works miracles?' Kamil couldn't keep the scepticism from his voice.

'No. I don't believe that. But they say it proves the existence of Allah for all religions and all doubters.'

'Even me?'

Ismail Hodja smiled. 'Even you, my son.'

'Well, now I'm even more anxious to get hold of it.' Kamil laughed, his mood suddenly exuberant. He reined in his voice, worried about such inappropriate behaviour when he should be mourning.

'All of our great religions flourish from the same trunk, a single vast tree inhabited by the spirit of Allah. Nevertheless every branch and leaf believes itself distinct.'

'And we're busy killing each other to prove it.' Kamil imagined an enormous oak tossing violently.

'Not everyone, thanks be to Allah. I've read your friend Malik's writings. He was truly a scholar and a friend of peace. He called for an ecumenical council that issued joint decisions, ecumenical fatwas, about what he called shared truths. Some of the religious scholars agreed, or at least respected him for trying. Others, as you can imagine, weren't happy with the notion of sharing their authority.'

'Unhappy enough to wish him harm?' And destroy something they thought might undermine their authority. But Malik had told no one outside his family about it, besides Kamil.

'I don't think so,' Ismail Hodja guessed. 'As long as he just wrote tracts, he was harmless. But with the actual Proof in his hands, he would be much more of a threat. People might have left their own religions to follow him, like a prophet. It's happened before. Very dangerous, indeed. The reliquary was stolen, you say?'

He wondered whether it would betray Malik's confidence to tell Ismail Hodja the rest. Malik was dead, he reminded himself, and there was nothing to fear from the scholar.

'The reliquary that was stolen was empty. The actual Proof was in a lead liner that Malik had taken out.'

'So the Proof itself wasn't stolen?'

Kamil wondered at the excitement in the sheikh's voice. 'What is it exactly?' Kamil asked.

'They say a prophecy of some kind. If only I could read it,' Ismail Hodja added wistfully. 'So close.' He sought Kamil's eye. 'If you find it, may I have the honour of seeing it?'

'I don't know, hodjam,' Kamil said reluctantly. 'I promised Malik I would keep its existence secret and, if I locate it, I'm to give it to Saba.'

Ismail Hodja nodded, unable to hide his disappointment. 'I understand. That's admirable of you, Kamil. Perhaps Saba will allow me a glimpse.'

'Of course, since you already know about it, it wouldn't be breaking a confidence.'

'No matter. What will you do now?'

Kamil thought for a moment. 'If you know about the Proof of God, then others must know about it too.'

'Tantalisingly small fragments of copies made by the Chora monks have turned up in Europe. Some scholars know of these.'

'Scholars aren't usually thieves.'

'Don't be so sure.' Ismail Hodja gave a self-deprecating smile. 'But it's certain they like to talk.'

'How much do you think European dealers would pay for something like this?'

Kamil saw a range of emotions chase across the old scholar's face: thoughtfulness, a stunned realisation, concern.

He laid his long fingers on Kamil's arm. 'It's not the dealers you should worry about. There are groups whose hunger for the Proof of God goes back hundreds of years, just like the Melisites. People who believe the Proof is the Ark of the Covenant or a rich treasure, or any number of ignorant legends. If their members heard it had been found, they'd stop at nothing to get it. They'd never sell it. It would simply disappear.'

IN THE PHAETON on the way home, Kamil considered the remarkable story of the Proof of God. He reminded himself that, fascinating though it was, it might be nothing more than a story. His real concern was the plague of thefts that were endangering the tenuous peace in the streets of the empire and the deadline Nizam Pasha had given him. The riot in front of the Aya Sofya and the melee by the Kariye Mosque showed there could be worse to come. If the Proof of God helped him break the case, it was worth pursuing. If not, he would have to seek out more promising avenues. He had only five more days.

He lit a cigarette. His mind felt sharp as a diamond, but multifaceted, as if his thoughts had fractured into a million pieces.

When he pulled up in his circular drive, he remained in the phaeton, staring at his house. The light of the lamps breathed in and out. A great sadness came to sit in his chest, crushing his breath. Sadness for Malik. For his father. For his mother, whose spirit he still caught out of the corner of his eye, in her bedroom, which was now his study, in the garden. He used to imagine her gentle voice in his head, but now he couldn't remember what she sounded like. He sorrowed for a loss greater than he could explain.

He looked down and saw Yakup's concerned face.

Yakup held up the lamp. 'Bey?'

Kamil climbed out of the phaeton, but found his sense of balance was distorted. He reluctantly accepted Yakup's arm to get into the house, then he staggered up the stairs to his bedroom. He disrobed and fell from the long succession of waking hours into sleep.

18

The blackness was so thick he couldn't tell if his eyes were open or not. The leaden weight in his hands and tongue was gone. He was naked. He could feel the air caressing his skin, then a breath or a hand – he couldn't be sure. Perhaps it was nothing. A dream. He dozed, then woke again. The darkness over him seemed thicker and his body had begun to glow in a slow, molten way, though it emitted no light. He felt it expand, first his chest and thighs, then his organ. His tongue swelled and thrust from his mouth. His back arched. His hands reached up to push against the blackness riding him and cupped two breasts, their nipples lying in his palms like pebbles. Kamil's eyes tore open. He bucked, but the centre of his body was no longer his. She had taken possession even of his voice, hoarse and strangled with lust until he brayed and lost consciousness. He remembered the nacreous gleam of a woman's back stained by a long smudge like a feather.

When he woke again, it was still dark. He got up to light a lamp. His sheets were wet. He touched them and sniffed his fingers. Too viscous to be sweat: an erotic dream. His mind cast back to his first memory of such helpless deliverance as a small boy, when he was little more than six or seven years old. His mother had taken him along to the hammam as she always did. But for the first time his childish eyes had registered the naked women stretched out on the bellystone, soaping and scrubbing each other's breasts and backs, applying aghda to depilate the area between their thighs. A blazing line of lust and desire had unfurled itself from that moment to the present.

He went to the washstand, filled the bowl with cold water, and cleansed himself, feeling strangely violated. In his dream, someone had used him like a tool, a vessel to be broken after use. Yet he wanted it again. He wanted her very badly, whoever she was. He shuddered. He had heard of incubi, male demons who sat on a woman's chest while she slept and engaged in intercourse with her. If he believed in that sort of thing, he would suspect he had just been visited by a succubus. It must be the Balat Balm, he decided.

He dressed and went downstairs. Instinctively, he checked his orchids. They seemed to watch him with bemusement, craning their long necks. He stepped outside into the back garden, carefully closing the door behind him so there would be no draughts. The pebbles on the path had been raked after Malik's departure and not been disturbed. What had he expected to find? Footprints?

By the time he went back inside, Yakup had lit the oil lamps. The windows were black wells into which the light fell, echoing faintly in their depths. Everything seemed slightly off kilter.

KAMIL STARED OUT of his office window, seeing nothing, his eyes focused inward. He had four days to break up the antiquity smuggling ring, and what had he accomplished so far? His friend and two, possibly three, policemen were dead. He knew that Amida had stolen the reliquary and was somehow involved, along with the thug Remzi and a brutal smuggling gang based in Charshamba, but Kamil had no proof of anything and now Remzi was gone. The marks found on bodies dumped in Fatih perhaps indicated a war between rival gangs. The mysterious Kubalou pulled strings somewhere in the background. Yet everyone Kamil met seemed obsessed by the battered reliquary they believed contained the Proof of God. Despite Ismail Hodja's enthusiasm, Kamil thought it unlikely that the Proof of God proved anything at all, but someone had been willing to kill Malik for it. To Kamil, that proved the ungodliness of man, nothing more.

He glanced at the files on his desk. In the past three days, a valuable, ancient Torah had been stolen, this time from the Ahrida Synagogue. This case was like a dog with ten tails. He had always liked the challenge of puzzles, the calm, exacting inevitability of logic winning over circumstance. What was the matter with him now?

He fell into his chair in exasperation and noticed Avi standing inside the door.

'Ah, you're well again. I see my sister has released you back to me.' He flung out his hands. 'But you find me pursuing the same case. What is it they say? "The church is dark, the letters in the holy book are small, the priest is blind, the congregation is deaf, so what good is shouting?"'

Avi approached Kamil's desk. 'There's another saying, bey. "However high the mountain, a road goes over it."'

'Well said. So let's find that road, shall we? I'll lay out the landscape like the blind priest and you can tell me what you see.' He took out a piece of paper and began to write down what he knew, separating the wheat from the chaff, as he put it to Avi, the true from the derivative. There were only two important questions: why kill? And who controls the flow of antiquities into Europe?

Underneath the first question, 'Why kill?', Kamil placed Malik's name and, beside it, 'Proof of God'. Next he wrote the names of the three policemen, including Ali, and beside them 'criminal arrogance' and Remzi's name.

Under 'antiquities' he wrote Kubalou and Amida. It was hard to imagine Balkis running a smuggling ring, but both Omar's and Malik's words pointed in that direction, so finally he added her name. Then he drew an arrow between Amida and Remzi – Remzi was involved in both the murder of the policemen and the antiquities gang. He underlined Kubalou.

Next to Malik's name he wrote 'wings'. Suddenly he remembered the feather on the woman's back in his dream the night before, and the feeling of unease intensified. It had seemed so real. He wrote 'Habesh, Wings, Proof of God'. He thought for a moment, then added 'drugs' and the name Courtidis.

Avi watched, fascinated, as the chart took form. 'What is the Proof of God?'

Kamil hesitated. 'A box of very special papers. Someone trying to find it probably killed Malik. You are not to speak of it to anyone.'

'Yes, bey. They couldn't open my mouth even with a hammer.'

Kamil winced at the metaphor and turned back to his chart.

'Who else wants it that badly, bey?'

'It seems the whole world wants it.' He sat up suddenly. 'It would be worth a fortune in Europe, not just to antiquities dealers, but to people who believe it's a sacred object.' He drew a circle around 'Proof of God'.

'Are those people here?'

'That's an excellent question, Avi.'

What did a member of a secret religious society look like? He imagined them to be rough, gullible, and ignorant, but then remembered that the Crusader orders had been made up of knights and educated men.

'If Kubalou is after the Proof of God, I bet he has a foreign buyer.' Kamil doubted someone like Kubalou had many scruples, much less a religious bent. 'The buyer could live anywhere.'

Kamil wrote down the only European names connected to the case so far: Magnus Owen, cultural attaché, and Joseph Ormond, Metropolitan Police. He added Rettingate and Sons, the dealers in London.

'I wonder how central the Habesh and the Charshamba men are,' he mused out loud. 'Who actually runs the gangs and who's just a hired hand? Remzi said Amida had hired him.'

Avi's eyes moved between Kamil's face and the chart. 'Maybe they both work for Kubalou.'

'Hmm. You might be right. If they're rivals, they'll try to undercut each other. Remzi would try to pin all the blame for the Tobacco Works fiasco on Amida. Although, I think Amida would sell the Proof of God without blinking an eye. He probably stole it on order for Kubalou. Why else would he take an old box and not the valuable pieces next to it?' He drew an arrow between 'Proof of God' and 'Kubalou'. 'But who killed Malik? Did Kubalou come back and tell Amida the reliquary was empty and to get the real Proof of God? Then Amida asked Malik for it and when he wouldn't give it to him, he killed him?' He shook his head and clicked his tongue. 'I can't see Amida killing his uncle.' He looked down the list. 'And I doubt Kubalou ever gets his hands dirty. That leaves Remzi.' Remzi who had escaped from jail the same night Malik was killed. He drew an arrow between the names Remzi and Malik. The murders were linked to the antiquities smuggling, of that he was sure. There was also the mysterious symbol that had been carved on the bodies and on the wooden chest they had briefly captured behind the Tobacco Works. He drew that on his chart beside Kubalou.

Saba wanted the Proof too, but why? Malik had trusted her enough to teach her how to read it. Saba would be the next priestess. Malik must have believed she'd use the Proof to strengthen the sect. If it was as important as Ismail Hodja said, it would indeed elevate the Melisites. He could imagine people making pilgrimages from all over the world to Sunken Village.

Kamil shook his head. Once people knew it had been found, it would never rest peaceably anywhere on this earth without people trying to steal it. He had to find it before Malik's killer did. Malik's letter to Saba rested in his jacket pocket. He took it out and turned it over in his hands. He wondered if Saba would allow him to read it. He returned the letter to his pocket and stood back from the chart to reflect on the thick inked lines linking Malik's death, Remzi's brutality, Kubalou's network, and the priceless Proof of God. He was convinced that all the others – the Charshamba gangs, Balkis, and Amida – were bit players. He leaned forward and wrote at the very top, above Kubalou, the word 'buyer'.

Avi stretched out his hand, palm up, and commented shyly, 'It's a problem that doesn't fit easily in the palm, bey.'

Kamil stroked the boy's soft hair. 'What was it you said? "However high the mountain, a road goes over it." If we use our heads, we'll get there.'

'And our feet.'

Kamil laughed and felt the tension fall from his shoulders.

19

Saba lay naked and sweating on the hot bellystone, arms by her side, legs pressed tightly together. Steam enveloped the small chamber and weak columns of light fell towards her from the round windows in the dome. She stretched luxuriantly, arching her back, letting the steam and the heat caress her. It was early and only the servants were awake. She was alone in the hammam at the back of the house.

She felt languorous. Slippery with soap, she began to explore. Her hand trailed slowly across her collarbone, then her breast and her belly. She reached between her thighs and let her fingers slide across the damp swollen flesh, the delicate mounds and mysterious valleys. Her body charged up to meet her touch. Her fingers fell into the ready space, the opening that flared with exquisite pain, obliterating all else. She cried out. The pain was irresistible.

Once, while Malik was out, she had discovered hidden in his library a folder of graphic miniatures. She had frozen with shame, but only for an instant. Then she had become intrigued, stealing back several times to memorise every detail. The images colonised her dreams, making them lush gardens in which she lingered wilfully long after the dawn call to prayer. Although Malik's death darkened her mood, it had also heightened her senses.

Suddenly, a short, heavy figure emerged from the mist

and pressed a bath mitt against her face. Saba struggled but couldn't get away. She felt a rough hand push her legs apart. When the finger impaled her, her back arched in pain and terror.

'Slut, slut, slut.'

Saba recognised Gudit's voice. The mitt covered her mouth so she couldn't scream.

'I saw you try to seduce the pasha with your honey cakes,' Gudit said in a harsh tone. 'I know everything and you, you little slut, know nothing. Someday you'll be grateful that I stopped you.'

She took the flesh between Saba's legs between her fingers and pinched and pulled at it as if she were trying to tear it off. The pain was intolerable. Saba fought and this time managed to pull the mitt off her face and wriggle out of Gudit's grasp.

Gudit slapped her. 'You belong to us.'

The two women struggled on the bellystone. Saba was amazed at the old woman's strength, but pushed her off again. A knife clattered to the floor. Slipping across the wet marble, Saba ran through the door to the cooling-off room. She turned, slammed it in Gudit's face and bolted it. Heaving with terror, Saba fell to her knees, the marble beneath her blooming pink with blood.

Saba didn't tell her mother about the attack. She was ashamed and, she acknowledged to herself, nervous about what other subjects such a conversation might open up. She said nothing because she knew her mother relied on Gudit, her lifelong friend who had helped her carry the burden of leading the Melisite community. Instead, Saba avoided the midwife, who had been released from the hammam by a puzzled kitchen maid. Saba concealed her bruises with fine clay under her veil. Although the physical pain began to subside, her fury multiplied. When she became priestess, she vowed, she would see to it that Gudit regretted her cruelty.

20

Kamil took Avi to the Brasserie Europe for lunch. Avi was fascinated by the mirrors, and his eyes were continuously drawn from the complicated choreography of knives and forks on the table before him to the reflections of other diners. He ordered the same as Kamil and copied his table manners exactly.

Afterward, they took the phaeton to the Fatih police station. Omar wasn't there – he had gone home for lunch – but Kamil was restless and decided to look for him instead of waiting. They left the phaeton at the station and followed the directions they had been given. They walked down a dirt lane between dilapidated two-storey houses, passing under colourful washing strung across the street. They arrived at a small square in the middle of which stood a fountain. A woman in wide flowered trousers and a hand-knit vest leaned towards it, filling a large copper jug. With a nonchalant gesture, she adjusted her cotton headscarf, which had come loose at one side, and deftly hefted the jug on to her head.

When she saw Avi, she smiled, showing a gap between her two front teeth. 'Good day, my son,' she said warmly.

Avi ran over to her. 'Teyze, does Police Chief Omar live here?' he asked, politely addressing her as aunt.

She paused, her eyes flicking to Kamil, who waited a short distance away. 'What do you want with him?'

'Kamil Pasha is a friend of his,' Avi explained.

'Ah, so you're Kamil Pasha.' The woman turned to him, the smile again lighting up her face. Toil had aged her prematurely, but she was still a handsome woman. 'I'm his wife, Mimoza. I'm sure he's complained about me.' She laughed. 'Come. I hope you're hungry.'

'May I take the jug, teyze?' Avi asked.

Mimoza looked him over, then gave it to him to carry. It was clearly heavier than he had expected, but he didn't complain.

They came to a wooden gate and passed through a garden deep in late-season blooms to a small cottage.

'Is that you, wife?' they heard Omar boom good-naturedly from the window. 'I'm dying of hunger.'

'I've brought company,' she warned him. 'You'd better put on your honey face.'

Omar appeared at the door in a loose robe that was open at the neck. The thin skin over his collarbone betrayed his age. 'Pasha,' he cried out. 'Well, this is my honey face. Wouldn't you rather the old one?' He laughed. 'Come in. You are welcome in my home. And who is this young lord?' He bent down towards Avi.

'Avi, Chief.' The boy saluted.

Omar laughed and clapped him on the shoulder. 'If I'd had that kind of respect in the army, we would have won all those bloody wars.'

The house was painted a cheerful blue, inside and out. Kamil slipped off his boots at the door and his stockinged feet sank deep into brightly patterned wool rugs. They were tribal rugs, traditional wedding gifts from the bride's family. The central room was lined around three sides with cushioned divan benches beneath large windows that looked out into the garden. White crochet-work curtains hung along the bottom of the windows for privacy. Each cushion was draped with a white cotton cloth embroidered with carnations. High above the entry door hung a tablet on which Mashallah – by the will of Allah – was written in fine calligraphy. Next to it hung a large blue glass bead, with contrasting circles of dark blue, turquoise and white glass, to ward off the evil eye. They were taking no chances. Kamil wondered which had been placed there by Omar and which by his wife. Two closed doors led off the middle room, as did a long hallway down which Mimoza disappeared.

They took their places on cushions on the floor around a low table. Mimoza brought bowls, spoons, and a single glass, which she filled with spring water from the jug. They tucked the crumb cloth across their laps and waited while she brought out a pot of yoghurt soup. This was followed by peppers stuffed with rice, dill, and currants in a warm yoghurt sauce.

Neither Kamil nor Avi mentioned that they had just eaten, but spooned yoghurt on to the peppers and ate them with pleasure, if not an appetite. The next course, a plate of rice, gave Kamil more difficulty, although he saw Avi and Omar wolf down theirs.

'Health to your hands,' Kamil complimented Mimoza.

She watched Avi eat and looked pleased. 'I was in Sunken Village last summer. I was buying vegetables at Charshamba market and happened to look down into the cistern, where I saw these amazing birds strutting about in someone's yard. Their tails were like enormous shimmering fans. I'd never seen anything like it, so I went down the stairs into the village and asked the woman who lived there if I could see them close up. She let me into the yard. They're called peacocks. They're vain birds.' She laughed. 'Just like people. The more beautiful a woman is, the more likely she is to peck out your eye. She let me have one of their feathers.' Mimoza got up and disappeared again. After a moment, she returned holding a gleaming green and blue feather. She gave it to Avi, who turned it back and forth, catching the light. 'She said they raise them for a local festival.'

Avi laid the feather carefully aside then jumped up to help Mimoza carry the dishes to the kitchen. Kamil had a glimpse of Mimoza patting Avi's hair and cupping his cheeks in her hands. Omar had seen it too, and Kamil caught a worried frown passing over his face.

As Avi came back into the room eagerly balancing a tray of glasses, Kamil felt an unworthy tick of jealousy. Avi seemed so comfortable here. He marvelled at the resilience of children.

Finally, they sat in the garden drinking their tea, and Kamil laid out his plan. If he wanted Omar's help in catching Malik's killer, he would have to tell him something about the Proof of God. He had considered carefully what could and could not be revealed. It would be a tricky conversation.

'We've been doing this haphazardly,' he began, 'following tips like the tobacco raid, or individual people, like Remzi and Amida. But as soon as we have a lead, it leaps sideways and we don't know where it's headed. It's like herding rabbits. Too many murders with too many motives, too many people, too many stolen objects. We need to focus on the European connection. We need to act, not just react. One antiquity that the thieves are after and that we have a decent lead on is the Proof of God.'

'The Proof of What?'

'The reliquary that Malik reported stolen. It contained papers that some people believe are sacred. Malik took them out to study them, so when Amida stole the reliquary, he didn't know it was empty. Whoever hired him to steal it, presumably this Kubalou, went back for the contents.'

'Are you telling me he was killed for some papers?'

'That's what it looks like.'

'Well, what else? What's in these papers? Aren't you going to tell me any more?'

Kamil hesitated. 'I can't.'

'You can't?' Omar's voice was incredulous.

'Malik made me promise not to tell anyone. He thought it would put his community in danger.'

'I should bloody well think he trusted me too,' Omar bellowed, getting to his feet and overturning his tea glass. 'Now what the hell is all of this about?'

Mimoza, with a concerned look on her face, leaned forward and righted the glass.

'Sit down, Omar. I'm not going to tell you anything while you're stamping about like a wild boar.'

Omar crossed his arms and remained standing. 'Well?'

Kamil calmly sipped his tea. Finally, Omar sat back down, still frowning.

'Ismail Hodja said these papers are important enough that secret societies have been following the reliquary for centuries, and that some of them would even kill to get it.'

Omar threw out his arms. 'You told Ismail Hodja, but not me?'

'He already knew about it. All but the connection to the Habesh. I'm sorry, Omar. Malik was adamant that no one should know.'

'Fine. I can respect a man for keeping his word.' Omar sounded disgruntled, but resigned. 'What do you propose to do?'

'I think the only way to control this is to find the document ourselves. Then we can decide what to do with it. Malik asked me to give it to his niece, but now I'm not sure that would be wise. She'd be in danger, and if she puts it in the prayer house, it would be stolen again. Ismail Hodja thinks it would be safer in the Imperial Museum.'

'Where is it now, do you think?'

'Either in Malik's house or in the Kariye Mosque.'

'We should take another look at his house. We didn't really know what we were looking for the last time,' Omar pointed out. 'At least I didn't. And if we don't find it?'

'We pretend we have it and dangle it in front of Amida's nose, then follow him when he tries to sell it.' Kamil looked at Avi, who was stroking the peacock feather. 'I thought the boy could help tail him. He'd be less visible.'

'He's just a child,' Mimoza protested. 'Let a man do the dangerous job.'

'It's not dangerous, teyze, really,' Avi spoke up eagerly. 'And I'm good at this. No one will see me.'

Kamil saw Omar meet his wife's eyes. Being married, Kamil thought, must mean learning an entire new vocabulary of words, looks and gestures known only to husband and wife, each couple a nation with its own language, government, and history. He wondered whether modern life would bring families out of their self-imposed exile and whether that would be a good thing. If the language of family faltered, he couldn't imagine what would take its place.

When Mimoza went to the kitchen, Kamil offered Omar a cigarette and they smoked in companionable silence. Avi sat beside them, still intrigued by the feather, which Mimoza had told him he could keep.

When she returned, Kamil stood up. 'Thank you for

your hospitality. Sadly I have to go.' He leaned over and looked steadily into Avi's face. 'Are you sure you want to do this? It's perfectly all right if you don't.'

Avi scrambled to his feet. 'Yes, bey. You can rely on me.'

Kamil turned to Omar. 'I'll set it up.'

'Agreed. You know where to find me.'

Kamil nodded.

'I'm glad to have met you, Kamil Pasha. And thank you for bringing us this young man.' Mimoza reached down and put her hand on Avi's shoulder. 'You're welcome here any time, my son.'

Avi beamed. 'Thank you, teyze.' He buttoned his jacket carefully over the feather, then took it out again and handed it back to Mimoza. 'Would you keep this for me, please?' he asked politely. 'I don't want it to get crushed.'

Kamil and Avi filed through the gate into the dusty square. Mimoza looked after them, twirling the peacock feather in her fingers.

KAMIL RAPPED ON the door. After a few moments, Amida opened it, unshaven and in a hastily donned robe.

'What do you want?'

'Peace be upon you.'

'Upon you be peace,' Amida responded lazily.

Avi stood in the shadow of the oleander, where he could see Amida but not be seen. He was wearing patched brown trousers too short for him and a ragged sweater and his feet were bare. He looked like any one of the hundreds of poor village boys sent to earn a kurush for their families on the city streets.

'Forgive me for disturbing your sleep,' Kamil said. 'I've come to speak to your mother and I thought you'd like to be present.'

Amida stared at him for a moment, suddenly alert. 'Give me a moment. I'll be right over.'

Kamil went next door to Balkis's house. Avi again took up position, this time under a thick ilex by a window that looked into the receiving hall. From there, he could hear and see whoever was sitting on the divan.

A servant led Kamil into the receiving hall. Balkis, dressed in a formal robe and kaftan, came to meet him. He smelled almond oil on her hair, mingled with a faint sourness. She looked exhausted. They exchanged the standard words of greeting.

'I wanted to speak with you and your son.'

'Amida isn't here. What is it about?'

'Good day, mother.' Amida came in, sat on the divan, and looked at Kamil expectantly.

'I wanted to let you know that we're very close to finding the Proof of God.'

'You mean that worthless reliquary?' Amida scoffed.

'No. I mean the Proof of God.'

'And what is that?' Amida asked, a sly grin on his face.

'Stop this,' Balkis snapped. 'You know what it is, and I wouldn't be surprised if you know where it is.'

Amida looked at her with alarm. 'Mother, what are you saying? How would I know where it is? Malik had it.' He rose to his feet. 'And if you're implying I killed him . . .'

She waved her hand at him. 'Sit down. I don't think you have it in you to kill anyone, let alone your uncle. But you said you wanted to sell it.'

'Well, where is it?' Amida asked Kamil impatiently.

'Malik left instructions about where he had hidden it.'

'Is this true?' Balkis asked, surprised. 'Why would he give that to you and not to me?'

'I don't know.'

'I'd be happy to help you look,' Amida offered.

'Thank you, but we don't need your help. We might even have it by tomorrow.'

'What do you plan to do with it?' Balkis asked. 'Malik must have told you it's central to our community.'

'I'll have to consult with my colleagues,' Kamil responded. 'The final disposition will be a matter for the court. But Malik did tell me how important it is to you, so I wanted you to know.'

These words, addressed to Balkis, found their mark. Out of the corner of his eye, Kamil saw Amida shift his position on the divan.

'You can't tell the court about it,' Balkis cried out in alarm. 'No one must know about the Proof. It's the core of our faith.'

'I'll do my best, but you must admit it would be safer in a museum.'

'It belongs in the prayer house, in the Holy of Holies.'

'We can discuss that later.' Kamil bowed formally and took his leave.

Amida caught up with him at the door. 'It's in Malik's house, I assume?'

'I'm not at liberty to say.'

Amida accompanied Kamil as far as the village square, looking frustrated. Kamil feigned interest in the architecture of the prayer house until he saw Amida climb the stairway to Charshamba and disappear from sight, then he walked back down the lane to Balkis's house.

BALKIS STILL SAT on the divan, smoking a chubuk pipe.

'I'm sorry to disturb you again, but I wonder if I might speak with Saba.'

Balkis looked at him blankly. 'Saba? What do you want with Saba?'

'I have something to give her.'

Balkis held out her hand. 'I'll give it to her.'

Kamil hesitated. Malik had told him to give it directly to Saba. 'I'd rather give it to her myself.'

'What do you have to give her that her mother can't see?'

Offended and embarrassed, Kamil responded, 'I'd prefer to conduct my business directly with her.'

'Spoken like a pasha,' Balkis muttered. She told the servant to fetch Saba. While they waited, she gave Kamil a long look that made him uncomfortable.

A few moments later, Saba swept in wearing a brown-striped robe belted with a yellow sash. A veil hid the lower part of her face. He remembered her oddly seductive behaviour in the garden the day before. As she came closer, he saw smudges of grief beneath her eyes and what looked like scratches and bruises only partially hidden by the veil.

'Come over here,' Balkis commanded. 'What's happened to you?'

Saba waited obediently while her mother pulled aside her veil. 'Nothing, Mama. I tripped and fell in the brambles behind the house.'

Kamil saw that Balkis wasn't satisfied but had decided to postpone further discussion until after he had left. He took the envelope from his pocket. He had wished to give it to Saba privately in the hope that she would share its contents with him.

'Here's the letter I told you about.' He handed it to her.

Balkis leaned over to take a closer look, but Saba slipped the letter into her sash.

'Who's that from?' Balkis asked, the tension in her voice apparent. 'Are you having a tryst?'

'It's a letter from Uncle Malik, Mama. I'm going to read it now.' She touched Kamil's sleeve, sending a jolt through his arm. 'Thank you for bringing the letter, Kamil Pasha.' Her green eyes looked directly into his. Kamil resented the hold she seemed to have on him and forced himself to look away.

Saba disappeared into an adjoining room and Kamil got up to leave.

'Please keep an old woman company for a few minutes, Kamil Pasha,' Balkis pleaded.

He sat down reluctantly, dreading another interrogation about his family, but her question surprised him.

'Did you notice Saba's eyes?'

'Should I have?'

'They're green. Like yours.'

Kamil mastered a powerful desire to leave.

'I have something important that I must tell you. When I was sixteen,' she began, 'I was given in marriage to my uncle, the old caretaker of the Kariye Mosque. Did Malik tell you it's a hereditary position?'

Kamil nodded, wondering where this was going. 'Amida will be caretaker now.'

'That's right. Amida. My son by my husband. I was young then, Kamil Pasha, and beautiful, although that may be hard for you to believe now. I had an elderly husband who paid little attention to me, and I was lonely.'

Kamil felt uncomfortable at being privy to such personal information. He should have left straight away, but now it was too late.

'One day, I was selling fruit near the mosque up there,' she pointed with her chin. 'After prayers, the men often buy fruit to take home to their families and I had many customers.'

She laughed lightly at the memory. 'I caught the eye of a pasha leaving the mosque. Yes, it's true. He left his retinue and came over to me. He bought some fruit and asked me if I would meet him later that afternoon behind the türbe. He assured me that he was an honourable man, filled my hand with gold liras, took his parcel of fruit, and rejoined his companions.'

Kamil got to his feet. This was entirely inappropriate. 'Why are you telling me this, Balkis Hanoum? You shouldn't be telling me this.'

'Sit down, Kamil Pasha!'

Kamil was startled at her tone.

'It's important that you hear this,' she said in a commanding voice. 'Malik was going to tell you, but I foolishly asked him to wait.'

Kamil was both mesmerised and repelled.

'The pasha was very kind. I ran away with him. He brought me to live in an apartment in Pera, on the Rue Tom-Tom.' She looked at Kamil. 'He was a very kind man. You have the same eyes.'

Kamil was no longer concerned whether he was being rude. 'I must go. This is none of my business.'

Balkis rose from the divan and with surprising speed blocked the door. 'It's very much your business. Hear me out.'

Kamil was uncertain what to do. He couldn't push Balkis aside without taking hold of her. 'I don't mean to be disrespectful, Balkis Hanoum. But I don't want to hear this. It's too personal.'

'That's right. It is very private. But I forbid you to leave, and when I finish, you will understand why. Ten months later,' Balkis continued, still standing before the door, 'I learned I would have a child. And soon after that, there was a knock on the door. It was the pasha's wife. A sweet woman, in her way, but nobody's fool. She saw I was pregnant. She told me that her husband wouldn't be coming again and left a sack of five hundred gold liras on the table. A gift, she called it. The remarkable thing is that she assured me the child would be looked after and would have an inheritance. I didn't believe it, of course, and, as things turned out, the pasha and his wife both passed away and no one came to offer Saba an inheritance. But that isn't important. We do well enough in our village. No one starves.

'Malik brought me back here. My poor husband had died while I was gone. I knew he was ill when I left him, to my great shame. In a last kindness, he had hidden my betrayal by telling everyone I was visiting relatives, so when Saba was born, no one guessed the baby wasn't his – no one except my brother and my mother, who was priestess at the time. After that, every bayram I received a bundle of fine cloth and a kerchief into the corner of which was knotted a gold lira. Three years ago that too ceased. I never saw him again.' She shrugged, but her eyes told him that she had loved this pasha. 'They're both gone from this world now,' she finished.

'Why are you telling me this?' Did she expect him to comfort her, or to exact retribution from the pasha's family? And what was this about eye colour, Saba's, his own? It was nonsense and he rejected the insinuation he knew she was making.

'I was going to tell her today.' Balkis slumped against the door. 'Please, Kamil Pasha, sit. I'll take only a few more moments of your time. You must hear the rest. I've waited a lifetime to tell you this. I'm an ill woman and there might not be another opportunity.'

They heard a wail from the other room, and suddenly Saba stood in the hall, a piece of paper dangling from her hand.

'Tell me what, mother?' she cried out. 'Tell me what?' The bruises showed livid against her chalky skin and deep lines scored the side of her mouth. The transformation from a few minutes earlier was so extreme that Kamil was afraid she had been attacked in her room. He held a hand out to her as if she were a frightened animal.

'Saba Hanoum, what's happened?' He stepped towards her. 'Is someone in there?'

'Stay away from me,' she screamed with such anguish that Kamil feared she had lost her mind.

Balkis stood by the door like a statue.

'You told him?' Saba asked her.

'Sit, my daughter,' Balkis said calmly. 'I haven't finished the story yet.'

'Leave,' Saba screamed at Kamil. 'Leave now.'

Balkis walked over and slapped Saba with such force that she fell against the wall.

Kamil grabbed Saba's arm to help her up. 'I've had enough of this,' he exclaimed angrily. 'Would you like to leave, Saba Hanoum? I can escort you wherever you wish to go.'

Balkis stood before her daughter. 'It's important,' she said, dwelling on every word, 'for you both to know.'

Saba refused to meet her eyes. Instead, she concentrated on smoothing her robe and adjusting her headscarf. Her breathing sounded laboured.

'Your brother is here,' Balkis announced, 'in this room. I was Alp Pasha's lover and Saba is your sister, Kamil.'

Saba bent over and pressed her fingers to her forehead.

'Right after she visited me, your mother left your father and moved to Beshiktash with her children,' Balkis told Kamil.

'How do you know that?'

'I made inquiries.' She lowered her eyes. 'I loved your father. He was the only man I ever loved. I still wait for him to come out of that mosque, even though I know he's gone.'

Moving as if in a trance, Saba passed Kamil and went to her mother's side. Balkis clutched her hand. 'I never told him about you.' Balkis rocked back and forth, crying without tears. 'I wish I had.'

'I don't believe this.' Kamil headed for the door.

Saba ran after him and pressed Malik's letter into his hand. 'Return it when you've read it.'

KAMIL HAD ALMOST forgotten Avi, who waited until Kamil had climbed up to Charshamba before coming to walk wordlessly beside him. Kamil was too stunned to speak.

'I saw them, bey,' Avi said. 'Do you want me to follow Amida?'

Kamil looked down at Avi's eager face and at the small bandage that still adorned his head. He squatted beside him. 'Yes, follow Amida. But don't take any chances. These are dangerous men. I just want to know where Amida goes and, if you can manage to overhear any of his conversations, who he talks to and about what. But this isn't a game. If anyone notices that you're hanging around or following Amida, I want you to leave immediately and take a carriage to the Fatih police station or the courthouse. Find me or Chief Omar.'

Avi smiled broadly. 'Yes, bey. Don't worry.'

'It'll be for no more than a few days. For the time being, I think you should spend the nights at my house. It's more convenient than Feride Hanoum's. I can bring you here in the morning. So once Amida is in his house for the evening or if you're feeling at all tired, come back to Beshiktash, and Karanfil will make you a good meal.'

They walked to the stable at the corner of the main boulevard. While the stable hand retrieved his phaeton, Kamil had a whispered conversation with the owner, a fat man in a stained leather apron. Kamil indicated Avi over his shoulder. The owner leered, but nodded in agreement. Money changed hands.

Kamil took Avi aside. 'I've arranged for you to have a carriage and a horse whenever you want.' He gave him a small sack of coins. 'And this is to buy food and whatever else you need.'

Avi tried to give it back. 'I don't need that, bey. I'll be fine.'

Kamil pressed it into his hand. 'Think of this as a job, Avi. You're a working man now.'

'Thank you, bey.' Avi proudly secreted the coins under his sweater. 'I won't use many, I promise.'

Bemused and grateful for the distraction of the boy's company, Kamil shook his head. 'Use as many as you need.'

KAMIL CLIMBED INTO the phaeton and steered it through a jostling hive of pedestrians, overloaded porters, carriages and carts. He tried to push all thoughts of Balkis's revelations firmly from his mind. He told himself that there was no proof that any of it was true. His father would never have betrayed his mother. But what did he really know about his father's life?

A memory ambushed him. He was a young boy and he was telling his father something important – he couldn't remember what. In mid-sentence, his father had turned away to attend to an aide and then, without another word to his son, had left the room. Kamil felt again the piercing disappointment that had overwhelmed him at the time, mixed with anger at his father's suicide the year before. Had his father walked away from his mother too?

He reached into his pocket for his watch and checked the time. His hand brushed the letter, but he didn't take it out. For some reason, the thought of reading it caused him great anxiety. He remembered the shocked look on Saba's face; he felt unprepared for any further revelations.

As he approached the suburb of Nishantashou, the streets opened up and allowed the horse to move more quickly. Finally, holding the reins in one hand and allowing the horse its head on the mostly empty street, he took Malik's letter from his jacket pocket. He held it for a long time before unfolding it, then pulled the phaeton over and read it. After his stomach settled, he read it a second time with greater attention. The letter verified what Balkis had said. It also appeared to contain advice for Saba on her duties as priestess, including an odd prayer. He scanned it for clues to the whereabouts of the Proof of God. Surely, Malik would have left instructions for Saba to find it? But if they were in the letter, they were too obscure for Kamil to understand. A second piece of paper enclosed with the letter had dropped on to the seat. On it, Saba had drawn a map of the basement of the Ottoman Tobacco Works.

FERIDE RAN TO meet him in the corridor, more animated than he had seen her in a long time. She kissed him on both cheeks and drew him in by the hand.

'Oh, I love having Elif here, Kamil. It's like having a sister.'

Kamil found himself scanning the hall for Elif and was disappointed when she didn't appear.

'Let me go get her,' Feride suggested eagerly.

Kamil pulled his mind back to the reason he was there. 'Feride, can we talk privately for a few minutes?' He hoped his distressing news wouldn't throw her back into a black mood.

Feride stopped, alarmed by his tone. 'Has something happened?'

'Not exactly.'

She led him into the parlour and sat apprehensively on the sofa. Kamil closed the door and moved a chair so he could sit opposite her.

Before he could say a word, Feride began to cry. 'I'm sorry, Kamil. Since Baba's death, I just keep waiting for the next blow. Last week, I wouldn't let the governess take Alev and Yasemin to the park. I had a vision of one of them falling out of the carriage and being crushed by the wheels. Now there's Elif and Avi and I'm afraid something will happen to them too.'

Kamil moved to the sofa and put his arm around her. He was now very worried about how she would take the news about Saba. He wasn't sure what to make of it himself and had hoped to discuss it with Feride, but that might be impossible considering the state she was in.

'Ferosh,' he said softly. 'Nothing that happened was your fault. I wish you'd accept that. I told you, if you want to blame someone, blame me. It was my suggestion to reduce Baba's opium. But remember, he had stopped eating. We were trying to save his life.'

'But we killed him.'

Soon after Feride cut her father's opium supply, he had walked off a balcony to his death. Witnesses reported that he had been smiling. Kamil knew with certainty that his father had been walking towards his wife, the woman whose absence and then death he could never accept and whose image he conjured up in his opium dreams. Now Kamil added a new scenario, that his father had also taken to opium out of guilt.

After their father's death, a sadness had settled on Feride. He knew she had always been lonely, despite her large household and a constant bustle of teas and social visits. She used to press Kamil to get married, begging him to give her a sister-in-law, a companion, but had lost interest even in that. She seemed to have no dreams left, he thought, as he held her hand. He handed her a clean handkerchief from his pocket and passed his forefinger across her brow.

She pressed the linen against her face, then placed it on the sofa beside her, calmer now. 'How do you stand it?' she asked Kamil, trying to laugh. 'Your sister is a lunatic.'

'Not at all. My sister is as lovely as the moon. And sometimes as enigmatic.'

'Where did you learn to draw butter like that?' she teased him, but he could tell she was pleased.

'So what was it you wanted to tell me?'

Kamil hesitated.

'I promise not to collapse, cry out, or otherwise cause a scene. Seriously, I'm fine, brother dear.' She pressed his hand. 'Whatever it is, you can tell me.'

Kamil decided it would be better to tell her now, rather than risk having her find out some other way. He took a deep breath and asked, 'Feride, do you remember when Mama took us to Beshiktash?' Kamil still lived in the small villa his mother had inherited and in which she and her children had spent their mother's last years.

'A little. I was only eleven. You were older. Why?'

'Do you know why Mama moved there?'

'Living in the governor's mansion was too much for her. There were always dozens of women trying to see her or inviting her over. I don't think they cared about her at all. They just wanted to use her to influence Baba. I saw her crying a few times. I remember that very clearly.'

'Do you think Mama and Baba were happy?'

'Of course,' she exclaimed. 'Baba started on the opium after she moved to Beshiktash, remember? And after she died, he was inconsolable. He loved her. That's what killed him in the end.'

They let that conclusion settle between them. Feride gave Kamil a small smile and blinked back tears.

Then Kamil asked, 'Yes, but did she love him?'

Feride looked puzzled. 'Of course she did.' But she sounded unsure. 'What are you saying?'

'It's possible that Baba had a mistress.' Kamil braced himself for Feride's response.

She was silent for a moment, her face unreadable. Then, to his surprise, she said simply, 'I suppose that's possible. Most men have them. You know, there's a saying, "If your husband has two coffee cups, break one." As soon as a man has enough money, he buys a mistress. In the old days, it was a second wife or a concubine. I suppose having a mistress is more modern.' She seemed lost in thought for a moment, then looked up again. 'Do you think that's why Mama left?'

Kamil wondered whether Huseyin had a mistress. 'Yes,' he said. 'And she has a daughter.'

Feride sat up straight. 'You think it's Baba's child?'

'I'm not sure. I think she might be.'

'How old is she?'

'Eighteen. So she would have been born around the time we moved. Her name is Saba.'

'That's a strange name.'

'It's an Abyssinian name.'

Feride was silent for a moment. 'Mama had an Abyssinian slave at the governor's mansion. Do you think it was her? She was very beautiful.'

'The woman's name is Balkis. I met her brother, Malik, a couple of years ago. He was a good man. He was killed two nights ago.'

'I'm sorry, Kamil. Was he a friend?'

'Yes.' Kamil allowed himself to grieve for a moment, as much for his friend as for his friendship. 'But he never said anything about this to me.'

'So maybe it isn't true.'

'I don't know. He came to my house that night. He wanted me to find an object that had been stolen from him and that he wanted his niece Saba to have. He seemed to want to tell me something else, but decided to put it off. We were supposed to have breakfast together the next day and he was going to invite Saba. It's possible that this is what he wanted to tell me. When he left that night, he asked me to take care of her and gave me a letter to give her in case something happened to him.'

He pulled out Malik's letter and handed it to her.

'I gave it to her this morning. From her reaction, I'm sure she didn't know. Her mother told me the whole story, but I didn't believe her.'

He waited while Feride read. It occurred to Kamil that Malik had sought him out and befriended him not because he had any interest in orchids, but in order to judge his character. He thought Malik had been his friend. Instead, he realised with a shock, he had been a relation.

When Feride finished, her face was white. 'Can I keep this?'

'There's some information in there that I need. But there's no rush to return the letter. I'll bring it back to you. Are you going to show Huseyin?'

'Of course. And Elif.'

Kamil realised that next to Elif's arrival, this was the most exciting thing that had happened to Feride in a long while.

'What did the mother . . .'

'Balkis.'

'What else did Balkis tell you?'

'She said she met Baba as he was coming out of the Mosque of Sultan Selim.'

Surprised, Feride asked, 'What was Baba doing in a mosque?'

'I don't know, Ferosh. It was probably part of his official duties.'

'Did Baba know about the child?'

'I don't know. Balkis said she didn't tell him.'

Feride considered this. 'I think he must have learned about her, don't you?'

They sat for a few moments without speaking.

'Do we want to acknowledge the girl?' Kamil asked finally. It seemed the decent thing to ask Feride, although what he desperately wanted to know instead was whether his parents had been happy and why his father had taken up with Balkis. He couldn't imagine his father with her. It was another man, another father he didn't recognise. He felt grief, as if he were losing his father all over again.

'Is there any proof of this story?' he heard Feride ask.

'I don't think so. But there is a resemblance.' He remembered Saba's eyes, so like his own.

'She's beautiful, isn't she?'

'Yes. She looks like you.'

'Do you think she'll want an inheritance?'

'She's illegitimate, so she has no legal right.'

'There's law,' Feride pointed out, 'and there's justice. We'd need some kind of proof, though.'

Last night's nightmare came back to him with the force of a hallucination. He could see the feather on the woman's back. He fought the images by trying to picture his mother's face, but found the memory of her pulsing faintly in and out of focus, displaced by the stronger impression of Elif's small golden head.

21

Omar and Kamil pored over the map while the men placed dozens of lanterns around the perimeter of the Tobacco Works basement. Omar hadn't bothered to get permission from the French owners. When Kamil showed him the map, he simply gathered his men, rode there, and broke down the door.

The rusted machines, pillars and capitals, piles of bricks, clotheshorses, and a hundred other objects were revealed as nothing more than rubbish in the bright light, not the mysterious overlaid voices of grand civilisations. It all meant nothing, except obsolescence, decay, bad design. That was what the basement of the Ottoman Tobacco Works represented – a museum of dead machines.

Omar was clearly in no mood to reflect on any of this, Kamil observed. The police chief walked through, upending and kicking over objects until they came to the wall marked on Saba's map with an X. It was right next to the cavalcade of dummies. Omar hurled each one through the air like human projectiles.

The policemen waited tensely, hands on their guns and truncheons, as Omar stood nose to the wall, looking for an entrance. Instead of brick, the wall here was made of limestone blocks as long and high as his arm, fitted together without mortar.

'Son of a bitch. Where's the door? There's got to be a door.'

Kamil told the men to bring more lamps. He peered at Saba's map. Beneath the X was an arrow pointing down. He looked at the floor. Most of the basement was paved with cracked slabs of marble and stone but at the base of the limestone wall, he could just about make out a mosaic. It was so layered in grime that the design was almost invisible. He squatted and began scraping at the dirt with his knife. Omar quickly joined him.

'The design goes right to the wall, do you see? As if it goes through it.' Kamil uncovered the image of a naked child riding a dolphin, but this was no time to look at pictures. He thought of Elif again. She would have appreciated the adventure of uncovering this art. A curled seahorse with the head of a bearded man emerged from beneath the dirt. He could hear Omar on his knees beside him, grunting with concentration. Two policemen, looking puzzled, scraped energetically nearby. Kamil looked at what they had uncovered. It was a seascape with fish and mythological creatures and in the centre, Poseidon holding his staff. One of the fish seemed to be swimming into the wall.

'What does it mean?'

'It means that this wall is new,' Kamil said, pointing to the block above the half-submerged fish.

'In this place, new could mean a thousand years,' Omar snorted. He went over and kicked the wall, hard. It resonated dully.

'That's it. Right here,' he crowed. He took a large hammer from one of the men and was about to swing it into the wall when Kamil stopped him.

'Wait. There has to be a way to open it.' He squatted and brushed his fingers across the mosaic. Poseidon's staff looked different from the rest.

'This is some kind of metal.'

'And it's cleaner,' Omar observed, reaching down. He pushed the tip of his knife into the grout beside it and gave a satisfied grunt when the staff popped up.

He tried to pick it up, but it was attached to something. He knelt down and examined it in the light. 'It's brass.'

'Not Byzantine, then,' Kamil surmised.

The policemen circled them, watching curiously.

Omar took the small brass rod in his hands and pulled, felt resistance, pulled harder, and then lost his balance when whatever it was attached to gave way. They heard a whirring sound. Omar found he had a length of greased cord in his hands that stretched from the rod into a hole in the floor. He pulled on the cord and they heard whirring again, then a grating sound.

The policemen shouted and reached for their guns.

Omar and Kamil swung around. One of the granite blocks had disappeared, leaving an opening just high enough that they could enter it bent double.

Omar grabbed a lamp and ducked inside. 'Pulleys. Very clever.' His voice came from inside the wall. 'They swing the block backward and up. There's a release mechanism so you can let it drop back once you're inside.'

'Wait.' Kamil crowded in after him.

'Don't worry. I have no desire to close this damn door now that we have it open.' He pointed his lamp upward. 'Look how shallow this block is. Probably not very heavy.'

'I still wouldn't want it falling on my head.'

Kamil didn't say what they both thought. That they had no time to lose and all the time in the world. Kamil remembered Remzi's face when he had asked him about Ali. He was sure Ali was dead.

Omar didn't meet Kamil's eye. 'Let's go find the poor bastard.'

'Are you coming with the lamps?' Omar shouted impatiently.

The other policemen followed behind them. The light revealed a narrow vaulted tunnel that stretched ahead. The bricks were weeping dampness and the air was rank. Kamil's feet stepped into shallow puddles, but the water seemed to seep continually away, perhaps into a cistern farther down. If this had been the foundation of a palace, he thought, it was likely to have been built on top of a large cistern, its water supply. He looked down and imagined layers of such structures beneath his feet, enormous vaulted underground cities, sealed for a thousand years.

As they advanced, they saw signs of recent occupation. A piece of mouldy bread. A silver coin not yet tarnished. An empty cigarette tin. The air became more foul. Kamil and Omar said nothing, but pushed ahead. Behind them, some of the men coughed and pulled their shirts over their mouths and noses.

Kamil stumbled into Omar's back.

'The bastards have blocked it off,' Omar said, but Kamil could tell by his voice that he had seen something more in the tunnel before him.

Kamil pushed forward to stand beside Omar. The tunnel was blocked from floor to ceiling with bricks, stones, and debris. But what Kamil saw first was a head resting on the bricks. Below it, shoulder width apart, were two hands. One hand still gripped a stone, as if the man had attempted to defend himself. Or dig himself out. What was most disturbing of all was that Ali's eyes, nose, and ears, and the fleshy tips of one hand had been chewed off by rats.

Part of his tongue protruded where the rats had burrowed into his mouth.

Kamil was sickened. He and Omar were speechless for a few moments. Then Omar exploded into a string of curses. 'The sons of bitches buried him alive.'

There was a commotion behind them as the other men shared the news.

Omar dropped his lamp and began to haul rocks from the pile.

'Be careful,' Kamil cautioned. 'We don't want to have to dig you out too.'

But Omar was beyond listening or caring. He tore into the pile and Kamil handed rocks back to the line of men who passed them along the tunnel, through the door, and into the basement.

They pulled Ali from the rubble. His body and limbs, frozen in a sitting position, had been protected by the stone and were unmarked, except for a cut on his forearm encrusted with blood. Kamil took a closer look at the wound, then motioned Omar to do the same. Four straight cuts in the shape of two mountain peaks. 'The mark of Remzi's boss,' Kamil noted.

'The son of a bitch likes to advertise,' Omar snarled.

'He wants us to know who he is. What use is an empire if no one knows you run it?' Kamil said. 'I think his need to be acknowledged will make him easier to catch.'

'"A puffed-up chest makes a bigger target", we used to say in the army. One way or another, we'll get him and then I'll break his bones one by one.'

Omar took off his jacket and pulled off his shirt. He wound the shirt around Ali's head, then lifted the body under the arms. Kamil took the legs and they carried Ali awkwardly through the narrow tunnels, the corpse's stiff arms grazing the walls. The policemen were frightened. When Omar and Kamil reached the basement, they put the body down and Omar bellowed for someone to get a closed carriage to take it to the mosque.

Kamil forced himself to look at Ali's ruined face. He accepted as due punishment the nausea and anxiety this aroused in him. Maybe he should have pushed harder, had Amida arrested and beaten until he revealed the location of the tunnel. It wouldn't have saved Ali, who appeared to have been dead since the night he was snatched, but they would have found his body sooner. This, Kamil thought, was what happened when you didn't have a plan, when you relied on luck or fate to solve a case. He vowed that would never happen again. He would become more vigilant, look at things more closely, ask more questions. He didn't believe in fate, and this should never have been Ali's. All the same, beneath the words in his mind, a disquieting murmur flowed through his chest and heart, finally taking up residence in his stomach: out of control, out of control. He had a sudden vision of himself as a passenger on the Gravity Pleasure Ride, forced to go wherever the train sped, unable to get off, completely helpless.

He stood and pressed his handkerchief against his mouth. After the nausea subsided, he tossed the dirty cloth in a corner. Omar was berating two policemen for not bringing a large enough board to carry the corpse. If he had seen Kamil's distress, he made no mention of it.

Ali's body sat bent over, hands stretched forward, on the mosaic of fish above the ghost of a cistern, looking for all the world as if he were fishing.

22

By the time they brought Ali's body to the Fatih Mosque and handed it over to the imam for washing; by the time Omar and Kamil had located his family in a shabby two-storey wooden house up a steep, narrow lane; by the time Omar had delivered the news of Ali's death to his elderly parents and to his shy, young wife, her face hidden behind a veil, in the sparsely furnished sitting room of the house they occupied together, it was nearly night. A scruffy boy with wide eyes and Ali's ears pressed himself against his mother's legs. She bent her head low over the baby in her arms and rocked back and forth. Ali's mother went over and put an arm around her.

Kamil couldn't help but look for the hole in the floor from which Ali claimed to have fished, but saw only a threadbare carpet.

He and Omar stepped out to find an orange sky blazing across the landscape as if the whole city were on fire. From this height, they could look down through the tight canyons of streets to the Golden Horn, which at this moment channelled not water but molten copper. Without a word, they both stopped and watched. Omar took out a cigarette but didn't light it. Kamil thought about the looting and burning of Constantinople by the Turkish armies. He wondered whether someone, a Byzantine, had stood at this very spot and watched his city go up in flames.

'Want one?' Omar murmured. When Kamil nodded, Omar handed him the cigarette, took another out of a battered silver holder, and clamped it in the corner of his mouth.

When they'd finished smoking, they began to walk down the steep hill. The sky had quietened too, matching their mood. Shades of grey bled into feathers of pink, slowly smothering them. Kamil was aware of Omar walking beside him, but in the twilight he felt invisible, alone. Sounds seemed to come from a long distance away, or were muted, as if from another room. Children cried out and pots clanged from a kitchen window; a street vendor called out, 'Melons like honey, melons.'

'Should we head over to Malik's house or leave it for tomorrow?' Omar asked.

'Might as well go now.'

A pigeon had somehow managed to get into Malik's house and fluttered about like a dispirited ghost as the two men systematically searched the rooms. They were in no hurry this time, so they moved slowly and deliberately, Kamil on one side, Omar on the other, lifting each object and examining it carefully before placing it on a cotton sheet that Kamil had spread on the floor. The pile grew: shattered crockery, worn leather slippers, a broken pair of spectacles, the detritus of a simple life.

'What does this Proof of God look like?'

'A box of some kind, probably lead, or individual pages of a very old document written in Aramaic.'

'And what does that look like?'

'Like odd Arabic.'

'Well, that narrows it down,' Omar huffed, picking up a book in Ottoman Turkish, written in Arabic script.

'Just look for anything you can't read.' Kamil wished he

could show Omar the letter – maybe Omar could see clues that escaped him. But Malik's letter contained too much information that Kamil didn't want anyone to know about. It was too new, too raw.

After he and Omar had finished with all the other rooms, they stood at the entrance to the study and eyed the sea of paper with trepidation.

Kamil bent over and picked up a fragment of old linen parchment, brown and crumbling at the edges. His eyes had been caught by the brilliant colours that surrounded the Greek text – vivid purple, green, and red, ornamented in gold leaf.

Omar looked over his shoulder. 'Malik collected those. He said they were done by monks at the Kariye when it was a church.'

Kamil wondered what the monk who had copied this particular page had been thinking when he painstakingly painted the flowers and vines, the tiny distorted faces peering from behind highly elaborate letters. Did monks have a sense of humour? Were they bored by the texts and looking to entertain themselves? Why would their superiors allow such a thing?

According to Ismail Hodja, the Chora monastery had been built by Theodore Metochites, a Byzantine minister of state and diplomat who in his later years became a monk there. Had he devoted himself to studying these texts or did he while away his remaining days painting whimsical designs around their edges? Perhaps he had written his memoirs, as ageing statesmen were wont to do in any age. If so, they hadn't survived. Only his image on the wall of his church and on the reliquary had survived him.

Kamil picked up another illuminated page. They were beautiful.

'Well, the old rake,' Omar exclaimed, throwing on the table a depiction of a man penetrating another from behind in an explosion of colourful robes.

'This is Japanese,' Kamil commented, noting the eyes and elaborately knotted hair of the two men and their exquisitely detailed kimonos.

'Well, I guess the Japanese aren't choosy.' Omar dropped another page on the pile, an ink sketch of a woman holding up her kimono and straddling a man. She was leaning forward and every detail of their joined organs was lovingly depicted. Discomfited by the memory of his dream, Kamil placed a page of Latin text on top of the Japanese drawing.

Omar looked at him with amusement. 'I didn't know you were so squeamish, Magistrate.'

'Let's not forget what we're doing here,' Kamil responded irritably.

Omar shrugged and lumbered back into the pile of papers on the study floor. He picked out the spines, shook each one, then laid it out flat on the table.

After an hour, the table was covered in papers and book spines, but the piles on the floor didn't look much smaller.

Omar rubbed his back and stretched. 'Guess I'm not going to smoke here,' he observed. 'Back in a minute.' He tramped down the stairs.

Kamil heard the iron entrance doors clang. After a few moments, he heard voices, Omar's deep bass and a rapid-fire response. He opened the window and looked out. The night air, tinged with coal fumes, filled his lungs and he had to wrestle a desire to cough. The yellowish haze was illuminated by the moon and seemed almost alive, twining itself around the ruined Byzantine arches and foundations.

He could make out the top of Omar's head and broad shoulders by the door, and the top of a fez and long hair of a man facing him. The latter glanced up and Kamil saw it was Amida.

'Greetings, Magistrate,' he called out. 'I saw a light and thought I'd investigate. Could have been thieves or the murderers, back for another go. I didn't expect it to be you.'

Kamil went downstairs and set a lamp down just outside the door so it illuminated the nattily dressed Amida and a wary Omar, his eyes locked on the young man.

'What are you doing in this part of town?' Kamil asked, noticing Amida's stambouline jacket and trousers. 'It's not somewhere you get dressed up to go promenading.'

Amida shrugged. 'I had some business around here.'

'At this time of night?' Omar's eyes flicked to a nearby Byzantine arch, then returned to Amida.

'I was concerned that someone was breaking in,' Amida said defensively. 'Why am I suddenly under suspicion?' He pulled open his jacket. 'There's no crowbar in here. What are you doing here, anyway?'

'Getting a haircut,' Omar said in a tone that warned Amida not to ask further.

'Fine.' Amida shrugged. 'I'm glad to see our civil servants are burning the midnight oil. I'm going home.' He turned on his heel and disappeared into the dark lane.

Kamil turned to go back inside, but Omar grabbed his arm and indicated he should wait. Omar sauntered down the lane in the direction Amida had disappeared and when he'd assured himself that he was gone, he walked back to the dark hulk of the Byzantine arch and smiled. 'You can come out now, you rascal.'

Avi emerged, dressed in rags, his face and hands filthy.

Omar smiled broadly and boomed, 'A disguise worthy of Saladin!'

'Well done, Avi,' Kamil said. 'Let's go inside.'

'Have you eaten, son?' Omar asked as they trooped back up the stairs.

'Yes, Chief. Thank you.'

Kamil wasn't so sure. The boy looked pinched. He decided to take him home and ask Karanfil to feed him. He and Omar could return the following day to sort through the rest of the papers.

But Avi was almost jumping with excitement. 'Can I report now?'

'So, my son,' Omar asked obligingly, 'where was our friend Amida this evening in his fancy suit?'

'He was in Beyoglu.' Avi turned to Kamil, his eyes alight. 'He met with a Frank and they agreed to meet again tomorrow night at eight o'clock by the Galata Tower. I didn't hear his name but Amida is supposed to bring him something.'

'Well done, Avi,' Kamil said, patting his shoulder. He wondered if this Frank was the mysterious Kubalou. 'Let's get you home.'

'If you permit, the boy could stay with us,' Omar suggested shyly. 'We're close by and he's tired.'

Kamil hesitated. He felt strangely disappointed and realised he had been looking forward to Avi's company. 'Well, Avi, it's up to you. If you decide to stay with Omar, I'll have some clothes sent to you there.'

Avi looked at the floor and said nothing, but Kamil had seen the flash of pleasure in his eyes at Omar's invitation.

'He might as well stay with you, then,' Kamil said, smiling. 'Set him on Amida's trail again tomorrow morning.'

'In case the little pimp changes his plans.'

'Right. Let's meet at the courthouse at seven.'

'Yes, bey,' Avi chimed in.

'Not you, Avi. You'll have done your job by then. This might be dangerous.'

Avi looked disappointed.

'If we manage to arrest this Frank and if he's the central player we think he is, then you'll have done your empire and your sultan a great service. How many other young boys can say that?'

Omar motioned towards the door. 'Shall we look some more?'

'None of those papers looked like they might be the Proof of God. I suspect they're too delicate to be lying around in a heap. They must still be in that lead liner. If the thief had found it, he wouldn't have turned the house upside down.'

'There's no lead box in there. We were thorough.'

'I'll search the Kariye tomorrow and I'll also check the bazaar.'

'You won't find anything in the bazaar.'

'Maybe the reliquary?'

'We know it'll trace back to Amida.'

'It's part of the puzzle. And you never know what else might fall into our hands.' He wished again that he could share Malik's letter with Omar. He had seen nothing in it that indicated where the Proof was hidden. Had Saba? More than anything, he understood, Saba wanted the Proof. Perhaps she had already retrieved the Proof from its hiding place.

'Searching for the Proof of God,' Omar chuckled. 'You and a thousand theologians. Good luck, then.' He put his hand on the boy's thin shoulder and steered him out the door. 'You'll make a fine policeman, son,' Kamil heard him say.

23

Kamil slept deeply with, thankfully, no disturbing dreams and awoke refreshed for the first time in days. It took him a moment to realise that it was past daybreak. It was raining and a muddy yellow light clogged the windows.

After breakfast, he took Karanfil aside and asked her discreetly what she knew of an Abyssinian woman named Balkis. Karanfil bore little resemblance to her son Yakup. Where he was tall and angular, his profile sharp as a hawk, Karanfil was round, with delicate features.

'That was a friend of your father's, bey.' She seemed reluctant to say more.

'Come, Karanfil. My parents, may they rest in paradise, are no longer with us and can't be hurt by such revelations. I've heard the story from others but I'd like to hear what you know of it.'

'Why would anyone tell you such a thing, bey? It was all over with such a long time ago.'

When Kamil wouldn't let the matter rest, she said finally, 'Your mother found out. Everyone talks, so the news that her husband kept a mistress was bound to come to her ears. But she was such a good person, at first she didn't want to interfere. Me, I would have kicked my husband out and thrown his water cans after him, may Allah give him rest.' Karanfil's husband, a water carrier, had died in a fire. 'When the affair continued she thought that if she left your father, he might end it, so she moved the family to Beshiktash. But your mother never denied your father anything and whenever he came to visit, she treated him like a sultan. It didn't stop anything. So one day, your mother decided she wanted to see this woman herself. We went to her apartment. I waited outside. When she came out, your mother said the woman had agreed to give your father up. I don't know what she said to her, but sure enough, we heard that the woman had moved out of the apartment, and after that, your father spent all of his free time at Beshiktash. It's sad that your dear mother was too ill to move back to the city, but your father took care of her here until the end.'

'Was there a child?'

There was a long pause while Karanfil deliberated. 'Your mother sent this woman gifts every year and I saw what she put in the bundle. She never said anything to me, but you don't send gold liras to your husband's ex-mistress. There had to have been a child.'

'Why didn't anyone from the family help the child after my mother and father passed away?'

'Your mother had left instructions for the gifts to continue, but somehow the name and the location were lost. It was in Allah's hands. There was nothing to be done.'

'Lost? You must have known where they were delivered. That's not something you can easily forget.' Kamil's voice rose. He was overcome with an emotion he couldn't identify, anger at his father's betrayal, mourning for the lost purity of his childhood, and a sense of loss that came with the realisation that he hadn't known his parents at all.

He couldn't bear Karanfil's sympathetic look. 'Tell me what happened,' he demanded.

'After your mother passed away, your father found her account book where she had recorded the gifts. He tore it up.'

'Did he tell you to stop sending the money?'

Karanfil fidgeted. 'He never spoke of it directly and the very next day he moved to Feride Hanoum's house. We assumed that's what he wanted.'

'You assumed that my father, when he found out he had a child, would want to stop supporting her?' he asked incredulously. 'What kind of a man did you think he was?'

'He was a good man, your father. Everyone knows that. But this was in Allah's hands.'

Kamil stood and quickly left the room, shouting for Yakup to bring the carriage. He threw a waterproof cape around his shoulders and waited by the door, slapping his gloves impatiently from one hand to the other. Everything he thought he had known about his parents had been erased and rewritten in one day.

Just then, a carriage drove up that was not his own. He recognised his brother-in-law's scarlet and blue livery. The driver dismounted, ran up the stairs, and handed Kamil a note.

It was from Elif.

'Kamil,' he read, 'Today's rain reminds me of Paris, wet cobblestones, enormous black umbrellas, the steam from my coat when I took it off. It's a day to draw the new, the stalwart, the invisible. I think I should start here, if I am to go back to my art. I can't yet bear to paint in the sunlight where all is exposed. May I sketch your orchids this morning?'

Kamil dropped the letter on a table. Elif, of all people, now when he felt least composed. He took out his watch. It was eight in the morning.

The driver waited with downcast eyes.

'Is she in there?' Kamil indicated the carriage.

'Yes, bey.'

Taking a deep breath, Kamil went out to get her.

24

Balkis never saw Alp Pasha again. Often she daydreamed that he came back to the mosque, that they met again, and she showed him his child. That he was so enraptured by his daughter, he offered to support them and they left the village to live in a small house away from prying eyes. But after what had been done to her, Balkis no longer dared to dream the pasha would find anything at all attractive about the girl he had once compared to a peach. She no longer had a life outside the village, outside the sect. She was a monster, like the eunuchs, who were known to be loyal to their masters to the death because they had nowhere else to go.

After Balkis had given birth to Saba, Gudit had come to see her. Gudit with her powerful arms, short neck, and broad shoulders that gave her the appearance of a man or a bull. Like most of the villagers, she wore wide shalwar trousers, but eschewed the bright flowered cotton of the women. The villagers treated the midwife with elaborate respect. Balkis had been afraid of her.

'Your mother is weak, Balkis,' Gudit had told her. 'We need to prepare you to take her place as priestess.'

Over a period of two weeks, the midwife had tattooed enormous folded wings on Balkis's back with ink made of wood ash, indigo, and Balkis's own breast milk.

Needle in hand, the midwife promised her, 'Soon you'll be like a houri, a winged virgin, eternally pure.'

'Don't be ridiculous, Gudit,' Balkis said through teeth clenched against the pain. 'I have two children. Even Allah can't perform the miracle of making me a virgin again.'

The midwife frowned and explained earnestly, 'Only a virgin can touch the Container of the Uncontainable. She must herself become the Container of the Uncontainable.'

'Don't talk such nonsense. It's bad enough I have to endure this.'

The day the wings were done, the midwife dressed Balkis in a cotton robe and served her a cup of bitter, honey-laced tea. When Balkis felt drowsy, Gudit helped her walk to the sacrificial stone behind the temple and bade her sit. Three strong women who had been waiting there held Balkis down, covered her mouth, and pulled her legs apart. Balkis saw Gudit take a knife, and what followed was a pain so intense she thought they had killed her. They wrapped her in her robe and carried her to her house. Through her delirium, Balkis thought she saw the midwife empty a bowl into the pillars flanking the door to the prayer house.

Balkis had lain curled in bed in a ball of pain, refusing to speak with anyone. She could keep nothing down but simple broth. They brought four-year-old Amida to her, but she didn't acknowledge him. She refused her breast to the baby Saba, who had to be given to a wet nurse.

When Balkis finally kept down some bread and yoghurt, the midwife sat beside her and fed her morsels with her own hand, since Balkis was too weak to sit up. When she needed to urinate, she screamed and wet her bed. The midwife lifted the covers and pushed her legs apart. Balkis could feel her manipulating her flesh, but was too weak from pain and hunger to protest, although no longer too weak to wonder what had happened to her.

When she was alone, she reached between her legs and was shocked to feel sharp needles pinning her flesh together. She cried out with fear.

'What have you done?' she wept. 'What have you done to me?'

Gudit, who slept in the next room, ran in and stood by the bed, her arms crossed. She looked proud. Balkis never forgot that look.

'You've been cleansed in the way of our ancestors,' she explained portentously. 'You're a virgin again.'

'What ancestors? What did you do?'

'It's an ancient Abyssinian custom. We cleanse a woman by removing her extra flesh, just as boys are circumcised. To close you up, I used special thorns brought from Abyssinia,' she boasted.

'There's a stick,' Balkis moaned.

'A reed so you can urinate and other fluids can drain. I'll take it out when the wound is healed. You'll see. It'll leave just a small opening. Very beautiful, like an ostrich egg.'

'Are you . . . ?'

'Oh, no,' she responded, shaking her head. 'I'm not important enough. Back home in Abyssinia, every girl is circumcised, but here it's the privilege only of the priestess, once she has provided for the succession. It's shameful to let such an old custom die. We've been doing it since the pharaohs.'

When Malik was finally allowed to see her, Balkis saw that he was shocked, but she was too embarrassed to tell him what had been done to her. Too weak to sit up, she simply grasped his hand and cried, Balkis remembered, feeling again her helplessness. 'Stay with me,' she had begged her brother through the miasma of pain.

Malik had confronted Gudit. 'What's the matter with her? Why is she so ill? Why didn't you tell me? And why haven't you called a surgeon?'

'It's my duty to continue the traditions. You have your duties as caretaker,' Gudit responded smugly. 'The initiation of a priestess is none of your business. There's no need for a surgeon. She'll be fine.'

'She doesn't look fine. I'm going to get Pericles Fehmi.'

'That man doesn't know how to grow a moustache, much less cure anything. I told you, I forbid anyone outside the family from seeing her.'

Malik stepped closer and looked down at her unyielding face. 'And who are you to forbid anything?'

She smiled, showing a mouthful of stained but perfectly aligned teeth. 'I am the only person alive who knows all of the traditions of the Melisites. You need me. She needs me.'

Balkis waited in vain for the surgeon to arrive. When Malik came again, she asked him why he hadn't sent for him. Malik said that he had, but that Gudit had locked the doors and Fehmi had gone away.

'You look better,' he commented, gently sweeping a strand of hair from her forehead. 'You must have had a bad reaction to the tattoo.'

Balkis realised then that no one else besides the old priestess and the midwife knew everything the initiation involved.

'I know the tattoo is painful,' Malik continued, 'but look, I have it too.' He turned, pulled down his tunic, and showed her the powerful line of a wing at the top of his shoulder.

'You fool. What about this?' She pulled aside the sheet and spread her legs.

Malik clutched the side of the bed, his knees buckling beneath him. 'Who did this to you?'

'Gudit said that this was the initiation,' she replied through clenched teeth. 'Now I'm ready to be priestess, but my life is over.'

'Oh, my dear God.' He tried to caress Balkis's hair, but she jerked her head away. 'I remember Mother being ill when we were young, but I never thought . . .'

'Stupid,' she wailed. 'Stupid. The only way they can get the priestess to go through with this is not to tell her, to tell no one. That old bitch Gudit has all the power.' She began to cry.

Later that day, her mother had come to see her for the first time since the initiation, the bones of her neck so frail they seemed barely able to hold up her head.

'Mother, how could you let them do this to me?' Balkis had pleaded tearfully.

'Hush, child,' she replied. 'I went through this. So did all the women who were priestesses before us. In exchange, we have power, honour. We alone are allowed to enter the Holy of Holies. To be in the presence of the Proof of God, you have to be pure.'

The ceremony of accession was held in the prayer hall one month later. Three animals were sacrificed on the stone, the blood draining from their throats into a bowl before they were butchered and set to grill for the feast.

The caretaker and the new priestess stood before the iron gate adorned with a weeping angel and led the congregation in prayer.

Balkis turned to face the angel gate.

'Behold Balkis,' Malik intoned. 'Behold the Proof of God, Container of the Uncontainable. Behold the Key to all religions.' He lifted the cape from her shoulders, revealing the wings tattooed on her back.

She heard the congregation gasp and whisper.

He let his own cape fall.

Two winged creatures with their backs to the hushed congregation.

She unlocked the gate, beyond which lay the Holy of Holies, and went inside alone.

25

The back of Elif's head barely moved as she became an instrument of her art, capturing the shapes and colours of Kamil's orchids amid grand grey shadows and the trickle of moisture over the back of the windowpanes. She wouldn't allow him to watch while she painted, but once, when she briefly left the room, Kamil had taken a quick look. He was stunned by the powerful thoughts and feelings these simple lines and fields of colour evoked in him. Sadness, hope amid ruin. Before she returned, he sat back down in his wicker chair on the other side of the winter garden, facing away. He pretended he was reading and watched the reflection of her head in the rain-darkened glass.

After an hour and a half, Yakup signalled to Kamil that a small meal was ready. Elif put her brush down and busied herself with cleaning the trays of watercolour. When she looked up at him, it was as if from a great distance, but by the time they had sat at the table and sampled Karanfil's lamb-stuffed pastries, Elif was chatting gaily. She looked, Kamil thought with pleasure, as if she had finally come home.

Afterwards, they sat on a sofa in a room overlooking the back garden. The rain had turned to mist, fogging the windows. Yakup had lit the wood in the fireplace. Kamil brought several of his watercolour sketches of rare orchids to show Elif. Occasionally he sent a sketch and description of particularly interesting orchidaceae to H. G. Reichenbach, the world's leading authority on orchids, who directed the botanic gardens at Hamburg University. Kamil had never received a response, but hoped through his persistence to interest Reichenbach in the many varieties found only in Ottoman lands.

He held out a sketch of an orchid with yellow-green sepals. 'This is an *Ophrys lutea*. I drew it in a cemetery in Bursa.'

'It's lovely. You have such a delicate touch that I can almost feel the weightlessness of the bloom. They're remarkable flowers.'

Embarrassed by her praise, which he was convinced he didn't deserve, Kamil put his drawings away.

Elif rotated the glass of tea in her hands, warming them. Kamil could sense her appraising him.

'Would you like something more, Elif Hanoum?' He was beginning to worry about the time.

'Please call me Elif. I've stopped calling you pasha.'

Kamil was amused. 'I've never much liked the title myself. It sounds pompous.'

'I've always disdained rank and titles and authority. I've never understood why they're necessary.' Suddenly her voice became serious. 'But I learned about that during the troubles at home.' She twisted around and faced him, tucking her feet under her on the sofa. 'What I learned was that no matter what country you live in in your head, you can't afford to ignore the one on your doorstep. If you do, it will punish you. People who have power are proud and they want tribute. You can pay it in respect or you can pay it in blood. That's your choice.' She stared into the fire. 'It's the people who don't have power and who suddenly get it that you have to watch out for. They never give you a choice.'

Kamil saw tears sliding down her cheeks and wondered again what she had lived through in Macedonia. He handed her a handkerchief. Elif wiped the tears from her face. He put his arm around her as if it were the most natural thing to do, and they sat silently, engrossed by their thoughts. Her shoulders under the jacket felt thin and fragile.

After a while, Elif said, 'That was the first time I was able to cry since ...'

Kamil reached over and pulled his finger across her forehead as he did to Feride when she was sad. 'Even to grieve, you need to feel safe. You're safe now.'

'I didn't tell Feride and Huseyin the whole truth about what happened,' she admitted.

'You don't need to tell anyone anything.'

'I would like to tell you.'

'I would be honoured.'

'My husband wasn't killed by the Christians. He was killed by the Ottoman army as a deserter.'

Kamil wasn't surprised. He had heard that the armies in the provinces were so desperate for men that they were conscripting even boys and old men. It was a fatal symptom of what Huseyin had pointed to the other night, the inevitable decline of Ottoman power. How much longer could a government hold on when it had to force its citizens to abandon their own families in order to fight their neighbours?

'That's nothing to be ashamed of. The conscription is unjust.'

'He was an artist who didn't know the butt end of a gun from the barrel.' She shook her head. 'That's not an excuse.

I had to learn. Sometimes you have to do things that kill you inside. But whatever else I thought about him, he cared about his son.'

She shifted her feet and sat coiled into herself with her arms around her knees.

'He would have done it, but he didn't want to leave us unprotected. Guerrillas had put flags up all over the district, like dogs leaving their mark. There was a little flag stuck into our front gate. I'm sure if I had plucked it out, they would have shot me. But it wasn't just the flags. We heard rumours of terrible things that had happened to Muslim families in the next town. The guerrillas shot the men and then . . .' She grasped her knees tightly. 'Anyway, Dimitri told the Ottoman patrol that came to our door that he wouldn't go, that he had to stay and protect his family. They asked him his name and he told them the truth, that his father was a Slav and his mother a Muslim. The soldier leading the patrol was very young. He didn't even have a moustache. And here was this man telling him no and all the men in his patrol hearing it. So he had to put his foot down. He had to show them he was a man. So he said to Dimitri, "Well, you're not one of us anyway", and just shot him point blank in the chest.' She looked up at Kamil with fathomless eyes. 'And do you know what he did then?' she asked incredulously. 'He pushed Dimitri aside and walked up to me and made this formal bow. I was wearing a charshaf and standing in front of the door. He bowed and said, "My apologies, hanoum. You're safe now." Can you believe it? A polite murderer.'

'Allah protect us from people who mistake cruelty for duty and politeness for compassion. Unfortunately, our administration is full of people like that.'

She didn't seem to hear him. 'I had a gun in my hand

under my charshaf. If my son hadn't been inside, I would have shot that man. My finger was on the trigger. I've never felt such a powerful desire to kill someone. It's remarkable, as if you're standing on top of a mountain and one more breath will bring on Armageddon. You can choose. Destroy or not destroy. It does something to you.'

She sat hunched up, leaning against Kamil's chest.

'Later, when they killed my boy, I was beyond that. To kill someone else or to kill yourself, sometimes there's really no difference.'

'What did you do after your husband died?'

'Oh, he didn't die. Not then. He lost a lot of blood, but not enough to kill him. I went next door to our neighbour, who was a surgeon. He had delivered my son. Dimitri's paintings hung in his house. In the summers, we drank wine together under our grape arbour. His wife was my best friend.'

She stopped speaking, unfolded herself from the sofa and walked over to the fire. She took off her jacket, then took a poker and stabbed angrily at the glowing coals. The faint shadow of her body showed through the cotton shirt and Kamil was shocked to realise how thin she was under all that material.

'Shall I send for fresh tea?' he asked. The day's imperatives had receded. He was caught in the anguish of her reminiscences.

She shook her head and sat down beside him, keeping her eyes on the fire.

'He refused to come. They wouldn't even open their door to me. They were Christians, you see. Even though they saw what had happened, that Dimitri had been shot by Muslims, they wouldn't come out. I pulled Dimitri inside the house and took care of him as best I could, but the wound festered and he died, but much later. He was in great pain.' She held her hands over her ears. 'I'm sure they must have heard him next door. I didn't have the strength to bury him, so I covered him with his paintings, oils mostly, and set them on fire. I didn't want the neighbours to get his paintings, to get anything. But I stole their carriage and two of their best horses.' She grinned, tears running down her face.

Kamil's mind raced with images of Elif, hair cut short and dressed as a man, loaded revolver in hand, bundling her son into her neighbour's carriage and driving away as her house went up in flames. He took her hands in his and said, 'I can't tell you how much I admire you, Elif.'

'I don't deserve any praise. I lost everything. We got as far as Edirne before we were attacked by bandits. I don't even know who they were.' She shrugged. 'Bandits have no religion. I shot two of them, but there were too many. When I woke up, we were lying in the bushes by the side of the road.'

Kamil waited, but when she didn't continue, he offered, '*Bashiniz sagholsun*. What was your son's name?'

Her voice shuddered. 'I can't say it.'

'I understand.'

She let her head rest on his shoulder for a long while, their hands entwined.

'I'm grateful to you, Kamil. I feel you are truly my friend.'

'I'm honoured by your trust.' Kamil felt his response was stilted, but in the emotionally charged atmosphere he didn't know what else to say. 'I'm your servant in all things.'

She sat up suddenly and said, 'How selfish of me to take up your morning like this. Please forgive a woman who's been living outside of time for so long, she's forgotten that other people have duties. I can be such a bully when there's something I want to do. I'm sure Huseyin would claim it's a family trait.' She realised what she had said. 'Oh, I didn't mean that Huseyin is a bully.'

Their eyes met and they laughed. Her face was flushed, her eyes brilliant. Kamil thought she looked like an archangel, both beautiful and frightening. He reached for her hand and pressed it to his mouth.

He wished he had something to offer that would pull her back into the world. He had a sudden thought. 'Did Feride tell you about the woman from Sunken Village?'

'Your half-sister Saba? Yes. She was very excited. Other women might have been jealous or afraid, but not Feride.'

He told Elif he would be right back and left the room. In the hall, he took out his watch and was horrified to discover that it was eleven o'clock.

He returned a few moments later with Malik's letter. He explained who had written it and what had happened. 'We're looking for two things, a reliquary and a lead sleeve that fits inside the reliquary and contains a valuable old document. Malik took the document out and hid it for safety. He wanted me to find the reliquary so he could reunite it with the document and give it back to the sect. But now that he's gone, both are missing.'

'What is this document?'

'People refer to it as the Proof of God, but I'm not sure anyone really knows what it is. The important thing is that a lot of people seem to be after it.' He was about to warn Elif that this might be dangerous, then bit his tongue. 'We looked through Malik's house and didn't find anything, so he must have hidden it somewhere else after the reliquary was stolen. I thought there might be some clues in his letter, but I couldn't find them. Maybe you'll see something I've missed.'

In addition to the story of Saba's birth, Malik had reminded Saba of her duties as priestess.

'They have a priestess?' Elif asked. 'Are they Christians?'

Kamil shook his head no. He didn't want to go into the complications of that now; some things were not his to share.

At the end, Malik had included a prayer:

Hail Mary, Mother of the Word,
Hear those who bear your message,
Container of the Uncontainable,
Grant us your intercession.
Raise your eyes to the slain children,
O Samaritan,
In the dwelling place of the living and the dead.

and a notation: 'Matthew 2:16'.

Kamil hoped that Elif, with her knowledge of art, might see something in the imagery of the prayer.

When Elif had finished reading, she said, 'Malik could have given this directly to his niece. I think he meant it for you too. To help you find the Proof of God in case something happened to him.'

'But why make it so cryptic?'

'He didn't know who'd see it, did he?'

'What do you make of the prayer?'

Elif asked him for a piece of paper and, referring back to the letter, made some notes. She handed it to him.

'Do these words mean anything to you?'

He read:

Mary
Mother of the Word

Message
Container of the Uncontainable
Slain children
Samaritan
Dwelling place
Matthew 2:16

'I think Matthew 2:16 might refer to something in the Bible. Do you have a copy?' she asked.

'I'm afraid I don't. But what about "dwelling place"?' He pointed at the term. 'The Kariye Mosque was once the Church of Chora, which Malik said meant Dwelling-Place of the Uncontainable. So maybe we can assume it's in the mosque. That's a start.' He took the poker and stirred the embers in the fireplace. 'That's where he was killed. I never understood why he left his house in the middle of the night to go to the mosque. Someone must have called him there.'

'I'm sorry.'

He read through the list again. 'Maybe the rest refer to the mosaics.' Kamil told her about the Byzantine images.

'Fascinating. Would it be a burden, I mean, would you consider ... might I accompany you sometime or would I be a hindrance in your work?'

Kamil was taken aback. In his mind, he had already moved on to business and assumed she would go home.

KAMIL AND ELIF sat side by side in a closed carriage. Kamil was glad of her company, but also anxious, not only because she was dressed as a man, but also because he worried she would draw time away from his investigation. He had already lost too much of it to waste more on chivalry, explanations, and playing tour guide. The Old

City was also much more conservative than Beyoglu and the modern suburb of Nishantashou, where Feride lived. Kamil wasn't entirely sure Elif meant her costume to be an impersonation, it just seemed to be the way she had decided to dress. Turkish women wore trousers, but they were very wide and draped with shape-concealing sweaters, vests, robes, and tunics. In the street, even these were covered by a cloak and veil.

Elif had taken off her hat and was looking out the window. He looked at the back of her small, neat head resting against the back of the seat. He wondered whether his feelings for her were appropriate. A woman who had faced the worst that humankind could offer didn't need his protection.

He told the driver to let them out at the Nurosmaniye entrance to the bazaar. He had to stop himself from helping her out of the carriage. She hopped nimbly down on to the cobbled lane. As a precaution, Kamil asked his driver to accompany them a short distance behind.

They walked past the Nurosmaniye Mosque and fountain, then ducked through an enormous gate with iron-studded doors. Inside, a great vaulted street, lit by numerous lamps, burrowed down one side of the small city that was the bazaar. This was the gold market and the reflected light was dazzling.

As Kamil had feared, Elif dawdled at the shop windows, her hat drawn low across her forehead. When shopkeepers came out to ask politely if they could assist her, she walked quickly on without responding, only to be captured by the next display.

Kamil stopped and waited for her to catch up. 'We're going to the Inner Bedestan. That's where they keep the antiques and the rare, precious items. It's a building within a building that is locked up at night, with its own guards.' He could see the bazaar spinning in her eyes. It was too much, he knew. There were over five hundred shops under one roof. He hurried her up and down the connecting streets until they came to another large iron gate that stood open. Inside, the atmosphere was calmer, the shops smaller, the displays less prosaic. Porcelain vases, mirrors with carved silver backs, Roman coins, sturdy old books in leather covers, illuminated Greek manuscripts, Persian and Ottoman miniatures. Elif gravitated to these, fascinated by the brilliant colours and minute details. There were also some oil paintings.

'I don't recognise these,' she whispered, 'but they're in the Impressionist style. They're very good. See that one?' She pointed to one of a woman dressed in white, hand in hand with a child, standing on the side of a grassy hill silhouetted against the sun. They looked like clouds scudding across the landscape.

'I check the shops here regularly for stolen antiquities. This is where they end up if they're sold locally. I'll be back in a little while. Will you be all right?'

She nodded without looking away from the painting.

'The driver is nearby if you need anything and I'll be just around the corner.' He motioned to his driver to keep an eye on her.

Kamil made his regular round of the shopkeepers. They knew the magistrate and why he was there, but they never knew when he would come by. After a while, even the most cautious of them brought their best items out and displayed them, hoping for buyers. Kamil had discovered several important objects here – a fifteenth-century Iznik tile taken from a mosque in Bursa, two icons from a Greek Orthodox church in Albanian Village, and several gold crucifixes. The shopkeepers always claimed they didn't know the objects were stolen and bewailed their lost money when Kamil confiscated them. Only rarely could Kamil work his way through the thicket of middlemen to discover and sometimes even apprehend the actual thief. The bazaar was a closed world whose inhabitants protected each other against outsiders.

'Good day, Serkis,' Kamil greeted the shopkeeper of a tiny store.

'Good day, Magistrate. I hope you are well.' Serkis didn't look pleased to see Kamil.

Kamil accepted a glass of tea. Serkis stood, ceding the padded bench to Kamil. They exchanged ritual greetings and pleasantries. Finally, Serkis said, 'What can I help you with today, Magistrate?'

From where he sat, Kamil could see the contents of the entire shop. The walls were hung with framed illuminated manuscripts and shelves held trays of coins, old jewellery, and silver objects. 'I'd be pleased to see whatever you have that's new.'

'Are you looking for anything in particular?'

Kamil sipped his tea as the most valuable missing antiquities ran through his head, like the diamond-studded chalice and the solid-gold plate still missing from the Fatih Mosque. Instead, he said, 'A silver reliquary.'

'Nothing like that has come to me.' Serkis's face was a mask.

Kamil reflected that the merchant had had a lifetime of experience in hiding his emotions. He waited.

'Perhaps I can interest you in something else? As a small token of my appreciation.' The merchant pulled out a tray of silver jewellery and placed it on the table by Kamil's elbow. Kamil's eye was drawn to an intricate and unusual pin.

'What kind of design is this?' he asked the merchant.

'I believe it's Celtic. Excellent choice, Magistrate. I'll wrap it for you.'

Kamil felt sure it was Malik's and a great sadness descended on him, as if it were his friend's spirit trapped on this profane tray.

'Where did you get it?' He dreaded the answer.

Alerted by Kamil's tone, Serkis's hands stopped their practised dance of laying out paper. 'I don't know where it came from. I bought it two days ago as part of a job lot from another dealer.'

'What else was in the lot?'

'Some manuscripts. Nicely illuminated. I've sold those already. There are collectors just waiting for things like that to come on the market.' He gestured with his hand. 'I send a message and a few hours later, they're sold.'

'What else?'

Serkis ducked behind the curtain at the back of the shop and returned a moment later with a ledger. He leafed through it until he found the right page. 'Here it is. Three more pins, a silver-backed hairbrush and matching mirror, and a cigarette holder.'

'Let me see them.'

Serkis bent over and pulled open some drawers. Before long all the objects were arrayed on a piece of green baize. Kamil didn't recognise any of them.

'Is the dealer here in the bazaar?'

'Gomidian on the Street of Mirrormakers.'

'Please invite him here.' It was a command.

Serkis sent an apprentice the few steps to Gomidian's

shop. Almost immediately, a large head, topped by a fez, pushed through Serkis's door.

'What's new, what's not?' Gomidian asked wittily.

Kamil introduced himself and saw Gomidian's smile disappear. 'I'd like to know who sold you this pin.'

The three men were crammed into the store, Kamil sitting on the only seat.

'I don't remember.' Gomidian's hair was thick with pomade, and like all of the shopkeepers, he wore trousers and a jacket. He had a thick moustache and a gnarled nose that looked as though it had been broken several times.

Kamil had a sudden urge to break it once more. He crossed his legs and leaned back. 'I have plenty of time.'

The men began to sweat. Serkis told the dealer in an agitated whisper, 'What does it matter? This is just chicken crap.'

'I have to protect my sources,' Gomidian exclaimed.

Serkis raised his hands in acquiescence. 'Of course.'

When Gomidian turned and headed for the door, Kamil rose and blocked his way.

Serkis fluttered about nervously, worried about damage to his shop.

Gomidian shrugged. 'A crazy blood from Charshamba named Amir or Amid or something. A virgin. Didn't have a clue how to negotiate a deal, but loud as a rooster.'

Kamil's disquiet deepened. He asked for a description, just to be sure, then dropped the pin into his pocket. He thanked the men and left the shop. They looked visibly relieved.

Two streets over, he saw Elif, hands in her pockets, head poised over a display of enamelled French clocks.

'Shall we go?' he asked distractedly. Seeing the surprise

on her face, he felt guilty at rushing her and was relieved when she smiled and nodded.

They returned to the carriage.

Kamil was anxious to tell Omar about the pin and all that it implied, and he wanted to search the Kariye without Elif to distract him.

'Something's come up,' he told Elif. 'I'll get out at the Fatih police station, but the carriage is yours for the day.' He leaned out and gave the driver instructions.

'Are you still going to the Kariye Mosque?'

'Later this afternoon.'

As the carriage jerked into motion, he reached down and took out a parcel the driver had stowed there.

He handed it to her. 'A gift for your new life.'

'May I open it now?'

'As you like.'

She drew out the oil painting of the woman and child in the sun.

'May you be happy,' he said softly.

She leaned over and kissed him on the cheek.

26

Balkis drained the last of the diluted powder from the glass and put it aside. It was her third potion in two hours. She knew it was more than the surgeon allowed her, but the pain was relentless. She knelt heavily on the divan, her body aching with the effort, and reached up to take the monstrance from the shelf. She ran her fingers over the sharp gold tines, letting them linger on the tine black with her mother's blood. The heart of the monstrance was empty. Balkis pushed her finger into the circular opening where the Christians had suspended the wafer they believed to be the body of Jesus, the man they considered God. This too, she mused, was a Container of the Uncontainable. This too, like the Melisites, like her own body, was based on a lie.

Her body had been consecrated to an empty space that had slowly devoured her. There was the continuing pain that made even her daily ablutions a trial: the pus, the smell, the leaking urine. And more recently, sharp pains in her joints, her abdomen swelling up like a summer gourd. Gudit treated her with herbs, but it was Constantine Courtidis, with his Balat Balm and knowledge of western powders and medicines, who gave her the will to go on. She was too ashamed to reveal herself to the young surgeon, but he treated her nonetheless. She wondered whether Courtidis could take over from Gudit. Perhaps the Melisites should modernise, as Amida wished. In the modern world, no one had secrets anymore. What difference did it make?

She gasped and doubled over as the terrible pain burrowed through her. She lay groaning in a foetal position until the worst had passed, then slowly loosened her cramped limbs. She felt light-headed and was bathed in sweat, too weak to sit up. A barrage of thoughts pummelled her, drawing in their wake anger, fear, regret. Feelings she thought she had harnessed and defused over the years returned to run roughshod over her accomplishments. Her pain had cut them loose.

She had made the best of what fate had begrudged her. When she became priestess, she had learned the smuggling business. She was a good leader, discreet, firm, and fair. They had well-trained workers and loyal customers. Her one accomplishment was that under her leadership, the struggling sect had become secure and relatively well off. She had done it on her own, with no help from Malik. Now even that was being undermined by people like Kubalou, and by Amida, who in his foolish arrogance and ambition had brought these thugs and, as a consequence, the police into their community. Saba had told her that after she had refused to make a deal with Kubalou's representative, Amida had taken him to meet the village men and they had brokered their own deal. The idea that Kubalou would send someone else in his place to negotiate without letting them know was galling. Whenever she thought of the charade of her discussion with the flame-haired impostor, she felt shame. She had been treated disrespectfully and duped, but her son's perfidy was worst of all.

Her sweet, wide-eyed son whom she had sent to the monastery when he was twelve had come back a hard, compassionless stranger. She tried to remember the milky scent of his little body, slippery like a baby dolphin in the bath. She had licked his delicate chest, tickled him to make him giggle. 'I'll be your bride, won't I, little lion?' The desire of mothers everywhere. Those years he was gone, she had grieved as if he were dead. Now Amida seemed to despise her. She had even caught herself wondering whether he had killed Malik. Her son had announced his readiness to sell off the one thing that would have given her life meaning, if it truly existed. Without the Proof of God, what was she guarding? Malik claimed to have found it after all these centuries. Was Amida right? Was it nothing more than an empty box? Malik said there were papers inside. What miracle could be contained in a pile of papers? If truth was the enemy of faith, she had neither.

She turned on to her back and stared at the ceiling, her body heavy and listless, afloat on a sea of pain. She had to remind herself to breathe. What was there left to live for?

Her daughter had become a woman with religious ice in her veins, someone who would make a good priestess, who wouldn't snap like a weak branch. Yet the girl had fallen apart after learning that Kamil was her brother. Balkis blamed herself for not telling her daughter sooner, and she blamed Malik for bringing them together. How little she had understood her children.

Tears trickled from the corners of her eyes and down her neck. She had always wanted too much. Her own mother had tried to warn her. She had said love is a fig full of worms. When you pull it open, you see delicious flesh studded with seeds. You sink your teeth into the fragrant fruit and when you look again, the seeds are alive with motion. There wasn't just one snake in the Garden of Eden.

The emptiness inside her seemed truly uncontainable. She lay there, her eyes drawn to the opening in the middle of the monstrance that rested beside her like an uncaring mate. She heaved herself on to one elbow and pulled the monstrance towards her. She pressed the tip of her finger to the sharp tine until it pricked her skin. A tiny bubble of blood welled up. She pushed back her left sleeve, exposing the tender flesh of her wrist. She imagined the pain would be terrible, but purifying. What she didn't know was whether she'd have the strength.

27

Omar turned the pin over in his hand. 'This is Malik's. If Amida had it, then he must have taken it from Malik the night he died. What a pimp. First he steals from his own uncle, then he kills him.'

They sat under the scarlet leaves of the grape arbour in Omar's garden, eating a lunch that Mimoza had left for them before going to take some food to a sick neighbour.

'Why would he kill Malik? I mean, I can understand his motive for stealing the reliquary. Then when he or his buyer saw it was empty, it makes sense he'd go back for the contents. But kill his uncle?' He pushed his plate away. 'It doesn't make sense.'

'I agree. But here's the evidence that he was there that night.' Omar held out the pin. 'His associates from Charshamba are more likely. But why would they kill the old man? For his books?' He snorted in derision. 'There was nothing in it for them. Those thugs won't move unless they're paid. There's something that we're missing. Well, we'll pick him up tonight and then we can ask him, together with that Frankish bastard he's dealing with.'

'Avi's out following him again? You think the boy will be all right?'

'He's a talented little kid. Heart like a lion. The wife has taken quite a liking to him.' He frowned. 'Are you going over to the Kariye to look for this Proof thing?'

Kamil nodded. He should have been pleased at finding

Malik's killer, but the whole thing felt wrong. He couldn't picture Amida murdering Malik or going along with others torturing him. Yet he had been there that night.

Omar put his spoon down and leaned back, replete. 'I have some business to see to this afternoon, a burglary. The house right behind the police station, if you can imagine. Brazen bastards. They won't be smirking anymore when I'm done with them.'

He lit a cigarette and offered one to Kamil, who declined.

'The sooner I get over to the mosque, the more light I'll have.' Kamil looked up at the ashen sky. 'It gets dark so early now.'

'October is the gateway to hell, we used to say in the army.'

'Why is that?'

'It starts to get cold and dark, and before you know it, you're frozen in a ditch hoping someone will pee on your hands to thaw them.'

Seeing that Omar looked serious, Kamil choked back a laugh. What did he know about the brutalities and absurdities of war?

Omar accompanied him to the gate. 'If you need me, send a message to the station. You know how to get to the Kariye from here?'

Kamil smiled and pointed up the hill where the plump domes of a little mosque were visible above the roof lines. 'Not far.'

'It's further than it looks. Sure you don't want to borrow my horse?'

'I need to stretch my legs. If I keep going uphill, I'll get there eventually.'

'Lots of hills around here,' Omar warned. 'But ask

anyone and they'll point you in the wrong direction.' He chuckled.

As soon as Kamil entered the narrow lanes, the mosque disappeared, as did the hill, and he became lost in the chaotic, ruin-choked streets. Every shopkeeper gave him different directions, but eventually he caught sight of the domes again and oriented himself. Before long, he rounded a fountain and entered the little square before the mosque. The door of the mosque was locked, so he knocked at the imam's house.

'He's not here,' a man shouted helpfully from a window of the neighbouring house.

'Where can I find him?'

The man shrugged and ducked back inside.

Kamil walked through the square under the gaze of a group of men who were playing backgammon in the shade of a plane tree. Their calls and the slapping of wooden pieces on the board punctuated the quiet afternoon. 'Shesh-besh!' 'Penj-u se.' 'Du-shesh!'

At the back of the mosque he found Malik's classroom. The door was shut but unlocked. Inside, Kamil stood for a moment, surveying the room. It hadn't been touched since he was last here with Malik. At that moment, Kamil felt the loss of his friend more deeply than before, when his emotions had been flayed by anger. Now he registered every nuance of the man who was gone, his intelligence and gentleness, his devotion to his community, his family, even to a poor street boy like Courtidis. Kamil wished he could pray for Malik's soul to whatever God was listening. He tried, but his mind wouldn't hold still. Look for his killer, he told himself. That's all you can do.

Kamil opened the cabinet. The key to the mosque lay

on the top shelf. He was surprised that the imam still left it here, when it was likely that Malik's murderer also knew its location.

Lips pressed in a thin line, Kamil picked up the heavy iron key and a lamp and made his way around the back, through the overgrown garden, to the front door. The men across the square watched him unlock the door and enter, but didn't interrupt their game.

Kamil locked the door behind him and lit the lamp.

ELIF WAS SWEATING under her hat but didn't dare take it off. Some children had gathered behind her, and were chattering and pointing at her easel. Two men approached and greeted her. She answered in French. Better that they think her a Frankish man, thin, blond, odd like all Franks, and untouchable. But she was getting nervous and this made it hard to concentrate on her drawing.

She had captured the four domes of the cheerful little mosque, its red-tiled roof, and the fat tower of its minaret with a narrow balcony around the top from which the imam called the faithful to prayer. The minaret was topped by an unusual ornament shaped like a drop of water splashing on to its roof. Behind the mosque, the city fell away in a tangle of red roofs and trees. She had traced the outlines quickly in pencil, then charcoal, and finally pastels, one study after another, allowing the shapes and colours to dominate her senses until she felt as though the landscape were painting itself.

The carriage was parked in the lane below, out of sight from her perch on the hillside. She had told the driver he could have lunch and drink tea at one of the cafés in the square, but he said he preferred to wait. She presumed he didn't want to have to answer the locals' questions. But there was no escaping them, she thought, glancing with exasperation at her growing audience. She would have to leave soon.

Just then, she saw someone come round the mosque from the back and walk towards the door. He turned and for a brief moment regarded the square. She recognised Kamil. Heart racing, she packed up her things and began to run down the hill.

KAMIL PULLED OUT a piece of paper from his pocket and unfolded it. He glanced down the list, written in Elif's sprawling script:

Mary
Mother of the Word
Message
Container of the Uncontainable
Slain children
Samaritan
Dwelling place
Matthew 2:16

He raised the lamp and, as before, stood transfixed under the lush garden of figures and scenes in gold and brilliant colour that crowded around him. He found the image of Theodore Metochites and stood before him for a few moments, wondering what kind of man he had been. He knew much more about him now. He wondered what it had been like for Malik to come face to face every day with his ancestor. Of all the caretakers before him, only Malik had worked out the location of the Proof of God. He needed Malik's help now to find it again. The thought resurfaced that perhaps Saba had already worked out where it was and had taken it. Or was she waiting for Kamil to find it and bring it to her? She had had Malik's letter only for the briefest time and had been distraught when she had given it to Kamil to prove the truth of her mother's story. No, he didn't think she had found the Proof.

He bade farewell to Theodore and returned to the outer hall. He planned to begin in the south bay and work his way systematically through all the mosaic panels. The figures were so lifelike, they appeared to move. Nonsense, of course, but he admired the workmanship that made such an illusion possible. He thought he could feel Malik's presence and he wished he could ask him to explain the images. Kamil realised he had little idea about Christian stories and iconography. Well, he would have to look for a word, a message, a container, and, improbably, slain children.

Just then, he heard a booming noise. Someone was knocking on the door. Annoyed at being interrupted, Kamil went to the door and pulled it open.

A slight figure in a broad hat slipped inside with a gaggle of children close behind. 'Close it.'

'Elif!' he exclaimed. 'How did you get here?' He tried to sound pleased.

Elif noted his tone and looked puzzled. 'You said you'd be here this afternoon, so I waited for you. I was up on the hill sketching the mosque. Weren't we planning to decipher the mosaics today?'

'Yes, of course.' Obviously he hadn't made it clear he wanted to do this alone.

She took a few steps forward into the corridor and looked around. 'Oh,' was all she could say in amazement.

She took her hat off and set her box of drawing materials on a ledge.

Kamil locked the door again. He found a second lamp, lit it and gave it to Elif. 'There are windows, but the corridors with the mosaics are dark. This is the outer narthex.' It was as if he could hear Malik's voice reciting in his ear. 'And that's the inner narthex.' He pointed at the inner corridor that gave on to the nave.

'These are wonderful,' she exclaimed breathlessly, walking up and down, shining the lamp on the walls.

'What do you know about Christian saints?'

She tore her eyes away from the mosaics. 'Quite a bit. My father-in-law was a devout Christian. He took my son to church and read him stories about the lives of the saints.'

He handed her the list of terms.

She scanned it, then looked around and said, 'Mary is everywhere. The whole church seems to be dedicated to her.' She pointed to the next term. 'Mother of the Word. That's Mary too. Maybe it means the words are in the church dedicated to her. Same with the next term, Message. But I don't understand Container of the Uncontainable.'

What had Malik shown him? Kamil tried to remember. They had walked through the inner and outer corridors, but Kamil hadn't paid much attention to the location of the mosaics Malik had spoken about. He remembered something about a clay container, an amphora, but he didn't see it.

'Let's start over here and work our way through,' he suggested, leading Elif to the north end of the corridor behind the door.

They stood in the first bay surrounded by panels and inscriptions.

'I wish I could read Greek.' She squinted at the panels. 'I think I recognise some of these. This looks like the story of Jesus' birth. That bearded man might be Joseph, Jesus' father. There's Mary pregnant.'

They followed the panels along the corridor. 'Here's a familiar scene.' She pointed.

'The birth of Jesus,' Kamil said, regarding the shepherds and, in the next panel, three richly clothed men, 'and the wise men from the east.'

Elif pointed up at the vaulted domes, 'We're not looking at the pictures in the domes. Look. There's John the Baptist. There's so much here. If we look at everything, we'll never finish.'

Kamil had no answer. They had reached the middle of the outer narthex by the front door.

Elif strained her head backward, exposing the arch of her throat. The mosaics in the vault were badly damaged, but a dazzling image of Christ guarded the entrance to the inner narthex.

'Come with me.' Kamil took her hand. 'I want to introduce you to someone.'

He drew her through the opening and they stopped beneath the lunette over the entrance to the marbled nave.

'This is Theodore Metochites.'

'What an extraordinary hat.'

Kamil told her what he could remember of the man.

'So he's responsible for all of this magnificent art!' she exclaimed. 'Bravo. That explains the hat too. An artist.'

Kamil thought she looked happy – vital and less vulnerable. He wondered why that should disappoint him. Was it that she needed him less?

Since they were in the inner narthex, they continued along that corridor, Elif reading stories into the images wherever she could. She was puzzled by some of the panels until she exclaimed, 'It's the life of Mary. Look, there she's born and there she's with her parents. An angel is feeding her.' She stopped before a panel that showed a rod sprouting jewel-like leaves.

'I know this story. I've always found it a bit risqué.'

'Risqué? In a church?'

'When it was time for Mary to be married, the high priest called all the widowers together and placed their rods on the altar.'

Kamil began to laugh.

'Then he prayed for a sign. Joseph's rod began to sprout green leaves, so the priest gave Mary to him.'

'Well,' Kamil said. 'I won't repeat that story to the devout gentlemen who pray here every Friday.'

They smiled at each other in the gloom. Kamil looked through the door into the nave and noticed the light failing through the windows. Elif followed his glance and found herself drawn into the marble-panelled room.

'Another time,' Kamil warned her. 'We need to hurry. The imam will be here before long for the evening call to prayer. Let's do this systematically. We're looking for very particular images.'

They went back to the outer corridor and began at the door, moving south. They passed an enormous mosaic of Mary and Jesus, whose eyes seemed to follow them. Kamil looked for the image of the clay urn that Malik had shown him. Somehow he thought it was important, perhaps as the Container on their list, but he couldn't see it. They were passing the panels quickly now, scanning them and moving on. He could see the stairway to the minaret. They must be near the spot where Malik died.

Suddenly he saw Elif in the final bay before the minaret, standing stiffly and looking up at something, her face aghast. He hurried to her side and followed her line of sight. It was an image of King Herod on a throne instructing his soldiers. To his left, a soldier held a baby aloft by its feet and thrust a knife through it. Behind him a black portal like a tomb opened into the rock. The baby's mother sat bereft on the ground, hands aloft, her head turned away in despair.

'The slain children,' Kamil exclaimed.

'The massacre of the innocents,' she said softly, her eyes riveted to the scene.

Kamil put his hands on her shoulders and turned her away. 'We're getting close.' He looked around. 'Do you see a Samaritan or a container of some kind?'

They raised their lamps and scanned the wall panels and domes. In the north-west corner of the bay was a damaged mosaic of Christ speaking with a woman at a well.

Elif looked at the image for a few moments, then said, 'I've always assumed the story of the Good Samaritan was about a man, but I remember another story about Christ meeting a Samaritan woman at a well. He told her she had many husbands. That's why I remember it. I noticed that the images in here all seem balanced. Wherever there's a man, there's also a woman.'

'So if there's a male Samaritan, there would be a female Samaritan?'

'I'm just guessing.'

'In the interest of balance, did the male Samaritan have many wives?'

'Don't be daft.'

Kamil squinted at the mosaic. There was no image of a container, clay or otherwise.

Below the dome, the walls bowed inward and parts were whitewashed. He remembered Malik telling him that the walls here had to be very thick to bear the weight of the church tower and now the minaret.

'Find a chair or a ladder,' he called out suddenly.

They hurried through the rooms until Kamil came back dragging a ladder he had found in a storeroom. It was spattered with white paint. He leaned it against the wall under the Samaritan woman and climbed until he came to the corner of the wall where it began to bow inward. 'Hold up the lamp.'

He felt along the wall, then rapped with his knuckles until he found what he was looking for. He pulled his knife from his boot and began to chip away at the plaster. It was fresh, so it came off easily. There was a pounding at the door. Elif looked around nervously.

He ignored the noise and concentrated on his task. Beneath the plaster, he exposed a hollow clay ring. Weep-holes, he remembered they were called. Clay jars embedded in the walls to wick off moisture. The pounding became louder and he could hear the voices of several men. He reached into the hole but felt only debris. Something scurried over his hand. He thrust it in deeper.

'Hurry,' Elif whispered, clutching the base of the ladder.

He was surprised by the depth of the jar. Finally, he felt something smooth and cold beneath his fingertips. Water had beaded on it and it was slippery and heavy. He pulled it out slowly. It was a slim lead box two hands' breadth long. He thrust it inside his jacket, slipped the knife back into his boot, and with one leap was on the floor. He pushed the ladder through the neighbouring bay into the storage room. Elif put out the lamps and slapped her hat on her head. She took up her painting box and they stood, panting, before the door. From the other side, they could hear raised voices.

'Well, there's no one in there now. I did not lose the key. Of course I know where it's kept. Do you think I'm senile?'

Kamil whispered, 'Wait.'

After a few moments, the voices stopped. Kamil imagined the imam walking behind the mosque to the classroom and rummaging through the cabinet, looking for the key. The men in the square would accompany him to prolong the excitement of their imam being locked out of his own mosque.

Kamil turned the key, pushed open the door, and peered out. As he had suspected, the square was empty, the backgammon boards abandoned. He locked the door behind them and dropped the key in the weeds beside the entrance where someone could easily find it. Keeping to the edge of the square, they slipped behind the fountain and down a narrow side street.

A man fell in step behind them.

'The carriage is behind the hill,' Elif said, her voice shaking. Her paint box was clutched under her arm.

Kamil's heart was beating hard. He felt exhilarated and lengthened his stride up the steep hill. He had the Proof of God in his jacket. He felt it move against his chest like a second heart.

He stopped and turned around. 'Come, let me carry that box.'

Elif was gone.

Kamil stopped short. 'Elif? Elif?'

He retraced his steps to the fountain and looked around

the corner into the square. The men had returned to their backgammon boards. The imam stood by the door looking puzzled. A boy tugged at the imam's sleeve, pointing down at the ground.

Kamil turned and surveyed the lane. The houses barely held together. They listed into the street and there were large gaps in the walls where boards had rotted away. Rusty stovepipes twisted from their sides and roofs. Clean sheets flapped from a line between facing windows, looking as though their weight alone could pull the houses in on themselves. All the doors were shut tight. No women sat knitting on the stoops here. The only sign of life was a scarred tomcat lying in a patch of sun.

The ground was still damp from the night's rain and Kamil made out what he thought were Elif's footprints, those of a very small man's shoes. He followed them. They disappeared suddenly, as if she had been plucked from the ground. Larger footprints overlaid hers, then led in the direction of a brick structure.

Kamil thought it might be an ayazma, a small chapel the Byzantines built around a sacred spring. There were many in this part of the city, and some were still in use. Kamil ducked inside. Areas of painted plaster were visible inside its partially collapsed brick dome. He could make out images of an angel and the bearded head of a man, his eyes scratched out, perhaps by Muslims who took the injunction against representing the human form seriously, or more likely by bored local youths eager to prove their manhood through vandalism. Down several stairs, he came to a stone well.

He touched a brown substance on one of the stones. Fresh mud. Kamil peered into the well. It looked deep. Something was caught on a protrusion part of the way down. He hung precariously over the edge, reached down and pulled out Elif's hat.

The image of Elif falling into the black pit below gave his actions the urgency of desperation. He flung his feet over the edge and lowered himself slowly, propping himself up with his arms, feeling with his feet. The stones were uneven and some had fallen in, so he found ready platforms. When he felt stable ground beneath both feet, he tested it, then crouched down to see, bracing himself against the stones.

He stood on a small ledge. Beneath him, he could sense rather than see the well open up. If someone had snatched Elif, they would surely have had a reason and wouldn't have simply flung her down the well. He remembered that ayazmas were often connected to underground cisterns.

It was dark in the well, so he squatted on the ledge and felt around with his hands. Before long, he discovered an opening just wide enough to crawl through.

He felt his way along with his hands. On the other side of the entrance, a thin object rolled under his palm. He picked it up. One end was soft. A paint brush, still damp. He rejoiced. Elif was alive and she was leaving a trail for him to follow.

After a while, the tunnel became higher, so he could walk upright. Fresh air circulated from somewhere, but it was pitch black. Kamil could see nothing at all, not even his hand before his eyes. His pupils created sparks and tiny spots of light that he knew weren't really there. He took deep breaths to still the panic rising in him. Keeping one hand on the damp stone wall, he slid his feet forward, testing for holes in the floor. The tunnel seemed to be intact. It led downward. He flinched as a rat fell on to his shoulder, then leapt off.

When he bumped into a sharp protrusion, scraping his nose, he stopped and reached both hands ahead of him. They met a wedge of stone directly in front of his face. He listened for a few moments, the blackness pressing in on his eyes like weights, but heard only a distant drip of water and the scurrying of rats. Small sounds seemed to carry from great distances.

Guiding himself with his hands, he knelt and began to systematically test the shape of the walls. The tunnel divided here, he decided. He crawled in one direction for a few moments to gain a sense of things, then backed up and tried the other tunnel.

A sharp object pressed into his knee. He picked it up and recognised from its shape the small wood-handled paint spatula he had seen in Elif's kit. He was relieved that Elif had kept her head, although it didn't surprise him. He felt around, but there was nothing else. He stood and, hands stretched before him, strode as rapidly as he could through the darkness into the tunnel she had marked. He guessed that whoever had taken Elif knew this tunnel and had used it before, so he doubted there were any collapsed areas.

There was a glow ahead, so faint that Kamil thought his eyes had invented it. As he approached, he heard voices. They were distorted, so he couldn't understand what they were saying, but he recognised Elif's voice. The other was a man's. Kamil slipped the knife from his boot.

He crept closer, keeping his eyes on the light, knife balanced lightly in his hand. His boots made no sound.

Something caught at his jacket. He swung around, knife raised, alert to the slightest motion. He heard scurrying, then a faint whisper.

'It's me. Avi.'

He reached down and found the boy's close-cropped head. He leaned close to Avi's ear and whispered, 'Don't speak. There's an echo.'

If Avi was here, Kamil guessed the man ahead must be Amida. But what did he want with Elif? How could he even know her? He had misjudged the young man, Kamil thought with exasperation. First Malik's pin and now this.

As he approached, the light gained brightness. He could see Avi beside him now, and gestured that the boy should stay back. Avi pressed himself against a wall.

Kamil could hear Elif and Amida more clearly. They were arguing.

'What do you want with this box? It contains drawings and my pens,' Elif said in a hard voice. Kamil realised that she was still keeping up her guise of being a man.

'Of course. And you're Rembrandt.'

'Ah, an art lover,' she responded lightly. 'Here. See for yourself. You dragged me into this hole for nothing.'

Kamil heard a crash, the sound of a wooden box splintering. He peered around the corner. Elif and Amida faced each other in a room lit by an oil lamp on the ground by Amida's feet.

'Where is it?' Amida asked. He looked enormous next to Elif.

Kamil pulled his head back. He didn't want to be seen until he had decided on a course of action. Elif seemed to be in no immediate danger and she didn't appear frightened. If he listened for a few moments, he might get more information.

'Where is what?' Elif asked.

'Don't play dumb. I know you have it. I saw you duck out of the mosque and drop the key. You think I'm as dumb as that imam? I know you've found it. It was written on your faces.'

'What is it you think we've found?'

Amida let out an expletive. 'You have the Proof of God. Kamil told me he knew where it was.'

'Well, I don't have it, as you can see.'

'If you don't, then he has it.'

'Why don't you ask him?'

'I plan to. I'm sure he's wandering the streets right now looking for his friend. What are you, English?'

'French.'

He heard the sound of a struggle.

'Look at that. You're a woman.' Amida laughed. 'What a scoundrel that Kamil is. And he makes himself out to be a holy man. I'm sure he'll trade the Proof for you. You do make a good boy,' he added admiringly.

Kamil put his head around the corner again. He saw Elif kneeling before Amida, who had grasped the back of her neck with one hand. In the other, he held a knife. Kamil reckoned the distance and decided Amida would be able to use the knife before Kamil could reach him. He edged forward and saw Amida let go of Elif and fumble at his trousers. Then, Elif, still on her knees, jabbed something into Amida's groin.

'You bitch,' he howled and raised his arm to strike her. The knife glinted in his hand.

Kamil leapt into the chamber and grabbed Amida's arm. They struggled, but Kamil managed to pull back Amida's thumb so hard he had to release his knife. Elif immediately picked it up. Kamil noticed she brandished it blade-down, like a street fighter. Her face was grim, somehow inhuman, and Kamil half expected her to thrust the knife into

Amida's chest while he held him. Instead, she stepped back into the shadows.

Amida bellowed and twisted in Kamil's arms. Kamil looked down and saw that the front of Amida's trousers was stained with blood. He let go of one of the young man's arms. Amida reached down and plucked out of his crotch a small knife of the kind used for sharpening pencils. Before Kamil could grab his arm again, Amida had thrust the pencil knife into Kamil's chest. Kamil shouted and let go.

Elif stood frozen against the wall, Amida's large knife still poised in her hand.

Amida grabbed the lamp and ran into the tunnel, with Kamil following right behind.

There was a crash and the light went out. Kamil heard scuffling, then someone running. There was a loud rattle, which sounded like heavy chains, and a crash of metal against stone.

'Elif, Avi,' Kamil called out into the darkness.

'I'm sorry, bey.' Avi was crying. 'I tried to stop him. I didn't think about the lamp.'

'Come over here, Avi. Follow my voice.'

'I'm here.' It was Elif's voice, her hand on his arm. 'Avi? Come, hold my hand.'

Kamil bent and felt around for the lamp, but couldn't get it to light. The fumes of spilled oil filled the air.

'We can find our way out,' Kamil said more calmly than he felt. He wondered what the noise had been. Perhaps a trap. His hand found the place over his heart where Amida had stabbed him. There was a hole in the fabric of his jacket, through which he could feel a deep nick in the lead case that had been in his jacket pocket. 'Let's hold on to each other.'

He stepped forward carefully, Avi's hand tugging at his jacket, Elif to the rear. After a while, Kamil felt a difference in the direction of the air and thought they must be approaching the fork in the tunnel. Abruptly, he walked into a set of iron bars. He ran his hands along them. They felt as thick as a child's wrist and seemed to reach from floor to ceiling.

'What is it?' Elif whispered.

'The bastard has shut us in. It's a gate. Avi, can you squeeze through?'

Avi pushed through his leg and arm, but his head and chest wouldn't fit.

'If we can't go forward, we go back,' Kamil announced.

'That room had a lot of shadowy corners,' Elif said. 'I was looking for escape routes, but it was too dark to see properly.'

Kamil admired her calm. He wondered, though, about the glimpse of violence he had seen earlier, a darkness he could only guess at.

They turned and felt their way along the wall until they encountered an opening. The smell of oil was stronger here. They entered the room where Amida had held Elif. She put her hands flat against the wall.

'We can start here and work our way around.'

'There's a slight breeze. Maybe it's coming from above ground. Let me see if I can trace it. Stay where you are.' Kamil put his hands out in front of him and took five steps directly into the darkness. He stood for a few moments, turning his face slightly, trying to catch a current of moving air, but he was sweating and could discern nothing. He reached inside his jacket, pulled out the lead case, and stuck it into the waistband of his trousers. Then he took off his jacket and shirt, placed them on the ground by his feet and stood again quietly, eyes closed, this time letting his body listen to the atmosphere. The air felt good against his naked chest. He turned slowly in a circle. Like a dervish, he thought, communing with the divine harmony.

It was barely noticeable, a fraction of a change in temperature against his skin, but the air was slightly cooler, the force of it infinitesimally stronger from one direction. He walked slowly towards the flow of air until it was right above him.

'It's over here. Come towards my voice.'

'Keep talking,' Elif said from somewhere to his right.

Kamil began to sing an Italian aria he had heard performed several times in a small establishment in Galata. He sang it badly and loudly.

By the time Elif and Avi arrived beside him, they were laughing.

Elif's fingers settled on Kamil's chest, grazing his nipple. Startled, Kamil stepped back and the hand withdrew.

'I'm so sorry,' Elif said in a thick voice, her breath fluttering on his chest.

'Don't be.'

He felt her step away from him, but imagined he could still hear her breathing.

'You're right,' she said, her voice coming from a few steps away. 'The air does seem to move more here. Where is it coming from?'

'I'll look,' Avi offered.

They could hear him scrabbling about, his feet bumping up against stone, scraping noises, then clambering. A falling brick landed with a soft chalky explosion.

'Be careful,' Kamil called out.

Suddenly, there was a shower of bricks. They jumped back and both called out Avi's name.

'I'm up here. I'm in a chimney, I think.'

Most likely it was an air shaft. 'How did you get up there?'

'There's a pile of bricks on the ground. They must have fallen out of the chimney. I was following the air and it came from up here somewhere, so I climbed up the bricks.'

'Does the chimney have stairs?' Elif asked, still puzzled.

'No, but there are a lot of gaps on one side where the bricks have fallen out. You can put your feet in them and hold on.'

'How wide is it?' Kamil asked, already visualising their escape. 'Can we fit through?'

'Sure, bey. Want me to climb up first and see where it goes?'

'Yes, but be careful.'

They listened as the scuffing and tapping sounds of his climb became fainter, then disappeared altogether. They settled themselves on the floor to wait. Kamil wished he had his shirt and jacket, but didn't want to leave Elif alone while he searched for them.

'Do you have the Proof of God?' she asked.

'Right here.' He pulled it from his waistband and patted it with his fingers like a dull, flat drum.

'I wonder who built this tunnel. And imagine that iron gate!' she exclaimed. 'They must have had a lot of enemies to go to all that trouble.'

After a few minutes, Kamil called Avi's name, but received no response. 'I hope that's good news.' Kamil was more anxious than he let on.

He searched the darkness for Elif's hand. He was chilled to the bone. Her hand was cold too and he rubbed it between his.

After a while, they heard scratching noises; Avi was coming back. They jumped to their feet.

'It goes outside,' Avi's voice announced happily. 'There's a small tunnel that crosses the chimney halfway up. We can crawl through there.'

'Wonderful,' Kamil exclaimed. 'Well done.'

Kamil consulted with Elif. 'I'm going to lift Elif up, Avi,' he called. 'Can you guide her so she has something to hold on to?'

'Sure, bey. Don't worry, Elif Hanoum. Nothing will happen to you.'

'I feel safe in your hands, Avi.'

Kamil cleared a space to stand in the middle of the pile of bricks. He wrapped his arms around Elif's legs and lifted her.

'Stop,' she called out. 'I have to find the opening first or you'll break my neck.' She was as light as a child.

She felt around the ceiling with her hands. 'Avi, say something so I can find you.'

Avi began to sing a lullaby. 'Dandini dandini dastana. The cows are loose in the vegetable garden.'

'To the right,' she directed Kamil. 'Back a little.'

Kamil pushed bricks aside with his feet and moved sideways.

Avi kept singing. 'O gardener, drive them away, so they don't eat the cabbage.'

'Here it is. I found it.' Kamil could hear the tears in her voice. 'Lift me up now.'

He put his hand under her foot and hoisted her above his head. She bounced twice in his hands, then was gone. He could hear her breath labouring as she pulled herself up through the shaft.

'I'm in.' Her voice sounded distant. 'How will you get up? I can't reach down that far.'

Kamil had already started stacking bricks. 'I'm making a platform.' The haphazard edifice Avi had clambered up had collapsed, and Kamil had kicked most of the remaining bricks out of the way to make room while he hoisted Elif into the shaft. The opening was little more than an arm's length above his head, but he needed a stable base to reach it. He marvelled at Avi's agility. The boy must have thought himself up into the shaft.

As Kamil fumbled around the floor for more bricks, he sang a few lines of the operetta, but soon stopped. Building in the dark required all his concentration. Before long, he was out of bricks. When he tried to climb the platform, the loose bricks shifted beneath his weight and came apart. He stood for a moment, sweat cooling on his bare chest, wondering how to stabilise the platform. Then he took off his shoes, socks and trousers, and tucked the Proof of God into the front of his linen drawers. He wrapped the trouser legs tightly around the pile of bricks, but there wasn't enough material to tie the truss in place. Frustrated, he tried again to climb, barefoot this time, his toes seeking crevices among the bricks, but then one tilted under his weight and Kamil toppled backward. He cursed as he landed awkwardly, twisting his ankle.

He had a sudden idea. 'Elif, throw me your sash.'

After a few moments, a length of soft material brushed his face. He pulled it down and measured it with his hands. As he had hoped, it was a single piece of silk, more than long enough. When he had secured the sides of the platform with the sash, he climbed up and, head bowed beneath the ceiling, scraped his fingers across it until he found the opening. He put his head inside and stood up straight. The shaft ended just below his shoulders.

He slid his fingers over the walls of the shaft until they encountered some broken brickwork, hooked his fingers into the gaps, then hoisted himself up. He swung his legs up, wedging them against the opposite wall. Back braced against one side, feet against the other, he worked his way up the shaft, crabwise. He was sweating profusely and his fingers started to slip. He tried not to think about falling.

Elif's hands touched his shoulders. 'Almost there. Here's the ledge. Can you follow my hand?'

Kamil pulled himself on to the ledge. He lay there for a moment, waiting for the spasms in his muscles to lessen. The skin on his back was shredded and throbbed with pain. He sat up.

'Watch your head,' Elif warned. 'It's high enough to walk, but only if you crouch.'

In the cramped space, he felt Elif's hand brush against his naked leg and then the Proof of God. He heard her small cry of surprise, followed by soft laughter.

'What's so funny, Elif Hanoum?' Avi's voice came from the darkness ahead.

'You'll see later, Avi. Why don't you show us the way out?'

28

Ismail Hodja couldn't hide his excitement when Kamil placed the flat, featureless lead container on the table before him. Kamil moved stiffly, hindered by the bandages on his back and arms. He had decided it would be a waste of time to chase after Amida when they knew he was meeting the Frankish dealer tonight in Galata. Amida was only sugar water to attract the bee. Besides, Kamil had to find out what it was that so many people were hell-bent on stealing.

Beside him, Elif was draped in one of Karanfil's charshaf cloaks. Kamil had been reluctant to bring her along to Ismail Hodja's office, but she insisted she had earned the right to be present when the container was opened. Karanfil had bathed Avi, who was almost unrecognisable under a coating of dirt and brick dust, then bandaged his hands and put him to bed.

Elif let the veil fall to her shoulders. Kamil noticed her hair was still dark with moisture from bathing. They sat expectantly on the divan, watching Ismail Hodja as he ran his fingers carefully over the container, examining it from all sides.

'This is the only damage.' He pointed to a dent on the top. 'That's remarkable, considering how old it is.'

'That mark was left by the tip of a knife aiming for my heart,' Kamil explained. 'I had the box in my jacket pocket. It saved my life.'

'Did it now?' Ismail Hodja smiled benignly at Kamil. 'Well, then, we already have proof of its miraculous powers.'

Kamil let himself believe, just this once, in the miracle of coincidence.

'You said it had an outer casing, a silver reliquary. That must have protected it. Did you find that too?' he asked Kamil.

'We're still looking for it. Malik said it was important to prove the validity of the document.'

'Any proof of its credibility would be useful. But no matter. I'll be able to tell something about it from the paper and ink and other signs, but above all from what's written on it.'

Jemal refreshed their tea and then stood by the door, his powerful arms crossed, watching his master.

'Jemal, are all the windows closed? If this is as ancient as they say it is, the slightest breath of air might prove harmful. Indeed, we're taking a risk by opening it at all. You said Malik had taken the papers out to examine them?'

'He wanted to copy them in case the originals didn't survive.'

'It's a terrible dilemma.' Ismail Hodja's hands hovered over the box.

Jemal finished checking the windows. 'All shut.'

Where Yakup was companionable, Kamil thought, Jemal was taciturn, yet there was a bond between Ismail Hodja and his servant. Jemal sometimes seemed to know what Ismail Hodja meant even before he spoke, and Kamil had noticed how protective he was of the old sheikh.

Ismail Hodja took out a thin blade and inserted it into a nearly invisible seam at the side of the container, twisting slightly. Then he gently prodded and pulled until the lid slid lengthwise along a track. When the container was open, he sat for a long moment and simply stared at the contents.

Kamil sensed that everyone in the room was holding their breath.

Finally, Ismail Hodja shook himself and seemed to return from a distant place.

'You have no idea how much it means to me to be allowed to see this.'

He took a piece of writing paper and slid it slowly and carefully into the side of the container underneath the document, then lifted it and placed it on the table.

Kamil and Elif cautiously approached. On the paper was a short stack of irregular brown parchment pages covered in writing, their edges black as if they were slowly combusting.

Ismail Hodja examined the papers, careful not to touch them. 'There appear to be twelve pages. Would you be willing to leave them with me? I can read them and then tell you what they contain.'

No one spoke.

'If you like I can try to translate them now, but it won't be exact, you understand.'

'If it's not too much trouble,' Kamil said politely. 'We're all curious.' He was also worried about leaving the Proof of God unguarded. He wanted no harm to come to Ismail Hodja.

'Very well. Give me a few moments.'

They moved back to their seats and waited, watching the scholar's bearded face hovering above the ancient text. He got up several times to consult a book, then sat again and continued to read using a clean piece of paper to lift each page slowly and carefully so he could read the one beneath.

Kamil took his string of beads out of his pocket and ran them through his fingers.

Elif sat back with her eyes closed. Kamil wondered if she was asleep.

When Ismail Hodja finally looked up, it was with a puzzled frown. 'I don't understand this at all. I can read it, but ...' He shook his head in consternation. 'Is it possible?'

Elif sat up. 'What is it?'

'"In the name of the merciful and compassionate God",' Ismail Hodja read, '"their reckoning comes ever closer to men, yet they turn aside heedlessly".' He lifted his head and said, 'That is the opening verse of the al-Anbiya Sura, The Chapter of the Prophets.'

'It's a copy of the Quran?' Kamil asked.

'No. If the text is to be believed, it was written six hundred years before the Quran was revealed to the Prophet Muhammad, blessings upon his name. Listen.' He continued to read. '"To every renewed message from their Lord, they listen to it as in jest. They say, let him bring us a Sign like the ones that were sent to the prophets of old."'

Ismail Hodja stopped and read quietly for a while, consulted a book, then nodded and began to read the text out loud again. '"Before thee, the Apostles we sent were but men, to whom we granted inspiration. We have revealed for you a Book in which is a Message for you. This is the Message of those with me and those before me. He has ordained you the religion that He commanded to Noah, Abraham, and Moses, and revealed also to the servant of

God, Jesus of Nazareth, whose testament lies revealed before you."'

'What?' Kamil rose and went over to stand beside Ismail Hodja. They both stared down at the text.

'It's written by Jesus?' Elif asked, astounded.

'Apparently. It's in an untutored hand, but it's clearly legible. I'm certain that's what it says.' He continued reading. '"We have sent down to you a Book in which is a reminder for you. He it is who created the night and the day and the sun and the moon. We will place just balances upon the resurrection day, and no soul shall be wronged. Though it be the weight of a grain of mustard seed, we will bring it."'

Ismail Hodja looked up from his reading. 'I can almost recite this from memory,' he said. 'It's not exactly the same as al-Anbiya, but many of the basic elements are there, sometimes word for word. It's also interesting that the language is more sophisticated than one would expect from the handwriting.'

'As if the author were copying down something being dictated to him. Why would he do that?' Kamil sifted possible explanations through his mind. Jesus as an untutored scribe?

'The Angel Gabriel dictated Allah's words to the Prophet Muhammad, peace be upon him,' Ismail Hodja reminded him.

'But the Prophet didn't write them down. He recited them. They weren't written down until much later. It's unlikely that Jesus was literate.'

'It's possible that this too was dictated to Jesus and that he then recited it to someone who wrote it down before he died.'

The notion of Allah dictating through an angel was not

one Kamil gave any credence to. There had to be an explanation for this text written by a person of flesh and blood who knew how to wield a stylus.

Ismail Hodja continued reading, sometimes stopping to reflect on a word. '"Man is created out of haste. I will show you my signs, but do not hurry me. We gave to Moses and Aaron a light and a reminder to those who fear. And we gave Abraham direction, for we knew about him. They said, 'Burn him.' We said, 'O fire, be thou cool and a safety for Abraham.' We brought him and Lot safely to the land that we have blessed for the nations. We bestowed on him Isaac and Jacob and made them righteous persons. And we made them leaders to guide men. We inspired them to do good deeds and be steadfast in prayer, and to give alms. And they served us. And when Noah cried out, we delivered him and his family. And to Solomon we gave judgement and knowledge. To David we subjected the mountains and the birds to celebrate our praises. To Solomon we subjected the wind to run at his bidding and devils to dive for him. And she who guarded her chastity, we breathed into her of our Spirit, and we made her and her son a Sign for all peoples. To her son we give this Prophecy that we have revealed to others before him. Verily, this your nation is one nation and I am your Lord, so serve me."'

When Ismail Hodja stopped reading, no one spoke. The light from the windows was grey and the room had become dark.

Jemal came in with a lamp.

'Put it on the other side of the room, Jemal,' Ismail Hodja directed. 'The light will damage the document.' The brown parchment had already begun to crumble and the paper on which it rested was covered in fine dust.

Ismail Hodja carefully replaced the pages in the lead case and shut it.

'Malik was right. These should be copied. The exposure to air has set their decay in motion. There isn't much time.' He looked hopefully at Kamil.

'Of course, but remember that other people are after this box. Are you sure you want to keep it here? You could be in danger.'

Ismail Hodja looked over at Jemal, who shook his head very slightly. 'I'll speak to Hamdi Bey and see if we can take it to the Imperial Museum tonight. It should be safe there and I can consult with the conservator about preserving it and having it copied.'

Kamil nodded, relieved to have found a safe hiding place. Jemal slipped out of the room, presumably to fetch Hamdi Bey from his home or office.

'Is it a fake?' Kamil asked. 'Someone who knew the Quran and copied it out in Aramaic as a kind of joke?'

Ismail Hodja looked at the box thoughtfully and said, 'It's possible. But I've had the privilege of studying a number of old documents written in Aramaic. It's very hard to create a fake if you aren't a scholar of the language, of Aramaic as it must have been spoken eighteen hundred years ago in the time of Jesus. I have only limited knowledge, of course, and it was such an unfathomably long time ago. But despite the unsophisticated lettering, this document has none of the errors you'd expect if it had been written by someone trying to adapt a later form of the language, that is, trying to make it appear older. I doubt any scholar would have attempted such a thing. A joke like this would have taken a lifetime to accomplish.'

'So you think this really was written by Jesus?' Kamil was in turmoil. His mind categorically rejected this possibility, but he respected Ismail Hodja too much to dismiss his opinion.

'Or someone from that period. Yes. That's the simplest explanation.'

'But what does it mean?' Elif asked. 'How could Jesus write or dictate part of the Quran, when it didn't even exist?'

'Ah, Elif Hanoum. You've come right to the heart of the problem. In the al-Anbiya Sura, Allah tells us that there were many other prophets before Muhammad, praise be upon him, including Jesus, and that they were all given the same message by Allah, but that they were ignored or worse by the unbelievers. In the Night Journey Sura, there's a passage about people who refused to believe in Allah because he sent them a Messenger who was a man like them, instead of an angel. The important point is that all the prophets were given the same message. In the Consultation Sura, it is written, "He has established the same religion for you as that which he enjoined on Noah, on Abraham, Moses and Jesus. Namely, that you should remain steadfast in religion and make no divisions therein."' He shrugged. 'Of course, it's pointed out that the people did become divided, but the idea is that Allah will bring them together again. The Islamic, Jewish and Christian God is the same God.'

'An optimistic message for our time,' Kamil commented drily.

'Well, there's also plenty about the ungrateful unbelievers and doubters and their unenviable fates in the flames of hell.' Ismail Hodja stood by the table, looking down at the lead container. He reached out and laid his fingers on it. 'My eyes are privileged.'

'I still don't understand why it's so important if it just repeats what's in the Quran,' Elif insisted.

Ismail Hodja surveyed the room, his eyes shining. 'It proves that Allah exists,' he said slowly.

'What?' Kamil exclaimed. 'How does it do that?'

'Think about it rationally, Kamil, as you always like to do. How else would Jesus have been able to produce such an exact copy of the text? Allah dictated it to him, but he was killed and unable to deliver the message, so another Messenger had to be found. That was the Prophet Muhammad, peace be upon him. Allah revealed the same message to him and he was able to deliver it.'

'Could the Prophet have known about this text?'

Ismail Hodja thought about that for a moment. 'There are teachings about a Christian monk named Bahira who, it is said, happened to meet the Prophet Muhammad, peace be upon him, when he was a child and recognised even then his coming greatness. Some say he taught the Prophet the Psalms of David. But this is quite a different matter. These aren't just lines that refer to similar things, but an entire text word for word. I think either this text disappeared soon after Jesus died or it was hidden by his followers who replaced it with their own gospels. If the Azhar chronicles about the Proof of God are right, then it was first hidden in Jerusalem, where the Christian armies found it and took it to Abyssinia to keep it out of Muslim hands. It came to Istanbul much later. So until then, it was in a dry climate that must have helped preserve it.' He thought for a moment. 'It's possible that the Prophet Muhammad, peace be upon him, knew of the existence of this document, but given what we know of its history and the Prophet's movements, I think it unlikely that he ever saw it.'

Kamil's eyes rested on the deceptively simple grey container on Ismail Hodja's desk. 'I'll have to give this some thought.' He felt engaged and excited by these revelations, but still deeply sceptical. He found himself hoping, but not believing, that Ismail Hodja was right.

'I don't think the hellfires are meant for men engaged in honest inquiry,' Ismail Hodja assured him with a smile.

'By the way,' Kamil asked Ismail Hodja, 'does Matthew 2:16 mean anything to you?'

'I believe it's from the Bible.' Ismail Hodja walked to a shelf, took down a thick book, and leafed through the pages. 'Here it is. "Then Herod, when he saw that he was mocked by the wise men, was exceedingly angry, and sent forth, and slew all the male children that were in Bethlehem and in the border thereof from two years old and under."'

'"The Lord giveth and the Lord taketh away,"' Elif's voice cracked. 'What's the point of proving he exists,' she asked bitterly, 'when he's that kind of God?'

29

At the Galata end of the Grande Rue de Pera, Kamil and Omar made a sharp left down a steep canyon of five-storey buildings, stone and plaster interpretations of the traditional wooden houses. Candlelight shimmered in the windows. It was almost eight o'clock. They passed a rococo fountain in front of a small mosque. The buildings might be taller, but this place is still a thieves' den, Kamil thought, looking around at the men sitting in the dark. The men's eyes followed them suspiciously.

A street of steps spilled into the square before the Galata Tower. Built in 1348 by a Genoese colony of traders, the round stone colossus dwarfed even the tallest buildings in its vicinity. Enormous arches circled the top. Above them, a terrace wound beneath two small chambers stacked there like warming pots. The ground was littered with stones from the collapsed Genoese walls that had once connected to it.

'Gustave Flaubert wrote about the view from up there,' Kamil whispered when they reached the square.

'Well, that's not very original,' Omar replied. 'You can see up a swallow's arse from there.' He looked meaningfully at Kamil. 'Now that's original.'

Kamil laughed quietly. 'Where did Avi say they were going to meet?'

Omar pointed to a short stretch of wall, about ten feet high. At one end was a vaulted arch, a deep scallop scooped from the wall. 'I came earlier to have a look. No back exit.'

He nudged Kamil. A figure was hurrying along the street towards the arch. There were few lights in the square and the night sky was obscured by clouds, so the man appeared and disappeared, stepping between shadows. He was tall and wore a coat, and his hat was pulled low around his face, which was obscured by a scarf. Another man appeared inside the arch and motioned to him.

'Amida,' Omar mouthed.

The sight of Amida made Kamil's hand twitch in anticipation of landing a blow. Amida must believe that he and Elif were still locked behind that iron gate, where they would eventually die. Kamil had told Omar what had happened, although not about the translation of the Proof of God.

They crept closer. Kamil pointed to a low wall by a tree, where they would be close enough to hear without being seen.

Already there was a quarrel in progress.

'You said you had the Proof of God last time, but it was just a piece of junk. You'll have to do better this time.'

The voice spoke Turkish, the language of the street, with a foreign accent. English, Kamil thought.

They couldn't hear Amida's reply.

'If you can't deliver it, I'll take my money back and we won't be doing any more business. I don't deal with amateurs.'

'I have it. I've got the Proof.' Amida's voice rose with excitement.

'That's what you say. Let's see it.'

'No. I mean I know where it is.'

'You told me you'd have it tonight. I agreed to meet with

you for that reason alone. Otherwise you deal with Ben and Remzi.'

'I can get it.'

'You insufferable idiot!' the man said in English. Then, in Turkish, 'Why should I believe you?'

'Because you need me.' Amida sounded defiant. 'I'm the only one who knows where it is.'

There was a lull. Kamil imagined them sizing each other up.

Finally, Amida said harshly, 'I want more money up front.'

The man huffed into his scarf. Kamil realised he was laughing.

'You have your money.'

They couldn't hear Amida's reply.

'How much?' the man asked.

'Ten thousand gold liras.'

Kamil and Omar looked at each other in surprise. Omar pointed to his testicles and raised his eyebrows.

'Don't fuck with me,' the man snarled in English.

'Other people want it,' Amida responded. 'I could take it to them.'

'You have no idea what you're getting into, do you? I'm the only one who can get it out, you fool.'

'Suit yourself,' Amida said and walked out of the alcove.

'Two thousand.'

Amida turned. 'Five.'

'Four. I've already paid you a thousand for that worthless reliquary.'

'Where do you want me to bring it?'

'I'll pick it up at your house.'

A note of wariness entered Amida's voice. 'I'll bring it to you. It's not a problem.'

'I know where you live. I'll be there tomorrow after five. And if you don't have it, my associate Ben will talk to your sister.' The man's voice remained ominously pleasant, as if he were only discussing the weather. 'He's taken a liking to her. Or maybe Remzi. He dislikes you for snitching on him.'

'My sister doesn't know anything.' Amida sounded nervous.

'Of course not. Now get out of here.'

As Amida stepped into the street, Omar ran from the shadows to intercept him, but tripped over a stone in the dark and faltered, giving Amida enough time to turn down an alley and merge into the backstreets.

Omar cursed. 'Son of a donkey, I know where you live,' he muttered as he ran back to the square.

Kamil approached the arch carefully. He wondered why the man hadn't come out. He must have heard Omar. Maybe he was armed and lying in wait.

Kamil took out his knife and nodded to Omar, who moved quietly to the other side of the alcove, holding his revolver. When Kamil stepped into the opening, Omar moved in quickly behind him, pointing the gun straight at the man who should have been there. But the arch was empty.

'Well, go fuck a donkey,' Omar exclaimed, turning about in the enclosed space. 'Where did he go?'

They lit a lamp and looked around. In the corner of the arch was a low opening in the wall just big enough for a man to squeeze through.

'How did I miss this?' Omar picked up a stone and looked at it in the light, then felt around among the other stones on the floor. 'The son of a bitch. He stacked them so they looked like part of the wall. All he had to do was push them aside.' He threw the rock down in disgust. 'This damned city is full of holes.'

Kamil closed his eyes and threw his head back. 'I can't believe they both got away.'

'My fault, pasha.'

Kamil shook his head. 'There was something familiar about him.'

'English, right?'

'Sounded like it.'

'All English sound alike.'

'Bey, Chief.'

They whirled around at the voice. Avi stood outside the entrance.

'What are you doing here, you rascal?' Omar asked sternly. 'Trying to be a hero twice in one day?'

Avi didn't respond and Kamil saw that he was embarrassed. His pockets were bulging.

Kamil went over and laid his hand on the boy's shoulder. 'We didn't have much luck, Avi. Let's take you home. It's been a long day for all of us.' He sounded dispirited.

Avi pulled an engraved silver money clip from his pocket, that was bulging with British banknotes, and handed it to Kamil.

'What . . . ?'

Omar said nothing, but looked at Avi with a mixture of admiration and wonder.

Avi reached into his other pocket and fished out a key and a cigar.

Kamil turned the cigar over in his hand. It had a yellow and red label with a picture of a red rose and the word Cuba on the band.

'Where did you get these?' But Kamil already knew the answer. Cuban cigars, as Magnus Owen had pointed out to him, were rare. He found himself profoundly saddened by the realisation.

'I took them from the man's pocket when he got stuck in the wall.' Avi stood with his head bowed.

Omar burst out laughing. 'You pickpocketed him while he was stuck in the wall? Wonderful. Absolutely wonderful.' He stopped laughing when he noticed Avi was crying. 'No, no, my son,' he said gently, putting his arm around Avi. 'I meant that in a good way. I blundered and you saved the day. Again.' He punched him lightly on the arm. 'So, how many times are you going to be a hero today? Are you trying to show us up?'

'Avi,' Kamil chimed in, 'this is very helpful. I think I know who the man is, thanks to you.'

'Who?' Omar asked curiously.

'First I want to be sure. I need to check on something, but I'll let you know. Why don't the two of you go home and I'll see you tomorrow. You can take the day off, Avi.' He smiled at the boy, then frowned when he noticed his scraped hands. Some of the scabs had begun to bleed. 'Where are your bandages?'

'I took them off so I could work better.'

Kamil remembered the desperate, skinny boy who had accosted him on the street. He had wondered how Avi had survived. Now he knew or at least could guess. He would never truly be able to grasp that kind of life. He thought about the young refugee woman on the street with her baby.

Kamil watched Omar and Avi turn the corner, the police chief's big hand resting on the boy's shoulder, then set off in search of a carriage.

30

Hamida squatted over the cloaked figure sprawled facedown amid the weeds and listing grave markers in the old cemetery behind the Fatih Mosque. He lifted the cloak. Beneath it was a dark-skinned boy with a thick mat of tightly curled black hair, a dark fuzz of down outlining his upper lip. His neck was arched back coquettishly, one cheek pressed against the earth, lips parted in a grimace of what could either be pain or ecstasy. His eyes were closed but his face held nothing of repose, only hard absence. With trembling hands, Amida pulled the cloak back farther and saw that the boy was naked. Lines in the shape of two peaks had been carved into the boy's back. Amida crouched over the body, rocking back and forth on his heels, making a thin keening sound.

A breeze suddenly sprang up. The cypresses creaked and sighed. Amida sat up and looked around nervously. Seeing no one, he tucked the cloak around the body as if putting a child to bed, then stood and ran out of the cemetery, through the courtyard of the mosque, past the tomb of Sultan Mehmet II, and down the Street of the Lion-House.

31

Tailor Pepo's establishment was down a covered passage off the Rue de Pera that was crammed with shops selling bolts of cloth, ribbons, thread, buttons, and other items needed in the trade. It was only eight in the morning, but Tailor Pepo already stood at a long table, measuring lengths from a bolt of fine white linen. Three apprentices took up the rest of the small room, each hunched over a shirt, needle in hand. They looked up surreptitiously when Kamil entered, but immediately returned their attention to their work.

'Welcome, Kamil Pasha,' the old man said in a voice so low Kamil could barely hear him. 'Sorry.' He pointed to his throat. 'Doctor says I have a growth. Doesn't bother me, but can't speak.'

Kamil thought the tailor had aged since he had last come in six months earlier to be measured for a shirt. The man's face was grey and his white hair had begun to yellow as if stained with nicotine. He began to cough and one of the apprentices brought him a glass of water.

'Sit. Sit.' Tailor Pepo pointed to a stool.

Kamil explained that he was looking for someone he thought might be a customer of the shop. He took the silver money clip out of his pocket and laid it on the cutting table. The eyes of the apprentices flashed curiously in their direction.

Tailor Pepo picked up the clip and ran his hands over

the incised hunting scene, a leaping stag being dragged down by hounds. He turned it over. On the back was engraved the initial M.

'Monsieur Owen,' he said.

Kamil leaned in to hear him better.

'A cruel scene, *n'est ce pas*?' He leaned close to Kamil's ear. 'I didn't like this Monsieur Owen. I can tell a lot about a man by his shirts.'

'What can you tell me about him?'

'He first came here about two years ago. One of my regular clients recommended him, said he was the British ambassador's secretary.' He leaned forward. 'I think he wanted to butter Monsieur Owen up for a deal.' He shook his head knowingly, then started coughing again. 'I made Monsieur Owen a shirt to help my regular client, and we delivered it to my client's address. Then six months ago, Monsieur Owen came and ordered another shirt.'

The apprentice hurried over with more water. While Tailor Pepo was drinking, the young man glanced at the money clip.

'Do you remember this?' Kamil asked him.

The apprentice looked enquiringly at the tailor, who nodded his approval.

'He gave an address in Tarla Bashou. Not that it's a bad area, not like Galata. It's just families in Tarla Bashou. But there aren't many Franks living there. And since Monsieur Owen said he was employed at the embassy, I found it odd.'

Tailor Pepo stood suddenly and cried out in his diminished voice, 'We haven't offered the pasha any tea.'

The apprentice leapt to the door and called down the passage, then sat down and picked up his shirt.

'With your permission,' Kamil said politely, 'I'd like to ask the young man some more questions.'

'Of course. Take your time. We're all at your service.' Tailor Pepo went back to his measuring, his scissors biting into the material with a sound like tearing silk.

A boy appeared at the door, a tray of glasses swinging from his hand on a thin metal tripod. He plucked one off and handed it to the apprentice, who placed it before Kamil.

'What else can you tell me about this Monsieur Owen?'

The apprentice's hands continued their deft needlework as he answered Kamil's questions. 'I went to Tarla Bashou to deliver the shirt. The apartment was on the second floor. I knocked but there was no answer, so I went to leave the shirt with the doorkeeper. He told me the man who rented the apartment was an agent of trade by the name of Megalos. I wanted to make sure I was delivering to the right address, so I asked him to describe the tenant. The doorkeeper said he rarely saw him, but from his description it sounded exactly like Monsieur Owen. The doorkeeper didn't think he actually lived there but used the flat for business. He said the neighbours were always complaining to him about bulky trunks coming in and out and out and blocking the stairwell. It is odd. I mean, a proper business would have a depot.'

'What do you know about business?' Tailor Pepo rasped from his cutting table.

Agents of trade were go-betweens in business deals, paper shufflers and deal makers, not shopkeepers, Kamil thought. Owen was involved in something quite different.

'There's one more thing.' The apprentice looked uncomfortable. 'It's just gossip.' He glanced at Tailor Pepo.

'Go ahead,' the old man said. 'Leaves don't flutter unless there's wind.'

'I heard that Monsieur Owen lost his position at the embassy last year. He was accused of taking bribes.'

Kamil remembered the previous ambassador's daughter, Sybil, mentioning that her father had fired his secretary. Instead of returning to England, this man had stayed in Istanbul and set himself up as an agent of trade.

Tailor Pepo put his hands over his ears and shook his head. 'I knew it right away.'

'But he was rehired when the new ambassador arrived.'

'How do you know this?' Kamil asked.

'My brother delivers produce to the embassy kitchen, pasha.'

Kamil finished his tea, thanked Tailor Pepo, and left. In the passage, he stopped, took the money clip from his pocket and regarded the engraving, then flipped it over and looked at the initial. M for Magnus, he thought, but something else danced just offstage in his mind. Suddenly he saw it. Four lines in the shape of two mountain peaks: M.

Was this Kubalou's brand?

Hurrying out of the passage, he took a short cut to the British Embassy.

HE WAITED FOR the ambassador's secretary on an uncomfortable chair in the ornate receiving hall. The clerk behind the desk studiously ignored him. A clock ticked ostentatiously on the mantle. The previous ambassador had done most of his business from his rooms in the private residence at the back of the British Embassy compound, so Kamil had spent little time in the public rooms.

It gave him time to think. He was jumping to conclusions. Just because a man smoked Cuban cigars and his name had an initial that looked vaguely like a symbol cut into the bodies of dead men didn't necessarily mean he was guilty of killing them. Malik's name also began with an M. And perhaps all the trunks the tailor's apprentice had talked about really were just connected to Owen's business as an agent of trade. Why was he so ready to believe, Kamil asked himself, that Magnus Owen was Kubalou? Was it that Owen had lied about how long he had been in Istanbul? A useless lie. Kamil wouldn't have cared one way or the other. But the lie might have stopped Kamil from discovering that Owen had been fired for taking bribes under the previous ambassador.

After half an hour, a short, harried-looking man in a well-tailored suit rushed in. He had great brown whiskers on his cheeks and a bald head, across which lay two streaks of hair that looked as if they had been painted on.

'So sorry, Mister Pasha. Or should I call you Magistrate? Never know what form of address to use here, dash it. I'm Battles, the ambassador's secretary.'

Kamil had no idea if this was his last name, his first name, or a job description.

'Kamil,' he clarified, reaching out his hand to Battles. 'I'm here in my capacity as magistrate for the Beyoglu Court.'

'Well, do come in, man,' Battles interrupted him, leading the way towards a door at the back of the hall. 'I know I've kept you waiting, Magistrate. I do apologise.'

He swept Kamil into his office and offered him a chair. A very large desk shined to a high polish dominated the room. Three upholstered chairs were arrayed around a smaller inlaid table.

Battles sat down opposite Kamil and crossed his legs. He propped his chin on one fist in a caricature of total attention. 'Now,' he said, 'what can I do for you?'

'I'm here to inquire about one of your employees, a Mr Magnus Owen.'

Battles suddenly sat upright. 'Why is the Ottoman court interested in Magnus Owen? Look here, what's this all about?'

'I can't tell you anything at the moment,' Kamil explained. 'We're in the middle of an investigation. Right now I need some information.'

'But we have a right to know,' Battles spluttered.

'You'll be the first to be informed. I'm sure you can understand,' he said conspiratorially, 'that our actions must be circumspect. I'm working together with Scotland Yard on this matter.'

'Of course. Of course.' Battles laid his finger along his nose. 'No need to bother the ambassador with this yet. Scotland Yard, eh?' He looked impressed.

'Is Mr Owen here?'

Battles shot up and stuck his head out the door. 'Harbinger, is Owen here?'

A moment later, he came back shaking his head. 'No one's seen him all day. Never here when you want him.' He tilted his head and looked at Kamil. 'Is Owen involved in something? Drugs, eh? I won't tell a soul.' He leaned forward intently. 'I knew it. I could smell it on that man. I told the ambassador not to hire him.'

'Why did you do that?'

'He was secretary to the former ambassador, but said he had resigned. He was living locally, acting as an agent of trade. Apparently very respectable. As soon as the new ambassador arrived, Owen showed up and asked for his old job back. "Well, we have a secretary," I said. "Me. We don't need a second one."' Battles shook his head. 'No, I didn't like the man one bit. Shifty eyes. He went behind my back, convinced the ambassador he had more experience dealing with the natives. Not a lot of staff stayed over from the previous ambassador, you see, so it's true our sea legs were a bit wobbly, but we were getting the hang of it. The ambassador hired him as cultural attaché. I couldn't fathom it. He's about as useful as a two-legged stool.' He leaned forward again. 'And then one day I was talking to one of the men from the old days and guess what he told me? Owen hadn't quit. He was asked to resign, for taking a bribe. Well, when I heard that, I went straight to the ambassador, but he thought it was just gossip. Seems Owen made himself useful. Speaks the local lingo, you know.' Battles shrugged. 'I made the best of it. Kept him away from anything important. People like that. They think they're one of us, but you can smell the street on them. Gives himself airs, he does, plays the gentleman, but I did some checking around.' Battles lowered his voice conspiratorially. 'Born on the wrong side of the blanket. Father's a duke. Did the right thing by him, sent him to the best schools and all that, but beyond his public school manner, Owen's a fraud. He's no more a gentleman than old Harbinger out there,' Battles concluded, indicating the clerk in the hall.

Kamil wondered at the depth of his venom. Why would Battles hate the man so much? There was nothing in Owen's manner that had given Kamil cause to think ill of him. Perhaps, Kamil thought, he wasn't as finely attuned to the narcissism of minor class differences as the British were. They seemed to have the olfactory sophistication of hunting dogs when it came to sniffing out a man's standing. Kamil wondered whether a lifetime of harassment by his peers could drive a man to seek out associates like Remzi.

'Interesting information. Thank you,' Kamil said in a neutral voice. 'Could you tell me what his duties are here at the embassy?'

'Oh, translating, reaching out to the natives, cultural understanding – misunderstanding more likely.'

'What do you mean?'

'Well, we don't know what's really said, do we? He could tell the ambassador four is five and we'd have to accept it.'

'Is he the only Turkish speaker at the embassy?' Kamil asked, shocked.

'The others all left. The old ambassador worked them to the bone, cancelled their home leaves. Some of the poor buggers hadn't seen England in three years. The new translator shipped out from London last week. Oxford trained. When he arrives, we won't have to rely on Owen anymore. He'll be restricted to his other duties where he can do no harm.'

'What other duties?'

'Diplomatic pouch, post, shipping. He said he had done it before, and truth be told, it's the one thing he does well. We can always count on our post being on time.'

Kamil tried to keep the excitement from his voice. 'Would you be able to obtain a list of everything he's shipped for the embassy over the past month – what, where, when – without him knowing?'

'Certainly,' Battles said. 'It might take me a week, maybe two.'

'I need it this afternoon.'

'I'll see what I can do.'

On his way out, Kamil turned back and asked, 'Is Owen married?'

'I doubt it,' Battles replied. 'He's always chatting up the ladies at embassy functions. He's a dark horse, that one. Has an apartment somewhere in the city. Never invites anyone over.' He thought for a moment. 'I suppose he could have a native wife. I hear they don't mind that sort of thing.'

Kamil nodded curtly and stepped out the door before a suitable rejoinder could form on his lips.

KAMIL LEFT A police guard outside the building in Tarla Bashou, then he, the local police captain, and a fresh-faced policeman climbed the stairs to Owen's apartment. The hall was narrow and dark, but the steps were scrubbed clean. The stairwell was fragrant with the scent of freshly baked pastry and the noon meal. Every door was slightly ajar and women peered out, their children pressing their faces through the opening.

Kamil knocked on Owen's door.

A woman spoke from the apartment across the landing. She had a scarf draped around her face and her body was hidden behind the half-closed door. 'He's not home.'

Kamil turned towards her. 'Do you know where he is? When he'll be back?'

'He's rarely here, but he came in late last night. He'd lost his key so the doorkeeper had to let him in. He made a lot of noise in his apartment and right before the first ezan, a carriage came and they took down some big chests. It woke me and the children up.' As if on cue, a baby began to bawl behind her. The door closed for a moment, then opened again, a bit wider. Kamil could see she had a baby in her arms. A little girl clung shyly to her mother's shalwar.

If Owen was rarely here, Kamil thought, he must have another apartment somewhere. 'Does he get a lot of visitors?'

'I've only seen an orange-haired man and some rough local types. They haul large chests up and down the stairs at all hours. I'm afraid one of the children will get trampled underfoot some day. Up and down. Up and down. I sent my husband over with some stuffed peppers once, but he just took them and didn't even thank us. Didn't return the plate either. Not that we expected thanks, mind you. But I thought my husband could talk to him about being careful of the children on the stairs. I don't like the look of those men. This is a respectable house.'

She cocked her head and suddenly ran back inside. He could hear the clatter of pans in the kitchen, then a burnt odour wafted on to the landing.

Kamil took out the key Avi had taken from Owen's pocket and inserted it in the lock. He told the policeman who had accompanied him to interview everyone in the building. 'I want a description of these men. Get the doorkeeper's wife to sit with the women while you talk to them.' Then Kamil pushed the door open and he and the police captain stepped inside.

The room smelled of unwashed clothes with a hint of flowery cologne. There was little furniture, just a table with one chair, an old sofa covered with a purple silk quilt stitched with flowers in silver thread, a wardrobe, and a mattress on the floor with some grimy bedding. On the table was an empty enamel plate. Dust padded the windowsills and collected in drifts in the corners of the room. The wardrobe was empty. Dirty laundry was piled on the floor beside it and Kamil recognised one of Tailor Pepo's shirts. The wooden floor was scored from heavy objects being dragged across it.

A door led to another room. Kamil pulled back the dusty drapes to let in light. This room was piled high with chests and wooden crates. He opened one and found a cache of ancient coins. Another chest was full of jewellery, not all of it old. Owen must be dealing in stolen jewellery as well. In Europe, it would be nearly impossible to trace.

'Take an inventory of everything in this apartment,' he told the police captain. 'Then box everything up and deliver it to the courthouse as evidence. I'm holding you responsible for the safety of these objects.' Kamil was reluctant to leave this undocumented treasure in one man's hands, but Owen was on the run and he couldn't spare the time to stand guard over the inventory.

The captain stood to attention. 'Of course, Magistrate. You can rely on me.'

As he crossed the room, Kamil noticed an iron stave with an odd-shaped cross at the top. It looked familiar. Then he remembered seeing something like it in the picture Ismail Hodja had shown him from the sect that worshiped the weeping angel. An Abyssinian cross. Perhaps Balkis or Saba could help him identify it. He wrapped it in a sheet and took it with him. He also took the plate from the table and, on his way out, placed it before the neighbour's door.

A guard was left to keep watch on the apartment. If Owen did return, Kamil would have him turned over to the British Embassy, since by law he wasn't allowed to arrest a British national. If Owen didn't return, and Kamil didn't expect that he would, he would share his evidence with Scotland Yard.

On his way back to the Grande Rue de Pera, Kamil passed the French Hospital.

The gatekeeper called out a greeting: 'Peace be upon you, Magistrate.'

Kamil stopped. 'Upon you be peace.'

The man put his hand on his heart and bowed. 'I wanted to thank you, Magistrate, for opening my fate.'

'I'm pleased for you, but what have I done?'

'Remember the young refugee woman you asked me to care for?'

'Of course. What happened to her?'

'She has accepted my offer of marriage.' The gatekeeper's smile was so broad it lit up the street.

Kamil was taken aback, thinking that the man had taken advantage of the wretched girl's situation. But the alternatives ran quickly through his mind. Would it be better for her to be housed in a convent with hundreds of other women and children, being taught a skill that would bring her little money, even if she could find work? Instead, here was a gentle man who seemed genuinely pleased that she had accepted him.

'Congratulations,' Kamil said, trying to sound enthusiastic.

The gatekeeper didn't notice his hesitation. 'She's living with my mother for now. The baby is a boy, a boy like a lion. My mother is crazy about him. She's always wanted a grandson. So, Magistrate, I would like to thank you for my family. We would be greatly honoured if you would consent to come to the wedding.'

'I'd be delighted.'

Kamil pictured the young woman being absorbed by this family – being fed, protected, embraced – and wondered how she felt about it. He hoped they would be gentle with their love.

KAMIL SAT AT his desk and eyed with dismay the stack of papers that had accumulated over the past few days. He sifted through letters and messages. One was from Hamdi Bey. He eagerly ripped it open and read it.

Hamdi Bey wrote that he had inquired through some trusted friends in the antiquities business in London about the firm of Rettingate and Sons. It was owned by Lionel Rettingate and a silent partner whose name no one appeared to know and whom no one had ever seen. Although nothing had ever been proved, the shop was suspected of selling stolen goods and no reputable dealer would openly buy from them. It was no secret, though, that these same dealers would pass money under the table if Rettingate had something they really wanted.

Kamil was disappointed. He had hoped for a direct link of some kind to Owen.

He sat back and lit a cigarette, then unwrapped the long package containing the cross and carried it over to the window to examine it in the light.

'Good morning, bey.' He heard Avi's voice behind him. 'Would you like me to bring you some tea?'

'Good morning, Avi.' Kamil didn't turn. He was looking intently at the cross on top of the long stave. It was made of iron and brass in a flat diamond shape and decorated with a pair of stylised birds, little more than pairs of tiny iron wings. He touched the edge of the diamond and the wings, then held it up to the light and studied the shape from the side and from above.

'Come over here and hold this steady.'

Avi stood beside him and wrapped his hands around the

stave of the cross. Kamil noticed the boy's hands were still scratched and covered in scabs, but they seemed to be healing. He took a clean handkerchief out of his pocket and slipped it carefully between the wings of one of the birds. The white linen came away stained a rusty black. He did the same to other parts of the cross.

He examined the stains for a few moments. 'Blood,' he announced. 'We'll get the police surgeon to verify it, but I think it's blood.'

He suddenly had an idea. 'You know the bakery behind the stables?'

'Yes, bey?' Avi said, clearly puzzled.

'Run over there and bring me an unbaked loaf of bread, one that's already risen. Tell them to wrap it up so it doesn't fall flat before you get back.' He reconsidered. 'Bring two, just in case. Run.'

A few minutes later, Avi and Abdullah watched with fascination as Kamil placed a tray on the floor. The yeasty dough wobbled in his hands. He set it on the tray. The imprints of his fingers disappeared as the dough puffed itself up again into a flawless beige mound. Then Kamil took up the cross by its stave, turned it over so the cross was facing downward, and plunged it like a spear into the dough.

In the moments before the dough repaired itself, they could see a pattern of incisions. It was the same as the pattern of cuts on Malik's body, the sets of tiny bite-like punctures made by the miniature wings.

When the bread had risen again, they saw that its beige surface was mottled black in a pattern that echoed the cuts. Kamil had Abdullah record what he had done, then gave him his handkerchief to send to the police surgeon for analysis.

And he added murder to the charges against Magnus Owen.

'DOES THAT MEAN Amida didn't kill Malik?' Omar asked, looking disappointed.

Kamil had ridden to Fatih station to fill Omar in on the news, and was eating a portion of stuffed mussels he had purchased from a vendor. He swallowed and said, 'It appears that way. I don't understand, though, how he got hold of Malik's pin.'

'I think it's time to ask him.' Omar buckled on his revolver and threw on his jacket. 'By the way, the watchman found a body behind the Fatih Mosque this morning, with that mark carved into his back. So either Owen or his henchmen are still around. Probably that testicle Remzi,' he added darkly.

'Owen will stick around to see if he can get the Proof of God,' Kamil predicted, wrapping the shells in a piece of newsprint. 'He's probably holed up in his other apartment. I wish I knew where that was. Who was the victim?'

'Dark-skinned boy in his early teens, naked. Might be Habesh. He looked familiar. Probably from Sunken Village. While we're there, we can ask if anyone's missing.'

AS SOON AS Saba saw the cross in Kamil's hand, she exclaimed, 'It can't be. Where did you get that?' She went to a long box in the corner of the room and opened it, then turned to her mother. 'It's empty. Did you know the sceptre was missing, mother?'

Balkis was propped on the divan and covered with a quilt, one of her wrists bound in a thick yellow-stained bandage.

'Missing?' Balkis exclaimed. 'That's not possible. I used it on Friday.'

Kamil and Omar stood just inside the door, Kamil trying unsuccessfully to keep his eyes from Saba. He couldn't quite grasp that this was his sister. She wore a brown charshaf that covered everything but her face, which was pale and drawn, her pallor accentuated by the dark frame of the veil. She no longer looked like a child.

'It's the sceptre we use for our ceremonies,' Saba explained to Kamil. He noticed she avoided looking at him. She reached out for the cross. 'I'll put it back in the box.'

'I'm sorry. I can't give it to you just yet. It's evidence. We thought you might help us identify it.' He gave the cross to Omar, who wrapped it in a piece of oiled cloth. 'We're actually here to see your son,' Kamil told Balkis.

It was late afternoon. He and Omar had searched Amida's house and looked for him in his usual haunts in Charshamba. Kamil didn't think he had gone far. He was sure Amida still hoped to pluck the golden apple, to sell Owen the Proof of God Kamil had dangled before him. Four thousand gold liras was almost a minister's salary. It would buy Amida travel and a life far away from here. Four thousand liras would make a modern man of him. He was probably out looking for the manuscript right now. Kamil was certain that had been Amida's reason for coming to Malik's house two nights ago. He had probably planned to break in and hoped to find the Proof before his meeting with Kubalou. By now it was safely locked up in Hamdi Bey's museum.

'Did he take the sceptre?' Saba asked.

Kamil remembered that Saba had wanted him to arrest

Amida and thought she'd be pleased to know they were here to do just that.

'We don't know,' Kamil said in a neutral voice. 'That's one of several things we'd like to ask him.'

'I'll take you to him,' Saba offered.

'Don't,' Balkis croaked.

'Mama, Amida is a man, so let him take responsibility like a man.'

Saba slipped on her shoes and told Kamil and Omar to follow her.

When they reached the path that led to Amida's cottage, Kamil stopped and said, 'He's not home. We were just there.'

Saba didn't answer, but continued along the path. Pushing open Amida's door without knocking, she went inside. Kamil shrugged and followed. Omar took up a position inside the door.

Saba strode to the piano in the sitting room, lifted the lid and brought her hands down several times on the keys, creating an explosion of noise.

She crossed her arms and they stood waiting in the dying echo.

Amida appeared blinking in the corridor. He seemed surprised to see Kamil.

Kamil and Omar exchanged glances and Omar gave an imperceptible nod.

Kamil was shocked at the change in Amida since last night. His face was unshaven, his eyes bloodshot and swollen and shaded with circles as dark as bruises. He looked shaken and, Kamil thought, anguished.

'Brother, Kamil Pasha has some business with you,' Saba said, her voice taking on a note of concern. She too looked surprised at Amida's state.

Kamil took Amida by the arm. 'Let's go next door.'

Amida tried to shake him loose, only to find Omar hoisting him by his other arm.

'So where were you?' Omar asked him in the tone he reserved for naughty children. 'Hiding in your rabbit warren?'

Amida struggled. 'You have no right.'

'Of course not,' Omar agreed. 'You're such a good boy.'

They brought him into Balkis's house and thrust him into the receiving hall. Omar disappeared back outside.

Balkis's face was white and slick with sweat. 'My son,' she croaked.

Saba turned to Kamil and, for the first time, looked at him directly. Kamil found himself lost in her green eyes, so like his father's. He blinked and looked away.

'We found this,' he said, and took Malik's pin from his pocket.

Amida looked surprised and then relieved. He clearly had expected to be arrested for kidnapping Elif and attacking him, Kamil thought, watching his face. The harder an animal squirmed to get out of a trap, the more it entangled itself.

'Malik wore that all the time,' Balkis said, stretching out her hand. 'A friend gave it to him, an Irish monk. Where did you get it?'

'The pin wasn't on Malik's body, so either the killer took it or someone took it from his house. Whoever killed him was after something much bigger and I doubt they would have bothered with a pin. I think someone went to Malik's house that night after Malik had already taken the pin off and stole it. Was that you, Amida?'

'What would I want with a cheap pin like that?' he grumbled.

Kamil took it back from Balkis. 'I found this in the Covered Bazaar. A dealer named Gomidian had it.'

'We've done business with him for thirty years,' Balkis said. 'He's always been fair. What was he doing with it? Did he kill Malik?'

Amida looked wary.

'He said he bought the pin from Amida.'

Amida's eyes shifted rapidly around the room. 'If I tell you, what'll happen to me?' he asked.

'We'll arrest you for theft.'

'The theft of a pin?' Amida scoffed.

'Not just that. We can start with the reliquary.'

'You can't prove I took it.'

'You were seen leaving the mosque, and in your house you have the carpet that was stolen along with the reliquary.'

'I borrowed that carpet from the storeroom at the mosque.'

Omar had returned and stood blocking the door. From the look on his face, Kamil knew he had found the tunnel. He caught Kamil's eye and nodded.

Saba came to stand before her brother. 'I know you took the reliquary, Amida,' she said sadly. 'How else could you have known it was empty? Uncle Malik told only me about the Proof of God. You overheard us, didn't you? But you thought he meant the reliquary. You didn't know there was a manuscript inside.' Saba's voice rose. 'You have no idea what the Proof of God is and you're not worthy of being its caretaker.'

'I'm not saying anything,' Amida said, folding his arms.

'Then we'll arrest you for murder.'

'What? I had nothing to do with that.'

'We think otherwise,' Omar said pleasantly. 'You can

talk now or you can come with me and talk later. You'll need bigger shoes, though.'

Amida clearly understood the reference. Beating the bottom of the feet made them swell, sometimes permanently. 'All right. All right. This man wanted the reliquary, so I took it. I gave it to him. He paid me. That's all.'

Kamil felt his pulse rise. Much as he hated to admit it, Omar was right. The bastinado worked.

'You stole it,' Saba corrected him.

'It was going to be mine anyway. It's not stealing when it's your property.'

'It belongs to the community,' Saba insisted. 'It belongs to the world. You have no rights over it.'

'What's this man's name?' Kamil asked.

'I don't know. I gave it to his go-between.'

'What's this go-between's name?'

'How would I know? He always contacted me.'

Kamil let the lie go. What he wanted right now was an explanation for Malik's death.

Kamil lifted the Abyssinian cross. 'Did you take this?'

'He's the only one besides me and Mother who knows where it's kept,' Saba confirmed.

'So maybe you took it,' Amida suggested. 'Malik knew where it was too. Maybe he borrowed it and took it to the mosque for some kind of ritual.'

'How did you know it was in the mosque, Amida?' Kamil asked softly.

Amida was flustered. 'It was just a guess.'

'That's ridiculous,' Saba exclaimed. 'Uncle Malik would never take the sceptre out and carry it around town. It's a sacred object. It has to stay here.'

'I went to ask Malik about it and I left it in the mosque by mistake. So what? I'd have had it back in the box by

Friday service. No one would have noticed it was missing.'

Kamil lifted the sceptre. 'Malik was killed with this.'

There was a shocked silence, then all eyes turned to Amida.

'You killed Uncle Malik?' Saba asked, aghast. 'Why?'

'I didn't kill Malik,' he cried out. 'I would never do that. He was my uncle.'

Balkis tried to stand, but fell back on to the divan. Her face was a deathly white and she was breathing with difficulty. Saba brought her mother some water, then sat beside her, holding her arm.

'I believe you, Amida,' Kamil said.

Amida looked at him in surprise.

'We can help each other, but I need you to tell me the whole story. What happened the night Malik was killed?'

'Otherwise we arrest you for theft *and* murder,' Omar interjected pleasantly.

Amida got up and began to pace, arms folded protectively across his chest, his jaw working compulsively. When he walked towards the door, Omar blocked his way.

'Just make sure no one's out there,' Amida appealed.

Omar shrugged and stepped outside. He came back a few moments later and nodded. 'No djinns, no demons.'

'He'll kill me if he finds out.'

'Who?'

'I told you, I don't know,' Amida said in an anguished voice. 'They call him Kubalou. The man you asked me about, Remzi, is his go-between. I sold the reliquary through him to Kubalou, but then Remzi came back and told me it was empty and accused me of trying to cheat his master. They made me go with them to the Tobacco Works that night, but I swear I had nothing to do with killing those policemen. That was Remzi. He did this too.'

He pushed up his sleeve and thrust out his arm.

The raw edges of the wound were in the shape of an M. Kamil was certain now that it stood for Magnus.

'Remzi told me this was a message from Kubalou, although I think he says that to cover up his own crimes. He's a vicious son of a bitch.' Amida's eyes found the door. He looked hunted. 'I didn't know there was supposed to be anything inside the reliquary. Saba's right. I overheard them talking and Malik referred to it as the Proof of God. Kubalou wanted it for an English buyer.'

'You fool,' Saba said softly.

'If I don't get him the real Proof of God now, I'll end up like . . .' Amida leaned his forehead against the wall.

'Who?' Omar enquired impassively.

Amida shifted and looked nervously at his mother. 'He knew some things about me.'

'That you lie with boys?' Saba suggested.

Omar raised his eyebrows in amusement. Kamil glanced at Balkis, but she didn't seem to notice. She was staring straight ahead as if she had nothing to do with the conversation.

Amida stared angrily at Saba.

'There are no secrets in a village.' She became subdued, as if realising what she had said.

'Was that your boyfriend we found in the graveyard this morning behind the Fatih Mosque?' Omar asked.

Amida nodded miserably.

'Bilal?' Saba exclaimed. 'Bilal is dead?' Kamil thought he heard a note of compassion. He remembered the polite, dark-skinned boy who had served him whisky at Amida's house.

'Yes.' Amida's voice broke.

'You saw the body?' Omar stepped to the door and glanced outside.

'Bilal left me a note to meet him there at the first ezan, that he had something important to show me.' Amida's voice was strained. 'I thought it was odd. I see him every day and he could have shown me anytime. But I went anyway and when I got there, I found him dead.'

'How did you know the note was from him?'

'I recognised his hand. Or . . . I thought I did.'

'So someone happened to find him alone in the graveyard, waiting for you, and decided to rob him?'

'No,' Amida groaned. 'No, I don't think that's what happened. I saw his back.' He held out his wounded arm. 'It was the same.'

Kamil could see him struggling for control and, despite his outrage at Amida's despicable behaviour, he felt sorry for the young man. Omar hadn't seen the joyous smile on Bilal's face before he noticed Kamil coming through Amida's door. Bilal and Amida had been close, and Amida was grieving. Just as others might be grieving now over Elif, Kamil reminded himself, if they hadn't managed to escape from the tunnel.

'You think this is Kubalou sending you his calling card?'

'That bastard Remzi killed him.'

'That must upset you.'

Amida shrugged, but the skin around his mouth twitched. 'He helped me at the monastery.' He turned to Balkis. 'You have no idea what goes on there. The monks . . . Bilal took my place so I wouldn't have to.' He couldn't continue. 'I owed him better than this. I promised I'd take him to Paris,' he sobbed.

The room was silent as they absorbed what Amida had revealed. Kamil couldn't imagine the dapper Owen killing and maiming anyone, and wondered whether he was aware of the brutality engaged in by his hirelings. Still, Owen must have had a sense of what Remzi was capable of, and Kamil had witnessed the veiled threats Owen had made to Amida beneath the Galata Tower.

Kamil gave Amida's reserve a last push. 'Tell us what happened the night of Malik's murder,' he prompted.

Amida stood with his back to the wall, away from the window. His eyes flitted about the room as if his tormentor might appear at any moment.

'Remzi told me Kubalou wanted him to search Malik's house for the Proof of God, so I thought of a ruse to get Malik out that night. I unlocked the mosque door and then went to Malik and told him there was a thief in the building. I left the sceptre there to make the story believable and to keep him occupied working out how it had got there. I thought he'd take it back to the village and that would give us at least an hour to search his house. I waited for Remzi, but no one showed up, so I left.'

'You didn't think to go and look for Uncle Malik?' Saba demanded.

'I didn't know anything would happen,' Amida answered in a subdued voice.

Saba sat on the divan beside her mother, her expression hard. Balkis was hunched over. Kamil thought she looked broken. What must it feel like for a mother to discover her son was involved in murdering her own brother?

'Why did you take Malik's pin, then?' Kamil asked.

Amida didn't answer.

'Did you go back to the mosque?'

'Yes,' Amida whispered.

'You didn't look inside?'

'It was dark. I thought Malik had gone to return the sceptre.'

'And forgotten to lock the door? Was your uncle usually that forgetful?'

'No.' He looked at Kamil with a strangled expression.

'The pin?' Kamil asked again. 'Did you go into Malik's house again?'

'I was worried about him.'

They waited. No one looked at Amida.

'You knew, didn't you?' Kamil asked softly. The stupid boy, unable to face what he had done. Whatever compassion Kamil had had for Amida was gone.

'Malik wasn't there so I took some things to make it look like it was a robbery.'

Saba walked up to her brother and slapped him on the face. 'You didn't even check to see if he was still alive, you bastard.'

Amida dropped to his knees before Balkis. 'Mother, you believe me, don't you? I swear to you, I didn't kill him. Why would I do that?' He began to cry in small, sharp gasps. 'I didn't do anything.'

Balkis nodded and let her hand rest in his hair, too exhausted to respond.

Kamil turned in disgust and left. Omar hesitated, then followed.

When they were outside, Omar asked, 'Aren't we going to arrest him?'

'He's more use to us as a decoy right now,' Kamil responded. 'We need a hare to attract the hound.'

Without another word, they hurried towards Amida's cottage. Omar led him into the bedroom and flung his arms out. 'Want to guess?'

'No.'

Omar walked over to the wall beside the bed and gave it a push. A panel swung aside revealing crumbling stone stairs leading down into darkness. Kamil grabbed a lamp and stepped inside.

Their feet crunched on debris. Unlike the others, this tunnel was dry. Instead of damp and mould, dust and the foetid smell of rat droppings clogged their noses and mouths. It felt airless and very hot. Kamil began to sweat. Omar tramped ahead, just inside the circle of light, treading on his own shadow. After about thirty minutes, they came to a wall of rubble that blocked the tunnel, the wall in which Ali had been entombed on the other side.

Kamil stopped, but Omar kept walking, right up to the wall, and began to haul the stones down, one after another. After a moment, Kamil joined him. They worked until they had excavated a hole big enough to crawl through. On the other side was utter darkness.

32

The messenger was waiting for them at Fatih station. The note was from Battles, asking Kamil to come immediately to the Customs House at Karaköy. Abdullah had taken the initiative to send a messenger to look for him. Perhaps he had underestimated Abdullah, Kamil thought, as he washed the grime from his face and hands.

A visibly distraught Battles met Kamil and Omar at the door to the customs building. He led them around a crowd of disembarking passengers, past scarlet-coated British guards, to a dock where a large black and red steamer was being loaded. A line of smoke trickled upward from its fat chimney.

Battles took them down into the hold, which was piled high with sacks and bundles. These were bound with thick twine, the ends of which were encased in fragments of lead into which had been impressed the official seal. Several large trunks stood open, their seals broken. The air was dank and musty. Oil lamps hung from the low ceiling, their flames burning fitfully, as if gasping for air.

'He's been using the diplomatic pouch to send whole trunkloads back to England,' Battles exclaimed, drawing his hand across his streaks of hair and setting them adrift. 'He's been doing it for months. Delivered them right to the docks and told the staff it was official embassy post. He had the seals, so no one questioned him. Take a look at this.' He led them to one of the open trunks. It was crammed with objects hastily flung together; a tangle of religious objects, jewellery, and coins.

'Where the devil did he get all this stuff?' Battles huffed. 'If you hadn't asked me to look into Owen's shipments, we'd never have caught on.' He pulled out a handkerchief and wiped his sweating forehead. 'How did you know?'

Kamil was busy examining the contents of the hold and didn't answer.

On two of the chests, Kamil found tags with the address: Mr Lionel Rettingate, 58 Smythe Street, Kensington. He called Omar over to show him. 'Scotland Yard will love this. Here's the proof they need to shut down the other end of this business.' The seal was impressed with the initials VR. Did Lionel Rettingate have a brother? Kamil checked the other trunks, then the sacks. All the seals had the initials VR on them, regardless of address.

'Whose initials are these?' he asked Battles.

Battles looked shocked. 'Victoria Regina, of course,' he spluttered. 'Queen Victoria.'

'Naturally.' Feeling slightly foolish, Kamil leaned into the first trunk addressed to Rettingate and went through the contents more carefully, then did the same with the second. Omar busied himself with slicing open the sacks, ignoring Battles' distress. Kamil thought Omar was enjoying himself.

After a few minutes, Kamil plucked out a diamond-studded chalice and held it up for Omar to see. 'Fatih Mosque,' he announced with enormous satisfaction.

Omar unclasped a box and unwrapped the small bundle inside. He called Kamil over and handed him a tiny icon, an exquisitely painted Madonna and Child.

'With a little patience, the egg on the ground becomes

a bird in the sky,' Omar remarked with satisfaction.

Kamil felt elated. This discovery would do more to quell the unrest in the streets than the entire Ottoman army. He wrapped the icon carefully and put it back in its box.

They returned to their search.

'Hold on a moment, what's this?' Kamil pulled something from a trunk, a misshapen silver object with niello engraving. It was Malik's stolen reliquary.

He and Omar grinned at each other.

'Hail to the Queen,' Kamil declared, but quietly so Battles didn't hear.

33

Balkis shivered under the covers despite her fever. Saba sat beside her and pressed her hand against her mother's forehead. 'You're very hot, Mama,' she said worriedly. 'Gudit is making you some apple and rose water compote.'

'Gudit,' Balkis whispered. 'Tell her.'

'Tell her what, Mama?' Gudit had found Balkis the day before lying on the divan and bleeding from a deep cut in her wrist. The midwife claimed her mother had tried to kill herself but Saba didn't believe her. She couldn't imagine her mother, who had so much strength of will, turning her back on them just when they needed her. It must have been an accident. The top-heavy monstrance must have fallen on to the divan, and her mother must have reached up to ward it off and gouged herself. The cut itself wasn't deep enough to be life-threatening and Saba could think of no other explanation. She had found the monstrance on the floor, one of its tines broken and bloody, the others bent. She had kicked it vengefully, then thrown it into the storeroom.

Saba sat for a moment, frowning, then sent for the old servant and told him to fetch Courtidis. Her mother was shaking uncontrollably and an unpleasant odour clung to her. Saba sent another servant to heat some water.

Balkis twisted back and forth on the divan and muttered,

'Container of the unbearable, hail Mary, I can't bear it, I can't bear your message, I can't . . .'

The servant arrived with the bowl of hot water, along with washcloths, a towel, and some gauze. Saba sent her away, then locked the door and made sure there were no draughts. She felt embarrassed at what she was about to do, for she had never seen her mother naked.

'I'm going to bathe you, Mama.' Her mother had quietened. She lay with her eyes closed, breathing erratically. Saba wondered if she had fallen asleep. She took the bandage off her mother's wrist and carefully washed the torn flesh, then wrapped on fresh gauze, securing it with a strip of cloth. Next, she lifted the quilt and laid it aside. The smell was stronger. She quickly peeled off her mother's kaftan and chemise. The foetid stench hit her like a blow and she jerked her head away.

When she turned back, she froze. Her mother's body below the waist was a ruin. Balkis turned slightly and her legs opened enough for Saba to see that she had been horribly mutilated. Instead of the natural contours of a body, there was only a scar. It was infected and inflamed.

Saba was speechless. When her mother began to moan, Saba pulled herself together and focused on washing Balkis quickly so she wouldn't catch a chill. She dipped the cloth in warm water and began her task, starting with her mother's forehead and working down the sagging folds of grey skin until she came to her legs. Consumed equally by pity and disgust, Saba cleaned away the pus that seamed the scar.

She had just finished dressing Balkis in a clean chemise, when there was a peremptory knock at the door. Saba quickly covered her mother with a clean quilt and unlocked the door.

Gudit hurried in, carrying a dish with a lid. 'The compote,' she explained. 'The apples will break her fever. Why was the door locked?'

'She's delirious.'

Gudit put the dish down and went to Balkis's side. 'Oh,' she said, surprised. 'You've changed her clothes.'

'I washed her,' Saba said. Gudit knew. She was the one who usually helped her mother with her toilette. 'I saw. What happened to her?'

Gudit gave her a sly look. 'That's not for you to know.'

'Don't be ridiculous,' Saba shouted. 'She's my mother.'

'She's the priestess,' Gudit responded in a haughty voice.

'In the name of Allah, what does that have to do with anything?'

When Gudit didn't respond, Saba suddenly remembered what her mother had said about the priestess being celibate after initiation. What had been her exact words? That after her initiation, she would no longer *want* to have relations with her husband.

'Is this part of the initiation?' she asked, appalled at the thought.

Gudit turned her leathery face towards Saba and smiled.

It had to have been Gudit. She was the only one who knew how to do the special tattoo of ashes mixed with mother's milk. She was the one who knew all the steps of the ritual. This squat, sour woman who had always seemed so devoted to her mother, who had taught Saba the Melisite prayers when she was a child, and under whose blue-tipped tattoo needle Saba had suffered for weeks – Saba was now seeing her with new eyes. She remembered with a chill Gudit's attack in the hammam and the knife she had spied on the floor as she ran away.

'Did she know?' Saba asked, guessing the answer. If the

ritual had allowed it, her mother would have prepared her long ago. 'Of course not,' she said, answering her own question. 'No one would go along with it, would they, if they knew?'

'The women of this family have been purified for hundreds of years. No one has ever complained.'

That was so ludicrous that Saba had to laugh. 'That we know of. That's not counting the ones who were killed because they refused or who died of infections afterward. Have you taken a look at her?'

'What do you mean?' Gudit stroked Balkis's forehead. 'She's been ill for a long time. Only Allah knows when it's her time.'

'I'm not a doctor, but I know an infection when I see one. You never said a word about it. Constantine might have been able to do something. Instead, you let it fester.'

'That man thinks opium cures everything,' Gudit grumbled, propping Balkis's head up on a pillow. 'I've been treating it. The old ways are best.' She got up to ladle the apple compote into a bowl and sat beside Balkis with a spoon. 'Eat some of this, dear.' Gudit's hand shook and she spilled juice on the fresh sheets.

'Begging your pardon, may I enter?' Courtidis's voice boomed through the doorway.

'Come in, Constantine.' Saba was relieved to see him. 'Thank you for coming so quickly. Mother is delirious. She has an infection. I'm very worried about her.'

He walked in and put down his leather bag. He had taken off his shoes in the entry and Saba noticed his socks had holes in them. He faltered a moment when he saw Gudit sitting by Balkis and blocking his access. 'Begging your pardon, I'll just take a look at the patient, shall I?' he said meaningfully, approaching the divan.

Gudit didn't budge.

'Get up, Gudit,' Saba said with surprising authority.

Gudit hesitated, but obeyed. She hovered at the edge of the room, looking on sullenly.

Saba regarded Courtidis's back as he bent over her mother, soothing her as he looked into her eyes and mouth and palpated her neck and chest through the quilt. His low, calm voice talked on and on about nothing significant, like a chant. She could imagine her mother taking hold of this rope of words and hanging on.

She walked over and put her hand on his shoulder. He stopped moving for a moment.

'Thank you, Constantine,' she said softly into his ear.

Courtidis took a deep breath and continued what he was doing. His brief smile was quickly replaced by a frown.

'She's had a low-grade fever for a long time,' he said. 'There's probably an infection, but she wouldn't let me examine her, so I've just given her powders to bring her temperature down.' He hesitated. 'This is something different.'

Saba squatted by his side. 'What do you mean?' She wanted to tell him about the infection, but she was paralysed by embarrassment and fear. She tried to think what her mother would want her to do.

'I don't know. It's a violent attack on her body. What happened today or yesterday? Did she eat something and become sick? Did something happen to her?'

'She seemed very fatigued, more than usual. She said her muscles hurt.' Saba tried to remember. 'She'd never complained about that before . . .' She grasped the quilt. 'And there's a . . .'

Gudit broke in defensively, 'I gave her boiled barley and

camomile and willow extract. It brought the fever right down.'

'That may be, Gudit. You're not wrong. But this is something much more serious. She's burning up and her breathing is laboured.' He lowered his voice. 'She might, I beg your pardon, Saba ... she might pass away.'

Saba froze at his words. 'No, that can't be. She was fine before. It's just a fever.' She pulled back the quilt, revealing Balkis in her thin chemise. Saba was dismayed at the unpleasant odour rising from her mother's body again, even though she had just washed it.

Gudit ran over and pulled the quilt back over Balkis. 'You can't,' she yelled at Saba. 'It's not proper.'

Saba tried to yank the quilt out of Gudit's hands. When she wouldn't let go, Saba slapped her across the face.

Gudit retreated across the room. Courtidis looked on in consternation.

'There's an infection here,' Saba folded the quilt back again and pointed. 'I'm sorry, Mama.' She cradled her mother's head.

Courtidis lifted Balkis's chemise. 'Beg your ...' He stared down at the circumcision scar, then looked at Saba. He followed her eyes to Gudit standing against the wall.

'There are lots of ways to kill someone,' he said softly, his eyes never leaving Gudit's face, 'but the slow ways are the most merciless.'

He examined Balkis, then gently tucked the quilt around her.

'What is it?' Saba asked desperately. 'Is that what's making her ill?'

'Possibly, if it's infected her blood or if there's something wrong internally.' He startled Saba by pounding his fist on a chest of drawers. 'Why didn't you tell me about this? If I had caught it earlier . . .'

'I didn't know myself until today,' Saba whispered. 'Mama never told me. But if it's an infection, surely there's something you can do. Even now.'

'Saba, I'm sorry, but my skills fail me here. I know of no powders or techniques that can bring down such a high fever and bring order back to her heart and lungs. But I can tell you that whatever it is, it couldn't just be the infection of her . . . lower parts, since that appears to have happened some time ago.' He glared at Gudit. 'Her condition is much worse from the last time I saw her.'

'She can't die, Constantine,' Saba begged. 'Please don't let her die.' What else could she have done to help her? Saba asked herself. Her mother had never countenanced interference from her family. At least she had let Constantine treat her. Could he save her now? He must.

'This must have been brought on by something. Think.'

Saba struggled to focus. She went to the storeroom and brought out the monstrance. 'She cut herself on this.' She held up the discoloured gold tine.

Courtidis took it. 'Show me the wound.'

Saba pulled her mother's arm from beneath the quilt and pushed back her sleeve, revealing the bandage. Courtidis examined and cleaned the wound, then instructed Saba on how to care for it and bind it properly. Saba was glad to follow orders as it allowed her mind to go numb.

He took the tine over to the window. 'This is dirty,' he observed.

'That's Mama's blood.'

'No, I mean there's older dirt underneath, see?' He pointed to the sheath of granular black material beneath the streaks of fresh blood. 'Do you know what that is, Gudit?'

Gudit's face was grey. 'Her mother's blood. She never let me clean it.'

Courtidis waved the tine in the air. 'Come on, Gudit. Let's have it all at once. Why was Balkis's mother's blood on here?' Saba noticed the authority in his tone, so different from his usual shy manner.

'She scratched herself.'

'And?' Courtidis said with elaborately mimed patience. Saba could see he was sweating.

'Well, she died a day later. A red line crept up her arm and then she was gone. I never saw anything like it.' Gudit stepped back towards the door. 'Do you think there's some kind of bug on there that gets under people's skin? It was seventeen years ago.'

'Sounds like blood poisoning.' Courtidis studied the tine again. 'This might have been contaminated with something. It would explain her rapid decline.'

'You mean it was on there for seventeen years and then poisoned Mama?'

'Nature has a thousand ways of betraying us. I wish I knew.'

He took a small vial from his bag. Seeing the compote, he poured a small amount of the yellow syrup into a glass, then added the contents of the vial.

Saba watched his every move, as if by sheer will she could infuse his hands with the power to heal her mother.

'I beg your pardon, but I don't know what else I can do,' he admitted. 'This will relax her.' He felt Balkis's forehead and shook his head. Suddenly he dropped the glass.

Balkis had started to choke. Her face turned bright red

and her tongue swelled, blocking her throat. Her eyes protruded with the effort to get air.

Courtidis lifted her head and turned it to open her airway while a frightened Saba held on to her mother's shoulders. Finally, in desperation, he pushed his finger into her mouth to depress her tongue, but nothing helped. Saba watched in anguish as her mother's body bucked beneath her hands.

Finally, the violent writhing ceased and Balkis's arms fell away. Saba kept her arms around her mother as if the connection through her own body could somehow fool death. She felt an intense bitterness towards the midwife, blaming her for keeping her mother's condition secret for so long, for putting her mother's life in danger. Gudit had killed her mother. Saba turned her head, but there was no one in the room besides Courtidis.

'Mama,' she said in a thick voice, 'don't go. I need to talk to you.' She began to sob.

Courtidis put his arm around her. They sat like that for a long time. When Saba finally stood, she had made a decision about Courtidis. She needed him now, for many reasons.

She went to find Amida.

34

It was dark and had begun to rain heavily by the time Kamil arrived at the Imperial Museum, a dull, leaden rain that insinuated itself into the collar of his waterproof cloak.

The museum was housed in a two-storey structure built into the west slope of the hill above the Golden Horn. Hamdi Bey had already arrived, having received Kamil's message, and had lit the lamps. The light glanced brilliantly off the turquoise and dark blue mosaic tiles that covered the walls. The tiles were partially hidden by glass-fronted cabinets, within which Greek, Roman, early Christian, and Byzantine objects were neatly laid out, categorised, and labelled.

Hamdi Bey led him to the room he used as his office. Despite being roused from his home at a moment's notice, he looked dapper in a neat wool suit and pressed fez. His grey-streaked beard and moustache were freshly trimmed. He peered at Kamil through his spectacles.

'Hang your cloak over there. I apologise for not offering you tea. There's no staff here at this time of night except the guards. I've tasted their tea and I'm not sure I can recommend it to ordinary mortals.'

'I just wanted to make sure this is in a safe place,' Kamil said and took out a bundle wrapped in oiled cloth. He unwrapped it and placed the silver box on Hamdi Bey's desk.

'Ah, Theodore Metochites's reliquary.' Hamdi Bey examined it carefully. He found the latch and opened it. 'Let's see if the lid fits the kettle.'

He disappeared for several minutes. Kamil heard voices and a key turning, then heavy footsteps. Finally, the door opened and Hamdi Bey returned.

'Wait here.' A lean uniformed guard with alert eyes and a rifle stood to attention outside the office door. 'We take no chances,' Hamdi Bey explained as he placed the lead container on his desk beside the reliquary.

'They're about the same size,' Kamil noted, standing over the boxes.

'I have no doubt they were made to fit each other,' Hamdi Bey said as he slid the Proof of God into the reliquary, 'like a hand in a glove.'

He clicked the reliquary shut. They stood for a moment, regarding the miracle of this convergence.

'This is an extraordinarily important object,' Hamdi Bey said solemnly. 'It's rare that a document of this importance is found intact, and of course for humanity its value is beyond price. Imagine,' he said with mounting excitement, 'this could solve all dispute between religions.' He looked chagrined. 'I know what you're thinking, Kamil, but I'm not one of those devout believers. I try to live a moral life but I don't have much time for the trappings of religion. I delegate that to Ismail Hodja.' He smiled at Kamil. 'I suspect we're much the same in that regard.'

Kamil returned his smile. 'I'm afraid so. This Proof of God is an odd thing, isn't it, regardless of whether it proves anything or not. Do you think it really was dictated by Jesus and never seen by the Prophet Muhammad?'

'Ismail Hodja is convinced of its authenticity. There is no higher authority, to my poor mind.'

'He'd never make a judgement like that if he wasn't entirely sure.'

'And just the fact that people believe in the truth of it, which apparently has been the case for centuries, means it's an enormously powerful force for good and for evil.' He laid his hand reverently on the reliquary. 'Perhaps with this document, we can bring some peace to this world.'

Kamil thought about the difficulties he had preventing people from harming each other on his small patch of turf in Istanbul, and thought it unlikely that any document, however special, would be able to bring about that miracle, but he didn't wish to undermine Hamdi Bey's extraordinary dream. People like Hamdi Bey had a special way with dreams and could somehow make them become reality. Like the Imperial Museum and the Academy of Fine Arts. In the meantime, they had to keep the Proof of God safe.

'Where do you keep it?' he asked.

'In a locked room in the basement under continual armed guard. At least two men are on duty at all times – one guards the perimeter of the building, the other stays right by the door to the basement. The walls of the room are solid stone with an iron door and another at the top of the stairs. I hate to think what that room was designed for when this place was built. We've ordered a safe, but it'll take at least ten more days to deliver.'

Hamdi Bey called the guard into his office, then picked up the reliquary and its contents and took it back outside, followed closely by the alert-looking guard. Kamil heard the same sequence of sounds as before, but in reverse. After a few minutes, Hamdi Bey returned without the guard.

As they walked through the museum towards the front door, Hamdi Bey told Kamil its history. In 1472 Sultan

Mehmet II had built it as a pavilion for his new palace, a platform from which his pages could watch games of jirit on the field below. He had built his first palace on the ruins of the Great Palace of Byzantium, already decayed beyond repair when he took the city in 1453, but before too long he moved to this acropolis above Topkapi Gate. He laid out his second palace like a nomadic encampment, one jewel-like pavilion after another set within magnificent gardens.

Outside the front door of the museum, Hamdi Bey pointed to a cluster of ancient columns and capitals in the courtyard. 'We found those when we restored the building. They say when Sultan Mehmet the Conqueror walked through the ruined halls of the Great Palace, he became so sad he recited a distich by the Persian poet Saadi: "The spider is the curtain-holder in the Palace of the Caesars. / The owl hoots its night call on the Towers of Aphrasiab."'

Kamil took his leave and, after Hamdi Bey shut the door, stood for a while in the entrance alcove, pondering the calligraphy above the door. It was in the old Cufic style and he couldn't decipher it. Behind him, the rain pattered forlornly on the paving stones. Kamil found that he couldn't face going home to his orchids and the *Gardener's Chronicle*; to an empty house. He wished Elif were waiting for him there, ready to lean her head against his chest. A small, intimate surrender.

Kamil shivered and peered out through the rain. On the hill above the museum loomed the walls of Topkapi Palace. He could just make out the tightly shut Gate of the Watchmen of the Girls, a reminder that beyond these high walls was now a city of women – the widows, sisters, and daughters of deceased sultans. Like the Byzantine palaces,

Topkapi too was slowly crumbling, along with the lives of its melancholy inhabitants. Later generations of rulers and their families had built spacious new palaces and villas strung along the Bosphorus like pearls. The old came to Topkapi to die.

A bleak urgency seized Kamil. He clutched his rain cape around him, mounted his horse and turned towards home.

35

A night bird called outside her window. Saba drifted in and out of dreams. In one, from the waist down, she had become the lion from over the doorway. From the waist up, she was a woman with wings instead of arms, naked and ashamed. Without hands, she couldn't cover herself. She felt increasingly frustrated and angry at her predicament and opened her mouth, only to find that instead of speech, what issued was a roar. People ran from her. She tossed under the quilt and threw it off, then awoke. She pulled the quilt back over her body and tried to settle. Her stomach had been restless all evening. Gudit and some of the servants had brought her mother's body into the prayer house. She would be buried today in the little cemetery behind the Kariye Mosque.

Saba had had no appetite for dinner, so Gudit had brought her a dish of quince stewed in pomegranate juice. Even the clotted cream hadn't cut the tartness of the pomegranate, however, and the quince had an odd medicinal undertone. When Gudit wasn't looking, Saba emptied her bowl back into the serving dish. She realised then for the first time that she was alone. It was a devastating moment. No one cared what she did now. All the people she had relied on were gone – Uncle Malik, her mother. Her brother was out and hadn't returned, unaware that his mother was dead. Courtidis had been called to tend to the victims of an accident at a tannery outside the city walls and wouldn't be back until the following day. After the shock of her mother's revelations and Kamil's rejection of them, she no longer felt she could call on him, even though she supposed she now had some claim on him as her brother. No, there was only Gudit.

Saba finally understood the root of Gudit's power over her mother – she had mutilated more than Balkis's body. She had weakened her spirit as well, and then turned herself into her mother's only friend. Gudit's attack in the hammam now made more sense. She needed to impress herself into the flesh and spirit of the next priestess. Saba pressed her face into her pillow and rocked back and forth under the quilt until she dozed off again.

It must be near morning, Saba thought, startled awake by the renewed flapping of the bird. She froze. There it was again. A creak. Her floors didn't creak and her door was locked. She willed herself to pull the quilt slowly from her face and set her ears to listening. There it was again, from the direction of the wardrobe. Had a cat crept in during the day and nested in her folded robes? She raised her head. As her eyes adjusted to the darkness, she saw movement, a shadowy shape approaching her bed. Saba's heart hammered and her limbs felt paralysed.

She ran through the contents of her room quickly in her mind, but could think of no object that might serve as a weapon. She thought of using the quilt as a net to trap the person's head. That might give her enough time to run to the door and unlock it. The key was old and unwieldy. Could she get out in time? If she screamed loudly, the servants in the quarters at the back of the house would surely hear, but they might be too late.

As the figure approached, Saba recognised the smell of bitter herbs that always accompanied Gudit.

'How dare you come in here,' she shouted. 'Get out. Get out.'

She threw off the covers and tried to get up from the bed, but found herself pinned by the midwife's powerful grip. Gudit tied Saba's hands above her head to the wrought-iron headboard with a thin strip of cloth, stuffed a wad of cotton in her mouth, then slit her nightdress down the front with a knife.

The deep chill of fear settled in Saba's spine. Remembering the knife, she ceased to struggle, afraid to move, but also afraid not to move. She fought her panic and willed herself to think. What did Gudit want? Was this how the ritual cutting was carried out, with force and stealth in the night? Was this why her mother had refused to talk about her initiation, because it was violent and humiliating? The thought of her mother at the mercy of this madwoman enraged Saba. Remembering that the wrought-iron edges of the headboard were sharp where the repeat design ended, she moved her bound wrists up and down, focused on finding one of the sharp edges.

Gudit lit a lamp and balanced it on the bed by Saba's feet. Then she took hold of Saba's left ankle and pulled it roughly aside. Her face was illuminated in patches as it disappeared between Saba's legs. Saba felt her flesh being pinched together and then pulled painfully like dough. Shadows flew across the room like enormous winged creatures.

Saba kicked her free leg upward and connected with Gudit's face. The knife bit into her thigh and she felt something wet flowing down her leg. Gudit's grip on Saba's ankle weakened for just a moment and Saba took the opportunity to twist her lower body away, her hands still bound to the headboard. She heard a rending sound as the strip of cloth tore on the rough iron edges.

But Gudit had regained her balance and, kneeling over Saba, pressed the knife to her breast. 'Slut,' she hissed. 'Just like your mother.'

With one free hand Saba reached for the quilt and with the other pushed hard at Gudit, knocking her backward. She pulled the quilt over herself to guard against the blade and rolled backward, trying to get away from Gudit.

A moment later, the midwife had pinned the quilt around Saba, trapping her against the wall.

'What are you doing, Gudit? Is this how the priestess is initiated?' Saba was surprised at how calm her voice sounded.

'You'll find out.'

'Why do it like this? Why not properly, in the prayer hall?'

'Of course that would be better, but as you can see, I don't have assistants anymore, not like in your grandmother's day. Everyone respected me then. I am the left hand of the Melisites.'

'You could train assistants,' Saba suggested, squirming inside the cocoon, looking for a way out. 'You have important skills. People want to learn from you.'

Gudit knelt on the bed holding the quilt shut with both hands, the knife resting on the mattress beside her.

'You'd never have been chosen to be priestess in the old days. People obeyed the rules then. It was a partnership. I was the left hand, the priestess was the right hand.'

'It can still be like that,' Saba said, putting as much feeling into her voice as she could muster.

Gudit lifted one hand from the quilt and stroked Saba's tangled hair back from her forehead. 'Maybe. But first you must become pure.'

Pushing her feet against the wall for momentum, Saba launched herself towards Gudit and rolled on top of the knife. She freed her arms and tried to throw the quilt over Gudit's head, but Gudit had found the knife again and sliced the quilt in half, emerging from it like a snake hatching from its egg. She lunged for Saba's legs and gripped her ankle once more. With her free leg, Saba kicked the lamp hard. It fell to the ground, the light went out, and the acrid smell of oil filled the air.

Blinded, Gudit paused, and at that moment Saba pushed her backward off the bed. She saw the gleam of the blade as it fell on to the carpet and lunged for it. Gudit grabbed her wrist, but Saba refused to let go of the knife. They struggled on the floor in the dark, each pushing the blade close to the other, the midwife's powerful grip trying but unable to force Saba's wrist backward.

'Kill me and you'll have no priestess at all,' Saba whispered hoarsely. 'All you'll have is Amida.'

The balance shifted for just a moment and Saba's hand jolted forward. Gudit uttered a piercing cry and scrambled to her feet. Saba could hear her harsh sobbing, then it was gone. Entirely gone.

She tried to stand, but her legs were shaking too hard. Saba realised she still held the knife. Her hand was wet and sticky.

Finally, she managed to get to her feet. Footsteps sounded outside. The servants.

Someone knocked and tried the door. 'Is everything all right?'

'Just a moment,' she croaked.

She lit the lamp again and almost dropped it. Her hands were covered with blood. The room was empty.

'A nightmare,' she called through the door. 'I'm fine now. Go back to sleep.'

Saba followed the trail of blood across the carpet. Bloody palm prints were strewn across the wall like roses on English wallpaper. Saba pressed her hands between the prints, adding the pattern of her own smaller ones. The wall gave and a panel tilted inward. Beyond she saw ancient stone stairs descending into the ground. She knew where they would lead.

Putting her shoulder to the heavy wardrobe, she pushed it in front of the panel, surprised at her own strength. Then she stripped off the remnants of her nightdress. Her inner thighs were streaked with blood. The cuts weren't deep, but they hurt. She reached into the wardrobe, put on a fresh nightdress, then sank to the floor, her arms around her knees, her back to the wardrobe. A grey light washed the room.

After a few minutes, she got up, wrapped herself in a robe, and unlocked the door. She told the shocked servants to clean the blood from her room. She didn't care what they thought. She was the priestess now.

36

'Owen is still in the city,' Omar pronounced. 'I can feel it in my bones.'

They sat on stools in the small square behind the Fatih police station, enjoying the dusty autumn light filtering through the yellow leaves. It was a warm morning. Steam from the previous night's rain misted the air so everything looked, Kamil thought, like an Impressionist painting. He unbuttoned his jacket and took another sip of tea.

First thing that morning, he had presented the icon to the Greek Orthodox Patriarch and watched with satisfaction as it was reinstalled in the church before a weeping congregation. Then he had ridden to the Fatih Mosque and convinced its reluctant imam that the diamond-studded chalice and other Christian artefacts he had recovered were better off being displayed in the Imperial Museum than locked away in his storeroom.

Kamil had one more day before he had to face Nizam Pasha, but he no longer cared about that. So much else had happened in the past few days that Nizam Pasha's demands seemed as distant as the chirp of a sparrow in the shrubbery. Kamil wanted Owen brought down before he infected anyone else with his rabid insouciance, inspiring atrocious acts in his name, then branding them with his initial as if they were works of art. Ottoman law wouldn't allow Kamil to arrest him, but he would like to make sure he was put in the hands of the British police and punished.

'He's not going anywhere until he gets his hands on the Proof of God,' Omar went on. 'He's like a wolf that's smelled blood. He thinks Amida's a sheep and he's got one claw through his hind leg. So we set the bloody sheep out, pinch it to make it squeal, and wait for the wolf to come for its meal.'

'Omar, you should have been either a butcher or a zookeeper.'

'Not a farmer?'

'Farmers don't risk their sheep to catch a wolf.'

'Point taken. What do you think?'

'You mean we let Owen think Amida actually has the Proof of God?'

'Exactly. The problem is he knows someone tried to arrest him when he met with Amida, so he's not going to trust him to set up another meeting. He'll come to Amida, just as he said. At his home. Tonight.'

'Owen must know we're on to him.' They still had no clues as to his whereabouts.

'Of course someone will have squealed that the great Magistrate Kamil came looking for him and discovered he was smuggling stuff through the diplomatic post. That kind of news spreads like wildfire. Even the embassy kitchen maid will know, and if she knows, everyone knows. That he killed Malik, Ali, and the boy in Fatih, those cards are still in our hands. We have him for smuggling. He doesn't know we have him for murder too.'

'There's no proof that Owen killed anyone himself,' Kamil reminded him. 'You weren't able to extract a confession from Remzi, even with your modern methods.'

'What about the murder weapon, that cross thing, right in his living room?'

Kamil shook his head. 'The Tarla Bashou apartment was rented under another name and the descriptions we got of the owner are too vague to prove that it was him.'

'Remzi couldn't have killed Malik alone. He couldn't have walked two steps after the special treatment we gave him. He would've had to be carried out of jail. I bet Kubalou was there that night.'

Kamil considered this. 'You're probably right.'

He wondered about the buyer Amida said Owen had lined up in England for the Proof of God. Could it be one of the sects Ismail Hodja had warned him about? Arresting Owen wouldn't be the end of the story and he worried about Hamdi Bey. Did the gentle old man realise how dangerous possession of the Proof of God could be? It would make the museum a lightning rod for unscrupulous people like Owen and fanatics willing to stop at nothing to get their hands on the treasure. He hadn't shared this with Omar, who was still unaware of the contents of the Proof. Omar knew only that it had been placed in the museum with the other antiquities.

'Kubalou has no idea where the Proof of God is and Amida made a pretty good show of knowing where it was the other night. So let him think you still have it. That way he still believes he can lay his hands on it.'

'By attacking me or Elif Hanoum again.'

'So now you're fainting at the first sign of danger?'

Kamil didn't rise to Omar's jab. Omar would understand he was concerned about Elif, not himself. 'Let's talk to Amida again.'

'Like I said, send a thief to catch a thief. One nail drives out another.'

*

IT TOOK SEVERAL hours to track down Amida. He had spent the night in an apartment in Balat. A boy with a harelip answered the door and told them Amida had already left, but then they found him hiding behind a wall in the back garden. They brought him to the Fatih police station.

The ruse was simple. They made a deal with Amida. He would let Omar know if Kubalou contacted him again about the Proof of God, or they would throw him in jail for theft and murder.

'What do I tell him if he asks me?' Amida looked nervously at the window. 'I don't have it.'

Kamil smiled pleasantly. 'Arrange a meeting where you promise to hand it over, then tell Chief Omar about the meeting. Didn't Kubalou say he was going to be visiting you this evening?'

Amida gulped and nodded. 'How do I tell you he's there?'

'Send someone to the station with this.' Kamil handed him Malik's sketch of a fox. Avi would also be watching and report back if the Frank appeared.

'If Kubalou finds out I'm lying, he'll kill me.'

'Not as long as he thinks you know where the Proof is.'

'The minute you tell him you don't, smartarse, you're a dead man,' Omar added. 'And don't think we're blind. You won't see us, but we'll be watching you.'

Amida didn't move. 'What if there's more than one guy? What about Remzi? And Kubalou has another man, named Ben. If you arrest one, the other one might still kill me.'

'We can lock you up,' Omar offered. 'You'll be safe here.'

'No thanks.' Amida buttoned his jacket and waited uncertainly.

'Go home.' Omar gestured towards the door.

Kamil and Omar stood at the window and watched him walk away.

'Do you think we should have told him about his mother?' Omar asked.

'No.' Kamil thought of how great Saba's sorrow must be and wished he could comfort her. She was his sister, after all. And he was the better brother.

Amida hesitated in the square and looked around, then hurried down Kemer Altou Street. Behind him strode a tall man in a cloak and turban. A beggar boy ran up and tugged on his robe, asking for alms but the man brushed him away.

37

Saba saw Amida stride into the compound. She also caught sight of a turbaned stranger behind him in the lane before he turned and disappeared. She walked stiffly across the courtyard, her bandaged legs rubbing against each other beneath her robe. She followed the oleanders to Amida's cottage and, finding the door ajar, pushed it open and went in.

'Amida,' she called.

Amida came to the door, unbuttoning his jacket. 'Hello, little sister,' he said, regarding her grim face. 'Has something happened?'

'Mama is dead.'

'What?' Amida sank against the door frame. 'What happened? Did someone . . .'

Saba wondered what he suspected. Whatever it was, she was sure, was nowhere near as bizarre as the truth.

'Constantine thinks she was poisoned by something on that monstrance above the divan. It fell and she cut herself on it.'

'Poisoned?' Amida repeated in a disbelieving voice. 'But she was strong and healthy.'

'She was ill, Amida. Very ill, even before the poisoning.' She paused. 'We just didn't see it.'

Amida sank shakily on to the sofa. He sat, unmoving, head in his hands.

Saba sat beside him and waited.

'I should have known there was something wrong,' Amida admitted finally, lifting his head. 'When Kamil Pasha brought the cross back, I thought maybe the shock had done that to her. I wish . . .' He choked down a sob.

Saba sat closer and put a tentative hand on his shoulder. When he didn't react, she left it there.

'I wish I'd had a chance to explain things before she passed away. I can't bear the thought that she died thinking I was responsible for Malik's murder.'

Saba said nothing. He was responsible, she thought, but her anger had leached away under the onslaught of sorrow. There was room only for one measure in every cup, she mused, and hers was filled with grief. There would be no room for anger until she had drunk this cup dry.

She went into the kitchen, poured a glass of water, and gave it to him. He stared at the glass in his hand, but didn't drink. His shoulders heaved. She took the glass from him and laid a hand on his arm. There would be time for recriminations later.

38

Omar jumped up from sleep, fully alert. Avi was pulling at his arm. 'Chief, Chief. The Frank is at the village. He followed Amida from the jail and then he left and came back again with two men.'

Omar was immensely relieved to see Avi. 'All right. Calm down and tell me what you saw.'

Mimoza had been asleep on a mattress in the corner. She sat up and asked drowsily, 'Where's the fire, husband?'

'Right here,' Omar retorted. 'Where else would it be? Don't worry, I'm not going to see my mistress. She's still asleep. Like you should be.'

'Avi.' She blushed to see that the boy had overheard. 'What are you doing up so late? It must be midnight.' When she saw Omar and Avi turn to leave, she jumped up and tried to block their way. 'He's a child, Omar. Not a policeman.'

'Worry about me. I'm the policeman.' Omar kissed her on the cheek and pushed past.

A carriage waited in the lane. Omar leaned down and asked Avi, 'How did you get the driver to bring a beggar boy across Fatih in the middle of the night?'

Avi pulled out his sack of coins, which had shrunk considerably. 'I went to the station first, but they said you had gone home.'

'Good boy. Now I need you to go get the magistrate.' He

gave the driver directions and told him to hurry. This mission would keep Avi out of harm's way.

As soon as the carriage had pulled away, Omar ran for his horse. They had waited at the station all evening for Amida's signal or Avi's return. Finally, Kamil had suggested they each go home, in case Avi had gone there instead. Omar had left instructions at the station to inform him at once if the fox sketch or Avi arrived.

One mistake after another. Most of all, Omar berated himself for falling asleep before Avi had returned safely. Allah was right not to have entrusted a son to him. If he went to the station now to fetch his men, Owen might slip away before they reached Sunken Village. He cursed. He should have sent Avi to the station first. He decided to go to Sunken Village and keep an eye on Owen until Kamil arrived. He'd stick to Owen like a nit.

When he got there, Omar tied up his horse, ran down the stairs into the village and, keeping his back against the wall, moved slowly towards Amida's cottage. He crept up to the windows. The curtains were drawn and he couldn't hear any voices. He checked the other cottages and Balkis's house. There was no sound or movement, as if this were a normal chilly autumn night and everyone was asleep.

Suddenly the sounds of a piano drifted from Amida's cottage.

Omar found an open window to a back room, and climbed over the sill. The door of the room was ajar, and he saw a light and heard voices that he guessed were coming from the direction of the sitting room. Pressing his back against the wall, he edged towards the light. He heard footsteps approaching in the corridor. Just as someone pushed open the door, Omar disappeared into the wall.

KAMIL GALLOPED THROUGH the black, deserted streets of the city over the back of Pera hill, past the cemetery, and down to the Old Bridge. Avi had said three men, so Kamil had taken Yakup with him. They were both armed with revolvers. Avi had strenuously objected to being left behind.

They clattered across the Old Bridge, through Oun Kapanou Square, and down Djoubalou Boulevard. Finally, the enormous shadow of the Sultan Selim Mosque rose before them. Kamil and Yakup jumped off their horses and ran down the stairs into the open cistern.

It had taken them over half an hour to reach Sunken Village. Add to that the time it had taken Avi to get to Beshiktash, and Kamil reckoned Omar had already been in Sunken Village for an hour. He hoped the Police Chief had taken reinforcements, but knowing Omar, he had barrelled in like a bear after honey. He supposed he might have done the same. It was their only chance to arrest Owen and neither of them wanted to let him slip away. For a moment, he pictured a satisfied Omar with three criminals all trussed and ready to be carted to jail. No, he thought, three men were too much even for Omar to handle by himself.

The village was still and dark, the central square deserted. There was no sign of Omar. Kamil and Yakup split up and made a circuit, keeping close to the walls, then converged on Amida's cottage.

Kamil froze. From the curtained windows he heard the strains of a sonata, perfectly executed. Not Amida. Owen.

Kamil told Yakup to wait outside the front door, then

crept around the side of the house. He found the open window, climbed in, and felt his way through the room. Light seeped under the inner door. He pushed it open slowly and peered out. He was in a corridor leading to the sitting room. Cautiously, he edged his way forward until he could see into the room beyond.

The room was brightly lit by Amida's Venetian lamps, two of which stood beside each other on a table by the sofa, as if someone had needed extra light there. Owen was sitting at the piano. Behind him was a man Kamil had never seen before, idly flipping a deck of playing cards. He didn't see a third man, or Amida, or Omar. Kamil's eyes were drawn to the floor, where a leg protruded from behind the sofa.

Suddenly his head exploded with pain and he dropped to his knees. His vision was blurred, but he recognised Remzi standing over him, cudgel in hand.

The piano playing ceased. 'Kamil,' Owen called out, his voice betraying his surprise. 'Is that you?' He got up and came towards him. 'What the blazes are you doing here?' He reached down his hand to help Kamil up.

Kamil struggled to stand on his own. He pressed a hand to his head and it came away bloodied. He felt nauseous, but his vision gradually cleared. Remzi had disappeared. Behind Owen stood a tall, powerfully built man with ginger hair who was wearing a suit too small for his massive shoulders. He had sharp, wary eyes in a blunt face and the revolver in his hand was pointed at Kamil.

Owen turned and frowned at the man. 'Put that away.' To Kamil, he explained, 'This is my associate Ben. He acts as my bodyguard. You can't be too careful in this part of the city, especially at night.'

Kamil waited.

'Why don't we go somewhere and you can have a wash?' Owen suggested, blocking Kamil's view of the body behind the sofa.

'No, thanks.' Kamil had no intention of confronting Remzi, who was somewhere behind him. To reach the front door he'd have to get past Ben, who was eyeing him intently. His weapon was still in his hand, although it was no longer pointed at Kamil. Still, Kamil could sense Ben was aware of his every move.

Owen and Kamil stood facing each other. Through his blinding headache, Kamil regarded the tall, lanky Englishman's face, his pale eyes, patrician nose, and ever-present smile. Kamil thought Owen looked momentarily lost.

Owen's smile grew wider. 'What's the use,' he said lightly. 'You're always one step ahead of me, Kamil.' He settled back on the piano stool and reached for a glass and a bottle on a nearby table. 'The Ardbeg is almost gone, I'm afraid, but there's a drab left. The beggar has good taste in whisky, at least.' He poured some of the amber liquid and reached the glass out to Kamil. 'This'll help.'

Kamil took one step and staggered as a jagged edge of pain ripped through him. The next step was passable and the third bearable. He could see more of the body behind the sofa now. It was still hidden from the waist up, but from the slender calves Kamil could tell it wasn't Omar. He was relieved.

He took the glass of whisky from Owen and drank it down.

'Your gun? I presume you have one.' Owen put out his hand. 'Please.'

Reluctantly, Kamil drew the Colt from the holster under his jacket and handed it to him. Owen placed it on the table next to the bottle. Kamil reached out his glass and Owen refilled it, a parody of the gracious host at a dinner party.

'Why are you here, Kamil?' Owen asked. 'I really wish you hadn't come,' he added sadly. 'I was rather fond of you.'

Kamil noted the past tense. 'Where's Amida?'

Owen nodded towards the sofa. 'There he is, poor chap. Had a bit of a whack.'

Taking his glass, Kamil approached and bent over the body. Amida lay on his stomach between the sofa and a low table, illuminated by the two Venetian lamps. He was naked from the waist up. His back was tattooed with wings, one of them complete, the other an outline waiting to be filled in.

'Impressive, isn't it?' Owen commented. 'Wouldn't mind having a set of those myself. Bet it'd be a big hit with the ladies.'

'Is he . . . ?' Kamil turned Amida's face to the side and examined it.

'Dead? No, I don't think so. There appears to be life in the fellow yet. "And cheeks all pale, which, but an hour ago, blushed at the praise of their own loveliness,"' he recited.

Kamil set his glass of whisky within reach on the table. He sat on the arm of the sofa, facing Owen on the piano bench across the room, and fished in his pocket for his cigarette case. Ben tensed and took a step closer. Kamil held up the cigarette with a thin smile, then leaned over and picked up Amida's ormolu device to light it. 'What do you want with Amida?' he asked Owen.

'We had some business to discuss.' Owen flapped his hand in the air. 'I know, I know. It seems a devil of a way to discuss anything, but believe me, it was necessary. That fellow was playing me for a fool.'

On the floor, Amida groaned. Kamil knew how he felt.

'He'll have a bump in the morning,' Owen explained apologetically, 'nothing more.'

'What business does a cultural attaché have in Charshamba in the middle of the night?' Kamil asked.

'I could ask the same of the good magistrate.'

Tired of the standoff, Kamil decided to place his cards on the table, 'You're here for the Proof of God.'

Owen looked impressed. 'Bravo, Kamil. Bravo.'

'Why do you want it?'

'Why does one want anything, Kamil? What do you want? Wealth? Fame? Glory?' He let his fingers trickle along the piano keys as he sipped his whisky and regarded Kamil's impassive face. 'No, I think not. You're not ambitious, my friend. And neither am I. We're nourished by the goodwill and respect of our fellow men. We're very much alike in that regard. This is nothing more than a simple business transaction.'

'Well, fill me in, then,' Kamil suggested calmly. 'Have you found what you were looking for?'

'Can't tell you that. It's a matter of some discretion. You understand.' Owen turned around, crossed his legs, and leaned towards Kamil. 'What have you got your heart set on, my friend?' he asked earnestly. 'I'm very well connected. Maybe I can help.'

'You haven't got anything I want. Your associate Remzi already found that out.'

Owen looked offended. 'I thought you and I were on the way to becoming friends. But clearly I haven't yet earned your trust.'

Kamil held out his empty glass and gestured towards the bottle. 'That's good whisky.'

Owen chuckled and handed him the bottle. 'Leave a finger for me.'

In filling his glass, Kamil managed to drop his cigarette and spill whisky on the sofa. Suddenly, his eyes froze on Ben across the room. He had taken out his gun and was training it on Kamil.

'What are you doing?' Owen demanded.

'He's up to something,' Ben grumbled, shoving the gun back in his waistband.

Owen craned his neck at Kamil. 'Surely not.'

Kamil took out his handkerchief and blotted the sofa. 'We were discussing the Proof of God,' he prompted, leaving the damp handkerchief draped over the back.

'I'm intrigued. How do you know about it?'

Kamil didn't answer, but took another cigarette from his case and lit it with a match, keeping the matchbox in his hand.

'I didn't think anyone besides these Melisite types knew about it.' Owen gestured towards Amida. 'Although this young man has exhibited more bravado than good sense. He told us he knew where it was, but I believe he knows nothing.' He looked at Kamil quizzically. 'In fact, he thinks you have it. He said he followed you, hoping to wrest it from you.' When Kamil didn't answer, he asked, 'Unlikely, I know, but what do you make of his assertion? Do you have it?'

'You're right,' Kamil answered. 'He doesn't know where it is.'

'And you do?'

'I do.'

'Ah. Will you tell me?'

'Maybe. First tell me what happened to Malik.'

'Who's Malik?'

The fact that Owen didn't even know the name of the man whose death he had occasioned infuriated Kamil. 'The caretaker of the Kariye Mosque.'

Owen took a deep breath and let it out slowly. 'Believe me, Kamil, that wasn't my idea. I simply asked one of my local associates to find a way to get the man to talk. He was uncommonly stubborn. Why should he care? It's only a packet of old papers. It's beyond me, really, why anyone should care. The buyer in London belongs to some kind of group that reveres – I'm not exaggerating, *reveres* – this thing. It's utterly ridiculous. I sense that you'd agree with me on that, at least.'

'Were you there?'

'Where? In the mosque?' Owen paused. 'I owe you the truth. I was there, with my two associates. And, believe me, I was disgusted. These Orientals have their own ways of getting things done but one mustn't interfere. Only in this case, it did no good. A waste, an utter waste. But that will all be redeemed now when you tell me where it is.'

'I don't think so.'

Owen began to pick out a tune on the piano with one hand. 'That's a shame. I have a lot of money riding on this, my friend, enough to finance a small kingdom.' He shook his head in amused disbelief. 'For a pile of paper in a crushed silver box. It's inconceivable to me why my buyer is willing to bankrupt himself to get it, but,' he gave Kamil a charming, lopsided smile, 'his loss is my gain. I'd be happy to share the profit with you.'

Kamil was becoming impatient. Where was Omar? He couldn't tackle all three of these men by himself. Yakup was outside waiting for his signal, but he wouldn't be fast enough to cross the room before Ben could fire a shot.

He had no choice but to stall for more time. 'What will you do with all that money?' he asked Owen.

'Retire to an estate and finally claim the position in English society that I should have inherited from my father. You know what I mean, Kamil. You're the son of a lord, just as I am. We're naturally drawn to one another. Birds of a feather.' He leaned forward. 'You should trust me.'

'You can let Amida go. He's of no use to you. I'm the only one who knows where it is.'

'He'll be fine here. How do I know you're telling the truth?'

Kamil looked offended. 'You know better than that.'

'Yes, I believe I do,' Owen said thoughtfully, regarding Kamil with a sad smile. 'I believe I do.' He turned back to the piano and played a few bars of what Kamil thought might be Mozart.

Kamil calculated the distance between himself and his gun on the table beside the piano. Owen could easily reach it from where he sat.

Owen turned around and gave a mock bow. 'What can I do to convince you, Kamil?'

'You can let Amida go and answer some questions about those chests full of antiquities and jewellery.'

'I thought that had to be you. No one else could have worked it out. Congratulations. And what about that flaxen-haired damsel, Miss Elif? Amida said you went out on a limb to rescue her.' Owen chuckled. 'My dear fellow, is that the mark of a casual acquaintance? But you can't be beside her every moment, old chap. I'd be honoured to ensure that no harm comes to her.' He began to recite, '"And thou art dead, as young and fair / As aught of mortal birth; / And form so soft, and charms so rare, / Too soon return'd to Earth!"'

'"Look around and choose thy ground, and take thy rest",' Kamil responded in a hard voice, furious at Owen's implied threat.

Owen looked enormously pleased. 'My dear friend. You know Byron too! How wonderful! That's from "My Thirty-Sixth Year", isn't it? What a delightful change from the rather uninspired company I'm forced to keep these days.' He gave Ben a toothy smile. 'Sorry, old man, but you're not exactly a poet, though you have many endearing qualities. Kamil, you know we'd be smashing good friends if you gave me half a chance. Tell me where the Proof of God is and let's split the proceeds. Right down the middle. No one will know.'

Kamil looked down at Amida.

'Oh, he won't say a word. I can guarantee you that,' Owen assured him.

The confidence of his prediction sent a chill through Kamil.

Suddenly a shot rang out. At Kamil's feet, Amida's body writhed, then lay still. The carpet pattern began to blur. Kamil turned to see his gun in Owen's hand.

'Not to worry. Nothing serious, although the next one will be. I'm in a bit of a rush. I'll trade you Amida's life, and Elif's, for the Proof of God. Now that's surely a bargain you can't refuse? It's a pile of paper, for heaven's sake. Surely it's not worth two lives.' Owen smiled. 'You see, Kamil, I do know you. I know your type.'

There was no more time to stall, Kamil decided. Omar or no Omar, he had to act now. He picked up one of the Venetian lamps and hurled it on to the sofa so that its delicate glass belly shattered and oil spilled over the cotton cover, already soaked with whisky. The second lamp followed. Kamil grabbed the ormolu device and ducked behind the sofa just as Owen released another shot. Out of the corner of his eye he could see Ben heading towards him. Kamil pressed the lever and a flame shot out. He held it to the oil-soaked handkerchief draped over the back of the sofa and when the cloth caught fire, he flung it on to the seat.

Ben was almost on top of him. Kamil scuttled around the other side of the sofa just as a bullet screamed by his head. He lit another part of the sofa with the flame from the device, praying that, in spite of everything he believed, this time there was a God, and he was looking his way.

Crimson and yellow flames shot up as the lamp oil caught fire and spread to the straw stuffing. Black smoke began to fill the room.

Owen slammed the piano lid down. 'You can't win this,' he shouted and ran towards the corridor, Ben behind him. They stopped briefly to confer with Remzi, then they were gone.

Kamil threw himself across the floor and tore open the front door.

Yakup burst into the room, gun drawn. The draught caused the fire to bloom.

Outside the cottage, excited voices shouted, 'Fire! Call the fire brigade!'

Kamil instructed Yakup to bring Amida outside, then turned to pursue Owen and his men.

In the corridor, he paused and listened. He heard a noise coming from the bedroom and peered around the door. Ben was trying to squeeze his girth into the opening in the wall that led to the tunnel.

Just then, smoke boiled into the room and the rafters cracked.

Ben disappeared, but the smoke had become so thick Kamil couldn't follow. Coughing, he turned and ran out of the house, his jacket singed, ashes glowing in his hair.

'DAMN,' KAMIL SAID, resting on a large stone beneath the cistern wall. 'Damn.' Spurred by the implied threat to Elif, he had sent Yakup to alert the guard at Huseyin's house while he helped put out the fire, part of a human chain that passed buckets of water from the well. Exhausted, his head aching, Kamil surveyed the damage both to the cottage and to his case. He was also worried about Omar.

It was sheer luck that Balkis's house and the other cottages hadn't caught fire. There had been enough men around to put out the blaze quickly. During the day, most of them would have been at work, but in the middle of the night, all were at home. The fire brigade arrived – a team of muscular young men running in unison, carrying a water pump on their shoulders – but by that time, the fire had been tamed. The piano remained upright like a large smouldering creature rooting in the rubble. Amida was being looked after by Courtidis and Saba. He had been shot in the lower back. Courtidis was not sure whether he would recover. There was no sign of Owen or his men. Kamil boiled with frustration that he had let them slip away. He had expected them to run out the front door, where Yakup was waiting. He should have remembered that Remzi knew about the tunnels.

It was almost dawn. A pall of white smoke filled the cistern like a bowl, making it difficult to see. A tall, thick-necked man in a ripped shirt approached him. His face was scratched and dirty, as were all their faces. Kamil assumed it was a villager coming to thank him. If only they knew he was the one who had started the fire, Kamil thought glumly.

'Well, where the hell were you?' Omar asked him with mock anger.

'Where was I?' Kamil jumped up and cried out. 'Where was I while you were getting your beauty sleep?' He took a closer look at Omar and noticed for the first time the cuts and bruises. His eye was beginning to swell. 'What happened to you?'

'You don't count punches in a fight.' Omar tried to smile, but ended in a grimace of pain. 'What happened to you?' He leaned closer and examined Kamil's blood-caked hair.

Kamil smiled bleakly. 'We can compare war stories later.'

'Well, come along, then. I have a present for you.'

He led Kamil through the smoke to a tumbledown cottage at the edge of the compound.

'It's used for storage,' Omar explained and flung open the door.

On the floor, bound like two neat packages, were Ben and Remzi, bloodied and black with soot. Ben's face was swollen like a cantaloupe. Remzi lay quietly with his eyes closed, blood trickling from his ear.

Kamil pounded Omar on the back. 'How did you do it?'

'There are those who can ride a horse, and there are those who can't,' Omar replied, making no attempt at modesty. He pointed to the back of the cottage, where steps led down into blackness. He shrugged. 'Two against one, in the dark? It was better than kissing a pretty woman.'

AFTER MAKING SURE their prisoners were under lock and key, Kamil and Omar sat at the back of the Fatih station, drinking tea. Dawn threw strange half-hearted shadows on the floor, as if the day were only practising and still unwilling to commit its full strength.

'I can't believe Owen escaped.' Kamil's voice was hoarse from inhaling smoke. He worried about Elif and wondered if Owen would make good on his threat to harm her or whether he'd just try to leave the empire the fastest way possible. Kamil had ordered every customs station, port, and train station to be watched, and sent gendarmes to notify every stable in the city where Owen might rent or purchase a horse and carriage. Huseyin's liveried guards were armed and on full alert.

'Why haven't we been able to find out where the bastard lives?'

'None of his associates ever met him there. And he has money. That buys you anonymity.' Kamil stood. 'I'll go and get cleaned up and this afternoon we can hand Ben over to the embassy. Remzi is all yours until his trial.'

'This time he'll squeal like a bitch. His Charshamba gang is out of business. When I round up the rest of them, believe me,' he added in a deadly voice, 'they'll be sorry they ever laid a hand on my men. At least I know Remzi will get what's coming to him when he goes to trial. Open and shut case. My friend, the warden at Sultanahmet Prison has reserved a nice dark cell for him in the basement where he can chat with the rats. But it really eats my liver about Owen. He's the one responsible for the murders, but we don't have a thing on him. I bet if we handed him over to the British, they'd fine him a thousand liras for smuggling, then cut the bastard loose.'

'At least we've severed his smuggling artery. The thefts should dry up now.'

'We'll make it so hot at this end that the bazaaris will

look like us if they so much as go near a stolen icon.' Omar pointed to Kamil's singed hair.

Kamil laughed, but his eyes were cold.

WHILE OMAR RETURNED to Sunken Village to check on Amida, Kamil rode through Fatih, across the New Bridge, and up the hill through Galata. The Grande Rue de Pera was still relatively deserted. Doorkeepers returning from the bakery carried loaves of fresh bread in string bags or tucked in paper under their arms. A few women, probably servants, hurried past, heads down.

Kamil turned into Agha-Hammam Street and dismounted before a wooden door.

'Your arrival pleases me,' the hammambashou Niko boomed, quickly hiding his surprise at Kamil's appearance.

A red-checked peshtemal towel hung around Niko's neck, doing little to hide his barrel chest. Another covered him from waist to knees. Kamil came here every week to bathe and to suffer brilliantly under the blows of Niko's muscled arms. This week, he was early.

Niko led Kamil into the cooling-off room and indicated a cubicle, a simple wood-panelled room with no ceiling that contained a comfortable padded bench, a wardrobe, towels, high wooden clogs, and a hammam bowl of tinned copper, indented in the centre to fit the bather's middle finger when he poured water from the basin on to his head and shoulders.

Kamil stripped. In the enclosed space, the stench of charred wool was foul. He piled his clothes in a corner and wound a towel around his waist. Then he lay on his back on the bench and looked up gratefully at the calm, blue-tiled dome above him. His head throbbed, but distantly, like a storm at sea. The voices of other men echoed about him, distorted by the marble and tile walls.

Restless, he got up and called Niko. He pointed to the pile of clothes and told him to dispose of them and to send someone to his office for new ones.

The air became increasingly dense as Kamil moved from the cooler rooms to the hot domed hall, where Niko waited with a silkweave washcloth and a bar of olive-oil soap.

AN HOUR LATER, Kamil arrived at his office freshly scrubbed and dressed.

A soft knock on the door announced Avi. 'This is from Mimoza Teyze.' He held out a packet redolent with the scent of freshly baked börek.

'Thank you.' Kamil unwrapped the börek and offered a piece to Avi. 'How do you like living at Chief Omar's house?'

'Mimoza Teyze lets me help,' Avi responded. 'I get to bring the water from the fountain. That's my job,' he added proudly, taking a bite. 'And the garden. I'm helping Omar Amja build winter beds. He showed me how to do it. See?' He held out his hand. The blisters had healed, but Kamil saw a new bruise. 'I'm not so good with the hammer yet,' Avi said, chagrined. 'But I will be.'

Kamil clapped the boy on the shoulder. 'Well, you've done a wonderful job for us. Who knows, you might end up a police chief instead of a magistrate.' He pushed the börek in Avi's direction. 'Now eat up. The padishah expects his officials to have meat on their bones.'

After Avi left, Abdullah handed Kamil a letter. It was from Nizam Pasha, reminding him that his seven days were up and ordering him to appear at the Ministry of Justice that afternoon.

Where could Owen live, Kamil wondered, without the

local muhtar, who registered everyone in the district, or the police being aware of him? The only answer was in a district of villas, konaks, and mansions like Huseyin's. The rich kept to themselves. But they had servants, and servants gossiped. There must be a way to find out.

Abdullah announced a visitor. Tailor Pepo's apprentice came through the door, hands clasped before him, head bowed.

'Pasha, Tailor Pepo sends his greetings. He asked me to tell you that Monsieur Owen has ordered two new shirts. He paid extra to have them made up right away.' He held out a piece of paper. 'Here's the address we delivered them to.'

Perhaps he should believe in miracles after all, Kamil thought.

THERE WERE NO servants and the house appeared deserted. It was a small villa in Nishantashou, not far from Huseyin's mansion and an easy ride to the apartment in Tarla Bashou and to the British Embassy. Surrounded by a great iron fence and set within an overgrown garden, the villa was barely visible from the street. Kamil asked a passerby if he knew who lived there, and was told that the place was empty, except for a caretaker. But no one had seen him for several months.

The gendarmes took up positions around the house. Kamil instructed Captain Arif to make sure nothing, not even a hare, got through. 'We believe there's only one man in there, an Englishman. Chief Omar and I will go in first.' He took out his revolver. 'I hope he'll come quietly. But if you hear shots, you know what to do.'

'Yes, pasha.'

Kamil and Omar circled around the back, where a carriage waited in the dusty lane.

'You can get in and out back here without anyone seeing you,' Omar remarked. 'But not anymore.' He grinned. Owen wouldn't escape again.

Suitcases and bundles were stacked inside the carriage, and the back gate was ajar. They ran to the house, keeping out of sight behind the bushes, and slipped in the back door. The notes of a piano sonata drifted through the hallway. They followed the sound to a large central room lit by French windows. Although the house was shabby on the outside, inside it rivalled a small palace in the opulence of its furnishings and the quality of the art that covered every surface.

Owen sat at a grand piano with his back to them, engrossed in his playing. A large suitcase lay open on the floor.

Omar circled the room to sneak up behind him.

'Going somewhere?' Kamil asked, pointing his gun at Owen's back.

The notes ceased. Owen froze, then turned around. 'My dear friend. I really am impressed.'

Before Omar could reach him, Owen suddenly pulled out a gun and shot at Kamil.

Omar leapt on to Owen's back and pulled him to the ground. He stamped on his wrist until the gun fell from his hand, then hit him on the head with his pistol.

Kamil lay on the floor. Captain Arif and ten of his men fanned into the room, guns out, unsure where to aim.

'Get the medical officer,' Omar bellowed. He turned Kamil and tried to staunch the wound. 'Still alive, I see. The high and mighty must be bulletproof.'

'Did you get him?' Kamil groaned.

Omar nodded towards the figure slumped beside the piano.

'Good.' Kamil struggled to rise. His jacket was soaked with blood. 'Did you kill him?'

'Maybe.' Omar looked unrepentant.

As two soldiers, led by a worried-looking Captain Arif, hurried Kamil's stretcher out of the room, he saw Omar standing over Owen's body. The last thing he remembered was hearing Omar's voice ordering the remaining soldiers to get out.

39

Instead of the reception hall, the clerk at the Ministry of Justice brought Kamil into Nizam Pasha's private chambers. Kamil had never been there before and wasn't sure if this change in routine was good news or bad. It might simply be that it was late in the day, and Nizam Pasha no longer had any reason to be sitting in the draughty hall.

Exhausted by pain, Kamil wore a cloak instead of his stambouline jacket to accommodate his bandaged shoulder. The military surgeon had assured him that the bullet had gone right through the muscle and that the wound would heal cleanly, but Kamil had refused to take anything for the pain. He wanted a clear head for this interview. In life, he mused, philosophers say that the straight path is best, but they didn't know Nizam Pasha.

The clerk ushered him into a room lined with books that had several comfortable-looking chairs and a modern desk piled with books and papers. The books were bound in soft leather and embossed in gold. A ladder used to climb to the higher reaches was propped against the shelves. Kamil stopped, assuming this was where he would be received, but the clerk urged him on through another door at the back.

They walked along a corridor, then emerged into a room in the old Ottoman style, with little ornamentation but an abundance of space and light. In the centre a fountain burbled inside a small marble pool. To one side, the floor was raised to make a room within a room. The higher room was furnished with only a simple divan that stretched on three sides around a large blue and yellow silk rug. Dressed in a subdued grey robe and turban, Nizam Pasha was propped comfortably against cushions, his legs tucked under him. He was puffing on a narghile and a tiny china cup of coffee rested within arm's reach.

Kamil struggled with one hand to take off his boots, then took the pair of finely tooled leather slippers the clerk held out. He stepped up to the room where Nizam Pasha waited, bowed deeply, and uttered the usual polite phrases.

'Sit, Magistrate, and give me your report.' Nizam Pasha snapped his fingers and told the clerk to bring Kamil coffee. He glanced at the bandage visible under Kamil's cloak, but said nothing.

Kamil sat down on the divan opposite Nizam Pasha, grateful to be off his feet. It would have been impolite to look at his superior directly, so he directed his gaze towards Nizam Pasha's right shoulder.

'We apprehended the thieves, Minister, and I've broken the connection to Europe.' He told him about Magnus Owen and his embassy export business. He detailed the many antiquities that had been recovered on the ship and in Owen's apartment and villa, including the icon, the Ahrida Torah, the chalice and other Byzantine valuables from the Fatih Mosque. He told him about the Rettingate shop. 'The London police are raiding it as we speak. I expect we'll get information leading to more arrests once they've had a look at their books. Much of the illegal trade from the empire went through this dealer's hands.'

Kamil didn't mention Malik's murder. Although he was a civil servant himself, he had an instinctive distrust of bureaucrats and what they might do with information about something as potentially inflammatory as the Melisites or the Proof of God. Be loyal to the state, he thought, but trust who you know. The Proof of God was better off in the hands of Hamdi Bey, who at least appreciated it as a rare antiquity that needed to be preserved, if not as a theological triumph or the heart of a religious sect.

Nizam Pasha listened with lowered lids, then looked directly at Kamil. 'The bodies of the two Englishmen will have to be handed over to the embassy.'

Startled, Kamil said nothing, still digesting the news that Owen and Ben were dead.

Nizam Pasha appraised him. 'You surprise me, Kamil.' There was a note of respect in his voice. 'It'll be a delicate matter.'

'Delicate, Minister?'

'You'll have to explain the ears.' Nizam Pasha pulled on his narghile, his eyes intent. 'Was that a joke? Why did you cut off their ears?'

At first, Kamil didn't understand. Then, in a rush of horror, it became clear to him – Omar must have taken his revenge for Ali's mutilation in the Tobacco Works tunnel. Omar had once mentioned, with a kind of admiration, warriors who strung up their enemies' ears and wore them as necklaces. Kamil struggled to hide his shock from Nizam Pasha, who was watching him intently. What possible explanation could he come up with to account for such brutality that didn't implicate Omar?

Kamil settled on a lie so close to the truth it was almost indistinguishable. 'An unfortunate incident. Before we could lock them up, they were killed by a rival gang. That was the gang's signature.'

'Good enough. The embassy will believe it.' He fixed

Kamil with his gaze. It was clear that Nizam Pasha did not believe this lie.

'Yes, Minister.'

'I had mentioned that there might be an opening in the Appellate Court. I regret that this opening did not become available after all.' Nizam Pasha examined Kamil's face for his reaction.

Kamil kept his relief to himself. 'I serve the empire in whatever capacity I can,' he responded, then added quickly, 'and the sultan, may Allah give him health.'

Nizam Pasha looked amused. 'I think you serve him best where you are at present, perhaps better than I had expected. But the padishah's benevolent eye is upon you. In his name, we thank you for your service.'

As Kamil stepped, pale and shaken, into the street, he had a disturbing thought. Had Omar cut off the men's ears before or after they died? What was the difference between atrocity and vengeance?

40

Kamil was feeling lighthearted. The air was brisk and redolent of autumn. The chestnut trees lining the approach to Huseyin's mansion hung limpid and golden, drawing in the light. His wound was healing, and he had in his pocket a letter from Detective Inspector Joseph Ormond.

Honoured Magistrate,

Acting on the information you provided to us, CID raided Lionel Rettingate's shop in South Kensington and went through its books, the official as well as the real ones. We were surprised at the extent of what appears to be a well-financed, sophisticated operation with global reach. We believe Magnus Owen and his associates were midlevel participants, Rettingate higher up. From your description, we believe the man Ben to have been a former East End pugilist by the name of Sam 'Big Ben' Hardacre. The Rettingate shop was a central distributor for stolen antiquities. We are following a number of leads that we hope will identify the ringleaders.

Given the extensive nature of the problem, CID has created a Special Antiquities Unit which I have the honour to lead. As such, I would like to express to you our gratitude here at Scotland Yard for apprehending Owen and his associates. I understand that you were educated at Cambridge and are familiar with our small island. If you would find it useful to follow up in London yourself, CID would be pleased to welcome you and your associates. (On a personal note, I have learned you share an interest of mine in Orchidaceae.)

Your devoted servant,
Detective Inspector Joseph Ormond
Leader, Special Antiquities Unit
Criminal Investigation Department
Metropolitan Police Force
Great Scotland Yard

Hamdi Bey and Ismail Hodja were expected to lunch as well, but Kamil was early. Feride met him in the entry hall. As he kissed her cheeks, he found himself looking over her shoulder for Elif. He had seen a length of cobalt brocade in a tailor's shop and had wondered whether she would like a vest made from it.

'Where are the girls?' he asked.

'They're taking a nap. Now that Elif is gone, it's so quiet here. You should bring Avi with you sometime.'

'Elif is gone?' Kamil asked, startled. 'Where?'

Feride tapped his face gently with her fingertips. 'Not far, brother dear. Don't worry. She has her own apartment now in Pera. Isn't that wonderful? I've just been to visit.'

'She never said anything to me,' Kamil protested, then realised how ridiculous that sounded. Why would Elif have told him?

'It's really lovely,' Feride prattled on. 'It's in the new Camondo family building, the one on the hill. You should see it. Her windows open right on to the sea. You could throw yourself into the blue. Oh, I'm so happy for her.

Huseyin offered to pay rent, but the Camondos wouldn't take it. They said they were proud to have such a famous artist as their guest.'

They arrived in the sitting room and Feride settled herself comfortably on the sofa. Kamil remained standing.

'How does she know the Camondos?' They were a wealthy and very distinguished Ottoman Jewish family.

'Hamdi Bey arranged it. She's going to start teaching at the academy, and, well, we are a bit far away out here in the suburbs. She needed a respectable place to live. The Camondos have taken her under their wing. She's painting again too.' Feride's excitement had taken on an element of wistfulness.

Kamil was speechless. Elif had leapt suddenly from Feride's dining table into a full-blown life of her own.

Feride said, 'She left something for you. I'll go and get it.'

When she was gone, Kamil pulled out his amber beads and walked aimlessly about the room, calming himself with the rhythm of the beads as they slipped one by one through his fingers. It wasn't like him to be set adrift by a passing swell.

Feride came back with a thin parcel and handed it to him.

'Thank you, Ferosh.' He sat and rested the parcel against the chair, intending to open it later, in private. He wished he could leave now.

'Aren't you going to open it?' Feride demanded.

It seemed somehow indecent to open it in front of Feride, yet he acknowledged that he could not focus on lunch until he did. Setting the parcel on his lap, he untied the string and removed the paper wrapping.

It was a watercolour. He recognised the image straight

away. '*Orchis pinetorum*,' he exclaimed. The pure white blooms flashed across the page like an arc of tiny startled birds. He felt her exhilaration there, her vulnerability. There was also a tensile strength in the arc that surprised him.

HALF AN HOUR later, Ismail Hodja and Hamdi Bey arrived in the same carriage. They greeted Kamil and their hosts effusively. They seemed in excellent spirits and the conversation at lunch was lively.

'It's too bad Elif Hanoum isn't here,' Hamdi Bey said as the servants took away the soup bowls. 'But I take full blame. She's needed at the academy.'

Kamil listened, but ate little. His headaches had returned. He planned to ask Courtidis for more Balat Balm. He hadn't liked the hallucinations and emotional untethering – he assumed they were side effects – but it had cured his headache, at least until Remzi hit him on the head and Owen put a bullet through his shoulder.

'The Proof of God should remain in the museum,' Hamdi Bey was saying, 'where it can be copied and studied. Above all, where it can be guarded. I've taken a look at that flimsy prayer hall in Sunken Village. An artefact of this historical value needs to be preserved and protected. Saba Hanoum is welcome to come to the museum to look at it whenever she likes.'

Feride nodded and looked interested. Kamil had told her and Huseyin only that the Proof of God was an important sacred object and that people had tried to steal it. He wondered what they made of the conversation.

Ismail Hodja told Huseyin that Saba was keeping up the tradition of Malik's ecumenical dawah.

'Ecumenical dawah?' Huseyin asked.

'Theological calls to discussion across religious lines,' Ismail Hodja explained, setting aside his fork. A servant whisked his plate away and replaced it with a clean one for the next course.

'I've taken the liberty of convening a discussion group made up of my Jewish, Muslim, and Christian colleagues, all scholars of the highest calibre. I reached out to as many denominations and sects as I could. We had our first meeting last night,' he added. Kamil could hear the excitement in the sheikh's voice.

Huseyin was uncharacteristically silent and Kamil found himself feeling sorry for his brother-in-law, who, on this subject, was clearly out of his depth. Kamil wondered what Feride thought about her half-sister being the leader of a religious sect. She had wanted to meet Saba, but Kamil wasn't ready to let her into their lives just yet. His feelings about Saba were too confused, wrapped up in some way with that profoundly disturbing dream and his father's betrayal.

Huseyin set to cutting up his meat with great concentration.

Hamdi Bey asked, 'Will Saba Hanoum attend these meetings?'

Ismail Hodja nodded. 'I asked her to come to the meeting last night. There was some resistance to having a woman in the group. But after I explained that Saba had authored some of the calls and was leader of her own sect, the others agreed that she should join us. They call her Sheikha Saba. Do you know what she told them? She said all the prophets point in the same direction, and if we look to where they point and go there, we all end up at the same spot. Remarkable insight for someone so young.'

'What is a sheikha?' Feride asked.

'A Muslim woman who is a spiritual leader,' Ismail Hodja explained.

'I didn't know there was such a thing,' she exclaimed.

'One of the most famous is Rabi'a al-'Adawiyya, who lived about two hundred years after the Prophet Muhammad, peace be upon his name, in the city of Basra. She was a servant of poor origin, but one night her master awoke to see the light of saintliness shining about her head and illuminating the entire house. He released her and she went to live in the desert. She debated with highly esteemed Sufi leaders, but outshone them all with her intellectual forthrightness and spiritual powers. It is said that one such leader, Hasan al-Basri, became envious and approached her as she was sitting on the bank of a stream with some of her followers. He threw his carpet on the water, sat on it, and called to Rabi'a to come and converse with him. Do you know what she did?'

Feride was rapt with attention. 'No, what?'

'She stuck a knife in the inflated sheepskins he was using to hold the carpet up,' Huseyin suggested, eliciting a scowl from Feride.

Ismail Hodja laughed. 'Excellent guess, but no. She threw her carpet up in the air, sat on it, and said, "Well, Hasan, come up here where people will see us better."'

Feride laughed in delight.

'Hasan couldn't do it, of course. And Rabi'a told him, "What you did, a fish can do, and what I did, a bird can do. The real work to be done lies beyond both of these."'

'A very wise woman,' Hamdi Bey applauded.

Huseyin tore off a hunk of bread. 'Thanks be to Allah, women can't be politicians.'

They laughed.

'The Quran doesn't forbid it, you know,' Ismail Hodja

commented, his fork pausing in midair. 'In verse twenty-three of the Sura of the Ants, the Queen of Sheba is described as a mighty ruler who, although she consulted with men, made all the final decisions. It is her ignorance of the true faith that is faulted, not her inability to govern.'

Feride said tentatively, 'I remember something about the Prophet's wife Aysha riding into battle on a camel.'

'And his first wife was a rich merchant, wasn't she?' Huseyin asked. 'Smart man.' He nodded approval.

Kamil leaned over to Ismail Hodja and asked softly, 'Have you told this ecumenical group about the Melisites or the Proof of God?'

'Unfortunately, the world isn't ready to become one nation,' Ismail Hodja responded. 'We need to plough the ground first before we plant the seed. The Proof is safe in the museum. I go there every day to copy and study it. It'll be my life's work. I can't think of anything more important. Hamdi Bey has kindly put a private room at my disposal where I can work on it undisturbed. It has to be handled with the utmost care, as you can imagine. At the moment, I'm preparing a report for the Azhar Archive. A most auspicious day, Kamil. I praise Allah that I should live to see it.'

41

The liveried guards saluted Kamil as he passed through the main gate into the courtyard of the Camondo Apartments. The building was shaped like a U, with one side of the courtyard open to the sea and sky. Built into the side of a steep hill, it seemed to float above the sparkling water. On three sides rose walls studded with French windows and balconies.

Elif was waiting for him in the courtyard, outlined against the immense cobalt sky. She wore a brown tunic over loose trousers, a coral-coloured vest, and a long, matching brown jacket. Her head was bare, her blond hair still short as a boy's. Her clothes were neither those of a man, nor those of a woman; perhaps different enough to avoid condemnation, he decided. He wondered if she had designed them herself.

'Kamil,' she breathed. 'I was so happy to get your message. Thank you for coming.' She looked like a figure from classical antiquity, yet more present than any woman he had ever met.

'Are you well?' he asked, although he could see the answer. Her eyes were still troubled, but her face had lost its hollows and her cheeks radiated health.

'Come. I'll show you.' She took Kamil's good arm lightly. They entered a grand entry hall and she led him up the marble stairway. Two well-dressed women stopped for a moment to greet her.

'We're off to the Café Lebon,' the younger woman said. With a curious look at Kamil, she added, 'Join us later, if you like.' The women continued down the stairs, their hats bobbing.

On the next floor, Elif pushed open a double door and stepped inside. Kamil followed. They entered a bright, high-ceilinged room, which ended in a set of large windows and French doors leading to a balcony. The walls were so alive with light, Kamil was momentarily blinded.

Then he saw the canvases. One was on an easel, others were stacked in a corner of the room. He walked up to the easel. It was an oil rendering of the French doors, open to the sea, but defined by light and colour rather than any realistic detail. It evoked exactly the same feeling he had had when entering the room, of falling into a brilliant sea of blue.

'Remarkable,' he said. 'You have enormous talent.' He felt humbled by it, and eager to support it in whatever way he could. He let his eyes follow the delicate curve of her head. He thought of her bravery and humour. She was unusual, eclectic, still wounded, but recovering. A strong woman. Remembering their intimacy by the fire, he wondered what it would be like if they were married. He imagined her in the winter garden, painting, then thought of his orchids, endangered by draughts and continual traffic.

'Elif,' he began awkwardly. 'Have you thought any more about your future?'

'Well, I love teaching,' she responded. 'I'm terrified, of course. But the students are talented and so kind. It's wonderful that Hamdi Bey has art classes for women at his academy. You know, it's so rare, even in Paris. I wouldn't have been able to get anywhere without the support of people like Mary Cassatt. I'll repay her by teaching these girls everything she taught me.'

'They're lucky to have you as their teacher.'

She flushed and lowered her head at the praise.

Kamil's heart caught at the sight of her slight smile.

'Have you thought about getting married again?' He could see the rapid rise and fall of her chest.

Kamil was suddenly overwhelmed with embarrassment. Who was he to ask Elif such a personal question, especially if he was not prepared to follow through himself?

She went to the window and looked out at the sea. 'I'm not ready yet,' she said softly. 'You know some of the reasons. There are others.'

'You don't need to tell me. I understand.'

'Do you?' She looked up at him. The blue of her eyes shot through him. 'It wasn't just my husband's death and then,' she paused and he could see her struggling with herself, 'my son's death. There were other things, things I thought I had to do but that in the end changed nothing. Except me. They changed me.' She laid her fingers on his arm, her eyes willing him to understand. 'I can't.' Her voice broke and she looked away. 'I just can't.'

Elif walked to the easel and regarded the scene from the window in the painting.

Kamil followed.

'Elif,' he said softly, 'I don't know what happened, but whatever it was, it created the woman standing before me for whom I have all the love and respect in the world.'

She nodded. Tears spilled over her cheeks.

'May I visit again?' Kamil asked, wondering whether he was taking unfair advantage of her distress.

'I'll send a message through Feride,' she answered without looking at him.

Trying not to let his disappointment show, Kamil turned towards the door. 'I'll go now. Be well.'

As he descended the stairs, he heard rapid footsteps behind him and looked back. It was Elif.

She bent her head to his and whispered, 'My son's name was Yunus.' Then she ran back up the stairs. He heard the door slam.

Yunus, dolphin.

She had given him the gift of her son's name.

LATER THAT EVENING, Kamil sat in his bed, idly turning the pages of the *Gardener's Chronicle and Agricultural Gazette*. He had propped Elif's watercolour on the dresser. In the half-light, *Orchis pinetorum* came to life, its white-robed blooms whirling like dervishes across the page. In the background, a basketry of shadows, stems, bracts, and nodes. He stood and placed the book of poems by John Donne beside it, as if each might draw comfort from the other.

42

'How are you, brother?' Saba asked, pushing Amida's hair back from his forehead.

He turned his eyes to her. 'As well as can be expected,' he answered bleakly.

'Do you want to sit up?'

Amida nodded and Saba gestured to the servant waiting by the door to come and help her. Together, they tugged and lifted him into a sitting position. His legs were still limp, but he was getting stronger.

The night of the fire, Constantine, with enormous skill and concentration, had extracted the bullet from Amida's back and closed the wound. He came by every day to check on his patient. Most evenings he and Saba sat together and talked. She found herself looking forward to his visits and relying on his advice.

'So, how does it feel to be in charge?' Amida asked her. She could hear a faint echo of bitterness that she knew Amida tried to hide.

'I'm not in charge of anything yet. The ceremony isn't for another two weeks. There's a lot to do.' After the ceremony that would make her priestess, they were planning an enormous feast for the Melisite community and several other important guests.

'Sorry I can't help.' Amida grimaced, gesturing at his legs.

The ceremony should also be the initiation of the

caretaker. She regarded her brother carefully. Should she include him or wait until he was better? Did they even need a caretaker anymore, now that the Proof of God had been found?

'You know,' he said, 'you don't need to walk to be caretaker. It wouldn't make any difference, would it? Malik could walk, but he never went anywhere.' Amida laughed, a desperate sound.

'You're right. It wouldn't matter.'

Amida looked relieved.

'There's no rush, though,' Saba added. 'Now that the Proof is safe, there's no need for a caretaker at the Kariye. It's not there anymore.'

Amida was clearly unhappy. 'How about caretaker of the Imperial Museum?'

Saba laughed to keep him company. 'I think that job's taken.'

'I can go through the ceremony,' Amida insisted. 'I can sit in the chair.' He pointed to a wheelchair beside the bed. It was made of wicker and polished wood with a small chamberpot built into the seat.

Saba pictured Amida being wheeled in beside her on her day of triumph. She leaned over and kissed his cheek.

'Later, Amida. There's plenty of time. Get well first.'

Amida closed his eyes and turned his head away. Tears gathered beneath his lashes. 'Leave me alone now,' he muttered.

Saba turned and walked to the door. As she passed the servant, she told him, 'Have him brought to the hammam this afternoon and make sure you find that special masseur Monsieur Courtidis recommended.'

'Yes, madam,' he answered with lowered head.

Since the day Saba had summoned the shocked servants

to clean her room after Gudit's attack, they had treated her with great deference. Perhaps, she thought with a tight smile, they were afraid of her.

Gudit hadn't reappeared, nor did Saba enquire after her, but she learned with surprise and some satisfaction that the midwife had sought out Constantine Courtidis to tend to her wounds. Gudit would have to carry out the ceremony of accession. There was no one else. Then she would no longer be needed.

Saba opened the box and took out her sceptre, which Kamil had returned to her.

It would have been easier to establish her leadership, she thought angrily, if Kamil had done the right thing and given her the Proof of God. It belonged to the Melisites.

43

The guard at the Imperial Museum put down his rifle and unlocked the front door. He looked up at the Arabic inscription over the lintel. He couldn't read it, but assumed it was a verse from the Quran, so he said a silent prayer before stepping across the threshold. Inside the other guard was asleep in his chair. He nudged him and went into the kitchen to prepare the morning's tea. It took him several minutes to light the brazier, set the water to boil in the bottom of the double-boiler teapot, and pour a cup of black tea leaves into the top. He stared out of the window, looking at nothing particular, but letting the golds and russets of autumn fill his eyes. When the water was hot, he poured enough over the tea leaves to cover them, put the teapot back on the boiler, and set it on the coals to brew for another twenty minutes. He glanced at the lay of the light to judge the time, then went back into the main room. He wanted to ask the other guard's advice about finding an apprenticeship for his son. It was time he learned a trade.

The other man was still asleep, head on his chest, arms loose in his lap. When the guard pushed his shoulder, he slumped further, then slid from the chair on to the floor.

KAMIL HELD HIS head in his hands. Standing before him was Hamdi Bey, his usually impeccable cravat askew and his vest buttons wrongly done up.

'It's gone,' Hamdi Bey repeated.

Kamil stood and walked around his desk, his headache flaring with each step. He offered Hamdi Bey a seat and some refreshment, but the old man wagged his grey beard and refused to be coddled.

'What happened?' Kamil asked, bracing himself against a table and wishing Hamdi Bey would sit so that he could.

'Someone drugged the guard.'

'With food?'

'I don't know,' Hamdi Bey cried out in bewilderment. 'There was no food anywhere. Just dregs of tea. We tested them and they're just tea. The man has always been completely reliable.'

'How is he?' Kamil asked.

'He's delirious. He's babbling about having been visited by an angel who showed him the gardens of paradise.' Hamdi Bey peeled off his thin leather gloves. 'I think the strain of watching the Proof of God must have been too much for him.'

Kamil was surprised. 'Does he know what it is?'

'We never told the guards what it was, but in the absence of real information, rumours are passed around.'

'What do you mean?'

'The other guard told me that they thought they were guarding a prophecy revealed to the Prophet Muhammad by an angel.'

'But that's the Quran.'

'I know. They think this is a newly revealed sura.' He put on his pince-nez as if that would clarify matters, then took them off again and massaged between his eyes.

'They're simple men,' he decided finally. He took a deep breath and straightened his shoulders. 'Now I have to go tell Ismail Hodja.'

Kamil stood at the window watching Hamdi Bey get into his carriage. When the horses moved off into the traffic, Kamil slammed his fist into the sill.

44

Two Weeks Later

The first snow of the season drifted over Sunken Village. Kamil, Hamdi Bey, and Ismail Hodja sat on stools in the Melisite prayer house in an unobtrusive spot where they could see past the worshippers and follow the ceremony unfolding at the front. Kamil could see Amida's disappointment as he watched the proceedings from his wheelchair, Courtidis hovering nearby. Omar had decided, as he put it bluntly, to live and let die, and not arrest Amida on any charges.

The hall was packed with villagers of all ages, dressed in their best. Earlier, to a wild crescendo of drumming and a steady undercurrent of prayer, an ox, a ewe, and a she-goat had been sacrificed and their blood poured into the pillars by the door. A blood-spattered peacock feather lay in the snow before the sacrificial stone.

After the ceremony, Courtidis had told them, there would be a feast in the hall and the community would dance and sing. Kamil noticed that he looked happy and relaxed and that his clothes were clean and neatly pressed. He wore a fashionable suit and a new fez. He slipped Kamil a small tin box, which he tucked into his pocket.

Suddenly, all conversation ceased. Kamil saw Saba enter the room. She was dressed in a magnificent linen cloak embroidered with gold. Two fillets of gold-embroidered linen fell on either side of her face. She looked like an empress. Kamil could feel the powerful impact her presence had on the people in the hall.

The crowd opened a path before her. In her hand, she held the sceptre, now innocent of Malik's blood. Near the front of the hall waited a stout old woman in a red robe. Her face was split from nose to ear by a wound, not entirely healed. Two apprentices dressed in red stood on either side of her.

When Saba reached the front of the hall, she turned, raised her arms, and led the congregation in prayer.

Ismail Hodja whispered to Kamil, 'Fascinating. They're praying in Ottoman, but they use terms like Adonai. That's from the *Tawrat*. It means lord. I've only heard Jews use it. And watch their hands. The motions are like a tour of all the religions.'

Of them all, Ismail Hodja had been the most philosophical about the disappearance of the Proof of God.

'In an odd way, the disappearance reaffirms my faith,' he had explained to Kamil. 'It's as if the Proof is travelling in the world incognito. It won't settle and reveal itself until humanity is ready to hear its message. We've been enormously blessed that it allowed us a glimpse before returning to occultation.'

Ismail Hodja's renewed faith was of little comfort to Kamil. Stealing the Proof was cheating humanity of peace, he thought, regardless of whether or not you believed in its divine origin. Malik would have understood. As he might have pointed out, this was a city that ate the soul of the past.

The woman in red came forward and placed Balkis's ring, engraved with a crescent and disc, on Saba's right forefinger, then bowed her head and retreated. Saba turned away from the congregation and faced an iron gate decorated with an angel that led, Courtidis had explained, to the Holy of Holies.

'Behold Saba,' the woman intoned loudly. 'Behold the Proof of God, Container of the Uncontainable. Behold the Key to all religions.'

'Adonai, help us,' the congregation responded. 'Virgin of Chora, Container of the Uncontainable, keep us.'

Saba let her cape slip from her shoulders. A collective sigh of astonishment rose from the congregation. Kamil felt the hair on the back of his neck rise.

Saba wore a backless white robe. From her waist to her amber shoulders was a pair of powerful tattooed wings. They were the wings of a bird of prey, a falcon or a hawk.

'Behold the Proof of God,' Saba announced in a voice that carried to the back of the hall.

She took a key from a gold chain around her waist, unlocked the angel gate, and stepped inside.

Acknowledgements

I am deeply grateful to my editor, Amy Cherry; my agent, Al Zuckerman; and all the talented, supportive folks at W. W. Norton, especially Elisabeth Kerr, Ingsu Liu, Erin Lovett, and Vanessa Schneider, as well as Kirsty Dunseath at Weidenfeld & Nicolson. I have the best team in the world. Robert Ousterhout was extraordinarily generous in sharing with me his deep knowledge of Byzantium and the Kariye in particular. Roger Owen came up with intriguing historical details and Corky White bravely accompanied me below ground. They and Lydia Fitzpatrick, Stephen Kimmel, Star Lawrence, and Carl Leiden read the manuscript at various stages and, where I strayed, showed me the straight path. I also wish to thank Rosalyn Adam, Walter Denny, and Jordan Dimitrakov for sharing their expertise in names, carpets, and modes of death. Asli Baykal helped me track down everything from curses to weasels and Deniz Hughes offered up the contents of her house. I owe a special debt of gratitude to Linda Barlow, my mentor and role model, and to Michael Freeman, my secret weapon, who is always there and who always knows what to do.